THE GATES OF DAWN

Also by Michael J. Gowers

Non-fiction:

THREE GO TO KNOYDART

About the author

Michael J. Gowers worked as a business analyst in financial services for more than forty years, before retiring to become a full-time writer. *The Gates of Dawn* is his first novel.

Michael lives in Bristol and in his spare time plays the drums, and the occasional game of golf – weather permitting.

The Pre-Raphaelite artworks

For more information about the eight Pre-Raphaelite paintings featured in this book, including full-colour illustrations, please visit my website at **www.michaeljgowers.com**.

Published by
Michael J. Gowers

THE GATES OF DAWN

MICHAEL J. GOWERS

First published in Great Britain in 2023 by Michael J. Gowers
www.michaeljgowers.com

2

ISBN: 978-1-7393169-1-4 (Paperback)

Typeset in Constantia with Calibri Light for headings and
Cambria for numerics.

Cover design by Duncan Betts and David Gowers.
Painting images on cover © the Masters and Wardens,
Drapers' Company, London.

In memory of Betty

Mum, I think you gave me all your love of words.

Behind all great art lies a moment of truth ...

... behind all of human history lies a question to be answered.

∞

ACKNOWLEDGEMENTS

For those who know me well, and some who don't, you'll be aware that this first novel has been somewhat of a labour of love, these past thirteen years. For anyone who has tried to balance the challenges of work and 'play', you'll know it requires passion, dedication, hard work and a bunch of friends and family who will provide copious amounts of support, encouragement and the occasional kick up the backside when required. And for all of that, and more, you have my love and my thanks.

In particular, I'd like to thank the following people, in no particular order: all those friends who have heartened and inspired me to put pen to paper. My brother, David Gowers, for all of your valuable insights into the workings of the Ashmolean Museum in Oxford, where you worked as Head of Photography for twenty-three years. Sue Gowers and Roger Burdass for your helpful thoughts on my early drafts. Rachael Rowlands and Justine Cunningham, without whom my words would have fallen from the path. Della Hooper for your help with my research into the Pre-Raphaelites. Penny Fussell, archivist and the Master and Wardens of The Drapers' Company, for their kind permission to use the photographic image of *The Gates of Dawn*. Sandra Tredgett and Steve Howse, who always kept believing in my ability as a writer. And finally, my dear friends, Duncan and Karen Betts, and Richard and Penny Arnold, for your encouraging words, sound advice and shared love of music, books and film – all of which helped keep me going when my ardour was on the wane.

Prologue

Ardingly Hall, Sussex, England

8 July 1890

The rain came suddenly, riding the sea breeze like a ghostly shroud, sucking the hues and tones from everything in its wake. Near the old coast road, two girls took shelter by a small stream, watched over by their young male companion. He looked up at the angry sky and squinted as the rain stung his face like tiny daggers. Matilda pulled her moth-eaten shawl over her head and let her younger sister, Isabella, sneak inside. Matilda closed her eyes and slowly bowed her head, sensing the dark foreboding that would soon befall them both.

'Don't worry, Tilly, it'll soon pass,' said Isabella, clasping her hand.

Heartened by her sister's touch, Matilda placed her slender fingers on the keys of her concertina and began to play the haunting melodies of an old sea shanty. The chords of 'Leave Her, Johnny, Leave Her' rose into the air like the wrath of angels, banishing the storm clouds to the nearby marshes of Walland and Romney, and leaving a pair of brightly coloured rainbows etched against the slate-grey sky.

'You did it,' cried Isabella, peering out from beneath the shawl.

Matilda smiled as a shaft of sunlight caressed her cheeks, knowing she would never see its splendour. Blind since birth, she'd learned to take what little pleasure she could from her world of constant darkness. Placing the concertina in her lap, she let her hand brush the raindrops from a clump of purple harebells and felt the shadow of twelve lost summers surge through her fingertips.

'Come on, you two, we'd better get going,' said the young man, as he shook the rain from his jacket and marched up the grassy slope towards Winchelsea, and home.

Suddenly, a voice called out, booming through the clouds like thunder.

'James, James ... where are you?'

He looked round to see if the girls had heard it too, but Isabella was busy helping her sister cross the narrow stream. The voice called again, louder this time – a man's voice, dark and foreboding, yet strangely familiar.

'Answer me, boy, when I speak to you.'

*

James found himself transported back to the sumptuous drawing room at Ardingly Hall – his father, Charles Waltham, standing next to him with his hands behind his back.

'I thought I'd find you here,' said Charles, admiring John Millais's enigmatic painting of two young beggar girls, sitting by a stream, waiting for the storm to pass. 'Why didn't you answer me?'

'I'm sorry, Father, my mind was elsewhere.'

Charles gave a resigned smile. From the moment he'd first laid eyes on *The Blind Girl* at Christie's London saleroom, he knew he had to have it. But at eight hundred guineas, it was an extravagance he could barely afford. Not that you'd know it from the lavishly decorated room in which they were standing – with its richly coloured damask wallpaper, the ceiling covered in ornately moulded plasterwork, and two gas-lit chandeliers casting their warm glow on a selection of fine rosewood furniture and Persian rugs.

However, the facade of affluence and power belied a deeply troubled family, debt-ridden and on the brink of financial ruin. In a bid to endure the tide of the Great Depression that had ravaged Europe and the U.S. for nearly two decades, the Walthams had taken the advice of well-respected entrepreneur and MP, Baron Albert Grant, investing nearly all their savings in the ill-fated Emma Silver Mine in Utah. After two years of heavy losses, the mine finally closed, leaving its shareholders with nothing but worthless bits of paper, and the bankrupt Baron facing charges of fraud and corruption at the Old Bailey. With just a civil engineer's salary to fall back on, Charles had been forced to sell virtually all the family heirlooms in order to save Ardingly Hall. But time was running out.

'You like this picture, don't you, son?' said Charles.

James looked at his father with a growing sense of unease – so rare was it for him to show even the slightest interest in his well-being, let alone engage in intimate conversation. As sole heir to the dwindling Waltham estate, James was a sensitive, intelligent young man, but with no friends or siblings to keep him company during his parents' frequent trips abroad, the painted scene near the Sussex coast had become his playground; and Matilda and Isabella, his dearest companions. And yet, standing here in front of Millais's heartfelt portrayal of social depravation and child vagrancy, it felt like his father was reaching out to him for the very first time.

'Yes sir, I do – very much.'

'Your mother tells me the girls speak to you. Is that correct?'

James thought he saw Tilly turn her head in anticipation.

'Sometimes, when I'm feeling lonely, Father,' he said, fearing the consequences.

'Really? And what do they say to you, exactly?'

'Matilda is so brave and insightful. She reminds me that no matter how dark and solitary the world may appear, there's a light in our heart, and—'

'James, I'm afraid I have some bad news,' said Charles, turning his back on them both. 'I'm going to have to sell *The Blind Girl*.

James stared in disbelief as his father's words rose into the air, circling the room like vultures, ready to gorge on his wounded young heart. He looked up at Tilly, desperate for her to reach out and tell him that everything would be alright. But she sat there, stoic and serene; her head raised in defiance of her so-called benefactors.

Fear grew to rage, and James turned angrily to his father as the torrent of betrayal continued to spew from his lips, like fetid water from a gargoyle's mouth, putrefying the air with its filthy rotten stench.

'As soon as I can make arrangements, she will go to auction.'

'But Father ... you can't do that,' croaked James.

'I don't have a choice. When you're older, you'll understand that sometimes we have to give up the things we love. And, much as it hurts, well ...'

'Well what, father?'

'We do what needs to be done,' he replied, with as much sincerity as he could muster.

'What about the other paintings, can't you just sell one of those?'

Charles looked up at the gallery of ancestral portraits glowering at him with utter indignation, for it was he and his financial negligence that had blighted their good family name.

'This will fetch the best price.'

'Father, please—'

'That's enough, James. My mind is made up,' and he marched out of the room.

James looked up at the two girls dressed in their brightly coloured rags. Soon they would be gone, leaving him with nothing but his own pitiful imagination for company.

He sank to the floor, drew his knees up to his chest and stared blankly out of the window – the dull, hollow ache in his rib cage almost too much to bear. He couldn't understand it. How could his father be so cruel, abandoning these poor creatures in their hour of need? This was their home, their sanctuary. There had to be a way to save them. There had to.

A ray of sunshine came bursting through the window, bathing him in a pool of light. With tears rolling down his cheeks, he slowly got to his feet, touched his fingers to his lips and placed them gently on the tiny paper label pinned to Tilly's smock. It read simply, *Pity the blind*.

He gazed up at his two young friends and spoke the words of a solemn promise never to be broken. The vow had been made, their destinies had become entwined; and from this day on, he would endeavour to keep the girls safe, whatever the cost.

For as his father had said, "We do what needs to be done."

Chapter One

Wickwar, near Bristol

2 November 1999

Emily awoke with a strange sense of euphoria – that feeling you get when you realise you don't have to go to work today, or the next ten days, in fact. Wearing just an old T-shirt, she went downstairs to make some coffee, followed closely by Bill, who jumped off the bed the second he knew some cat treats were in the offing.

Emily rubbed the sleep from her eyes and gazed out of the kitchen window. After last night's wind and rain, leaves from the cherry tree lay scattered everywhere, covering the tiny cottage garden in a carpet of amber and pink. Tom, her partner, had left for work hours ago, slamming the front door as he went – much to Emily's displeasure. Snowed under with some end-of-year project or other, he'd made it quite clear there was no way he could take time off, this close to Christmas. Fair enough, she thought, and decided the next week and a half would be spent doing exactly what she wanted.

With Bill trotting alongside her, she walked through the curving passageway to the cosy little dining room, turned on the gas fire and sat down to check her emails.

'Why is it that whenever I open my laptop, you have to stomp all over it with your big furry feet?' she said, as Bill rubbed his head up and down the edge of the screen. In truth, she loved the cute way he marked his territory, and gave his chin a friendly rub.

She was just about to turf him off the table, when an email from her good friend, Rosa Martell, popped into her inbox.

> Hi babe. Saw this and thought of you twiddling your thumbs on your end-of-year break. And let's face it, you do love a bargain. See link to website, below.

She hadn't exactly planned on traipsing around a dusty old auction room during her time off, but the prospect of getting carried away and bidding on something utterly frivolous did have a certain appeal.

'Oh, what the hell,' she said, and clicked through to the website.

Forty minutes later, she'd printed off the auction catalogue and was parking the white two-seater Sunbeam Alpine, her father had restored for her thirtieth birthday, in the last available space at Barton & Cole.

As the heavens opened, she ran towards a metal door that had been left open to the elements and into a large building, housing the main saleroom. Breathing in the not unpleasant aroma of beeswax, antiques and dust, she stood there scanning the labyrinth of treasures. It was packed with potential buyers wandering the aisles of dusty brown furniture, occasionally stopping to pull out a drawer, peer into a faded mirror, or run a discerning finger along a section of decorative moulding. She spotted a group of people hunched over a glass-topped display cabinet, like magpies coveting the shiny trinkets inside. Each would point to an object, wait impatiently for a member of staff to hand it to them, then hold it up to the light – searching for hallmarks or the slightest imperfection with their jeweller's loupe, before handing it back with a feigned frown to deter the other punters.

On the far side of the room was a man in a green tweed jacket, Tattersall check shirt and copper-coloured bow tie, admiring a Victorian engraving that looked like it hadn't seen a duster in years. *Probably has his own antique shop somewhere in the*

Cotswolds, she surmised, as she made her way over to a large selection of second-hand books.

Where to begin? she thought, glancing at the woman standing next to her.

'Have you read it?' said Emily, seeing the copy of *Watership Down* in her hand.

'Good God no, I can't stand rabbits.'

'Oh, you should, it's wonderful. Terrifying, but a real classic.'

Without so much as a smile, the woman virtually threw Adams' masterpiece back on the shelf and walked off without a word.

'Rude!' said Emily and worked her way down the seemingly endless row of mahogany bookshelves hugging the side wall. The range of titles was enormous – everything from novels to poetry, children's picture books to paperbacks, encyclopaedias, art-house magazines and even a seventeenth-century Bible that was, quite literally, falling apart.

She ran her finger along one of the upper shelves, then stopped in her tracks. With a flutter of excitement, she pulled out a copy of *Dandelion Wine* by Ray Bradbury. She'd been a fan of the American science-fiction writer since reading a collection of his short stories at university. She flipped open the cover and scanned the frontispiece. It was a first edition, not in the best condition, but still a nice find. She noted the number on the shelf and took the printed catalogue from her coat pocket. Lot 143: Twenty-five titles – various, including Bradbury, Rankin and Wodehouse (£100–£150).

Her heart sank. She would have to buy the complete lot for just one book. Reluctantly, she placed it back on the shelf, remembering the promise she'd made herself before leaving the house – a maximum budget of one hundred pounds and not a penny more. She looked at her watch. The auction was due to start at 10.00 am. Still time for a quick scout around, in case something else caught her eye.

She found herself wandering over to the old sepia-toned engraving the bow-tied gentleman had been looking at, earlier. Originally painted by John Everett Millais – a member of the Pre-Raphaelite Brotherhood – *Ophelia* depicted a beautiful yet haunting scene from Shakespeare's *Hamlet*, with a young noblewoman lying motionless in a stream, her heart broken by the recent news of her father's death. Having lost her mind, not only to grief, but also the shame of becoming pregnant by the Prince of Denmark, she'd been seen wandering around Hamlet's castle, handing out rue, an abortive herb and symbol of regret, while singing,

> There's fennel for you, and columbines;
> there's rue for you; and here's some for me;
> we may call it herb of grace o' Sundays.
> O you must wear your rue with a difference.
> There's a daisy. I would give you some violets,
> but they wither'd all when my father died.

Pondering whether to rescue poor Ophelia and take her back to Wickwar, Emily stood back to get a better view and noticed an Edwardian washstand beneath the picture, with a box full of old prints sitting on top. Intrigued, she began flicking through the contents. There were pictures of birds, classical architecture, two portraits of Victorian judges, some old county maps and a wonderful lithograph of a Gloucestershire Old Spot pig. Not her particular choice of art, perhaps, but certainly some potential wall-hangers for the cottage.

Then her fingers came across an old book at the bottom of the box. She pulled it out and opened the red marbled cover. Inside was a beautifully penned inscription, *Sketches by Herbert James Draper*. Not a name she recognised, but it looked interesting and definitely had some age to it. Flicking through the book, she met with page after page of beautiful drawings depicting churches, seascapes, female figures and the face of a young girl, all appended with carefully handwritten notes from the artist. Emily knew then, this was the *something* she'd been hoping to find. She glanced round to see if anyone was watching, but everyone seemed to be readying themselves for the start of the auction. She closed the book and placed it carefully back in the box, making sure it was well hidden. Having noted the ticket number – lot 21a, she placed the box on the floor and nonchalantly kicked it under the washstand.

After registering her details at the office and armed with paddle number 1341, she took a seat near the side aisle, her heart racing with excitement. This was surely what auctions were all about – finding a hidden gem. The question was, had anyone else seen it?

Realising she didn't even know what the auction estimate was, she turned to the second page of the catalogue and ran her finger down the list of lots.

'Oh, you've got to be kidding,' she said, prompting a sideways glance from the woman next to her. There was a lot 21 and lot 22, but no 21a.

She quickly checked the notes at the back and all the other pages in between. The box of prints was nowhere to be found. Perhaps they'd withdrawn it. She was about to get up and walk out, when she saw the auctioneer take his seat at the front of the room, giving the microphone a gentle tap.

'Good morning, ladies and gentlemen,' he said, in a broad West Country accent. 'Welcome to this month's general sale at Barton & Cole.'

May as well hang on and see if it comes up, she thought.

'Firstly, thank you all for braving this awful weather. And, as long as you've kept your wallets nice and dry, we should be absolutely fine,' said the auctioneer, bringing a few chuckles from the patrons.

Soon, the auction was off to a rattling start, and Emily sat waiting, as the first twenty-one lots went under the hammer. Finally, this was it – she was about to discover whether the morning had been a complete waste of time. She rested her sweaty palms on her jeans, willing the auctioneer to call the number. He looked at his lot sheet, then placed his hand over the microphone and leaned across to talk to one of his colleagues.

Here we go, thought Emily, expecting the worst.

'Right, the next lot is ... twenty-one/a. A late entry, so some of you may not have this one listed in your catalogues. We have a box of framed prints, maps etcetera, there – estimated at sixty to eighty. What shall we say to start ... thirty? Twenty, then?'

Emily couldn't believe her luck. She was about to signal her bid, when the man with the bow tie, sitting just a few feet away, put up his hand.

'Thank you, sir. Twenty pounds.'

Emily glared at him, disparagingly. *How dare you bid on my lot!* The image of the sweet little antique shop owner from the

Cotswolds was gone. Now he was nothing more than a ruthless London art dealer, out to make a quick buck. And she, had competition.

'Do I see twenty-five anywhere?' said the auctioneer.

Emily raised her hand.

'Thank you, madam. I have twenty-five. Thirty, sir?'

The bow-tied 'art dealer' nodded.

'Thirty-five, madam?'

She raised her hand again.

'Forty? Forty-five? Fifty? Fifty-five?'

Before long, they'd gone well over the top estimate of eighty pounds, and there was a real buzz in the room as Emily and her opponent battled it out.

Then, as if woken from a dream, Emily heard the words, 'Four hundred, madam?' Suddenly, the limit she'd set herself was nothing but a distant memory. My God, this is what they must mean by auction fever, she thought, wiping tiny beads of sweat from her brow.

'The bidding is against you, madam, at four hundred pounds?'

The man in the bow tie turned to her and peered down his nose, as he waited for a response.

This is it, the moment of truth. I can bail out now and let the old man have his precious sketchbook. Or I can fight, fight to the death!

With her heart firmly in control of her brain, she nodded her assent at the auctioneer. She hadn't come this far just to give in.

'I have four hundred. Four twenty, sir?'

After a moment's hesitation, the man nodded.

'Four forty?' said the auctioneer, looking at Emily.

Sensing a hint of hesitation from her opponent, she confirmed with a wink, bringing a smile from the auctioneer.

'Thank you, madam.' He turned again to the bow-tied man. 'Four sixty, sir?'

The man stared straight ahead, looking calm and collected. A hush fell over the room as everyone waited for his answer. Would he? Wouldn't he?

To Emily's relief, he looked down at his catalogue and shook his head.

'No? Are you sure?' said the auctioneer.

Again, a shake of the head.

'Okay, I have four forty. Do I hear four sixty anywhere?'

Emily held her breath, praying there would be no more bids.

'No? Are we done, then? I will sell at four hundred and forty pounds to the young lady, here on my right.'

Bang! The gavel went down.

'Your number, madam? One-three-four-one? Thank you.'

She'd done it. Barely able to contain her excitement, she watched as her rival calmly closed his catalogue and stood up.

'Well done, young lady,' he said, as he passed her in the aisle, then walked out of the auction room.

Feeling quite pleased with herself, Emily made her way over to the office to settle her account. With the buyer's premium and VAT, the total came to just shy of six hundred pounds. Oh my God, how am I going to explain this to Tom? she thought, handing over her bank card.

After settling the invoice, she took the two copies of her receipt over to the porter and watched, intently, as he went off to retrieve the box of prints. Having placed it on the collection table in front of her, she plunged her hands to the bottom of the box and began rummaging around to check the sketchbook was still there – it was. She thanked the porter, tucked the box under her arm and strolled out to the car park.

The rain had stopped and the low autumn sun was starting to break through the clouds. She placed the box on the Alpine's roof and was just about to put the key in the door when there was a sudden screech of tyres. A black Audi A4 came hurtling out of its parking space and headed straight for her. She flung herself back against the car door and waited for the impact. But the Audi roared its engine and swerved out of the way at the last second, missing her by inches. Emily glared at the driver's dark piercing eyes as he fixed her with an evil stare.

Then she saw who was sitting in the passenger seat – none other than her arch-rival, the bow-tied art dealer. And from the fleeting glimpse she caught as the car sped away, he looked as scared as hell.

Chapter Two

The Cock Tavern, Great Portland Street, London
21 September 1848

With his eyes fixed firmly on the bosom of the serving girl with whom he'd spent the previous evening, Rossetti threw back the last of his gin and leaned in close to his two companions.

'And then, she slowly unbuttoned her blouse and revealed the most delectable pair of milky white—'

'For the love of God ...' said Hunt, thumping his fist on the table, and sending candlesticks and gin glasses flying in all directions, '... can we please get on with the business at hand?'

Rossetti gazed at Hunt through a semi-drunken haze and roared with laughter at his friend's sudden outburst. Born in London, the son of a warehouse manager, William Holman Hunt, or Maniac to his friends, was an exuberant character who generally had plenty to say on most matters. And tonight was no exception. The last of the trio, artist and fellow co-founder of the Pre-Raphaelite Brotherhood, John Everett Millais, knew Hunt better than Rossetti and could see something was troubling him.

'William, calm yourself,' Millais said. 'What on earth is so important that it warrants interrupting Gabriel's tale of Rubenesque passion with our lovely serving girl, here?' Millais lent in close to Rossetti. 'Who is, by the way, an absolute stunner.'

'Yes, come on Maniac, what's got you in such a state, this evening?' said Rossetti, using his finger to tease the last few drops of spilt gin from his jacket.

Hunt continued, 'Before I proceed, I must insist that what I am about to say be kept strictly between the three of us.'

Millais and Rossetti duly nodded their agreement.

'Good. Now, you will recall that at our last meeting, the Brotherhood declared in its manifesto, a complete lack of faith in man's immortality, except for the influence of those great men such as Shakespeare, Leonardo da Vinci, King Alfred, Dante and the like.'

'Not forgetting Homer, Chaucer and Browning,' said Rossetti.

'And Goethe, Keats and Shelley,' added Millais. 'Oh and—'

'Yes, yes. The point I wish to make is that we made a solemn vow to express genuine ideas of what is direct and serious and heartfelt, to the exclusion of what is merely conventional, self-parading and simply learned by rote. My concern is that, without a worthwhile cause through which to concentrate our endeavours, we can never hope to aspire to the heights of those paragons to whom we swore allegiance. Therefore, Brothers, I would like to propose a crusade.'

'Most intriguing. I just hope it warranted wasting three glasses of perfectly good gin in the process.'

Millais waved his hand impatiently in front of Rossetti. 'What kind of crusade, William?'

'If we are to be deemed worthy of our creed, then we must seek to create something truly extraordinary – and what better than a collection of uniquely symbolic works that enable the viewer to experience such profound enlightenment as he, or she, has never witnessed before? A moral feast for the soul, if you will.'

A contemplative silence fell over the table, as the idea permeated their eager, if somewhat gin-dulled, imaginations. Was this the opportunity they'd been waiting for – to not only further the cause of the Brotherhood, but also command the respect and admiration of influential sponsors such as John Ruskin, whom they all venerated so highly? A consenting smile grew on the faces of Millais and Rossetti.

'Gentlemen, I think this calls for more drinks, don't you?' said Rossetti, searching his empty pockets. 'Johnny, I seem to be a little short of coin.'

Rolling his eyes, Millais turned to the nearest serving girl and ordered a large jug of gin, and some bread and cheese to keep the wolf from Rossetti's door. With their glasses full, the meeting continued.

'William, tell us more about this feast for the soul,' said Rossetti.

Hunt thought for a moment then leaned in close, as though spies from the Royal Academy had infiltrated the gin house and were listening to their every word. 'My friends, I look around these streets and cannot help but be ashamed by the deplorable decline in moral values of the common man. He has become blind to the real issues blighting our society today – poverty, adultery and vagrancy among children and the disabled, not to mention salacious behaviour and general ill-treatment of women. We have to strike at the very heart of man's ignorance and greed.'

'Hear, hear,' said Rossetti, stuffing a large piece of cheese into his mouth.

'Gentlemen, we must conceive a collection of seven allegorical works, each symbolising a moral code that will inspire humankind and restore the spirit of compassion and goodwill within the soul of man.'

'Yes, and thereby lead them back to the path of righteousness, so that they may achieve true enlightenment,' added Millais, staring at the candle flame.

'That all sounds very commendable, but why seven paintings?' said Rossetti.

Millais tutted. 'Seven is a sacred number, of course, signifying the union of heaven and earth.'

'Not just that,' said Hunt, raising his finger in the air. 'There are a number of ancient Gnostic texts describing the soul as being bound by seven wrathful powers, from which it must break free in order to ascend to its final resting place.'

'And what are these powers?' said Millais.

Hunt was about to explain when a buxom serving girl walked over and placed a fresh jug of gin on the table. Rossetti, unable to resist an ample cleavage, grabbed her by the arm and pulled her onto his lap.

'Hello, my beauty,' he said, gazing into her fiery eyes.

Hunt coughed loudly.

'Ah, it appears my learned friend is keen to continue with our business. Perhaps some other time,' Rossetti said, pushing her away with a slap on the rear. She turned and gave him a wink that was every bit as good as a promise.

'Gabriel!'

'What?' said Rossetti, with a mischievous smile.

'Apparently, the moral degradation of which we speak is alive and well, and residing in the minds of some around this table,' said Hunt, glowering through his beard.

'My apologies, William – please carry on.'

'As I was about to say, the seven wrathful powers that seek to prevent the soul from achieving its spiritual awakening take the forms of Darkness, Desire, Ignorance, the Lust for Death, the Kingdom of Flesh, the Folly of Man, and finally, Wrath itself. And so, Brothers, it is with our God-given craft that I propose we portray the very nature of these challenges and show those with eyes to see, how they may be overcome.'

'That's quite an undertaking, William,' said Rossetti, conscious of the fact that he had yet to complete a single painting in oils.

'Doing the Lord's good work is, indeed, a weighty commitment. But, as educated men, we must stick to the task; for the sake of those poor unfortunate souls who have strayed into a life of degradation and debauchery.'

'Oh, no matter then. I'm sure with Johnny's prolific rate of production, we'll have the task completed in no time.'

Millais shot Rossetti a sardonic smile. 'Well, I think it's a wonderful idea,' he said, patting Hunt on the shoulder. 'And when all seven works are finished, we should hold a grand exhibition to display them to the world, don't you think?'

That sealed it – a public exhibition would be the capping stone to Hunt's glorious vision. And as the gin flowed and the trails of melted candle wax grew longer by the hour, glasses were raised and toasts made, to the three Brothers and their seven works of enlightenment.

Chapter Three
Wickwar, near Bristol
2 November 1999

Still shaken from the incident in the auction house car park, Emily drew up outside the small, terraced cottage she'd shared with Tom for the past four years. The Old Cider House, as it was known, dated back to the eighteenth century and had a red tiled roof and external walls of cream render. The one unusual feature, marking it out from other properties on the high street, was the old horse and cart entrance leading all the way to a courtyard at the back of the building. Emily always thought it looked barely wide enough to get a Mini Metro through it, let alone a horse and cart.

The huge rainstorm that had been moving up the Severn Estuary for the best part of the day had now reached the village, and with her coat draped over the cardboard box to protect the precious contents, she made a dash for the front door. After much swearing and fumbling with keys, she eventually got it open and burst into the living room to be greeted by Bill the cat nudging at her ankles.

'Hello, baby. You knew it was me, didn't you?' she said, placing the box on the coffee table and bending down to stroke Bill's furry white chin. 'I wouldn't go out there if I were you, you'd drown within minutes.'

Despite opening straight onto the high street, the front room was cosy and warm with a large stone fireplace at one end and a huge red settee along the side wall. Squeezed into the corner by the front window was a baby grand piano, decked with photo frames – one of Tom's family heirlooms, or so he claimed when it arrived out of the blue on moving-in day.

Purring loudly, Bill jumped up on the coffee table to check out the newly arrived object of curiosity.

'No, that's not for you,' said Emily, lifting him down again. 'We don't want cat claws ruining Mummy's ludicrously expensive purchase, do we?'

Having dried herself off and turned the heating up to full blast, Emily retired to the kitchen for a much-needed glass of wine. She stared out of the kitchen window, wishing Tom was there to comfort her, after her near-death experience. But if the last few weeks were anything to go by, she'd be lucky if he was home by seven. She picked up the phone and was about to dial his number when she thought better of it – a long distance hug was of little comfort to her, right now.

Feeling sorry for herself, she flopped down on the settee and emptied the contents of the cardboard box on the coffee table, ignoring the prints and making straight for the sketchbook. On closer inspection, it looked even more impressive than she remembered. Bound with red marbled boards, the spine and corners were covered in a beautiful dark brown leather, and the pages comprised thick white paper that had yellowed slightly at the edges. All in all, it was in remarkably good condition.

She opened it up and there, written inside the front cover, was a date, *1899*, and the words, *Trailing Clouds of Glory*.

Marvelling at such a delightful phrase, she began examining each page, carefully. The first half of the book included various pencil sketches of ecclesiastical scenes, including a large Gothic window, towering stone pillars and an impressive model galleon suspended by chains from a church ceiling.

The final section ended with a series of drawings depicting a young girl dressed in a traditional costume, illuminated by shafts of light from a stained glass window. The accompanying notes confirmed they were from Saint-Pol-de-Léon Cathedral in Breton, North West France.

With a rapidly growing admiration for Herbert Draper, she wandered into the dining room and fired up her laptop and modem to do some internet research. She typed his name into Lycos and waited to see what hits came back. Surprisingly, there weren't that many.

She clicked on the first web-link and began to read:

> **Herbert James Draper** (1863–1920) was an
> English painter in the Victorian era. He
> studied art at the Royal Academy in London
> and undertook several educational trips to
> Rome and Paris between 1888 and 1892. In
> the 1890s, he also worked as an illustrator and
> married his wife Ida in 1891, with whom he
> had a daughter, Yvonne. He focused mainly
> on mythological themes from ancient Greece.
> Though Draper was neither a member nor an
> associate of the Royal Academy, he took part
> in the annual expositions from 1897 onwards.
> During his lifetime, Draper was a well-known
> and respected portrait painter, but in the last
> years of his life, his popularity faded and now
> he is almost forgotten.

'Well, as far as I'm concerned, Mr Draper, you are forgotten no longer,' she said, and spent the next hour ploughing through various art history websites, trying to find out all she could about this enigmatic artist.

Just as she was starting to get disillusioned by her lack of progress, she heard the front door slam.

'I'm in here,' she said.

Tom walked in, looking absolutely shattered.

'Oh dear, bad day?'

'Can you tell?' he said, loosening his tie. '*Sick-note* was off again, today.'

Emily tutted. 'Why don't they just get rid of him?'

'God knows,' said Tom, shaking his head. 'Anyway, that's someone else's problem. What sort of a day have you had?'

'Oh, eventful, I guess you might say. I went to an auction this morning,' and she proceeded to recount the frightening incident in the car park.

'Fucking hell! Did you get the bastard's registration?' said Tom, looking outraged.

'No, I was too busy diving out of the way, at the time.'

'Well, you should contact the auction house. Maybe they've got it on CCTV.'

She'd thought long and hard about calling the police, but time had diluted her appetite for justice, and now she just wanted to let it go and move on. 'Look, it's fine. It had been raining all morning and perhaps his windows were steamed up.'

Tom looked far from convinced. And, in truth, so was she. She decided to change the subject. 'Actually, there's something else I need to tell you.'

Tom gave her a quizzical look. 'What have you bought?'

'Well ... I found this sketchbook buried in a box of old prints,' she said, proudly holding it up.

Tom glanced at it and shrugged. 'And what did you pay for it?'

'It wasn't that expensive, really ... and I am on holiday.'

'How much?'

'Errr, five hundred ... and eighty.' She winced.

'Bloody hell, Emily! Whose is it – John Constable?'

'No. I've been doing some research and I think it's a real find. He's a famous Victorian artist – Herbert James Draper. Surely you've heard of him.'

'Have you?'

Emily glanced down at the book. 'Well ...'

'No, I didn't think so. Look, I'm bloody starving, why don't you tell me about him over dinner?'

Emily carried on with her research while Tom heated up some leftover chilli from the freezer. An hour later, they were sitting on the settee, drinking red wine with The Sundays' album, *Blind*, playing in the background.

'Hey, listen to this,' said Emily, reading out some notes from the sketchbook. '"June, eighteen ninety-nine – the cathedral at Saint-Pol-de-Léon is truly enchanting. I try to capture the look of a local peasant girl standing by one of the stone pillars. As the light streams through the south window, she is a vision of innocence, illuminated in trailing clouds of glory."'

She picked up her laptop and called up the webpage she'd been looking at earlier.

'This must be it. My God, it's beautiful,' she said, showing Tom the painting of a young Breton girl dressed in local costume and bathed in a kaleidoscope of dappled sunlight. Underneath the image was a quote from the *Liverpool Courier* at the time:

... the sweetest thing he has ever done; one of the
truest and tenderest pictures of a child ever painted.

The more she read, the more she became intrigued by Draper
and his work. Even Tom showed some interest, reading a section
from the webpage:

> The portrait study of the girl's head was
> called *The Light of the World*. This
> strongly suggests the influence of
> William Holman Hunt, one of the Pre-
> Raphaelite Brotherhood, and his picture
> of the same name, painted some forty
> years earlier. Draper later changed the
> title to *Trailing Clouds of Glory* and
> appended the words, 'Heaven lies around
> us in our infancy' when it was exhibited
> at the Royal Academy.

Tom nodded. 'Okay, I admit you may have something here. But
I'm still not convinced it was worth paying six hundred quid for.'
    'Yes, but don't you think it's strange that something this
important would be buried at the bottom of an old box, in some
run-of-the-mill general auction?'
    'I tell you what I do think is strange – you spending all that
bloody money, so close to Christmas.'
    'No, seriously, why would they do that?'
    'Beats me. Perhaps they just skipped over it when they did the
cataloguing.'
    'Maybe. I'm seeing Rosa for lunch tomorrow – I'll see what she
thinks about it.'
    Tom smirked.
    'What?'
    'Rosa, having an opinion?' he said, dryly.
    'Don't get sarky – she's my best friend. And she knows a hell
of a lot more about art than you do.'
    'No doubt.'
    Tom had only met her once, at one of Emily's work dos at the
Royal West of England Academy. His initial observation was that
she was far too up-her-own-arse for his liking. But he did admit,

later, that she was intelligent and funny, in an all-consuming kind of way.

Fighting the urge to fall asleep, Emily turned to the last few pages of the sketchbook. These drawings were different from the others and comprised a series of nude studies of a rather voluptuous-looking woman posing on a pedestal. Some showed her gazing out from a doorway with a silken robe cascading from her waist. Emily couldn't quite explain it, but there was something extraordinary about this woman. She seemed to radiate an aura – so powerful, so elemental – it was as if hers was a story that would be told throughout the ages.

But, whatever it was would have to wait until morning; and as the Merlot took effect, Emily put her head on Tom's shoulder, closed her eyes and fell asleep.

Chapter Four

Ardingly Hall, Sussex, England
8 January 1901

James Waltham, now twenty-six and master of Ardingly Hall, stood looking out of the drawing-room window. The moon was full and cast a silvery glow over the formal lawns at the back of the estate – land that, following the death of his father, Charles, from a bout of chronic pneumonia on Christmas Eve, was now his.

The new year had barely begun and James could already feel a dark cloud hanging over the house. Out of respect, the decorations had been taken down early, and Christmas had brought anything but tidings of comfort and joy. At least their financial difficulties were now resolved, thanks to a loan from an old family friend, which Charles had used to pay off their creditors.

But, with his father not long laid to rest in the frozen earth, something else was troubling James – a personal vendetta that both excited him and filled him with dread. Indeed, the decision to see it through had not been an easy one, for he was no longer alone in the world – there was a wife and child to consider. However, recent events had crystallised his thoughts, making him more determined than ever to complete the long-awaited reinstatement of what was rightfully his. And now, the day of reckoning was at hand.

'James, darling,' called a voice from the doorway.

He turned from the window and smiled.

In walked an elegant young woman wearing a long flowing mourning dress, with waves of dark brown hair fashioned into ringlets around her smooth pale neck. Caroline Waltham looked down at the little boy whose hand she was holding, and with reassuring words, led him over to his father who was beaming with pride.

'William, have you come to say goodnight?' said James, picking him up and twirling him round, making him giggle with excitement.

'Don't get him too excited, or Mrs Argyle will never get him down,' said Caroline.

Normally, James would have ignored her, for nothing gave him greater pleasure than to share such joyous moments with his son, in a way his parents never had with him. But tonight, there were more pressing matters. He kissed William on the head and ushered him back to his mother.

'I'll join you for dinner shortly, my dear,' he said, and returned to face the window.

Caroline watched him for a moment, then left him to confront whatever demons had been troubling him, these past few days.

Staring out into the darkness, he gazed upon his own shadowy reflection – a tall, melancholy figure, accompanied by a succession of identical images stretching out in the mirror behind him. As a boy, he would often stand here, scanning the empty gardens, wishing he'd been blessed with just one sibling to play with. But his attention would always return to Millais's painting – to Matilda and Isabella, those poor unfortunate creatures who did so much to stave off the interminably, gut-wrenching loneliness of his childhood. And now, they were gone.

If he harboured any doubts about the chain of events he had set in motion, all he had to do was cast his mind back to that fateful day when his father told him, "We must sell *The Blind Girl.*"

There had been a number of interested bidders, with the painting eventually going to a Mr Albert Wood for the sum of nine hundred guineas, a fraction of its true worth as far as James was concerned. After just one year, Wood sold the picture to William Kenrick, chairman of the committee at the Birmingham Museum and Art Gallery (BMAG), who later gifted it to the gallery. And there it remained, despite a number of more than generous offers from James to buy it back.

He had long since convinced himself that what he was about to do was utterly defensible, and beyond reproach. Of course, some would have called his plan audacious and foolhardy – the product of a criminally insane mind; but in truth, he couldn't have cared either way. As far as he was concerned, there was only one way to be reunited with his beloved painting – he was going to have to steal it back.

*

After a quiet dinner with Caroline, James made his excuses and retired to a small, but comfortable, bedroom on the second floor. The butler had been given the night off, so that suspicions wouldn't be roused. Not even his wife knew what he was about to do – it was better that way, in case the police tried to implicate her as an accomplice. Having packed his bag with a selection of working men's clothes he wouldn't normally be seen dead in, he finished his glass of brandy and sat on the bed. Everything was ready. The men had been briefed, a one-way train ticket to Birmingham New Street station was in his coat pocket and a single room in a small, family-run hotel in Edgbaston had been booked for the following night. He lay back and closed his eyes. Of course he was concerned about getting caught, but all that mattered was to right the wrongs of his father and rescue *The Blind Girl* – the painting he had loved virtually all his life.

Moments later, he was dreaming of newspaper headlines, and what would, perhaps, someday be called "the most daring art theft in one hundred years."

Chapter Five

College Green, Bristol

3 November 1999

Emily approached the Bristol Central Library, the second oldest public library in Britain, and glanced up at Charles Pibworth's gloriously sculpted panels, each containing a group of historical figures. On the left was Chaucer, together with six characters from *The Canterbury Tales*. In the centre stood the Venerable Bede and other literary saints. And on the right, Emily's personal favourite, King Alfred 'The Great' leaning on his sword, next to William of Malmesbury and other famous bards.

Her mind was full of questions: was Herbert Draper a member of the Pre-Raphaelites? Why was he virtually unknown, these days? And just who was the voluptuous woman gazing out from the final pages of his sketchbook?

She crossed the tiled lobby and headed straight for the reference library on the first floor. The art section lay at the back of the massive vaulted reading room, with its glorious cathedral-like columns and glass canopy ceiling – a towering construction that even Isambard Kingdom Brunel would have been proud of.

Savouring the ambience of old books, she dumped her coat and bag on one of the leather-topped reading desks, and went in search of reading material on Draper. Having found his name in the index of a large illustrated book on Victorian art, she took it back to the desk and switched on the small reading light to study it properly. She sat down, took out her notepad and pen, and began to scan the artist's brief résumé.

Interesting though it was, it didn't really tell her anything new – the only paintings listed were three of his most notable works: *The Lament for Icarus*, portraying the myth of the young Cretan prisoner who fell to his death after flying too close to the sun; *Ulysses and the Sirens*, an erotically-charged depiction of three naked temptresses launching themselves at Ulysses as he struggled to free himself from being lashed to the mast of his own ship; and finally, *Pot Pourri*, which Emily recalled from a birthday card she'd once received from a school friend, who'd written inside:

An old-fashioned girl in an old-fashioned dress –
reminds me of you, Emily.

She wandered back to the bookcase and continued her search, until she came across a book called, *The Influence of the Pre-Raphaelite Movement*. She took it back to the reading desk and began to immerse herself in the lives and works of three daring young artists.

William Holman Hunt, John Everett Millais and Dante Gabriel Rossetti were the founding members of the Pre-Raphaelite Brotherhood – a small group of like-minded young men who had become increasingly tired of the overt romanticism of English art. Bound by a set of common beliefs and a sworn covenant, the PRB, as they liked to call themselves, abhorred the dark, lifeless creations that filled the walls of the Royal Academy, believing their so-called creators had become blinded by artificial and outdated conventions, and were completely lacking in the devotion and skill required to capture nature's beauty in its truest sense. In their view, it was the overt sentimentality of sixteenth-century artist, Raphael, and his piece, *The Transfiguration*, that had heralded the regrettable decline in Italian painting. In protest, the Brotherhood would rise like a phoenix from the flames and be recognised as the true advocates of Pre-Raphaelite art – forever paying homage to the work of those painters who plied their trade, before Raphael. But tarring Hunt, Millais and Rossetti with the same PRB brush did them a disservice, and history would ultimately judge them to be of far greater importance to British art than the mere sum of their parts. Millais, a child prodigy, was accepted as a student of the Royal Academy at just eleven years of age, and with such a precocious talent, could easily have achieved huge success in his own right. Instead, he chose to channel his passion into the furtherance of the Brotherhood, much to the benefit of the group's reputation. It was at the Royal Academy that he eventually met Hunt, with whom he struck up a deep and lasting friendship. Rossetti, on the other hand, was a charming, flamboyant character whose desires as a painter and a poet were, if truth be known, the driving force behind the group of aspiring young artisans.

Having gained some insight into the origins of the Pre-Raphaelite Brotherhood, Emily turned to her notepad and paused for a moment. She could have sworn she'd left it open after her first visit to the bookshelves. Now it was closed. She scratched her head and flipped it open. There, right in the centre of the first blank page, someone had written a message, in ink:

Aurora, when will you wake up and see the light?

She looked round, expecting to see some student prankster smirking at her, but everyone seemed to be working away with their heads down. Then, she had a terrible thought. She grabbed her bag and began scrabbling around for the sketchbook.

'Oh, thank God,' she said, sitting back in her chair.

But how had she not seen someone at her desk? She'd only been standing a few yards away. Although, with her nose buried in various books for the last ten minutes, anyone could have done it without her noticing.

She leaned over to speak to the girl sitting opposite. 'Excuse me, did you see anyone at this desk, a few minutes ago?'

The girl looked at her blankly, shook her head and carried on reading.

'Okay, well thanks for that,' said Emily, derisively.

She studied the handwriting once more. *Why are they addressing me as Aurora? It just doesn't make any sense.*

She rubbed the back of her neck and gazed up at the ceiling. Out of the corner of her eye, she saw something moving in the upper gallery. There, in the darkness, was the outline of a man, staring down at her. She couldn't see his face, exactly, but he looked to be short and stocky, and ... was that a bow tie he was wearing? A shiver went down her spine. As she stood up to get a better look, the man merged slowly back into the shadows, and was gone.

What on earth was happening? In the last two days, she'd been almost run over, sent weird messages, and now she was being spied on by strange men in dark corners.

Feeling a little freaked-out, she quickly began stuffing her things back into her bag. In the rush, she knocked the notepad, sending it crashing to the floor. The girl opposite looked up and glared at her.

'Sorry, did I ruin your concentration?' said Emily, and marched off towards the reception area.

She'd only gone about halfway when she heard the sound of footsteps descending the spiral staircase in front of her. She stopped, expecting some dark shadowy figure to jump out and confront her, but it was just a librarian, carrying a pile of books.

For heaven's sake, Emily, ... get a grip, she thought, and walked calmly over to the glass barriers marked, EXIT.

Having reached the ground floor, she let out a sigh of relief, grateful to be back in the presence of 'normal' people milling around the lobby. As she buttoned up her coat, she glanced to her right and, for the briefest of moments, noticed a dark-haired man disappearing behind one of the marble pillars. If she did happen to see him stubbing out a cigarette with his shoe and zipping up his black leather jacket, it certainly didn't register, and she made her way out into the bright autumn sunshine.

*

At the far end of the reading room an elderly gentleman, wearing a tweed jacket, Tattersall check shirt and copper-coloured bow tie, emerged from the shadows of the medieval history section. He calmly walked over to one of the leather-topped tables and switched off the reading lamp that was still glowing brightly. The girl sitting opposite looked up.

'She was obviously in a bit of a hurry,' said the man, and quietly made his way to the exit.

Chapter Six

Hagley Road, Birmingham

10 January 1901

After a sleepless night, James Waltham walked out of the small Edgbaston hotel and climbed into a hansom cab, bound for the centre of Birmingham. The sky was thick with blue-grey cloud that looked like it was going to dump a mountain of snow on the city at any moment. As they made their way along the Hagley Road, he pulled up the collar of his tired old overcoat, beneath which was a selection of working man's clothes to help him blend in with the common people. For today, he wanted to be invisible – to become part of the great unwashed. Even his mop of wavy blonde hair, of which he was immensely proud, had been concealed beneath a plain cloth cap which made his scalp itch at the very thought of it touching his head. Such were the lengths he was prepared to go to, in order to rescue Matilda and Isabella.

As the cab pulled up outside the old Brasshouse on Broad Street, he spotted the other gang members waiting on the corner. A right motley crew, admittedly, but they were bought and paid for, and relatively unsung enough to avoid raising suspicion in the wrong circles.

Having alighted and paid the driver, he walked over to join them.

'Mornin', Mr Waltham,' said Jack Morden, stamping his feet against the biting cold.

Robert Morden turned to his younger brother, grabbed him by the collar and whispered in his ear, 'I swear that fuckin' house brick has more common sense than you. No names, remember?'

'Right, bruv. Won't 'appen again.'

James couldn't help but wonder if his decision to include Jack was a mistake. Their first choice, Bill Cotter, had recently been arrested for the murder of a local shopkeeper and they were suddenly a man down. Robert, begrudgingly, put forward his brother as a last-minute replacement. He was strong, fast and had a punch like a sledgehammer. A risky choice, but one James was willing to take, in the circumstances.

'Sorry about that,' said Robert, shaking James's hand. 'I did tell him to think before he opens his trap.'

James nodded. 'Alright, let's get going, before it gets too busy,' he said, glaring at the steady stream of people making their way into the city centre for the unveiling of an impressive new monument to their beloved Queen Victoria.

Being part of a crowd was alien to James. He could almost feel their footsteps, their coughs, their heartbeats, as the citizens of Birmingham surrounded him on every side. Tiny beads of sweat began to form on his forehead, searing into his skin like pinpricks in the chilly north wind. He wiped them away with the back of his hand and straightened his cap, his mind focused on what was to come.

As they crossed the Broad Street Bridge, he noticed a blind beggar huddled on the pavement. Heedless to his plight, the crowd continued to file past the old man, as if he was invisible. James pulled a shilling from his trouser pocket and lobbed it into the battered tin cup by his feet.

'God bless you sir, this fine day,' said the beggar.

James smiled, then, realising his charitable act was hardly that of a poor working man, he quickly merged back into the growing tide of loyal subjects.

Eventually, the four men entered the hustle and bustle of Chamberlain Square, cautiously making their way through the multitude of police, spectators and street vendors. They were close now. James could feel the adrenalin pumping through his veins as the clock tower next to the museum came into sight. It was just gone twenty past eight. There was no going back, now.

*

Keep calm, you can do this, Collins told himself and took another puff from the small clay pipe he kept hidden from Mr Briggs, his superior at the Birmingham Museum and Art Gallery. He checked his pocket watch – 8.24 am. One minute until he was due to let them in downstairs. He opened the lavatory window and gave his pipe a gentle tap on the metal sill, sending a shower of burning tobacco into the courtyard below. After splashing some cold water on his face, he did up his collar and made his way back through the series of galleries to the Round Room. He was about to enter the grand circular space when the tall, regimented figure of Samuel Briggs stepped out in front of him.

'Ah, Bob, I was wondering where you'd got to,' said the superintendent, responsible for the small team of attendants who monitored the building, and its precious contents, night and day. Ever the dutiful watchman, Briggs had gracefully declined the City Council's invitation for him to attend the unveiling ceremony; preferring instead to keep an eye on his beloved museum.

Little did he know that Bob Collins was being blackmailed by James's gang of thugs, using an affair he'd been having with his wife's sister as leverage for his favours. All he had to do in return was give up the security of the museum, and keep his mouth shut in the process. But could Collins trust these men? Somehow, he doubted it. He knew nothing of their intentions once he'd let them into the building. He assumed they were art thieves, but as to what they were planning to steal, he had no idea; and nor did he care, as long as they kept their promise to conceal his marital indiscretions.

'Is everything alright, Bob, you look a bit distracted?' said Briggs.

'Err ... just a bit tired, that's all; what with the new-born and all.'

'Ah yes, of course. I was the same when Annie and I had our first. I was like a bear with a sore head for a few months. Come on, you can help me check the other floors.'

'I just need to take a piss and I'll be right with you.'

'Alright, but hurry up, lad, we've got lots to do today.'

As Briggs marched off back to his office, Collins stood and looked at his pocket watch.

'Bloody hell!' he said, realising the time, and flew down the narrow stairs leading to the small side entrance.

*

James led his men away from the heaving crowds and into a side street next to the museum. Apart from a few latecomers taking a shortcut to the soon-to-be renamed Victoria Square, all was quiet.

'Is everybody clear on what to do?' he said.

'They should be, I went through it with them last night,' said Robert Morden.

'Good. I don't want any unnecessary rough stuff, is that clear? We do what we need to do and get out.'

'Shame,' said Hawkins, cleaning some dried blood off his knuckle-duster.

A truly vile character, Terrance Hawkins worried James the most. He'd been recommended by a friend of Morden's who had brokered a deal supplying gin to an East End pub. After the landlord reneged on the agreement, Hawkins was called in to apply a little persuasion and make him see the error of his ways. Three broken ribs and a fractured cheekbone later, the deal was back on, and Hawkins' savage reputation assured.

The four men followed the side wall of the gallery, past a couple of drunks pissing against the Darley Dale stone, until they reached a red-painted door marked, PRIVATE – Museum Staff Only. James gave three sharp knocks and waited. After a good half minute, he shot Robert Morden a concerned look and knocked again. Still no response.

'Where the hell is he? We said twenty five past.'

'Give it a minute, he'll be here,' said Morden.

James put his hands in his pockets and paced up and down, nervously. Another minute went by. He was just thinking about breaking a window when there was a loud clunk and the door swung open.

'I'm really sorry,' said Collins, standing to one side to let them in.

'We were beginning to think you'd forgotten about us,' said James.

'No, no – I got held up, that's all.'

The men entered the small foyer with Hawkins bringing up the rear. He walked up to Collins and shoved him back against the door, his blackened teeth and foul breath right in the young man's face.

'You came this close to never seein' your family again, matey,' said Hawkins, holding up two pinched fingers.

Collins froze, his eyes bulging and tears streaming down his cheeks as the vice-like grip on his genitals grew tighter and tighter.

'Leave him be, we've got work to do,' said Robert.

With one last excruciating squeeze, Hawkins let go and gave Collins a glare that he would remember for the rest of his days.

Hawkins and the two Morden brothers unbuttoned their overcoats and each pulled out a revolver.

'Alright, just calm down,' said James, sensing the rising testosterone levels. 'We're not here to act like a bunch of thugs.'

Hawkins shoved the barrel of his gun into the gallery attendant's ribs. 'Right, ... as long as they behave 'emselves,'

'You won't get any trouble from me,' said Collins, glaring at Hawkins' trigger finger.

'How many guards on duty?' said Robert.

'We're down to three – Superintendent Briggs, Ashcock and me. Just like I said.'

'Good, now if you'd lead the way,' said James.

Having finally been released by Hawkins', Collins bolted the side door and led them up a narrow staircase to the main gallery complex on the first floor.

'The office is this way,' he said, pointing down the corridor towards the magnificent Round Room.

As much as James loathed the museum for what it had taken from him, he couldn't help but admire this particular architectural wonder, with its impressive glass dome and red-painted wall that formed a perfect circle. It reminded him of the Pantheon in Rome – visited during one of the rare foreign trips on which, as a boy, he'd been allowed to accompany his parents. But there was no time to admire the cabinets of fine Chinese porcelain, or row upon row of old master paintings – a much more cherished treasure was calling his name.

They progressed through the double-arched doorways on the far side and into a large rectangular foyer at the top of the main staircase. Thinking his work was done, Collins turned and marched off in the direction of Briggs' office.

'Where do you think you're going?' said Robert.

'We agreed I'd be sat with the others, so Mr Briggs wouldn't get suspicious.'

'There's been a change of plan,' said James. 'To be quite honest, I don't trust you. So I'd like you to stay with us, if you don't mind.'

'I wouldn't let on, honest, I—'

Before Collins could complete his protestations, Hawkins grabbed him by the collar and rammed the barrel of his gun up his nostril.

'You heard the man. Now shut your fuckin' pie hole.'

Robert Morden, followed by the others, stepped quietly across the foyer towards a small office in the far corner. The door was closed but a light was shining through the frosted glass. He grabbed the handle, gave a nod to James, then burst into the room.

'What the hell?' said Briggs, getting up from his chair.

Sitting on the other side of the desk, Ashcock froze, then slowly raised his hands. Collins went and stood next to him, doing likewise.

'Sit down!' said James.

Briggs stared at him, as if trying to process the apparent contradiction between a well-to-do accent and a lawless thug, dressed in working man's clothes. He returned to his seat.

'As you see, we have come prepared,' said James, alluding to the three guns pointing at the museum employees.

'What do you want?' said Briggs.

'What I want, sir, is for you to keep quiet and do as I say. I've instructed my men to suppress their itchy trigger fingers during our brief visit to your gallery. But if you try to raise the alarm, or attempt in any way to hamper our endeavours, then I fear, gentlemen, it will be the last mistake you ever make. Is that clear?'

Collins and Ashcock nodded, followed reluctantly by Briggs. James gave the signal to Robert, who pulled three lengths of rope from his coat pocket.

'If you'd kindly stand and face the wall with your hands behind your back,' said James. 'You too, Bob.' Collins turned and glared at the mention of his name – his treachery now apparent for all to see.

Robert Morden and Hawkins pushed the two young attendants up against the wall and bound their hands tightly behind them.

'If you think you're going to get away with this, you're a bigger fool than young Collins, here,' said Briggs.

'Shut your trap, or I'll cut out your tongue and shove it down your throat,' said Hawkins.

Briggs stared at him and turned his face to the wall. 'I'll not forget your ugly mug in a hurry, that's for sure.'

Hawkins let out a hollow laugh, bringing the butt of his revolver crashing down on the back of Briggs' skull. The Superintendent hit the wall, then collapsed on the floor, unconscious.

'For God's sake man, control yourself,' said James.

'He fuckin' asked for it,' Hawkins replied.

'I don't care. Now get his keys.'

Hawkins unclipped the large ring of keys from Briggs' belt and tossed them to Robert Morden.

James stepped into the doorway. 'Bring those two out here,' he said, moving back into the foyer. 'And why don't you drag the unfortunate Mr Briggs along, too?'

With their hands bound behind their backs, Collins and Ashcock were escorted to a solid wooden door marked, STAFF ONLY, while Hawkins grabbed Briggs by the collar and hauled him across the tiled floor to join them.

'Down on your knees, please,' said James.

Collins and Ashcock duly obliged, helped by a swift kick from Hawkins.

Robert Morden pulled a small bottle of chloroform from his pocket and poured some of the clear liquid onto two rags. After handing one to Hawkins, they each grabbed the collar of one of the attendants and held the rag against their mouth, making them squirm and writhe in protest.

When the anaesthetic had done its work, Hawkins dropped Collins to the floor and pointed to Briggs. 'What about him?' he said to Robert.

'Tie his hands behind his back and gag him. We don't want him shouting his mouth off when he wakes up.'

Using Briggs' keys, Robert unlocked the door to the small store cupboard, revealing a row of shelves along the back wall and just enough floor space for three bodies to be laid out, side by side. They dragged the museum men inside and locked the door.

'Good,' said James. 'Now, Hawkins, Jack, ... you two stay here and keep an eye on things, while Robert and I go and get the painting.'

With the whole building to themselves, James and Robert made their way through the Round Room and into the Industrial Gallery – a magnificent balconied hall with cast-iron arches and huge gas lamps suspended from the glass ceiling. It looked more like a grand railway station than an art gallery.

James's pace quickened as he approached the small gallery at the far end. With a rush of excitement, he strode through the archway and looked to his left. There on the wall in front of him was *The Blind Girl*. He stood motionless, as if transfixed by some holy vision. To him, this was no mere painting – its two subjects were manifest, his long-lost friends in everything but flesh and blood.

'She's a beauty, sir,' said Robert.

Without responding, James walked up to the picture and held out his arms, as if to embrace a loved one. He took hold of the frame and gently freed it from its mounting, gazing at the palette of radiant colours.

'We'd better get a move on, sir?'

James looked round, suddenly realising where he was.

'Of course. We have a lot to do,' he said, laying the picture gently on the floor.

Robert Morden undid his overcoat and removed a small bag of tools; rolling it out in front of him. With the precision of a top Victorian surgeon, he took out a hammer and chisel, knelt down over the back of the frame and took aim. James held his breath.

The operation was about to begin.

Chapter Seven

83 Gower Street, London

9 December 1848

Rossetti held up the lantern and peered into the background of Millais's latest creation – a homage to John Keats' poem, *Isabella*.

'Now tell me, Johnny,' he said, his face pressed up close to the painting and contorted with concentration. 'What exactly am I to make of this pale, languid fellow sitting at the back, here?'

'Ah yes, a rather fine likeness, don't you think?' said Millais, not sensing the tone.

Watching from the other side of the room, Hunt grinned to himself. 'And holding that glass up to his lips, he looks just like you, Gabriel.'

Rossetti snorted, 'On the contrary. He is the most grotesque character I have ever had the displeasure of seeing committed to canvas. Have I done something to offend you, Brother?'

'No, of course not,' said Millais, looking hurt by the suggestion. 'There was just something in his demeanour that reminded me of you, that's all.'

'And what was that, exactly? The ghastly brown tunic portraying an appalling lack of style and grace? Or the way he is trying to extract every last drop from his wine glass? Or is it, perhaps, that unfeasibly large nose?'

'That'll be it,' murmured Hunt, enjoying the uneasy exchange between his two Pre-Raphaelite kinsmen.

'And do my eyes deceive me, or is that a scar on his left temple?'

Hunt could refrain no longer, and wandered over to the easel to have a look for himself.

'Be honest, Maniac. Tell me I'm not overreacting, here?'

'On the contrary, Gabriel, I think it's quite magnificent.'

Rossetti gave him a derisory sneer and slumped into an armchair by the fire.

'Then again, if you're looking for promotion to a character at the front of the picture, perhaps Johnny could cast you as the man kicking the dog,' said Hunt.

Rossetti picked up a log and hurled it into the hearth. 'Oh, why stop there? Why not get him to paint my face on the damned hound, and be done with it?'

Millais laughed. And then, for the sake of cordiality, thought he'd better change the subject. 'Is William Michael joining us tonight?'

'No,' said Hunt, stroking his beard. 'I hope you don't mind, Gabriel, but I told him we were otherwise engaged, so that we might discuss details of our forthcoming crusade.'

Rossetti nodded, approvingly. 'Although, can I suggest we move to more comfortable surroundings?' he said, not wanting to be in the presence of his wine-guzzling caricature a moment longer.

Having decamped to the warmly lit drawing room to enjoy some of Mrs Millais's legendary hospitality, Hunt went and stood by the mantelpiece.

'Brothers, you will recall when we met some weeks ago to discuss our latest venture, the details were a little sketchy. So, I have given the matter some thought and I have a proposal to put to you.'

Rossetti and Millais looked on as Hunt paced back and forth in front of the fire, like an expectant father awaiting the birth of his latest progeny.

'As you know, these paintings will have, as their inspiration, seven sacred doctrines with which to accompany the soul of man during its ascension, thereby arming it against the powers of darkness that wish nothing more than to avert its heavenly progress. With that in mind, I propose that we name these seven beacons of enlightenment – *The Lights of the World*.'

The proposition met with stunned silence. Hunt stood looking at his two friends, waiting for a reaction. 'Well, say something, for goodness' sake.'

Millais stood up and patted his friend on the back. 'William, that is indeed a worthy title.'

They both turned to Rossetti, waiting for the tirade of abuse, but none came. A wry smile grew on his face. 'It's perfect,' he said, standing up to embrace them both. 'It says everything about what we are trying to accomplish.'

As a poet, he sometimes frowned upon Hunt's habitual bark and bluster, but on this occasion, even he could not have chosen a more fitting epithet.

Hunt gave a smile of relief and joined his two Brothers in a toast to their newly christened enterprise.

Of course, artists being artists, the discussion went on long into the night; and after much debate and pontification, each of the seven works were duly granted their own bespoke title.

*

The following day, Hunt wrote to both of them outlining the pact they had made, together with a newly designed motif for their consideration. For they had conceived of an idea in which each held an unswerving passion and belief – firing their creative spirit and serving only to strengthen the brotherly bond between them.

More importantly, *The Lights of the World* would help to bring much-needed salvation to a nation of souls in dire need of restitution; whilst also providing a welcome boost to the three Brothers' respective careers, of course.

In reality, however, as was so often the case with the three young romantics, mere hope and aspiration were never enough to bring their dreams to fruition – for the human frailties of life and love would always seem to get in the way.

Dearest John, Dearest Gabriel,

At a meeting on this ninth day of December, 1848, we the undersigned, being the three principle founding members of the PRB, do hereby agree to produce a series of seven painted works, henceforth known as *The Lights of the World.*

Devout adherence to the sacred doctrines, portrayed therein, will empower man to discover the true nature of his humanity, preparing the soul for the seven challenges it must face on the path to enlightenment and true spiritual awakening.

Those with eyes to see, let them see.

<u>Darkness</u> – Blessed are they that harbour the beacon of hope, when all around them is desolation and despair.

<u>Desire</u> – A man's lust is his eternal shame, for the appetite of a licentious man will never be fulfilled.

<u>Ignorance</u> – The mind is not merely a vessel to be filled, but a vine to be nurtured for the most precious of fruit.

<u>Lust for Death</u> – All must dissolve into their beginnings, but only those with love in their heart may ascend the heavenly realms.

<u>Kingdom of Flesh</u> – When the body returns to nature and is resolved into its own roots, may the soul rise up, free from the bondage of man.

<u>Folly of Man</u> – Learned we may be with another man's learning, only wise can we become with wisdom of our own.

<u>Wrath</u> – eternal peace awaits those that cast off the bonds of oblivion, to follow the everlasting light.

Signed, this tenth day of December, 1848

William Holman Hunt
John Everett Millais
Dante Gabriel Rossetti

Chapter Eight

College Green, Bristol

3 November 1999

Emily wasn't one to get spooked that easily, but the strange goings-on in the central library, earlier, had definitely unnerved her. As she walked past City Hall, with its pair of gilded unicorns staring out across the city, she looked round to see if the bow-tied man was following her. Thankfully, he was nowhere to be seen.

Her lunch appointment with Rosa was only a ten-minute walk away, but all uphill, so she walked to the bottom of Park Street and hailed a cab. A few minutes later she was standing in the bar of Browns brasserie, ordering a large glass of Merlot. Rosa was rarely on time for anything, so she took a seat by the window and gazed at the passers-by. Normally, she loved people-watching, but her mind kept going back to the strange events of the past couple of days.

Just as she was starting to get herself worked up again, in walked Rosa wearing a mustard-coloured leather coat, jeans and a fluffy cream roll-neck jumper that accentuated her short dark hair. Swinging her handbag as though she hadn't a care in the world, she mouthed, 'Glass of Prosecco, please,' to the barman and walked over to where Emily was sitting.

'Hi there, babe. I'm not late, am I?'

Emily smiled to herself. 'No, you're fine.'

She always felt relaxed in Rosa's company. The two of them had clicked from the moment they first met, six months ago, when Rosa joined the Royal West of England Academy. There was something about her – the sharp sense of humour, the confident demeanour, the classy London accent, perhaps. She was a nice person to be around and just the tonic Emily needed right now.

'How's the holiday going?'

'Crikey, where do I start? Tell you what, let's order first and I'll tell you all about it.'

Rosa gave her a quizzical look. 'Sounds intriguing.'

A young waiter came and showed them to their table in a quiet corner of the restaurant. Formerly the old Bristol Museum, and with a frontage modelled loosely on the Doge's Palace in Venice, its high ceilings and aspidistras evoked the perfect atmosphere of grand Edwardian dining.

Rosa took a sip of her Prosecco, rested her chin on her hand and smiled at Emily. 'Come on then, what have you been up to?'

Emily explained about the auction at Barton & Cole, how she'd found the Draper sketchbook hidden in a box, and her subsequent bidding war with the bow-tied old man.

'Have you got it with you?' said Rosa.

'Of course I've got it with me.'

Emily fished the sketchbook out of her bag and handed it to her. With an expert demeanour, Rosa carefully turned each page and studied the delicate drawings.

'This is a real find,' she said.

'You think so?'

'Absolutely. These drawings are stunning.'

'I've been trying to find out about Herbert Draper, but there's nothing much out there,' said Emily.

'Well, I do know he was highly thought of by the Royal Academy. In fact, he studied there in his younger days, I believe.'

'So, he was well known in his day?'

'Oh yes, he was one of the most successful painters of classical mythology and portraiture in the early twentieth century.'

'Then why did he just fade into obscurity?'

'I suppose, in the end, he got overshadowed by the likes of John Waterhouse and Frederic, Lord Leighton, who painted in a similar style. And Burne-Jones, of course.'

'God, you know your stuff, Rosa.'

'Oh, not really. Just bits and pieces I've picked up along the way. Look, if you want to find out more about him, there's a chap I know who's a real expert on Victorian art – he's written books and everything.'

'Okay, who's that?'

'Doctor Julian Mountfield, he's curator of Western Art at the Ashmolean in Oxford.'

'Wow, how well connected are you?' said Emily, sitting back in her chair. 'And you think he'd meet with me?'

'Sure. I've only met him a couple of times, but he's a really nice guy. Richard has his contact details. I'll give him a shout when I get back to work, if you like.'

'Okay, thanks. But do me a favour; please don't mention the sketchbook to Richard.'

'No problem. I'll just say you're doing some research on Draper.'

Having finished their lunch, Emily went to the ladies' room, leaving Rosa to examine the sketchbook. When she came back, Rosa had a somewhat puzzled look on her face.

'What is it? Have you found something?'

'I'm not sure. This looks a bit strange, don't you think?' Beneath one of the sketches of the scantily clad young woman, Draper had written a tiny footnote:

Awaken, and see the light.

'What does that mean?' said Emily.

Rosa shook her head. 'I have absolutely no idea.'

'Hold on.' Emily fished in her bag for her notepad. 'It's a bit like ... yes, it's almost the same words, ... look.'

Aurora, when will you wake up and see the light?

'Sorry, I don't understand. What is this you're showing me?' said Rosa.

'Ah, I haven't told you what happened this morning, have I?

'Err, ... no, you haven't.'

'I mean, it's probably nothing, but it did freak me out a bit.'

'Okay, well spit it out then.'

'Right. So I went to the Central Library to do some research, and when I was sitting at one of the reading desks, I saw this man in the gallery upstairs, staring at me.'

'Some guy eyeing you up, you mean?'

'No, nothing like that. Anyway, before that, I went to look for some books on Draper. When I came back, someone had written this on my pad.'

Rosa re-read the handwritten note and laughed. 'Probably just some randy young student trying to grab your attention.'

'That's what I thought. But I had a good look round and there was no one – lecherous or otherwise.'

'So, why address you as Aurora?'

Emily shrugged. 'Not a clue. What do you think it means?'

'Well, it could be asking you to open your eyes to something. You know, wake up and smell the roses. Or ...'

'Or, what?'

'It might be some kind of warning.'

'Oh God, I hadn't thought of it like that.'

'Babe, I'm sure it's nothing. As I said, it's probably just someone playing a practical joke. Have you shown Draper's sketchbook to anybody else?'

'Only Tom, but he wouldn't have mentioned it to anyone. There is something else I haven't told you.'

Rosa rolled her eyes. 'Go on.'

'After the auction, the old man I was bidding against ... well, he just seemed a bit creepy, put it that way.'

'Okay. That doesn't mean he's been stalking you and leaving you strange messages, does it?'

'No, but when I walked outside, he was in a car with this other guy, a real hateful-looking bastard. Anyway, as they were leaving the car park, they kind of, well ... tried to run me over.'

'What?!' exclaimed Rosa, causing people on nearby tables to stop and stare. 'You're kidding? Did you get his registration?'

'No, as I said to Tom, I was too busy diving out of the way at the time.'

'Perhaps he wasn't looking where he was going?'

'No, he saw me alright. The more I think about it, the more this whole thing is starting to creep me out.'

'Sounds like the old man was a bit pissed off that you outbid him. On the upside, you got the sketchbook and he didn't.'

'But you should've seen the driver, Rosa. He looked as evil as anything.'

'Maybe he was just jealous of that clapped-out old banger you call a sports car.'

'Hey, that's my pride and joy you're talking about.'

'Of course it is. Look, I've got to get back to work, but I think you've stumbled on something truly wonderful, babe,' said Rosa, touching her arm. 'I'll give you a call when I've got Julian's number off Richard, okay?'

'Thanks, Rosa, I really appreciate it.'

They walked out into the cold grey afternoon and gave each other a hug. Emily wrapped her scarf around her neck and strolled along the Queen's Road, busy with afternoon shoppers. She thought about what Rosa had said, and decided to focus her attention on the meeting with Julian Mountfield at the Ashmolean. If anyone could enlighten her about Herbert Draper and his sketchbook, it was him.

*

Standing outside the entrance to the Bristol Museum, a man took a long, slow drag of his cigarette and watched as Emily strolled past. He unzipped his black leather jacket, pulled a mobile phone from his pocket and dialled a number.

'We're on,' he said, and hung up.

Flicking his cigarette butt into a nearby flowerbed, he calmly zipped up his jacket and walked on after her.

Chapter Nine

Birmingham Museum and Art Gallery
10 January 1901

Samuel Briggs felt the creeping dawn of consciousness peer over the horizon and hit him like a tidal wave. For a few dazed moments, he basked in the warm glow as his body awoke. Then came the pain – a dull throbbing river coursing from the top of his skull to the blood-encrusted estuary of his broken nose. He opened his eyes, but the world remained black, save for a handful of tiny stars zipping back and forth across his field of vision. Even the act of blinking was a struggle, as though his eyelids had been welded shut. His hands and arms felt strange too, refusing to function, as if no longer his own.

What the hell was wrong – was he paralysed? Was he dead? He couldn't tell. He tried to swallow, but something dry and musty had been stuffed into his mouth, cutting into his teeth and gums. Then it dawned on him – would a dead man feel this pain?

With his brain fighting a battle between consciousness and sleep, distant flashes of memory started to return. The men in the office. Three of them, or was it four? They had guns and Collins was with them. Oh God, the bang on the head. It must have been them who put him here – wherever he was. That was all he could remember.

After lying quietly for a few minutes, cognitive reasoning began to kick in – those bastards had tied his hands behind his back, gagged him, then dumped him somewhere. But where? His right arm appeared to be pressed up against a wall. The other was touching something soft and heavy. Most likely, Collins or Ashcock were lying there with him and, judging by the warmth he could feel down his left side, at least one of them was still alive. He gave the body next to him a nudge with his shoulder, hoping for some kind of response, but none came. No doubt, they'd been knocked unconscious, too.

Ignoring the pain in his hands and wrists, he hauled himself up into a sitting position and looked around for anything recognisable. Everything was black, except for a sliver of light beneath the door behind him. Then it came to him – the tiled floor, the smell of paint and cleaning fluids. He was in the storage cupboard off the main foyer.

Buoyed by his newly restored logic, he rocked back and forth on his backside in an effort to stand up. But he was not a young man anymore, and after a few attempts and with his head throbbing, he fell back on the floor, exhausted. He gazed up at the ceiling and thought for a moment. Perhaps he would do better lying on his side. He pushed against the wall and managed to roll himself over. Then, drawing his knees up to his chest as far as they would go, he leaned on his shoulder and pushed his weight forward, until, after much heaving and groaning, he finally managed to tip himself over into a kneeling position.

Having gotten to his feet, he took a few seconds to get some air into his lungs, whilst trying to picture the layout of the tiny cupboard; and, more importantly, what he could use to cut his hands free. If memory served him correctly, there was a toolbox on one of the shelves along the back wall. He turned round and took a step forward into the space where he'd been lying. Then another. And before he could take a third, the edge of one of the shelves hit him in the sternum. At least now he had a point of reference. He turned round the other way and, with his back to the row of shelves, felt his way along the edge, seeking out and identifying as many objects as he could reach. There were paint tins, candles, brushes, lampshades, even a paraffin heater; everything except a toolbox. He was just getting into his stride when his right shoulder bumped into the far wall – the end of the line. Unable to reach the top shelf, and with his head thumping, he slumped back down to the floor, catching his knuckles on something sharp. With blood oozing from the cut, he let out a muffled groan, and began cautiously investigating the offending object with his fingers. Cold, hard, lots of narrow ridges, one on top of the other – it appeared someone had stacked a pile of ceramic tiles against the wall. In which case, perhaps he wouldn't need the toolbox, after all.

Sitting up straight, and holding the rope tightly against the corner of the stack, he began moving his hands up and down on either side. The old rope was not in the best condition and began to fray quite easily. Within a couple of minutes, he'd already cut through one of the loops and tried yanking his wrists apart to try and loosen it. But the binding held fast. As his arms started to ache, he laboured on, taking a break every few seconds, until, finally, the rope loosened and with a jerk of his hands, it dropped to the floor.

After rubbing his hands and wrists to restore the circulation, he got to his feet and untied the gag from his mouth, searching the darkness for inspiration. With more than twenty years' service in Her Majesty's Army, he was damned if he was going to sit there like a coward, waiting to be released from a bloody broom cupboard. Whoever these men were, he was going to come out fighting. But it wouldn't be easy. Even if he could escape, far more dangerous challenges lay ahead. Experience had taught him that men like these were ruthless and unpredictable, but seldom intelligent – and that would be their downfall. It was time to think clearly. His one-man campaign was just getting started.

*

Jack Morden watched as Hawkins paced up and down the foyer, clutching his groin and muttering various obscenities.

'I'm goin' for a piss,' said Hawkins, finally. 'Stay here and don't move, got it?'

'Yeah, yeah. Take as long as you like,' said Jack, knowing full well that Hawkins' recurring bladder infection would mean he'd be gone for some time.

Jack Morden was a colourful character whose nervous disposition meant he couldn't sit still, not even for a second. People would often remark that he'd got the worst case of St Vitus' dance they'd ever seen. But when, on this day of all days, he should have been concentrating on the job in hand, the museum's treasures proved too much of a temptation; and, no sooner had Hawkins disappeared in the direction of the nearest toilet, Jack's mind and feet began to wander.

'May as well take a quick look around, while I'm here,' he said, peering through the marble arch into the Round Room.

He was about to abandon his post when he heard a strange squeaking sound behind him. He spun round and scanned the room. Any normal person would have gone to check it out, but the thought of all that naked female flesh on the gallery walls next door was too much for young Jack, and in the battle of lust over logic, there was only ever going to be one winner.

'Probably a mouse,' he muttered, and was gone, leaving the vicinity completely unguarded.

*

Birmingham Corporation's budget hadn't quite run to installing an electric light in the broom cupboard, so there was no point in Briggs feeling for a light switch. After checking the pulse of his two colleagues and loosening their gags, he knelt down to peer through the keyhole and could just make out a small section of the foyer leading to the main staircase.

Was anybody out there? He couldn't tell. It was a gamble he'd have to take. He took hold of the doorknob and gave it a gentle turn, causing it to emit a long dry screech, like a scalded cat. He froze, waiting for the sound of footsteps on the other side, but none came. He pulled the knob, only to find the door was locked. Not a problem, he thought, and reached for the ring of keys on his belt. His heart sank – they were gone. Once more, shooting pains coursed through his head. He rubbed the blood-encrusted wound on top of his skull and leaned against the wall to ponder his next move. Truth be told, he didn't have a next move.

With his hopes of a daring escape dashed, Briggs stood there, trying to cast his foggy mind back to what had happened earlier. How had the men gotten into the gallery? Was that right, that Bob Collins had colluded with the gang, letting them into the building while his back was turned? It would certainly explain why he'd been acting strangely, that morning. He must have sneaked into the office and stolen the spare keys from his desk drawer.

Then, it hit him. His heart pounding with anticipation, he reached across and felt inside the pockets of the man lying at his feet. Finding only a crusty handkerchief and a small wooden pipe, he turned to the jacket pocket. Tucked inside was a bunch of keys. Not normally one for overt displays of emotion, he punched the air and began picking through the ring. Four years of locking and unlocking every door in the museum was about to pay dividends, and, at last, he came to a likely candidate. His fingers danced over the warm steel of the O-shaped bow, two ringed shoulders along the shaft and a square bit with two turret-shaped teeth. He held the key between thumb and forefinger and offered it up to the little bead of light shining through the keyhole. It turned with a click. He smiled and pressed his ear to the door. Everything appeared quiet outside.

He slowly turned the doorknob once more and pulled until the tiniest gap appeared, scanning the open space for any sign of his captors – it was empty. He walked out into the foyer, following the side wall until he reached the entrance to the Round Room. Crouching as low as he could, he scuttled past the double archway and headed straight for his office, hoping the gang hadn't taken up residence in his absence.

Seeing the light off, he crept inside and sat down at his desk. There was no time to relax. He picked up the telephone and waited for the operator to connect him – silence.

'Hello, ... hello?' he said, frantically clicking the receiver. The line was dead. They must have cut the telephone wires, too. He felt the back of his skull and looked at his fingers. At least the bleeding had stopped, but his head still hurt like hell. There had to be a way to get out and notify the police. He examined the spare keys – all useful, but the ones to the exterior doors were on his main set, now in possession of the robbers. He fingered the empty metal loop still attached to his belt. It was as if one of his vital organs had been removed, not feeling the weight of those keys hanging from his waist. He knew then, there'd be no outside assistance – it was up to him to put an end to this atrocity.

Like a thief in his own museum, he crept back across the foyer and removed a large fire extinguisher from its wall mounting. Hiding behind a marble pillar leading to the Round Room, he saw one of the robbers, standing just a few yards away, jerking himself off in front of a large Titian nude.

Under cover of the loud banging noise coming from the nearby gallery, Briggs crept up behind the wanking man and brought the copper cylinder crashing down on his skull, sending him sprawling across the floor. Having checked he was out cold, Briggs grabbed his arms and dragged him back into the foyer.

'I know just the place for you,' he said, opening the store cupboard and hauling him into the space he, himself had recently vacated.

He bound the robber's hands and feet, then gagged him with the rag they'd used on him. A quick search of the man's pockets yielded a revolver. As he held it in his hand, it brought back memories of that fateful day at the Battle of Majuba Hill where, despite being shot at by a group of Boer snipers, he and a handful of fellow Gordon Highlanders had bravely stood their ground, contrary to Sir George Colley's orders to retreat, only for them to be captured later by a crack troop of Boer Commandos. Strengthened by the memory of fallen comrades, he stuffed the gun in his pocket and headed back to his office to plan his next move. The other gang members couldn't be far away, and when they did finally realise they were a man down, they were bound to come looking. His only chance of survival was to do what the Boer's had done, to bring about his own surrender, all those years ago – fire and manoeuvre, or *vuur en beweeg*, as they said in Afrikaans.

*

Rubbing his groin, Hawkins made his way back to the foyer, expecting to see Jack Morden standing guard, but there was no sign of him.

'Where the fuck's he got to?' he said, and marched off into the Industrial Gallery.

Also suffering from a severe ear infection, no doubt caught from the filthy bed linen at Madam Balzac's East End whorehouse – the source of most of his ailments – he cupped his hand over his ear, to shield it from the cacophony of bangs emanating from the end gallery. Standing in the doorway, he shouted over to Robert Morden and James, who were busy dismantling Millais's picture frame.

'You seen, Jack?' he yelled, wincing as Morden inflicted another precise hammer blow.

The two men looked at each other.

'Isn't he with you?' said James.

Hawkins shook his head. 'He disappeared when I went for a piss. Don't worry, I'll find him.'

'Tell him he's in for a right bollocking when I see him,' said Robert.

Hawkins walked back through the chain of galleries, cursing as he went. As he entered the foyer, a loud crash made him stop in his tracks. It seemed to have come from the superintendent's office. He approached the doorway and drew his revolver.

'Jack? Is that you?' he said, pushing the door open with the barrel of his gun.

It swung back revealing the small darkened room. Everything seemed as they'd left it. Then he noticed a fire bucket lying on its side, its contents scattered across the floor. He walked in, his eyes darting left and right, trying to make out shapes in the gloom. Something caught his eye – there in the shadows. Before he knew it, a shower of sand came flying out of the darkness, blinding him instantly. He stumbled backwards, trying to wipe the sand from his eyes and waving his gun aimlessly in front of him. With tears streaming down his pock-marked cheeks, he could just make out the dark grey outline of a man pointing a gun at him. He rubbed his eyes and saw it was the superintendent he'd locked in the broom cupboard, not fifteen minutes before.

'How the fuck did you get out?'

'Drop it,' said Briggs, 'unless you want to lose a kneecap.'

'I wouldn't get too cocky, if I was you, mate.' replied Hawkins, 'My gun's pointin' right at your bollocks.'

The two men stood either side of the small desk, their arms outstretched in the half-light, as if engaged in a duel.

Hawkins laughed. 'You ain't got the guts to shoot me,' he said, rubbing his nose on his sleeve.

'Just give me an excuse,' said Briggs.

Hawkins grinned. 'That gun you got there, ... belonged to the lad who was with me. Now, I dunno what you've done with him, and I really don't care. Trouble is, he's a bit of a fuckwit, see. And we never trusted him enough to put bullets in it. So you're holdin' an empty gun, my friend.'

'It feels loaded to me,' said Briggs, assessing the weight in his hand.

The two men continued to glare at each other across the desk. Hawkins, his eyes streaming and bloodshot, blinking continuously as though suffering from some kind of affliction.

Briggs, on the other hand, looking the epitome of calm – watching, waiting.

Hawkins was about to break the deadlock when a loud *clang* sounded from the clock tower above their heads. He put his hand up to his ear and glanced up at the ceiling. Briggs quickly grabbed the letter knife from his desk and thrust it into Hawkins' shoulder. The thug dropped his gun, howling in agony.

'Up against the wall, you piece of scum,' said Briggs, pushing the barrel of his revolver into Hawkins' temple.

Without a second thought, Briggs raised his arm and brought the butt of his gun down hard on the back of Hawkins' skull, sending him crashing to the floor.

'That was for earlier,' he said, and threw the gun on the desk.

He collapsed into his chair, took out his pocket watch and gave it a gentle tap; glancing up at the ceiling where the clock tower bells had just finished chiming.

'Good ol' Big Brum, ...' he said, with a satisfied grin, '... right on time, as usual.'

Chapter Ten

Birmingham Museum and Art Gallery
10 January 1901

Robert Morden knew the process of separating *The Blind Girl* from her wooden frame was not to be rushed. Even the slightest lapse in concentration could spell disaster, with a scratch to the paint, or worse still, a torn canvas. All the same, progress had been painfully slow. The 9.00 am chimes had sounded a short time ago, but he wasn't overly concerned. James Waltham had made it patently clear that he loved spending every precious moment with his beloved painting. Getting the thing out of there in one piece, however, was proving more of a challenge. Just as he was about to lay siege to the last stubborn nail, there was a muffled shout from the gallery next door.

James looked up. 'What was that?'

Morden shrugged. 'Probably just Hawkins giving our Jack a good hiding.'

'Mmm. Go and check, would you, Robert?'

Morden nodded, reluctantly, and swapped the hammer for a gun. He feared Jack would do something like this and having him wander off to, God knows where, was a distraction he could well do without. He entered the Industrial Gallery's towering iron nave, looking around for any signs of activity. Everything was quiet – too quiet.

'Hawkins, you there?' he shouted.

There was no reply.

'God help you, Jack, when I get my hands on you,' he muttered, and made his way down the corridor of glass display cabinets.

Suddenly, he heard a noise from the balcony above. 'Jack, is that you? Stop fuckin' about and get down here.' But the only response was the gentle *tap-tap-tap* of James' hammer and chisel from the room next door.

He walked over to the steps leading to the first-floor picture gallery and saw something move behind the balustrade overhead. Before he could raise his gun, a man jumped out from one of the pillars and hurled a large copper fire extinguisher down at him. He put up his hands but the sheer weight of it knocked him to the floor, sending the revolver spilling from his hand. Feeling somewhat dazed, he looked up, only to see the superintendent launch himself from the balcony above. Taking the full force of the impact, Morden fell back, cracking his head on the hard tiled floor. But all he could think about, as he clutched his dislocated shoulder, was: *Where the fuck did this guy come from?*

*

With his latest quarry deadening the fall, Briggs quickly got to his feet and felt for the gun in his pocket – it was gone. He scanned the floor and saw it lying beneath one of the display cabinets, twenty feet away. He ran over to retrieve it, then turned around, only to see that the felled villain had somehow managed to haul himself to the base of the stairs and was reaching for his gun. Briggs watched as the man slowly raised his arm and took aim.

The deafening explosion that followed, echoed through the gallery like thunder. Briggs had forgotten what it was like to kill a man – a bizarre rush of exhilaration, followed by revulsion and guilt. But as he stood looking at the motionless body, he felt no remorse – he was simply defending the City's treasures from this band of thieves.

He looked over to the end gallery. The hammering had stopped, and in the doorway stood the gang-leader, the last man standing. In one hand, he held the rolled-up canvas of *The Blind Girl*; and in the other, three sticks of dynamite – their slow-burning fuses belching a column of smoke and sparks into the air.

Briggs just stood there. When confronted by a raging psychopath who would obviously stop at nothing to get what he wanted, better to lose one painting than risk the whole damned gallery. Briggs raised his gun and pointed it at the man – it was all he could think to do.

'I underestimated you, superintendent. It appears you've single-handedly incapacitated all of my men. May I suggest you put the gun down – unless you want this gallery of yours reduced to a pile of rubble?'

Realising his brave show of resistance was at an end, Briggs tossed the gun down in front of him.

'Thank you. Just slide it over here, would you?'

Briggs did as he was told, kicking the revolver across the tiled floor. 'For God's sake, put that thing out, before you blow us to kingdom come,' he said.

James took a pair of snips from his pocket and calmly cut off the last few inches of unburnt fuse. Then, keeping a watchful eye on the superintendent, he slowly bent down to pick up the gun.

'A wise choice, Mr Briggs. Now, if you'd be so kind as to place the canvas inside here for me,' he said, handing him the painting and a leather carrying tube tucked under his arm. 'And do be careful not to scratch it.'

'You've got a bloody nerve,' snarled Briggs.

'I see it more as a birth right. And please hurry, before the police arrive to investigate your little burst of gunfire, earlier.'

Briggs carefully slid the rolled-up canvas into the cylinder and secured the end cap with its buckle and strap.

'There, that wasn't too difficult, was it?' said James, grabbing the leather tube. 'Now if you don't mind, I've got to get these young ladies back home where they belong,' and he waved the gun towards the marble archway.

But the superintendent didn't move; his expression impassive as he looked right through the pillager, like he was a ghost.

The second gunshot echoed round the walls like cannon fire. James stood there, motionless – his eyes glazed as a stream of blood spewed from the bullet hole in his chest. He remained upright for a moment, then fell backward, hitting the floor with a thud.

Briggs watched the leather tube spill from his hand, landing just a few feet from where he was standing. He looked over in the direction of the Round Room. There, holding a freshly fired revolver, was Bob Collins – staring wide-eyed at the body of a man whose actions had threatened to jeopardise his very existence. But no longer.

*

Two days later, following sensational headlines in the national press, the doors to the BMAG reopened to huge crowds. Everybody came, including lords, ladies, wealthy patrons, MPs, doctors, industrialists and even members of the Royal Family. But mostly, a morbidly curious public, desperate for a sight of even the tiniest drop of the gang's dried blood.

Having assisted the police in their investigations, Samuel Briggs was glad to be back to the humdrum routine of daily inspections, albeit with a slight limp sustained in the line of duty.

With his arms tucked behind his back, he made his way from the Round Room, through the Industrial Gallery and into the small exhibition space at the far end. Having completed a brisk circuit of the room, he went and stood by one of his favourite paintings in the whole museum – a Millais, depicting the all-to-common plight of child vagrancy. With the hint of a smile, he ran his finger along the recently repaired picture frame and gazed with admiration at the artist's eye for light and colour.

'Glad to have you back where you belong, ladies,' he said, and quietly proceeded with his rounds.

Chapter Eleven

Wickwar, near Bristol

3 November 1999

Despite Emily's best efforts to forget about the cryptic note at the library, it was still playing on her mind. As soon as she got home from her lunch with Rosa, she made herself a mug of tea and fired up the laptop, drumming her fingernails on the dining-room table as she waited for the search engine to respond. The question was simple enough: Who was Aurora?

She had a vague notion that she was some kind of Roman goddess, but that was about it. When the results came up on screen, she clicked on the first entry – a website dedicated to classical mythology – and read the description:

> Aurora was the personification of the dawn in
> Roman mythology. From the Latin [au'ro:ra], she
> renews herself each morning and flies across the
> sky, announcing the arrival of the sun to a
> waiting world. The Greeks called her Eos, and
> was said to be the daughter of the titans
> Hyperion and Theia, and the sister of Helios (the
> sun god) and Selene (the moon goddess).

She read on and eventually came to a selection of classical poetry devoted to her. The first, a passage from Ovid's epic narrative poem, *Metamorphoses*, referred to Eos, Aurora's Greek equivalent:

> Far in the crimsoning east wakeful Dawn threw
> wide the shining doors of her rose-filled chamber.

Another from, Virgil's *Aeneid*, described the Roman goddess:

> Aurora now had left her saffron bed,
> And beams of early light the heav'ns o'erspread,
> When, from a tow'r, the queen, with wakeful eyes,
> Saw day point upward from the rosy skies.

The words were beautiful, enchanting, but what did this have to do with the message left on her notepad?

Emily remembered what Rosa had said about it possibly being some kind of warning. On reflection, it sounded more like a request for Emily to be mindful of something, but what?

She glanced over at Bill, who'd leapt up onto the table and was currently rubbing his head against the corner of Draper's sketchbook, as if to say, *Don't be stupid woman, it's right here in front of you.*

Her mobile phone buzzed, lighting up the display. It was a text from Rosa.

> Hi babe, thx for lunch.
> Spoke to Richard, he wants to
> see u about mtg with Julian.
> Can u pop in tomorrow @12?

'Oh, great,' she said, hating the thought of having to go back into work during her time off. But according to Rosa, Julian Mountfield was pretty high-up at the Ashmolean – no doubt Richard just wanted to make sure she didn't go there and make a fool of herself, or the Academy.

After texting Rosa back to confirm she'd be there, something made her turn to Draper's sketchbook. She opened the front cover and flipped to the drawings of the semi-naked woman leaning against a pillar. There was something about that serene face gazing out from the page, as if she was looking out on the whole of eternity.

Emily kept tapping the down arrow on her laptop until up popped a quote from Homer's great poem, *Iliad*.

> Now when Dawn in robe of saffron was
> hasting from the streams of Oceanus,
> to bring light to mortals and immortals,

Thetis reached the ships with the
armour that the god had given her.

She read the first line again, *Now when Dawn in robe of saffron ...*

The woman in the sketch was almost naked, apart from a swathe of silken material wrapped round her waist – her robe of saffron. It was as if the sun's rays had suddenly illuminated Emily's thinking. Right there, in front of her, was the truth in all its glory.

Could the shapely young woman in Draper's sketches be none other than Aurora – goddess of the dawn?

Chapter Twelve

Birmingham Museum and Art Gallery

12 January 1975

A gusty, north wind blew down Great Charles Street, chilling everything it could grasp with its icy fingers.

'Why on earth did your father want to meet us here, anyway?' said Joanne Waltham, struggling with the door to the museum's rear entrance.

Luke shrugged, more concerned with getting the pushchair containing their three-year-old daughter, Kate, out of the cold. Joanne glared at him, demanding an explanation.

'I don't know. He just said we should meet him here at midday, and not to be late – which we are.'

'Well, it's a bloody cheek, if you ask me – dragging us all this way out of London. And I bet he's not even here yet, is he?'

'I don't know, Jo.'

Once inside the small lobby – its stark black and white marble walls doing little to raise their spirits – they went and stood next to an old Victorian radiator, providing a modicum of warmth for newly arrived patrons. If he was honest, Luke was also far from happy at having to travel all the way to Birmingham, just to see his father "... for a chat," as he put it. Particularly, as he too lived in London. But, they were here now, and he always enjoyed the look on Kate's face whenever she got to meet up with her favourite grandparent.

'Look, just humour him, okay? He's been struggling on his own since Mum died, and he's become a bit ... quirky in his old age.'

Joanne shook her head. 'Why couldn't we meet up at a nice family restaurant, instead of traipsing around this old dump?' she said, snatching one of the free museum guides from a nearby stand.

'Can we get some sweets, Daddy?' said Kate, struggling to free herself from the pushchair.

'In a minute, darling, we're just waiting for Grandad.'

Having finally conceded and lifted her out, the door burst open, sending an icy blast into the small atrium.

'Grampy George!' shouted Kate, running over to give him a big hug.

'Hello, princess. Oh, I do like your hat and scarf,' he said, picking her up and twirling her around to a barrage of giggles.

Noticing the frosty expression on his daughter-in-law's face, he set Kate down and donned his best diplomatic smile. 'Hello, Joanne, ... lovely to see you. I hope you don't mind me dragging you all the way up to Birmingham on a Saturday afternoon.'

'I'm sure you have your reasons,' she said, and gave Luke a sideways glance.

'Be nice,' he mouthed, and turned to his father.

'Hi Dad, how are you keeping?'

'Oh, fine. Come on, let's go upstairs. I've got something to show you,' he said, and proceeded to pick Kate up and tuck her under his arm, to her absolute delight; and Joanne's utter indignation.

At the top of the twisting staircase, George set Kate down and the Waltham family strolled through the maze of galleries to the oldest part of the museum. No sooner had Kate spotted the curved red wall of the Round Room, she broke free from her mother's hand and ran, full pelt, towards it.

'Kate, come here!' barked Joanne, causing an elderly woman to turn and stare.

Kate stopped in her tracks. She turned around, and with her head bowed, walked slowly back to her mother.

'No running in here, alright?'

George wandered over and crouched down to meet the gaze of Kate's big green eyes. 'This is a grown-up place, so I want you to be on your best behaviour. Will you do that for me?'

She nodded and gave him a little smile.

'Tell you what, Joanne, why don't you two go on through to the restaurant, while I have a chat with Luke, eh? We won't be long, I promise.'

Begrudgingly, she took Kate by the hand and marched off in the direction of the Industrial Gallery.

'I really don't think she likes me, you know,' said George.

Luke gave him a wry smile. 'Don't worry, she's just pissed off because you've dragged her out of London for the day. And, if you must know, she's never quite forgiven you for letting Kate make such a mess of your kitchen, that one time she stayed over with you and mum.'

'We were just having fun making cakes, that's all.'

'Joanne sees it as a lack of discipline.'

'Right. Well, that is a mother's prerogative, I suppose.'

'So, ... why have you dragged us all the way up here?' said Luke, as they strolled into the heart of the Western Art section. 'There are plenty of good museums in London, as I recall.'

'Yes, dear boy, but none with such a special connection to you and me. I want to show you something.' And he strolled off into a neighbouring gallery.

Luke followed, looking somewhat perplexed.

'This is it,' said George, beckoning Luke to come and stand next to him. 'Look at those colours. The definition in the foreground.'

'Very nice. What's it got to do with us?'

'Quite a lot actually. It's a Millais.'

'Yes dad, I can see that,' said Luke, pointing to the label on the wall.

'Enchanting, isn't it?' George put out his hand, as if to touch it.

Luke grabbed his arm. 'For heaven's sake, what are you trying to do, get us thrown out?'

'No, of course not. Now the story I'm about to tell is going to shock you. Way back in nineteen o-one, not far off this very day in fact, your great-grandfather, James Waltham, was murdered, quite close to where you're standing.'

Luke stared at his father, open-mouthed. 'You're kidding me.'

'No, son, I'm not.'

'Murdered ... how?'

'He was shot in the chest, from over there.'

Luke glanced at the handful of visitors milling around the gallery, next door. 'My God, that's terrible.'

'Yes; but, truth be known, he did play quite a significant part in his own demise.'

'Why, was he trying to steal something?' sniggered Luke.

'Actually, yes.'

'What? My great-grandfather was a thief?'

George nodded.

'Jesus, that's unbelievable.'

'Mmm, not one of our family's finest moments.'

'What was he trying to steal? Oh, hang on … it was this, wasn't it?' said Luke, pointing to *The Blind Girl*.

George looked at it, fondly. 'Part of me doesn't blame him for trying, you know. It is truly captivating.'

'Dad, you can't go around stealing paintings from museums. There are laws against that sort of thing, even back then. It sounds as though he got exactly what he deserved.'

'He was only twenty-six, you know.'

'So, you're putting it down to youthful exuberance, are you?'

'No, no, far from it. The painting was originally bought by your great-great-grandfather, Charles Waltham, in eighteen eighty-six. It used to hang in the drawing room of Ardingly Hall. Charles got into some financial difficulties and had to sell it to help pay off his debts. Apparently, young James was deeply upset by this and vowed that, one day, he would return *The Blind Girl* to Ardingly Hall, where she belonged.'

Luke gazed at the poignant summer scene as his father continued the story.

'After being sold to a Mr Albert Wood for nine hundred guineas, it finally ended up in the hands of William Kenrick, who gifted it to the BMAG. James did try to buy it, but they refused. So he hatched a plan to steal it back.'

'And it cost him his life.'

'Indeed. Apparently, he was about to make his getaway when he was shot by one of the gallery attendants.'

'So, was he acting alone?'

'No, there were three men with him. One was also shot and killed in the robbery. The other two were captured by a museum employee and later imprisoned.'

'God, this is mind-blowing. And all for this,' said Luke, staring at the painting of Matilda and Isabella. He couldn't help but wonder how an object made of canvas, paint and wood could drive a man to such extremes. And yet deep inside, there was a part of his ego that would relish the thrill of such an adventure

– to see if it could be done; and get away with it, against all the odds.

George continued, 'I've often wondered what made him do it? He must have known he'd get caught, even if he had managed to escape with the painting.'

Luke walked over to the Round Room, trying to picture the scene as the shot rang out and his great-grandfather fell to the floor.

'But, I guess we'll never know,' said George, following on behind. 'The painting used to hang in the gallery at the end there. Then they decided to move it here, for some reason.'

Luke shook his head. 'Poignant doesn't begin to describe it.'

'What do you mean, son?'

'Well, the two girls looking out on the exact spot where James was killed. One with her eyes closed, the other choosing to look away in shame.'

'Huh, I'd never thought of it like that.'

The two men fell silent, reflecting on the events of that day when their long-lost relative, for whom they both felt a curious respect, finally let go of his dream.

*

That night, Luke lay awake for hours, mulling over his father's shocking revelations. He was sure no one had ever mentioned the incident before. Not even a whisper at family gatherings. Perhaps they were embarrassed that one of their own was a criminal; a black sheep who'd brought the good name of Waltham into disrepute. If that wasn't enough to keep the family elders tight-lipped, nothing was.

As a junior lecturer at the Royal College of Art in London, Luke had mixed feelings about the whole affair. On the one hand, he hated the thought of someone trying to steal his own amateur daubs, or even those of his students. And yet, perhaps because he was a direct descendant of this maverick aristocrat, he couldn't help but feel a sense of admiration for James and his daring deed.

What was it about the painting that made him risk everything to possess it? No doubt, it was one of Millais's finest works, but was it worth dying for?

In his lectures, Luke would teach his students about *infusion*, the alchemy or transference of the artists' passion and inspiration through their materials, and into the very objects they were creating. Only by putting something of their own spirit into their art, would it truly come to life – physically, emotionally and intellectually.

There must be something hidden in *The Blind Girl* that James identified with. He could recall some details of the composition and the vivid palette, but nothing more. Proper research was required if he was to really understand Millais's inspiration for painting it. He would just have time to visit the college library before his lecture, tomorrow morning.

And wondering just where all this would lead him, he slept.

Chapter Thirteen

Royal West of England Academy, Bristol

4 November 1999

All those who ascended the Royal West of England Academy's grand marble staircase were duly rewarded with a view of Walter Crane's stunning lunettes – one on each side of the domed ceiling, representing the four pillars of the institution (RWA) – painting, craftsmanship, architecture and sculpture. On her first day at the Academy, Emily made herself a promise that she would never take them for granted, and whenever they came into view, she would always look up and savour their beauty from a distance. The artist and his imagination was owed that.

She had only been at the RWA for three years, but had got to know her boss, Executive Director – Richard Horsley, pretty well in that time. A likeable character, he was witty, intellectual and obviously a lover of art – with one exception. For some reason, he could never quite get his head around the growing tide of "street art" that was sweeping the nation, even though Bristol was home to Banksy, its most famous exponent. But, as the younger Academy staffers liked to remind him, he was duty bound to keep an open mind on the subject. And to his credit, he tried.

Having knocked, Emily walked into his office and took a seat, confident in her approach. Her strategy was to be one of restraint. She wasn't going to lie, exactly, but would avoid any mention of her discovery at the auction.

'So, how's the time off going?' said Richard, 'Been up to anything exciting?'

'Oh, nothing much, just relaxing really.'

'Rosa tells me you've developed a sudden interest in the Pre-Raphaelites?'

'Yes, I'm trying to find out about an artist called Herbert Draper. Have you heard of him?'

As soon as she said it, she regretted asking such an obvious question. Of course he'd heard of him!

'Yes,' he said, raising an eyebrow. 'One of the later Pre-Raphaelites, if I recall. Although something of a dim light now. Why him in particular?'

'I like his classical style. And, I suppose, I think he's been unfairly forgotten.'

'Really? I never had you down as a lover of the Romantic movement.'

'Well, you'd be surprised,' she said, trying not to sound completely ignorant. 'Rosa said you know someone at the Ashmolean who's a bit of an expert. I was wondering if you could arrange for me to meet him?'

'Ah yes, Julian Mountfield. He and I worked together a few years ago. He's a busy man, you know.'

'Of course. Do you think you could just—'

'Although, I'm curious as to why you'd want to bother someone like Julian, when there's a perfectly good library just down the road?'

'I tried that, obviously. But none of the books seem to say much about him – not that I could find, anyway.'

'I see. Well, if you want me to set up a meeting with Julian, I'll need a little more than that, I'm afraid. I'm guessing your research is pretty important, if you're going to all this trouble?'

That was it, he had her. How on earth could she justify her sudden taste for a little-known nineteenth-century artist, having shown no previous interest in him or his work? Was there an important project she was working on for the Academy? ... no. Was she conducting research for a postdoctoral thesis in British Art? ... of course not. She tried to think of any plausible excuse, but other than the sketchbook, nothing came to mind. Oh, what the hell – she could trust him, surely.

'Actually, Richard, I went to a local auction a couple of days ago and stumbled across something rather interesting.'

'Really? What was that?'

'An artist's sketchbook.'

'And you think it belonged to Draper?'

'I'm almost certain it did, but I need someone to authenticate it for me.'

'Do you have it with you?'

She retrieved it from her bag and placed it on the desk in front of him.

After staring at it for a moment, he leaned forward, opened the front cover and began examining the drawings, as Emily sat and watched.

Before even a couple of minutes had passed, her patience finally ran out. 'What do you think?' she blurted out, bracing herself.

'Well, I'm no expert, but if you want my opinion ...'

I do, thought Emily, I most definitely do.

'... it certainly looks authentic. Obviously Julian needs to cast his expert eye over it, but I would say you've got something pretty special, here.' He gave a little smile. 'And you found it at an auction, you say?'

'Yes, in a box of old prints – I almost missed it. Obviously, someone didn't know what they'd got.'

'Mmm ... did anyone else bid on it?'

'Yes, an old chap. He bailed out when it got to four sixty. I'm not sure he knew it was there.'

Richard looked up from the sketchbook. 'A box of old prints got to nearly five hundred pounds? Oh, I'd say he knew it was there alright. The question is, why did he stop bidding?'

Emily was about to ask him what he meant, when he got up and perched himself on the corner of the desk, next to her. She looked at him, quizzically.

'I'm going to give Julian a call and ask that he see you.'

'Okay, great; if you think he won't be too busy?'

'It's fine, he owes me a favour. But I want you to promise me something. I want you to take good care of this. Store it somewhere safe.'

'You think it could be valuable, then?'

'I do.' He looked her in the eye, as though choosing his next words carefully. 'I'm just a little suspicious, that's all.'

'What do you mean?' she said, her mind racing.

'Emily, you know as well as I do, there are some pretty unscrupulous characters in our business. And, although rare finds like this do materialise from time to time, they seldom pop up at auctions, uncatalogued and unvalued, if you get my drift?'

'Sure, but don't you think you're overreacting a little?'

'Possibly. I just don't want you to be taken for a ride. Why don't you ask Rosa to go with you to Oxford? She loves a bit of artistic detective work, so she tells me.'

'I suppose so, but I'm not sure she's got any holiday left, this year.'

'Oh, I'm sure we can spare her for a day on something as important as this, don't you?'

'Well, yes … absolutely.'

'Good. I'll call Julian and see if he can fit you in tomorrow.'

*

Emily made her way back down to the ground floor; her head spinning – what did Richard mean, exactly? She'd gone there to ask him to set up a meeting with a Draper expert and come away wondering if she'd inadvertently purchased a stolen artefact.

She crossed the marble entrance hall and headed into the bowels of the building – home to the Academy's administrative offices – where she found Rosa standing at the photocopier, staring blankly at the noticeboard.

'Hard at work, I see?' said Emily.

'I am, unlike some people. How did you get on with Richard?'

'Okay, I think.'

'You think?'

'He's arranging for me to see Julian tomorrow afternoon. And guess what, you're coming with me.'

'Oh, I am, am I? He does know I've got a stack of work to do, doesn't he?'

'He told me he's giving you the day off, so you have to come. Besides, I'm starting to get quite worried about all this. Especially after what Richard has just told me.'

'Really? What's he been saying?'

'He gave me the impression it might be stolen property.'

'Oh, for Christ's sake, what's he trying to do, scare the living daylights out of you?'

'Well, if he was, he damn well succeeded.'

'Don't listen to him. He's probably just jealous he didn't find it.'

'So, you'll come with me to see this Julian guy, assuming he's free tomorrow?'

'A day off work and a trip to the Ashmolean, you try and stop me.'

Emily smiled nervously and stared at her feet.

'Are you okay?' said Rosa.

'Yeah, yeah. I just hope I'm doing the right thing.'

'Look, honey, from where I'm standing, you've been lucky enough to stumble on something pretty amazing. Something most art lovers can only dream about. I say grab it with both hands and don't let go.'

'I know. I shouldn't be looking a gift horse in the mouth.'

'It wasn't exactly a gift horse, but no, you shouldn't.'

They hugged and Emily made her way back to the car, quite looking forward to her research trip to Oxford.

Heading out of Bristol city centre, she stopped the Alpine at some traffic lights and glanced over at a shop window, nearby. Hanging from two thin wires was a picture of a young woman in a beautiful summer dress, leaning against a pillar.

Strange choice for a winter collection, she thought.

The cardboard girl seemed to be looking straight at her, but instead of the usual vacant expression worn by most boutique models, hers was one of kindness and understanding – as if the goddess Aurora had appeared before her, dressed in saffron and silk. A tingle went down her spine, and she sensed a strange vibration in the air, barely discernible, like a whisper – *Follow your destiny.*

Suddenly, a car horn blasted behind her. She looked in the mirror and saw a young man mouthing obscenities and pointing at the lights, which were now green. As she pulled away, she noticed the sign above the dress shop. It read, DUSK TILL DAWN.

She laughed and berated herself for being so ridiculous. But try as she might, she couldn't help but think about Richard's cautionary tale.

Was it really happenstance that had led to her discovering the sketchbook, or was fate somehow lending a hand?

Chapter Fourteen

Clapham, London

24 March 1975

Trying desperately to ignore the melodrama brewing across the breakfast table, Luke Waltham sat watching one of his shirts perform a kind of maniacal dance on the washing line outside the kitchen window. He took a bite of toast and marmalade and thought to himself, *what the hell have I been doing with my life?* But, as he looked over at his young daughter, Kate – her arms folded in front of her and wearing a face like thunder, he knew.

'No, we can't afford it this year and that's the end of it,' said Joanne, hoping for some moral support from her husband regarding the purchase of a new bike for Kate's birthday, and getting none.

'Daddy said I could have one.'

Joanne shot Luke a Medusa-like glare that would have instantly turned him to stone, had he been bothered to look up.

'Did you?'

'Sorry, what?'

'Did you promise Kate a bike for her birthday?'

'No. I don't know … I might have.'

'Oh, well that's bloody brilliant. You do know how much debt we're in at the moment, don't you?'

'I've got a fair idea.'

'Ever since you took that teaching job, we've been struggling to make ends meet. We haven't had a proper holiday in years and do you give a shit? No.'

Luke returned his gaze to the other items of clothing that had joined in the washing line dance, whilst calmly considering his reaction. Should it be fight or flight? He couldn't decide; and to be honest, he didn't care. After all, she did have a point.

'I haven't been out with the girls for months,' she said.

'Really? That is a shame.'

'Yes, it bloody is. We've all got to make sacrifices, Luke. You're not part of the landed gentry any more.'

Okay, so, fight it was. 'What the fuck has that got to do with anything?'

Joanne gawped at him with a look of horror; not least because he'd said the F-word in front of Kate; something he never did.

'It's her birthday, for Christ's sake. Why shouldn't she have a new bike?'

'Oh, you would take her side, wouldn't you? You're as thick as thieves, you two. Sometimes I feel like a stranger in my own house, do you realise that?'

'Now you're just being ridiculous.'

'Am I? Well go ahead, do what you like. You can bankrupt us for all I care – your family were good at that,' she said, and marched out of the room, slamming the door behind her. Kate looked at her father and burst into tears. He knew she hated it when mummy and daddy rowed; which seemed to be something of a daily occurrence, these days.

Luke reached out and put his arm round her. 'Kate, don't cry.'

'It's all my fault,' she sniffed.

'No, no. She's angry with me. Come on – go and let Mummy get you ready for playschool, there's a good girl, and I'll talk to her about that new bike, okay?'

She gave him one of her 'thank you, daddy' smiles and ran upstairs to get her things. He watched her go and laughed at the ease with which she could wrap him around her little finger – a weakness he would willingly harbour for the rest of his life.

*

In the relative tranquillity of the Royal College of Art's library, Luke took a sip of his vending machine coffee and sat down to examine a large colour volume devoted solely to the Pre-Raphaelites. The RCA library was a modern, well-stocked archive of reference material situated on the south side of Hyde Park – the staggered metal-framed windows looking out onto a small triangular courtyard, just a stone's throw from the Royal Albert Hall.

He stretched out his legs under the table and began his search. He didn't know what he was looking for, but ever since his father had told him about James Waltham's daring attempt to steal *The*

Blind Girl, he'd become fascinated with the Pre-Raphaelite Brotherhood and their work. He'd always had an interest in the artistic influences of great painters and sculptors, and could regularly be found dispensing his views on the subject to a room full of first-year students. But since the revelations in Birmingham, he'd been able to think of little else. That, and, what was it that had driven his great-grandfather to commit such an extraordinary act of criminal behaviour – one for which he'd paid the ultimate price?

He had to admit, the more he studied *The Blind Girl*, the more it spoke to him. Not least because of its clever artistic symbolism and the subtle beauty with which it showed its heart-rending portrayal of homelessness among the young and disabled in Victorian England. Luke flipped the page over and there they were, the two beggar girls, lost in their own little world. For such a young man, the skill with which Millais had pictured their desperate plight and garnished it with a dash of hope and acceptance, almost brought a tear to the eye. It was all there in the tiniest details: the tortoiseshell butterfly on the blind girl's shawl, mirroring the innocence and frailty of its host. The two rainbows glowing against an angry black sky, a suggestion of the sunlight that had been denied her all her life. The wildflowers at her fingertips, a reminder that although her sight was lost, her remaining senses were very much alive. And, perhaps most poignant of all, the dusty old concertina resting on her lap, echoing the discord between the symphony of the countryside and the harsh musical tones she used to beg for a living, to survive.

Millais's message was simple yet powerful. He wanted members of Victorian society to wake up and open their eyes to a problem confronting them every time they walked down the street. But his cautionary tale went further – it warned that salvation could not simply be bought, it came from within. The beacon of hope resided in everyone, but only those willing to open their hearts could see it and be guided by it.

In that moment, Luke understood what his great-grandfather must have experienced all those years ago. As a young boy, James's loss of something so personal, so precious, must have been profound. And yet he never gave up hope of seeing *The Blind Girl* returned to its rightful place – with him.

Luke stood up and was about to return the book to the shelf when something fell from between the pages and landed at his feet. It was an old pamphlet entitled *The House of Life* by Dante Gabriel Rossetti. He picked it up and began flicking through the collection of sonnets, which mainly spoke about love and Rossetti's relationship with his wife, Lizzie Siddal.

Then he stumbled across one about his scriptural namesake, called: 'OLD AND NEW ART – 1. ST LUKE THE PAINTER'. It began:

> Give honour unto Luke Evangelist;
> For he it was (the aged legends say)
> Who first taught Art to fold her hands and pray.
> Scarcely at once she dared to rend the mist
> Of devious symbols: but soon having wist
> How sky-breadth and field-silence and this day
> Are symbols also in some deeper way,
> She looked through these to God and was God's priest.
>
> And if, past noon, her toil began to irk,
> And she sought talismans, and turned in vain
> To soulless self-reflections of man's skill,
> Yet now, in this the twilight, she might still
> Kneel in the latter grass to pray again,
> Ere the night cometh and she may not work.

Rossetti seemed to be saying that, since the dawn of Christianity, art had evolved from its primitive beginnings into something that could spread the word of God to those who could not read or write it for themselves. But over time, art had lost its way, succumbing to man's vanity and idleness. Yet there was still hope it could be saved, if it repented and went back to its long-forgotten principles. Could Gabriel have been declaring that the Pre-Raphaelites were in fact, the saviours of art itself? That, through their enlightened craft, they would illuminate the sacred teachings that had been diluted and lost over the centuries? That they alone could restore art's truth and purity? He let out an admiring laugh - even for these egotistical romantics, that was quite some claim.

With his curiosity piqued, he opened the reference book and began analysing the Brotherhood's most revered paintings, inspecting each one closely for signs of a hidden message. It soon became clear that the PRB's most iconic works had been produced by the three founder members: Rossetti, Millais and Hunt. Some were overtly spiritual in nature, such as Hunt's *The Light of the World* and *The Girlhood of Mary Virgin* by Rossetti. Others told a more moralistic tale, including Millais's *The Blind Girl* and Hunt's *The Awakening Conscience*.

Luke continued traversing the Pre-Raphaelite timeline until he reached the later years. Two particular paintings caught his eye. One was Hunt's *The Finding of the Saviour in the Temple*, a remarkable panoramic scene of a young Jesus debating scripture with Jewish elders in the Temple of Solomon. The other was a serenely radiant picture of love and death: Rossetti's *Beata Beatrix*, painted as a memorial to his wife, Lizzie, who died tragically of laudanum poisoning.

After an hour, Luke sat back and scratched his head. What was it about these three artists that made them stand out from the rest? They were young, intelligent and ambitious, but there was something else. To them, art had become degraded and corrupt. So much so, that they had taken it upon themselves to put things right; to forge a new path. If his interpretations were correct, the three artists were subtly communicating their aspirations for a better world by challenging the whole of Victorian society – demanding that the viewer open their minds to their particular brand of moral propaganda, by simply engaging with the detail and beauty of their work.

He walked back to the main college building, exhilarated by what he'd found. He hadn't felt like this in years. It was as though Millais's painting had given him a new lease of life. But this would require more research, and lots of it.

One thing was for sure, though; the students in his morning lecture were in for a real treat.

Chapter Fifteen

St. George's Gallery, Knightsbridge, London
24 March 1849

On this bright spring day, the Pre-Raphaelite Brotherhood was out in force to support one of their own. Dante Gabriel Rossetti's first major work, *The Girlhood of Mary Virgin*, was complete and hanging for all to see at the Free Exhibition of Modern Art, near Hyde Park. Not exactly the Royal Academy, but a public exhibition none the less. And Rossetti was in good company, as works by his friend, Ford Maddox Brown, were also on show to help attract the West London crowds.

Gabriel, dressed as smartly as his paltry artist's income would allow, in a light-brown jacket, white shirt with dark blue cravat and dark trousers, greeted Millais and Hunt as they approached the painting, followed closely by Gabriel's brother – William Michael, and also Frederick Stephens, both fellow members of the PRB.

'Brothers, I hope you are as excited about this as I am,' said Gabriel, shaking them each by the hand.

'We wouldn't have missed it for the world,' said Millais.

'Well, there she is,' he said, proudly. 'And in a most agreeable spot, I think you'll agree.'

Unlike the Royal Academy, where up-and-coming artists would find their work hung virtually out of sight, at the top of the wall or in a darkened corner, the Free Exhibition was much more accommodating and had hung Gabriel's picture at eye level, or "on-the-line". However, most patrons would agree that the light in the temporary building, comprising a single lofty saloon, was far from perfect. Despite its righteous title, St George's Gallery was a plain affair with gas lights hanging from the ceiling and a single row of pillars down each side. One journalist had called it, "... a sort of Brighton Pavilion with permanent fittings ...". How different from a few years before when a thirty-foot-high Chinese pagoda stood at the entrance to an exhibition entitled: *Ten thousand Chinese things* – a display of oriental art and culture, from one world empire to another very much on the rise.

But the somewhat drab surroundings mattered little to Gabriel, for there was more than just a desire for fame and fortune burning inside this young Brother. He wanted his work to be seen. To be recognised very much as a painter of his time, an artist driven by a passion to paint what he truly believed – and this certainly leapt out of the canvas in all its glory in *The Girlhood of Mary Virgin.*

And, if that were not enough, in order to demonstrate his artistry in both pictorial and poetical compositions, Gabriel had also attached a pair of sonnets to the frame – to assist those for whom the graphic symbolism was not so obvious – in what he called a 'double-work'.

'So what do you think?' he said, beaming with pride as the four Brothers looked on.

'Magnificent Gabriel; and hopefully the first of many,' said Hunt.

'You've done the Brotherhood proud,' added Millais.

'It does credit to our darling mother, and sister, Christina,' said William Michael, putting a congratulatory arm round his brother.

Fred stepped forward to inspect the tiny, yet compelling, monogram added to Gabriel's signature. 'I see you have signed it PRB.'

'A statement of intent to our critics ...' Gabriel replied, '... may they be few in number and blissful in their undoubted ignorance.'

'Has anyone shown any interest in buying it?'

'Not yet, Fred, but all it takes is for one discerning gentleman with the right amount of tin to walk past and take a shine to it.'

'And a few more visitors through the door, wouldn't go amiss,' said Hunt, scanning the rather empty gallery.

'Well, I could always drop a line to *The Illustrated London News*, to help pull in a few punters?' said Fred, whose talents, in truth, lay as an art critic, rather than the gifted artist he'd always hoped to be.

Gabriel nodded. 'And *The Times*, of course.'

'Mmm ... unfortunately, that particular institution has not yet seen fit to publish any of my articles, but I will give it my best shot.'

Looking over to the door, Gabriel spotted two modestly dressed ladies walking towards him, arm-in-arm. Recognising his Aunt Charlotte and sister, Christina, he put on a cordial grin and marched off to greet them.

'Sister, I'm so glad you came,' he said, kissing her on the cheek. Christina responded with the faintest of smiles, then walked over to the painting. The four Brothers stood aside so she could view Gabriel's touching portrayal of her as the young Mary. She stared at the Holy Family, showing not the slightest hint of emotion. But Gabriel knew better than to be offended by her apparent indifference and turned to his favourite aunt.

'Aunt Charlotte, I had no idea you would be accompanying Christina, this morning.'

'I thought I would surprise you, Gabriel.'

'Well, may I say how pleased I am that you did.'

'So, this is the masterpiece I've heard so much about,' she said, walking over to join Christina.

'Yes, the fruits of my labour, these many months. Do you like it?'

Teasing him a little, she tilted her head one way, then the other, as if to consider the subject more deeply.

'Why, it is a most noble work. I see a hint of your dear mother's face in St Anne. And, of course, lovely Christina as Mary – both so beautifully observed, don't you agree, Christina?'

'Yes, I suppose so,' she said, gazing blankly at the angel in the centre of the picture.

'So Gabriel, Christina tells me that your picture is full of allegory and mystery.'

'Why yes. I'd be delighted to tell you about its symbology, if you'd like?'

The Brothers, having heard him wax lyrical on the subject all too often, took this as their cue to leave and explore the rest of the exhibition.

Gabriel studied his painting, scratching his chin in reflection. 'The subject is, of course, the education of the Blessed Virgin, one which I cannot but think has been treated by Murillo and other painters, in a very inadequate manner. They have invariably represented her as reading from a book under the superintendence of her mother, St Anne. An occupation obviously incompatible with these ancient times, and which could only pass muster if treated in a purely symbolic manner.'

'Yes, I see,' said Charlotte, listening intently.

'In order to attempt something more plausible, whilst also less mundane, I have represented the future mother of our Lord embroidering a lily, with the flower she is copying being tended by a little angel. And there, at a large window in the background is her father, St Joachim, pruning a vine.'

Just as he was getting up a head of steam, Charlotte held up her finger and stepped forward.

'I wonder, Gabriel, would you indulge me in some rudimentary observations of my own?'

'Yes, of course. I would be delighted.'

Although not an immediate member of the artistically gifted Rossetti family, Charlotte Polidori did have a considerable appreciation for the arts and wrote poetry that she would often share with Gabriel – much to his delight. In fact, she needed no instruction, from the artist or otherwise, to understand the painting's overt symbolism.

'Well, I can see that in addition to the blessed Virgin, you also elude to the life of Christ, himself. For instance here, on the red cloth draped over the wall behind St Anne, you show three lilies, symbolising the Holy Trinity. And yet the second bloom is not quite perfect – perhaps indicating that Christ, the son, is not yet born?'

Gabriel nodded, sagely.

'And here, in the window, a haloed dove representing the Holy Spirit, and an oil lamp for piety. How am I doing so far?'

'Very perceptive, Aunt Charlotte.'

'Alright. Now, as you said before, St Joachim is tending a vine. Is this a reference to Christ as the True Vine – the giver of abundant life through its branches and fruit?'

'Yes, absolutely,' said Gabriel, looking slightly stunned.

'Aunt Charlotte, I fear that if you continue to show such insight into the workings of the artist's mind, your nephew may just discover something hidden in his work that even he was not aware of,' said Christina, wryly.

Charlotte put her hand to her mouth. 'Gabriel, I'm so sorry. I never meant to—'

'No, no. It gives me great heart to listen to someone as insightful as yourself, aunt. Please, do continue,' he said, running his fingers through his hair.

'Very well. Now here in the foreground is a potted lily standing on a pile of books.'

She took a step closer and peered at the canvas.

'Each one seems to bear an inscription and a colour of some significance. There is gold for charity, blue for faith and green for hope – the three theological virtues. And underneath, further volumes depicting three of the cardinal virtues – prudence, temperance and fortitude.'

Noticing her brother's edginess at having his work so astutely dissected, Christina leaned over and whispered in his ear, 'Talking of heavenly virtues, brother, you would do well to show a little patience and humility in your present demeanour.'

Gabriel smiled sarcastically, as his aunt continued her analysis.

'And what are these lying on the floor? It seems to be ... a briar with seven thorns, crossed with a palm of seven leaves, all tied together with a scroll.'

She paused and moved even closer, until her nose was just inches from the canvas.

'I can just make out the wording – it says *tot dolores tot gaudia*, which if my Latin serves me correctly means, *so many sorrows, so many joys*. Perhaps a reference to what, for Mary, will be a lifetime of mixed emotions – the palm signalling her joy on hearing of Jesus's triumphant entrance into Jerusalem on Palm Sunday. But also the pain and suffering she will witness from the crown of thorns; and, ultimately, his crucifixion.'

Just as she was about to step away, something else caught her eye.

'And what is this? Something carved into the portative organ – a Latin inscription beneath the letter M. And a rose, standing in a vase on the window ledge. Allusions to Isis and the Magdalene, perhaps?'

Gabriel looked at her and smiled. 'Your interpretations are faultless, Aunt Charlotte. But then, I would expect nothing less from one of my favourite poets.'

'Gabriel, you mock me. My amateur ramblings are nothing compared to yours and Christina's beautiful prose. But I must congratulate you on producing such a fine work. You must be very proud.'

'And would be more so, if only I could find a willing buyer,' he said, looking round the hall.

'Well now, I may just be able to help you in that particular quest,' said Charlotte.

Gabriel looked at her, quizzically – surely the salary of a governess could not stretch to such an extravagance.

'You are familiar with my employer, are you not?'

'The Dowager, Marchioness of Bath – of course.'

'Well, I happen to know that she is looking for a new picture to add to her collection – something noble yet righteous in nature, I understand.'

Gabriel could hardly believe his ears. He knew, from witnessing the relative success and failure of other young artists, that opportunities such as this came along all too rarely, but when they did, you seized them with both hands.

'Really. And how much do you think she would be willing to pay for such a painting?'

'My darling nephew, the Dowager does not entrust me with details of her financial affairs.'

'No, of course not. And I would not dream of compromising your employment by asking you to represent me in such a matter.'

Charlotte let slip the hint of a smile. 'But, I suppose I could recommend that she come and see the painting for herself, if that would help?'

'Yes! That would be ... wonderful,' said Gabriel, suppressing his desire to turn cartwheels down the length of the gallery.

'If, as I suspect, she likes it, then you can discuss a price with her, personally. Do you have a figure in mind?'

'Well, perhaps something in the region of ... eighty pounds would be a fair price,' he said, seeking a reaction.

She nodded. 'I'm sure the Dowager would find that a reasonable sum for such a fine work. Would you like me to make the necessary arrangements?'

Gabriel responded by giving her a huge kiss on the cheek.

'Then consider it done, my dear,' she said, and casually flicked over the pages of her catalogue.

'Well done, brother,' said Christina, quietly. And with that, she took Aunt Charlotte's arm and strolled off through the gallery to find Ford Maddox Brown's *Lear and Cordelia*.

Hunt and Millais, who'd been watching from a distance, walked over to where their elated Brother was standing.

'You look rather pleased with yourself,' said Millais.

'I most certainly am, Johnny. Aunt Charlotte is going to arrange for the Dowager to come and view my painting.'

'Really? Do you think she'll want to buy it?'

'Of course she'll want to buy it. Just think, gentlemen, this could be the first of our works of enlightenment to find its way into private hands. And not just any old hands – the wife of a peer of the realm, no less.'

Dreaming of future successes, the three Brothers linked arms and marched side by side through the main hall of the Free Exhibition.

A new era was dawning for the Pre-Raphaelite Brotherhood; and with it, the first rays of a moral awakening were just beginning to shine upon a dark and unsuspecting world.

Chapter Sixteen

Oxford City Centre

5 November 1999

Not that people hadn't remarked about it for hundreds of years, but on this particular November morning, Oxford had something of a mystical air about it. As Emily and Rosa drove into the city centre, a burst of late autumn sunshine washed over the vast array of domes and spires, giving them an almost alchemical glow – like the fabled City of Gold.

As guests of one of the Ashmolean's curators, and with a visitor's permit that had been faxed through to Rosa the previous day, they neatly side-stepped the city's usual parking nightmares and drove straight into a reserved space at the back of the museum.

'I love this place,' said Emily, turning off the Alpine's heater that had been on full blast since leaving Bristol.

'Oxford – really?' said Rosa, screwing up her nose.

'Yes, what's not to love?'

'Well, it's hardly London, is it?'

'No, and much to its credit, if you ask me.'

'I mean, don't get me wrong, it's all very nice ... if you like the provincial thing,' continued Rosa, as they walked round to the front of the museum.

Emily laughed. 'Come on, let's get you inside before one of the local dons has you thrown out of town,' she said, taking her friend by the arm and gazing up at the magnificent portico, where mighty Apollo – god of knowledge and light – offered a warm welcome to all who entered below.

Crossing the threshold of the main entrance, they walked straight into the rather splendid Randolph Gallery, with its bright red walls and alcoves – the perfect backdrop for a collection of Greco-Roman statues even Mount Olympus would have been proud of.

While Emily checked in at reception, Rosa wandered off to inspect the seemingly endless display of male genitalia.

'Good morning, can I help you?' said the young man on reception.

'Yes, we have a ten-thirty appointment with Doctor Julian Mountfield.'

'And you are?'

'Emily Bradshaw and ... oh my God,' she said, looking over to where Rosa was cupping a modestly-sized plaster penis in the palm of her hand. '... and my so-called friend, Rosa Martell.'

'Err ... madam, could you please not touch the exhibits,' said the receptionist, and carried on checking the computer screen. 'Here we go, ten-thirty with Julian. I'll ask his PA to come and collect you.'

Having finally managed to tear herself away from the parade of plaster phalluses, Rosa came and sat next to Emily on a bench at the foot of the main staircase. Emily just looked at her and shook her head.

'What?' said Rosa.

'Unbelievable.'

'I don't know what you're so embarrassed about. I was just checking.'

'Checking, for what?'

'To see if they were lifelike.'

'Oh, really ...? And were they?'

'Yes, surprisingly so, actually.'

They both burst out laughing, only to be interrupted by the clip-clop of high-heeled shoes descending the marble staircase behind them. Emily looked up to see a smartly dressed, middle-aged woman smiling at her.

'Emily, Rosa? Would you come this way, please,' she said, turning on her heels and making her way back up the staircase.

Without saying a word, Barbara, Julian's PA, lead the way through the maze of galleries to the offices in the restricted section. Reaching a solid oak door marked, Curator – Western Art, she knocked twice and ushered them inside.

Whatever expectations Emily may have had were immediately dissolved, the moment she walked in. The room was light and airy, and housed a mishmash of design styles ranging from art nouveau to Bauhaus, modernist to modern day. And Julian

Mountfield, far from being the stuffy professor type, was in his mid-forties, slim, with dark brown hair – swept back to reveal a high forehead, and wearing sand-coloured chinos, a plain white shirt and dark-blue fitted sports jacket. He stood up and walked round from behind a desk so cluttered with papers and books, barely any wood was visible.

'You must be Emily,' he said, pushing his designer glasses up the bridge of his nose and holding out his hand. Emily shook it and smiled. 'Richard has been telling me all about you. And Rosa, good to see you again. Now, do sit down, won't you?'

'Doctor Mountfield, it's good of you to meet with us at such short notice,' said Rosa, sitting in one of the two brown leather Barcelona chairs facing his desk at an angle.

'Please, call me Julian. We're quite informal here at the Ashmolean – not like that other lot up in London,' he laughed.

'I'm sorry, I have to ask, is that what I think it is?' said Emily, pointing to the sketch of a Camden-town whore on the wall behind him.

'Ah yes, Walter Sickert – the master of reinvention and the iron bedstead,' said Julian, turning round to admire it with her. 'We're fortunate to have the first of his *Brighton Pierrots* in the gallery upstairs. Are you a fan, Emily?'

'Well, yes; ... him, and the whole Camden Town Group, actually.'

'Excellent, me too. Now, Richard tells me you have something intriguing to show me?'

Emily was beginning to warm to the mild-mannered, yet quietly confident curator. On the way to Oxford, she'd been plagued with doubt about sharing her discovery with a total stranger, but now, having met the man, any misgivings had all but vanished.

'Yes, I'd be interested in your opinion,' she said, removing Draper's sketchbook from her bag and handing it to him.

Julian held it in his hands for a few moments, before turning it over to inspect the red marbled boards. Apparently satisfied, or so she hoped, he placed it gently on the desk in front of him and examined each page with the care and diligence of an expert in his field. Emily watched, fascinated, as each page was turned, trying to assess his reaction. Every now and then, he would raise an eyebrow, indicating surprise, or was it disappointment? It was difficult to tell.

Time passed; still no one spoke. Eventually, Emily took a sneaky look at her watch and couldn't believe it had only been three minutes since the inspection began – it felt like a lifetime. She sat back and suppressed a deep sigh. Should she say something? Perhaps a casual enquiry to end the agony? She gesticulated at Rosa to say, *how much longer?* Rosa shushed her, covertly, and turned back to observe the examination.

Finally, Emily could bear the suspense no longer and was about to blurt out a casual, 'How's it looking?' when Julian closed the book and sat back in his chair.

'You've stumbled on to something quite exceptional, Emily. Where on earth did you find it, if you don't mind me asking?'

'Believe it or not, it was in a box of old prints at an auction.'

Julian raised an eyebrow. 'Really?'

'So, it is genuine, then?' said Rosa.

'Oh, no question. If my memory serves me correctly, there are twenty Draper sketchbooks catalogued, but none that cover this particular year – eighteen ninety-nine.'

Emily touched Rosa's arm, glad that she was there to share the good news.

'From what I can see, most of the drawings relate to one of Draper's lesser-known paintings called the *Trailing Clouds of Glory*. Its whereabouts is currently unknown, although there is a small oil-on-canvas sketch believed to be in a private collection. But what interests me are the sketches at the back. They appear to be from a different painting, altogether.'

'The woman leaning against the pillar,' said Emily.

'Yes. I believe they're of the goddess, Aurora, which actually ties in perfectly with that year.'

Emily gave a little smile of self-satisfaction – her suspicions about the celestial dawn-bringer were correct.

Julian continued, 'As the nineteenth century was coming to a close, Draper started work on a new painting inspired by the writings of Homer. He wanted to commemorate, not just a new century, but the dawning of a new era, in what some say was his greatest work – *The Gates of Dawn*. It depicts Aurora, or if you prefer the Greek, Eos, standing between two golden gates and gazing out upon mankind, as if inviting them to join her in a brave new world.'

'That's incredible,' said Emily.

'There must be a picture of it on the web, somewhere.' Julian tapped the title into the search engine on his laptop. 'Ah yes, here we go,' he said, turning it round for them to see. They both leaned forward, captivated by the beautiful young woman looking out at them.

'Wow, that is ... so, powerful,' said Emily, marvelling at the folds of cascading silk hanging from Aurora's waist. 'Who is she? The model, I mean?'

'Her name is Florrie Bird. She used to pose at the Royal Academy Life Drawing School, and was quite something in her day, as you can see.'

'She is striking, I'll give her that,' said Rosa, 'These carvings on the gates, Julian – do you know what they represent?'

'Yes, each gate contains a gold sun disc, surrounded by figures representing the various planetary bodies. And that is the winged head of Time, supporting them all.'

Emily continued to stare at the picture, marvelling at the way Draper had used colour and light to show off the imperious beauty of the goddess. Framed by her gates of gold, she stood almost naked before the world, clad only in a swathe of crimson silk that seemed to emanate directly from the rising sun. At her feet lay a scattering of rose petals, representing the very fabric of nature that was hers to command. Draper was clearly paying homage to the power of the earth mother and her ongoing role in creation.

'Well, what do we have here?' said Julian, taking the sketchbook over to the window.

'What is it?' said Emily.

'There's something written in tiny writing below this sketch. It says ... Awaken, and see the light.'

'Ah yes, we, or should I say Rosa, noticed that the other day. Do you know what it means?'

'A reference to the dawn, perhaps. Or, given the year in which it was painted, maybe Draper was heralding the advent of a new era of enlightenment.'

'Oh yes, I like the sound of that, don't you, Rosa?'

'Yes, very interesting. Julian, do you have any idea what the sketchbook might be worth?'

Emily gave her a glare.

'What?' said Rosa. 'Don't pretend you're not itching to find out.'

Julian laughed. 'Don't worry, I'd be just as curious if it was me. That said, I'm not terribly *au fait* with the prices for Draper's work these days. If I were you, I'd take it to a specialist auctioneer and have it properly valued.'

'Yes, good idea,' said Emily.

'But, if you were to push me ...' he said, scratching his head.

Both girls leaned forward, a little.

'... I would say it would certainly be in the thousands.'

'That much?' said Rosa, turning to gauge Emily's reaction.

'Oh yes. I expect a number of galleries and museums would jump at the chance to buy this, if it ever came onto the market.'

Wait till I get home and tell Tom, thought Emily, trying her best to remain poker-faced.

'Emily, with your permission, I'd like to conduct some more research. Would you mind if I held on to it for a little while?'

'Err ... no, of course not. I'm obviously keen to find out as much as I can about it.'

'Thank you. And don't worry, I'll make sure it's kept safe and sound, here at the museum,' he said, getting to his feet. 'If you leave your contact details with Barbara, I'll be in touch as soon as I have more information.'

'Okay,' said Emily, realising their time was up.

'Have you had a chance to look around the museum yet?' said Julian, showing them to the door.

She shook her head.

'Oh, then you must take a look at our Pre-Raphaelite collection – it's superb, if I do say so myself.'

He escorted them over to Barbara's desk, bade them farewell and went back to his office. As they made their way out, Emily couldn't help but feel, in some bizarre way, that she'd just been finessed out of her prize possession.

After a light lunch in the coffee shop, they made their way up to the second floor to take in the Pre-Raphaelite collection. Despite agreeing with Julian's somewhat partisan recommendation, Emily was unusually quiet as she and Rosa walked round the room in opposite directions – finally meeting up next to *Convent Thoughts* by Charles Collins.

'So, what did you think of Julian?' said Rosa, pretending to gaze interestedly at the painting.

'Oh, he seems like a nice chap. And certainly knows a thing or two about Draper.'

'Stop being coy. He's bloody gorgeous, don't you think?'

'If you say so, Rosa. But I'm quite happy with the one I've got, thanks.'

Emily was bracing herself for a derisive comeback about her apparent predilection for geeky men, when the sound of *Mambo No. 5* began to echo around the gallery walls, causing a number of visitors to turn and stare.

'What the hell is that?' she said.

'It's my new ringtone. Do you like it?' said Rosa, rifling through her handbag. 'Oh, it's only Richard. Probably wants to talk to me about the new winter exhibition. Tell you what, you have a last wonder round and I'll see you downstairs.'

'Alright, I'll meet you by the main entrance in ten minutes.'

While Rosa wandered off with the phone clasped to her ear, Emily headed back down to the ground floor, in search of the gift shop.

Halfway down the Randolph Gallery, something made her take a last-minute detour into a small side-gallery. As she stood there, trying to assess what the Tradescant collection was all about, something caught her eye in the centre of the room. She walked over to the display case and peered at the curious iron object. It was blackened with age, and looked more like a piece of junk than an exhibit. On closer inspection, she realised it was an old lantern and glanced at the display card next to it:

> **Guy Fawkes' lantern** – sheet iron, English, early
> 1600s. Originally the lantern would have had a horn
> window, which could have been closed completely to
> hide the light (a dark lantern). Given to the University
> of Oxford in 1641 by Robert Heywood, son of the
> justice of the peace who was present at the arrest of
> Guy Fawkes in the cellars of Parliament House, when
> the Gunpowder Plot was foiled on 5 November 1605.

Instantly forgiving its tatty appearance, she recalled the textbook images she'd seen as a child, with Guy Fawkes standing next to the barrels of gunpowder, holding up his glowing lantern in one hand and a lit fuse, ready to blow James I to kingdom come, in the other. It was amazing to think that the object she was looking at had once played such a key role in British history.

She was just about to move on, when she sensed someone was standing beside her.

'How befitting,' said a voice.

Emily looked up and saw that it was none other than her bow-tied rival from the auction. 'I'm sorry?' she said, sharply.

'You, looking at Fawkes' lantern, on today of all days.'

She checked her watch – it was 5 November.

'To think, if all had gone to plan that night, world history would have taken a very different turn.'

'Yes, I suppose so,' said Emily, trying to work out where the conversation was heading and, more importantly, how to get out of it.

'You might say it would have heralded a brand new dawn,' he said, turning his head to face her.

The mere mention of that word in the context of the last few days held her rooted to the spot.

'You were at the auction,' said Emily.

'I was.'

'You knew the sketchbook was in that box?'

The man nodded.

'I'm sorry, who are you, exactly?'

'Of course, how rude of me not to introduce myself. My name is Henry Faber,' and he held out his hand. Emily shook it, begrudgingly.

'I hope you're enjoying our wonderful collection, here at the Ashmolean.'

'You work here?'

'Yes – I'm assistant keeper of the Western Art department.'

'How strange. My friend and I were just talking to your boss, Julian Mountfield.'

'Yes, I know,' he said, with a smile.

'I'm sure you also recall nearly running me over in the car park, the other morning?'

'Do you know, Miss Bradshaw, ...' he said, ignoring the allegation, '... I've studied thousands of paintings over the years, and one of the things I've learned about the Pre-Raphaelite Brotherhood is that their work is purposefully enigmatic. Nothing is ever quite as it seems.'

Emily stared at him. 'How do you know my name?'

'Ah, well, ... you don't get to work in a place like this without knowing how to do a little research.'

'I have to go,' she said, turning towards the exit.

'Did it ever occur to you, how a valuable Draper sketchbook could turn up at a small provincial auction, completely uncatalogued?' he said, calmly.

She stopped by the oak-panelled door. 'Yes, it did, actually. And I expect you're going to tell me it was stolen, or something.'

'No. Not exactly.'

'Mr Faber, I'm sorry I outbid you, but I won that book fair and square. And I would really appreciate it if you would just ... stop following me.'

'Of course.' nodded Faber, looking somewhat embarrassed. 'However, contrary to what you might think, I am as much in the dark about all this as you are. So my offer to you, Miss Bradshaw, is simply one of help—'

'Well, if you must know, I've left the book with Julian. He's going to research it for me. So, if it's all the same with you, I think I'll take my chances and see what he has to say.'

He nodded, with a look of quiet resignation. 'That sounds eminently sensible.'

She was about to give him one final piece of her mind when the phone in her pocket buzzed; it was Rosa.

'Where are you? I've been waiting here for ages.'

'Sorry, I got a bit distracted,' replied Emily. 'Give me two minutes and I'll be right with you.'

She turned round, but Henry Faber had gone. For a moment, she thought about chasing after him, but the prospect of having to face an irritable Rosa was not one she relished.

She gave Fawkes' lantern one last admiring glance, then noticed something on top of the display case. It was a business card. She picked it up and read the neat hand-written message, in ink:

Henry James Faber
Assistant Keeper – Western Art Department
Ashmolean Museum, Oxford. Tel. 07709 900176

*Aurora, some art requires you to look a little closer ...
to find the truth.*

93

Chapter Seventeen

'Come on, Dad, light a candle in that dark and dreary mind of yours, will you?'

George Waltham was a little hurt by the unwarranted slur on his intellect, but chose to ignore it – preferring instead to consider the small brass key poking out of his desk drawer. He desperately wanted to join in with his son's enthusiasm about the Pre-Raphaelites, and Rossetti's poem *St Luke the Painter*, but instead found himself pondering a dilemma that had plagued him for decades; and never more so than tonight.

'Can't you at least acknowledge the possibility that the Brothers were up to something?' said Luke.

'Such as?'

'Well, I'm convinced they were putting together a body of work which was underpinned by a series of moral codes.'

'And why on earth would they do that?'

'I don't know – to make the world a better place.'

George walked over to the study window, pulled back the curtain and peered into the night. A black cat, crossing the gravel path in front of the house, stopped and studied him with its amber eyes.

'Luke, the PRB's paintings have been open to academic scrutiny for well over a century. Even if there was some kind of esoteric agenda, don't you think someone would have found it by now?'

'Honestly? No, I don't. Sometimes, you don't see what's staring you right in the face. Christ, I should know.'

'Then perhaps you should widen your research, instead of basing all of your theories on a poem.' As soon as he'd said it, George knew he'd been unfairly dismissive and returned to the window. The black cat, its coat glistening with tiny droplets of rain, sloped off into the night.

'Research? I've done little else for the past six weeks. God, I've spent so much time in libraries and galleries, Joanne thinks I've got another woman.'

George turned and gave his son a look that posed the question without actually asking it.

'Oh, come on, really?' said Luke, offended by the insinuation. 'Anyway, I'm sure Millais, Hunt and Rossetti were up to something; I just haven't figured out what, yet.'

'Perhaps there's nothing to find.'

'I don't believe that, Dad, I really don't'.

George sighed and walked over to where his son was sitting. 'You're not going to let this go, are you?' he said, placing a hand on his shoulder.

'No, ... I can't.'

'In that case, there's something I need to show you.'

George sat down at his desk, turned the brass key and slid open the top drawer, removing an old cream-coloured envelope which he placed on the leather blotter in front of him.

'What's that?' said Luke.

'It was given to me by my father, just before he died.'

As Luke went to pick it up, George placed his hand on top of it. 'Before you open it, I want you to promise me its contents will never leave these four walls.'

'Oh come on, what is this, the Secret Service?'

'Please, Luke.'

'Okay, okay, I promise,' he laughed, curious at all the cloak-and-dagger.

George slid the envelope across the desk.

Luke picked it up and inspected it carefully. It had some age to it, and was made of good-quality paper with a small brown stain in one corner. As he turned it over and saw what was written there, in dark blue ink, his mouth fell open.

Meeting of the principle PRBs – 9 December 1848
83 Gower Street, London

He looked up at his father.

'Open it,' said George, still wondering if he'd made the right decision.

Luke did as he was told, removing the single sheet of paper inside. He could barely contain his excitement as he read what was written in the same neat hand:

'Dearest John, Dearest Gabriel,

'At a meeting on this ninth day of December, 1848, we the undersigned, being the three principle founding members of the PRB, do hereby agree to produce a series of seven painted works, henceforth known as The Lights of the World.

'Devout adherence to the sacred doctrines, portrayed therein, will empower man to discover the true nature of his humanity, preparing the soul for the seven challenges it must face on the path to enlightenment and true spiritual awakening.

'Those with eyes to see, let them see.

Darkness – blessed are they that harbour the beacon of hope, when all around them is desolation and despair.

Desire – A man's lust is his eternal shame, for the appetite of a licentious man will never be fulfilled.

Ignorance – the mind is not merely a vessel to be filled, but a vine to be nurtured for the most precious of fruit.

Lust for Death – all must dissolve into their beginnings, but only those with love in their heart may ascend the heavenly realms.

Kingdom of Flesh – when the body returns to nature and is resolved into its own roots, may the soul rise up, free from the bondage of man.

Folly of Man – learned we may be with another man's learning, only wise can we become with wisdom of our own.

Wrath – eternal peace awaits those that cast off the bonds of oblivion, to follow the everlasting light.

William Holman Hunt
John Everett Millais
Dante Gabriel Rossetti

'Is this for real?'

George nodded, sagely. He could tell by the look on Luke's face, there were so many questions buzzing round in his head, he barely knew where to begin. In the end, he decided on the most obvious.

'Where on earth did you get this?' said Luke, eventually.

'Well, it belonged to your great-great-grandfather, Charles Waltham. He was a keen art collector, and it was that passion which led to him becoming good friends with Sir John Everett Millais.'

'You're kidding.'

George shook his head. 'Some years after purchasing *The Blind Girl*, he contacted Millais to try and find out what had inspired him to paint it. He arranged a meeting at Millais's house, where they talked long into the night. Apparently, Charles's intelligence and enthusiasm must have impressed the great man, because he went on to tell him about a long-held secret between the three principal Brothers.'

'I can't believe this,' said Luke, scratching his head.

'Imagine how Charles must have felt when Millais described a series of secret meetings that had taken place between Hunt, Rossetti and himself. None of the other PRB members knew anything about it, not even Gabriel's brother, William Michael. You see the date on the envelope? It was at the trio's final meeting in Gower Street that they made a covenant to produce a collection of seven divinely inspired paintings that would speak to the world. A moral crusade, Millais called it.'

Anyway, the next day, Hunt wrote to Rossetti and Millais, confirming what they'd agreed. Millais showed the letter to Charles, so he would better understand the true meaning of *The Blind Girl*.'

'And this is Millais' copy of that letter?' said Luke.

'Actually, no. When Charles got home from his meeting with Millais, he ran straight to his study and wrote down the contents of the letter, exactly as he'd seen it. That's his note that you're holding.'

'My God, what a mind to be able to remember all that. So, let me get this straight. What you're saying is, ... I was right all along.'

George smiled. 'So it seems.'

'And would you have told me, if I hadn't started to figure it out for myself?'

'I'm sorry, Luke. I was afraid that, once I'd told you, you'd want to broadcast it to the world.'

'That's exactly what we should do, isn't it?'

'George shook his head. The Brothers wanted to bring about a radical change in the way Victorian society thought and behaved. They came to understand that, to achieve this, required a programme of carefully planned re-education, over a considerable period of time; perhaps decades. Such a marked transformation required subtle influence, not shouting it from the rooftops. And to stand any chance of success, they had to keep their grand plan a secret – and we must honour that wish.'

'Surely that wish, as you call it, was broken when Millais decided to blab the whole thing to Charles Waltham.'

'Not at all. Charles proved he was more than a collector of art – he was an intellectual and a humanitarian. And, more importantly, a man who believed in the ideals the Brothers were preaching in their art. I suppose, as the owner of one of the sacred works, Millais thought he had a right to know its true purpose. He made Charles swear he would never divulge the contents of their conversation to anyone. And, as promised, he took the secret with him, to his grave.'

'Then, how did you come by it?'

'As I've already told you, his son, James, was killed trying to steal *The Blind Girl*. And, as far as we know, he never knew the true meaning of the painting that consumed him all his life.'

'God, that's tragic,' said Luke.

'In fact, it's your grandfather, William, we should thank for keeping the secret alive. One day, he was in the library at Ardingly Hall, when he stumbled across a book by Hunt called *Pre-Raphaelitism and the Pre-Raphaelite Brotherhood*. Hidden inside the lining was Charles's note. He'd told no one about it, not even his wife.'

Luke thought for a moment. 'When we were at the BMAG a couple of months ago, you showed me *The Blind Girl*.'

George looked at his son, knowing full well where the conversation was heading.

'So, which one of these codes is it?'

'You've got the note, you tell me.'

Luke ran his finger down the list, then returned to the top. 'It's the first one, "Darkness – Blessed are they that harbour the beacon of hope, when all around them is desolation and despair." That's it, isn't it?'

George smiled. 'That would be my guess.

'And what's this symbol on top? ... it looks like a sun of some description?'

'The Brothers called it a sun mark. Apparently, it represents the enlightenment that was meant to emanate from their seven works. And, if you look closely, you'll see it spells L.O.W. Quite clever, really. There, now you know as much as I do. Perhaps as much as anyone outside of the Pre-Raphaelite Brotherhood ever did.'

'What, ... that's it? What about the other six paintings?' said Luke, waving the piece of paper in the air.

'Luke, call me an old romantic, but I like the fact that there's still a part of the Brothers' secret that remains undiscovered. I suppose I feel privileged to know this much.'

'Well, that's the difference between you and me, Dad. I couldn't just leave it hanging like that – I'd have to know.'

George took the note, put it back in the envelope and placed it in his desk drawer. 'That's fine, but I would ask you to respect the promise you've made here tonight. You will do that for me, won't you?'

'Yes, yes, of course I will.'

'Good. Now get off home, before Joanne really does think you've got someone else.'

*

As Luke left his father's flat and got into his car, all he could think about was Charles's note and the incredible revelations it contained. He opened the glovebox, scrabbled around for a pen and paper, and wrote down everything he could remember. When he'd finished, he sat and stared at the jumbled notes, just as his great-great-grandfather had done, more than a century before.

He couldn't believe his father had been party to such a precious secret and never told him about it. Now the truth was out and he was holding it, at least the bits he could remember, in his hand. One thing he did know – he would tell Kate, as soon as she was old enough to understand and appreciate the enormity of it. She loved secrets, and this would be the most beautiful of them all.

It was well past midnight, and as he drove back to Clapham, a strange mist had crept up the banks of the Thames, shrouding the Albert Bridge in a glowing white veil from the four thousand light bulbs along its span.

His mind was so scrambled, he made the turning into his road without quite knowing how he'd got there. As he put the key in the front door, he realised the usual dread of coming home to a woman he no longer loved had been replaced by something new – a remarkable discovery that would shock the art world, were it ever made public.

He switched on the hall light and looked up at the stairs in front of him. Suddenly, the constant bickering and arguments that had blighted his marriage were put to the back of his mind – buried, but not forgotten – much like the solemn promise he'd made earlier that evening, never to betray his father's trust.

Chapter Eighteen

Ashmolean Museum, Oxford

5 November 1999

Following her encounter in the Tradescant Room, Emily walked out of the museum's main entrance and spotted Rosa leaning against a pillar by the forecourt steps.

'Sorry about that,' she said, doing up her coat.

'Oh, don't worry, I've just been standing here, watching the world go by.' Then she saw the look on Emily's face. 'What's the matter, honey? Are you okay?'

'Not really. Something quite bizarre just happened back there.'

Rosa screwed up her face. 'Pray tell.'

'Well, I was looking at Guy Fawkes' lantern – you know, the one he was holding when he got caught with the gunpowder – when I spotted some old guy staring at me.'

Rosa laughed. 'They're like moths to a flame with you, aren't they?'

'No, listen. It was that man who was bidding against me at the auction.'

'You're kidding.'

'I'm not. His name is Henry Faber, and he's the assistant keeper in the Western Art department, right here.'

'Okay, that's bizarre. So, what did he want?'

'I'm not sure. I think he wants Draper's sketchbook.'

'I bet he does. Well, he can bugger off.'

'Damn right. I think he was trying to convince me that something wasn't right about it.'

'Yes, so you'd agree to sell it to him for peanuts. What else did he say?'

'Well, he muttered something about wanting to help me; so, I told him I'd given the book to Julian. Then, I turned away to take your call and he disappeared.'

'Mmm, ... all sounds very weird, if you ask me.'

'Then I found this,' said Emily, handing her the business card. 'I think it's the same handwriting as the note left on my pad in the library. He must have been following me all this time.'

Rosa read the card, '"Aurora, some art requires you to look a little closer ... to find the truth." What on earth does that mean?'

Emily shrugged. 'No idea.'

'Do you think we should call the police?'

'No, no, I don't think he's dangerous, and he seemed polite enough.'

'Yeah, for now. What if he turns nasty when he doesn't get what he wants?'

Emily shook her head. 'I'm sure it won't come to that. I may be wrong, but I didn't get the impression he posed any kind of threat – quite the opposite in fact.'

'Let's hope not,' said Rosa.

Emily glanced at her watch. It was coming up to 4.00 pm. 'Look, I hope you don't mind, Rosa, but I think I'm going to stay in Oxford tonight. If I drop you off at the station, would you mind getting the train back on your own?'

'Oh, ... okay. Why?'

'I'd like to have a proper talk with this Henry Faber guy and find out what he knows.'

'Well, if you're sure that's a good idea.'

'Yes, honestly – I'll be fine. Thanks, Rosa.' Emily leaned over and gave her a hug.

'Where are you going to stay?'

'Oh, I don't know, that one looks quite nice,' said Emily, pointing to the Randolph Hotel, opposite.

Rosa laughed. 'Five stars, yes that'll do.'

After dropping Rosa off at Oxford Station and seeing her on to the next train to Bristol Temple Meads, Emily drove back to Beaumont Street, parked the Alpine in the hotel car park and walked into the Randolph's impressive Gothic-style lobby to try and get a room.

'I'm afraid we only have a superior available, madam,' said the receptionist. 'But it does overlook the Ashmolean Museum.'

'Okay, how much?'

'For the one night, that'll be two hundred and seventy-five pounds, including breakfast.'

Emily nodded, nonchalantly. Sod it, I'm still on holiday, she thought and handed over her credit card.

Having checked in and hit the high street for a change of clothes, she went back to her modestly-sized double room, ordered a smoked salmon salad and a bottle of Prosecco on room service, and ran herself a bath.

As she stood at the third-floor window, dressed in one of the hotel's luxurious bathrobes and admiring the Ashmolean across the road, there was a loud bang outside. She scanned the street below, then noticed the red and white flashes in the sky above the museum. Of course – it was Bonfire Night. So much for a quiet night in, she thought, and grabbed a small bottle of Prosecco from the minibar, before pouring herself a glass and checking on her bath.

Waiting for the tub to fill, she picked up a small glass bottle from the shelf by the sink, and read the label. It said:

> *Rose Otto Bath Oil – made in the Rose*
> *Valley of Bulgaria, this is one of the*
> *world's most exclusive essential oils.*
> *The rose petals are mixed with water*
> *and distilled, having been first*
> *harvested by hand at the break of*
> *dawn, when at their most fragrant.*

After sniffing the contents, she poured a few drops into her bath, savouring the warm rosey scent as it filled her nostrils. She turned off the taps, hung her robe on the back of the door and slipped into the warm soapy water.

Taking a sip from her wine glass, she lay back and let out a deep, relaxing sigh. As her eyelids grew heavy, she slowly succumbed to the fragrant elixir, allowing her hands to slip beneath the water. With her mouth ever so slightly open, she gently drew her fingers along the top of her thighs, delighting in the sensuous, self-pleasuring touch of her own skin. As her emotions surrendered themselves to the waves of bliss coursing through her body, she began to lose all notion of time and space; her sub-conscious mind leading her like a stranger to some dark and distant land – to a calling that would ultimately become her destiny.

The Dawn-bringer

She had entered another realm – a heavenly place.
Naked, except for a silken veil wrapped around her waist,
She took her first steps, tentative, yet unafraid, on a
Carpet of rose petals billowing gently beneath her feet,
Its sweet perfume leading her deeper and deeper into the
Darkness, like the glow of scented candles. She followed
The mountain path, an innate sense of purpose building
Inside of her – a primal force, driving her onward, its
Power elemental, like the sun and the moon, and
As old as time itself.

Soon, she reached a rocky outcrop where the path
Narrowed. A gentle breeze, full of wisdom and guile,
Encircled her, whispering in her ear, *Aurora, use your
Power to banish the darkness. This is your destiny, your
Time to shine.* She stopped for a moment, but the voice
Was gone, like a faerie returning whence it came.

Up ahead, she saw a shimmering light, pulling her closer,
As if a siren held her name on its lips. Each divine step,
Taxing, yet sublime, as she drew on the well of fire within
Her, it's lifeblood coursing through her veins like a river of
Gold, screaming to be freed. Higher and higher she
Climbed, led by the whispering wind as it bewitched and
Beguiled her, lifting her veil and kissing her skin with its
Soft lingering lips, as a lover, caressing her very soul.

Exhausted and gasping for breath, she kept her faith in the
Steepening path, until a mysterious object appeared there,
Glowing at the top of the mountain. She gazed at its beauty
From a distance, entranced and shaking with anticipation.
Fighting the pain, she pushed herself on, until, all at once,
The ground beneath her burst into life, its carpet of petals
Dancing in celebration as their sweet perfume filled the
Mountain air. For, at last, the top was made.

The whispering wind fell silent, bowing its head in
Honour of her glorious arrival. And there, standing before
Her, were the golden gates, resonating like two colossal

Beacons in the heart of the gloaming. Hungry for their
Touch, she reached out her hand and ran her fingers
Up one of the tall, slender columns, feeling its energy
Pulsing inside her like celestial aether. Suddenly, her
Body began to glow, and with a deafening roar, a stream
Of fire burst from her fingertips, cleaving the night sky,
And scoring its mighty black canvas with veins of pink
And amber along its edge.

But the gates refused to yield, defying her god-like power.
She raised her fist and banged on the ancient sun disk.
The winged-head of time, glared down at her, as if to
Question her very existence. Defiant, she called on
Mother nature's forces and struck the gates again, but
Still the gods remained reticent. In one final, desperate
Act, she grabbed the two handles and pulled with all her
Might. As the huge gates swung open, carving deep
Furrows into the silent earth, a beam of light brighter
Than ten million stars tore through the sky, illuminating
Her domain for as far as the eye could see.

And as night became day, she fell to her knees and gazed
Upon the heavens, while the stars fell all around her.
And there, far below, was Terra Mater, in all her radiant
Majesty; beholding every living creature of land, sea and sky,
As they awoke from their slumber to bask in the quickening
Power of the sunrise. For Aurora's work was done – she had
Given birth to a brand-new day. And as the tears of joy ran
Down her cheeks, they fell as tiny dewdrops, glistening like
Diamonds in the early morning grass.

Triumphant, she gazed up at the winged-head of Time, his
Expression stoic, eternal; unlike the pantheon of gods whose
Universal truth came forth on the breath of the breeze,
Cavorting around her like a mischievous sprite, as it whispered,
Aurora, you are the dawn-bringer, the fire of life.
Behold the glory you have bestowed upon the world.
But do not dwell too long on your conception,
For Father Time will surely call on you again, soon.

*

With her heart pounding, Emily opened her eyes and stared at the bathroom ceiling – her face and neck flushed, and covered with tiny beads of sweat. She slowly removed her hand from the tepid water and placed it on the edge of the bath, her body tingling, her mind racing from the rush of her lucid dream.

Suddenly, there was a loud knock at the door. She stood up, sending a torrent of rose-scented bath water onto the floor.

'Be there in a second,' she shouted, grabbing a towel from the rail and wrapping it round her.

After hurriedly combing her hair through with her fingers, she opened the hotel room door, only to be greeted by a spotty-faced bellboy, barely old enough to be out of school uniform.

'Room service, madam?'

'Put it over there, would you?' she said, adjusting her towel.

The young man entered, trying quite unsuccessfully not to stare at her cleavage as he walked past. He placed the tray containing a smoked salmon salad and a large bottle of Prosecco on the table by the window, then turned and smiled at her, expectantly.

'Oh, right,' she said, scrabbling in her purse for some coins. All she had was a five-pound note. Begrudgingly, she took it out and handed it to him.

'Thank you, miss,' he said, taking a final peek at her towel-clad breasts, before closing the door on his way out.

Emily sat on the bed and smiled to herself – trying not to think too hard about the fervent sounds of self-pleasuring he may, or may not, have heard whilst standing outside her bedroom door.

'Oh well, ...' she said, pouring herself another glass of Prosecco. '... I've probably just made his day.'

Chapter Nineteen

St John Street, Oxford

5 November 1999

With its lights switched off, the black Audi crept along St John Street and slid quietly into one of the residents' parking spaces on the west side of the Ashmolean. The two occupants looked over at the main building and synchronised their watches; it was 7.45 pm.

Danny Forgan, the youngest active member of a notorious North London crime family, removed a parking permit from the glovebox and placed it on the dashboard. The driver looked at him with cold, dark eyes, but said nothing. Danny was about to get out of the car, when he felt a hand grab his arm and yank him back into his seat.

'Listen, kid, no screw-ups, okay?'

'Right, Marcus. No worries. Let's do this.'

The driver maintained his cold, hard stare and only when Danny's smile began to fade, did he finally loosen his grip.

'Fuckin' better not be,' he said, and got out of the car.

Marcus Tyburn was violent and unpredictable – not the sort of man to be crossed. The few who had tried were no longer around to tell the tale. Despite his desire to maintain a low profile, his reputation as a ruthless psychopath ensured a certain notoriety among the criminal fraternity, and the police. All of which meant Danny was more than a little intimidated by his accomplice – just the way Tyburn liked it. Danny's father, Frank Forgan, had arranged for him to be paired up with Tyburn on this job – told him it would be good experience, and even though he was hard as nails, Tyburn was one of the best in the business.

Trusting no one, Tyburn had made enquiries about his young protégé. Danny's criminal career started when he was sixteen, driving the getaway car for a jewellery heist in Birmingham. All went sour a couple of years later when he was caught holding up a security van in Brighton with another man. Given seven years, he got out in five. But by then, he'd got a taste for the action – it was in his blood. And here he was, on the comeback trail and eager for more.

Tonight was Bonfire Night and there was a hint of drizzle in the air, which would mean they'd have to be careful. Surfaces would be slippery and Tyburn knew this job was far from straightforward – maybe even as daring as the one hatched centuries ago by a certain Mr Fawkes. But if Tyburn had anything to do with it, this one would go off without a hitch.

Fortunately, the weather had done little to dampen the spirits of the Oxford residents and firework parties were in full swing right across the city. With loud bangs and whistles going off all around them, Tyburn and Danny each put on a black balaclava and head torch, slung a rucksack over their shoulders and walked briskly into Pusey Place – a small side street to the rear of the museum. In the corner was a building site with a large white hoarding protecting the perimeter. Knowing the site's gate would be locked, Tyburn climbed on top of a nearby skip filled with builder's rubble, and peered over the hoarding, scanning the area for security guards.

'Is it clear?' said Danny.

Ignoring him, Tyburn clambered over the wooden hoarding and jumped down into a small tarmacked courtyard. According to the building plans he'd memorised, the darkened structures on either side were brick-built and five storeys high, each with metal-framed windows which fronted storerooms, offices and conservation laboratories. An alleyway led off the courtyard, sloping gently down to a flat section of path that ran for about thirty yards, until it became entirely blocked by an enormous scaffolding tower covered in blue plastic sheeting. Erected as part of the museum's extensive renovation works, the temporary platform ran the entire length of the back wall and went right up to the roof.

Doing his best to listen out for any sudden noises over the booming fireworks, Tyburn made his way to a narrow opening at the foot of the tower and pulled back the blue plastic sheeting. Inside was a builder's ladder leading to the first-floor platform. Ever impatient to get on, he looked back, only to see Danny rolling around on the tarmac, having fallen from the top of the hoarding.

'Get a fuckin' move on!' he said, watching Danny get up and begin to hobble towards the blue plastic tower, rubbing his hip as he went. By the time he got there, Tyburn was already standing on the first-floor planking – his wild eyes glaring down at Danny through his balaclava. 'If you're not up here in ten seconds, kid, ...' he said, and without waiting for a response, began scaling the remaining network of platforms and ladders.

A few minutes later, both men were standing on the flat roof of the Ashmolean, their head-torches lighting the way ahead. Tyburn glanced at Danny, who was giving his sore hip another consoling rub. 'What's up with you?'

'Oh nothing, I just fell on my arse, getting over that fucking fence.'

'You'd better not slow me down,' said Tyburn, and took off across the rooftop like a panther towards a thirty foot high wall, built of limestone blocks. This was the museum's west wing, housing, amongst other things, a treasure trove of valuable paintings.

Danny quickly joined him and stared up at the massive stone wall in front of them. A huge firework exploded above their heads, making him jump.

'Fuck me, that was a close one.' he said. But Tyburn's focus was on an extendable ladder, purposely left by one of the construction workers – his loyalty secured by one of the Forgan brothers having a less than subtle word in his ear.

Danny retrieved it and propped it up against the wall, letting out the top two extensions as far as they would go.

'Oh, you're shittin' me,' he said, looking up at the topmost rung, which had come to rest a good five feet short of the ledge.

While Danny was busy turning the air blue, Tyburn had mounted the ladder and was nearing the top of the first section.

'Oy, shit for brains, hold this thing steady, will ya?'

Danny did as he was told and stood on the bottom rung, while Tyburn continued his ascent.

Moments later, he reached the top and began inspecting the sizeable gap. 'Fuck!' he said, thinking up a world of pain that was going to befall the poor construction worker, for selling them short.

Keeping his legs perfectly still, he carefully removed his rucksack and hurled it up on to the roof, where it landed with a thud, somewhere in the darkness.

Making his way slowly up to the very end of the ladder, he grabbed hold of the wall, as best he could, and stepped gingerly onto the top rung. Standing as tall as his six-foot, two-inch frame would allow, he reached up and hooked his hands over the row of capping stones running along the top of the wall. Using all his upper body strength, he then hauled himself up until both elbows were resting on top of the ledge. With one foot balancing precariously on top of the ladder's side rail, he took a few seconds to prepare himself, and swung his right leg up onto the ledge, gripping the surface of the wall with the sole of his boot. The concentration on his face quickly grew to a grimace and with one last desperate lunge, he managed to heave himself up on top of the ledge.

He lay there, gasping with exhaustion, then rolled over onto the narrow strip of slabs that bordered the sloping roof. Even for a headcase like Tyburn, it was a welcome relief.

*

Meanwhile, thirty feet below, Danny looked up into the darkness. Now it was his turn. And, unfortunately for him, there was no one to hold the ladder.

'Fuck it, here goes nothing,' he said, grasping the side rails, tightly. Placing each foot down, purposefully, he began to climb – one slippery metal rung after another.

'Come on, we 'aven't got all night,' said Tyburn, peering over the edge.

But, Danny wasn't listening. With his heart pounding, he slid both hands up the side rails, his one and only thought – the next rung of the ladder.

After what seemed like a lifetime of climbing, he looked up to see how far he had to go. 'Shit,' he said, returning his gaze to where his cold, white fingers were gripping the ladder. He'd barely reached halfway.

'Get up here, you fuckin' pussy,' said Tyburn, scowling.

'Alright, alright … just wait will ya!' replied Danny, desperately trying to keep calm as the wind buffeted his body, and sweat from his forehead ran down into his eyes. He tried to move his hands, but it was as if they'd become frozen to the sides of the ladder. He looked up to ask Tyburn for help, only to see him curse once more, then disappear out of sight. Danny rested his head against one of the steel rungs. *This is it – I'm going to die, right here on this fucking roof.*

It wasn't until a full minute later and soaking with sweat, that he eventually plucked up the courage to free his hands and continue his slow, juddering ascent.

Having finally reached the top, he looked up to the roof ledge. 'Oh fuck!' he said, seeing just how big the gap was.

He called out to Tyburn, but there was no response. Then, he looked down at the ground – that was a big mistake. He could barely make out the bottom of the ladder, as the rungs melted into the darkness. He called out once more – still nothing. In desperation, he thought about climbing back down, but based on how long it had taken him to get up there, not to mention the shit he'd get from his father for bailing on the job, he quickly ruled that out. A hollow ache gripped his stomach as he resigned himself to the fact that somehow, some way, he was going to have to climb onto that roof.

He took off his rucksack and with one hand, swung it as hard as he dared in the direction of the ledge. It was a terrible throw, landing right on the apex of the capping stones. Leaning over on one foot, he stretched out his arm to try and salvage it, but it was just out of reach. He was about to try again, when he saw the bag slowly topple backwards. He lunged out to try and catch it, but could only watch as it plummeted into the darkness, hitting the ground with a distant thud. He glanced up at the smoky orange sky and shook his head. What the hell was he going to do now?

With no time to go back down, he took a deep breath and stretched out a hand towards the ledge above. Feeling for the apex with his fingertips, he started to play out a plan of action in his mind. This was going to be a one-shot deal. At best, he'd be able to scramble up onto the roof. At worst, if he was lucky, he'd land back on the ladder. Failing that, he was screwed.

After a few moments spent preparing himself for the big push, he flexed his knees a little, and on the count of three, launched himself up off the ladder with his arms outstretched, ready to grab onto whatever he could. Getting a better lift-off than he'd hoped for, he hooked his fingers over the back of the capping stones and clung there for dear life, grimacing as the muscles in his arms and shoulders began to sear with pain. Recalling his weight-training sessions in the gym, he took a few deep breaths to compose himself, while he plucked up the courage for his next move. He closed his eyes and tried to picture it, but all that kept coming to mind was the fall, the long agonising fall.

He started to panic – his legs flailing about, uncontrollably, as he tried to locate the top of the ladder. Suddenly, there was a loud clang as his boot kicked something metallic. He stopped, waiting for the inevitable crash of the ladder hitting the roof below, but all was quiet. Thank God, he thought, and began to feel for one of the rungs with the sole of his right boot; eventually managing to locate the top of the ladder's side rail. More in hope than expectation, he gently placed his weight down on the rail's plastic end-cap – the ladder held firm. Barely daring to breath, he stretched out his leg and searched for the top rung with his left foot. Feeling something flat under the toe of his boot, he let his body gradually slide down the few precious inches, until his foot came to rest on the top rung of the ladder. He'd made it.

Still clinging to the very edge of the capping stones, he said a quiet *thank you* to whatever gods were watching, up there.

Suddenly, the world shot from under him, like the trapdoor on a hangman's gallows.

'Oh fuck ... oh fuck!' he said, as the ladder scraped down the gallery wall, hitting the ground with an ear-splitting crash.

With just his ten aching fingers between him and death, he looked up at the ledge as a huge blood-red firework exploded overhead. In sheer desperation, he let out one last blood-curdling cry. 'Maaarcuusss!' But no one came.

This was it – time to meet his maker. Through tear-filled eyes, he watched the firework melt into the sky and wondered if there was any chance he would survive the fall. As the agony in his fingers took control of his mind, he closed his eyes, prayed for a quick death ... and let go of the ledge.

He waited for the cold rush of air, for the sudden impact to shatter his body into a thousand pieces. But something was wrong – he wasn't falling. Feeling a vice-like grip on his wrist, he opened his eyes to find himself suspended in mid-air.

'Goin' somewhere?' grinned Tyburn, and quickly hauled him up onto the gallery roof.

Danny lay there on the narrow strip of paving slabs, staring at the night sky – that big, beautiful, fucking, orange smoke-filled sky.

'Christ, Marcus … I thought I was a goner there.'

'Until we've got what we came for, you're not goin' anywhere, matey,' said Tyburn, brushing the dust off his black leather jacket. 'But I'll tell you one thing – if you say my name out loud again, I'll throw you off this fuckin' roof myself,' and he walked over to the four large skylights, glowing in the darkness.

Danny wiped the sweat from his eyes. 'Sorry … I wasn't thinking.'

'Yeah, well, do us both a favour …' said Tyburn, peering down into the brightly lit University Gallery, '… turn on that tiny fuckin' brain of yours, and start, … right now.'

Chapter Twenty

Cuckmere Haven, East Sussex

4 July 1982

Standing on the stoney beach and watching his daughter, Kate, stare blankly out to sea, Luke knew she was hurting inside – as was he. In all her short life, she'd never experienced grief like this – that all-consuming heartache of losing someone you love. Sure, his break-up with her mum, Joanne, had hurt her deeply, but nothing like this – this was death; and that feeling of *gone forever* would remain with her, always.

After wrapping her up in a long consoling hug, he bent down and picked a piece of sea kale out of the shingle, remembering how he always used to tell her it was protected and shouldn't be touched. But today, it didn't matter. Nothing mattered, apart from the love for his beautiful little girl.

'Grandad loved this place,' he said, clasping her hand tightly. 'He used to bring me here when I was a boy and we'd follow the bends in the river, all the way from Exceat. He'd tell me stories of the smugglers taking contraband upriver to Alfriston in the dead of night. And how the customs men would try and stop them.'

'Well I think it's a strange place for him to end up,' she said, tossing a smooth glass-like stone into the waves with frustration.

'Not really. You see those white cliffs up the coast there, that's the Seven Sisters. He used to say they were the gatekeepers of this great land. And here, right where we're standing, this is the place where England ends and the rest of the world begins. That's why he wanted to be laid to rest here, you see?'

She pursed her lips and nodded.

'Your Grandad was a wise man, Kate, and if he said it was true, it most probably was. Shall we set him free?' said Luke, picking up the stoneware urn, decorated with stylised willow trees – a Celtic symbol of clarity, understanding and strength.

They walked the few paces to where the gently flowing Cuckmere River cut its way through the pebble beach, and stopped to gaze into the blue-grey water.

'Okay, ... ready?' said Luke.

Kate nodded, reluctantly.

Accompanied by the chatter of fulmars on the nearby cliffs, he removed the lid, tucked it in his pocket, and saying one final goodbye in his head, began to relinquish the last remains of George Waltham to that most sacred of places – where the river meets the sea.

'Can I?' said Kate, holding out her hands.

'Okay, but be careful, it's heavy,' he said, handing her the urn.

She took it with both hands and stared solemnly at the contents. Then, keeping a tight hold of the urn, she launched it skywards, sending her grandfather's ashes billowing into the air. Luke watched in disbelief as the small grey cloud caught the breeze and broke into a thousand pieces as it made its way towards the sloping chalk cliff of Haven Brow. He looked at Kate, enquiringly.

'I didn't want Grampy George to drown in the sea. He'd have wanted to fly up there, with the birds.'

'Huh, ... well, you're probably right. I think he would have liked that,' said Luke, searching the sky for the last remnants of the tiny ashen-coloured veil.

Seeing his father literally disappear in front of his eyes brought a chilling finality to the proceedings.

'Come on Kate, we should be heading back,' he said, and tucked the empty urn under his arm.

They slowly made their way back up the steep rise from the beach, past the coastguard cottages and along the gorse-lined path towards the car park at South Hill Barn. As they approached the top of the hill, Luke stopped and looked back at one of his favourite views in all the world – the Seven Sisters from Seaford Head. Perhaps it was the solemn occasion, or witnessing the grief in his daughter's eyes, earlier; but suddenly, he felt very alone. Both his parents were gone – his mother from cancer when he was just twenty-one, and now, his father from the same evil fucking disease. Yes, he had Kate, and as long as there was breath in his body, she would want for nothing. But deep inside, there was also solitude and a slow-burning resentment at the things that had gone wrong in his life. By his own admission, his marriage to Joanne had been a disaster from start to finish. And, quite honestly, divorce had come as a blessed relief. But losing his job as a lecturer at the Royal College of Art had dealt him a bitter blow. He thought he'd done the right thing by covertly supplementing the coursework of one of his favourite students, when her drug-addled boyfriend's violent outbursts caused her to skip most of her final-term lectures – the College Dean, however, saw it somewhat differently. Not his smartest move, he had to admit.

And now, there was a chance he was going to lose Kate, too. Joanne was a bitch of the highest order, and had taken great delight in filing a petition for full custodial rights, claiming he was an unfit parent, having left his young daughter home-alone on at least three occasions. Of course, that was utter bollocks, and he would fight her all the way to the courts. Being unemployed, he had very little money, but all that was about to change, thanks to his father's inheritance. Now, he'd be able to hire the best divorce lawyer he could find. And there'd be plenty leftover to start his own business – restoring and selling old paintings – something he'd always dreamed of doing. It would be a new start, for him and Kate.

'Daddy look, a yellow wagtail,' she said, chasing it along the chalk bridleway.

'Alright sweetheart, be there in a sec.'

Watching a bank of high cloud coming in from the Channel, he thought back to that night, some years ago, when his father had shown him the copy of the Millais letter. He'd sworn never to disclose it to another living soul, and while his father was alive, he'd kept that promise. But his own research had unearthed more and more of the Pre-Raphaelite Brothers' remarkable secret, and now, he was the only person alive who knew about *the sun mark* and the seven paintings in their sacred collection. It was like being the only member of a secret society. Not only did he know the name and location of each of the pictures, but also their purpose. However, being sole guardian of such esoteric knowledge begged an obvious question: what on earth was he going to do with it?

Somehow, spending time here with his daughter, and saying his last goodbyes to his father, had helped crystallise his

thoughts. He would look to do what the Brotherhood had not –
to bring the collection of seven paintings together for the very
first time.

Obviously, such a grand scheme couldn't be rushed. He would
need to bide his time, build up the business and become a
respectable art dealer. He couldn't risk losing Kate; that would
destroy him. Once the custody battle was over, he would devote
himself to her upbringing, and under his careful tutelage, she
would grow up to be an intelligent, single-minded young woman
– there was no doubt about that. Then, when she was old
enough, he would tell her about his plan for *The Lights of the
World*, and she would be a part of it.

He took in a lungful of sea air and went in search of Kate,
who'd disappeared over the brow of the hill. He found her sitting
quietly on a patch of grass, watching an Adonis blue butterfly
feeding on some vetch.

'I've never seen anything so beautiful,' she said, tilting her
head as the butterfly probed and prodded for nectar.

'Come on you, let's go and get some tea.'

She jumped to her feet and walked with him back to the car.

'Can I do it, Dad?' she said, holding out her hand, as they
reached the indigo-blue, Mark II Jag.

'Alright, but don't scratch the paintwork.'

'I won't,' she said, with a playful look of disdain.

Luke dropped the keys to his father's car into her hand. As she
slid it carefully into the lock and pulled open the driver's door,
the smell of old leather and walnut veneer hit him like a tidal
wave of nostalgia – comforting and familiar.

After playing with the steering wheel for a few seconds, Kate
clambered over to the passenger side, allowing Luke to flop
down into the red leather driver's seat.

'Crikey, wind that window down, Kate, it's like an oven in
here,' he said, placing the urn on the back seat.

She did as she was told, and with the warm salty air filling her
nostrils, she took a last look at the white-chalk cliffs peeking
through the gorse.

'Bye, Grampy George,' she said, soulfully, and blew him a kiss.

As she handed the keys back to her father, the late afternoon
sun picked out one in particular, making it glitter like gold.

'One day, I'll tell you all about the secret that this unlocks,' said Luke, and facing a barrage of questions from an inquisitive ten-year-old, he started the 3.8 litre engine, released the handbrake and set off down the narrow country lane – the key to his father's desk swinging gently from the ignition.

Chapter Twenty-One

Ashmolean Museum, Oxford

5 November 1999

Three of the four skylights on top of the museum's west wing were fitted with reinforced security glass. The one Marcus Tyburn was focussing on, however, was not. Contrary to the architect's plans, this particular unit was fitted with a clever imitation that could be easily cut, like normal glass.

Tyburn removed a pair of suction pads and a diamond-tipped cutter from his rucksack and applied the pads to the centre of the glass panel. Flicking the two levers to create a vacuum, he gave the handles a sharp tug. They were stuck firm. Meanwhile, Danny used the glass cutter to score round the edge of the skylight.

With the last side nearly done, Tyburn took a tight grip on the suction pads, as Danny carefully tapped round the score mark with the end of the cutter. Accompanied by a long, dry cracking sound, the huge panel finally gave way. They were in.

All of a sudden, a burst of sirens came drifting up from the street below. Tyburn froze, tensing his forearms to support the large panel as it hovered above the open skylight. Seconds later, a fire engine tore past the front of the museum, no doubt on its way to another out-of-control bonfire. The two men glanced at each other. Danny exhaled and shook his head as Tyburn carefully lowered the glass sheet onto the sloping roof.

They looked down into the brightly lit picture gallery and caught sight of their target, hanging on the far wall.

'Where's your rucksack?' said Tyburn.

Danny grimaced and gestured to the fallen ladder on the roof below.

'For fuck's sake,' said Tyburn, shaking his head. 'Lucky for you I brought some spares.'

He took two smoke grenades from the side pocket of his bag, pulled the top off the first canister and struck the fuse against the abrasive top, causing it to erupt in a fountain of sparks. He peered over the edge and tossed it down onto the gallery floor, where it came to rest against an old radiator, belching plumes of dense white smoke. He lit the second, got down on his stomach and lobbed it into the far corner of the room, directly beneath the wall-mounted CCTV camera. It wasn't long before the dense fog had spiralled up the walls and along the ceiling, completely filling the picture gallery and most of the adjoining room.

The two men waited; then it came – the piercing screech of the fire alarm. With the power supply cut, the brilliance of Gallery 55 dimmed to a faint glow from the emergency lighting. Now their every move was against the clock.

Danny took the rope ladder from Tyburn's rucksack, hooked it over the outer frame of the skylight and tossed the rungs into the swirling smoke below. Tyburn, meanwhile, wiped the moisture from the sole of his boots with a dry rag. He lived for these moments – the confrontation, the danger, pitting himself against the establishment; it was better than sex, made him feel alive.

After being handed a ski mask and respirator by Danny, Tyburn put them on and climbed into position on the edge of the skylight.

'Take it easy down there,' said Danny.

'Just concentrate on what you gotta do,' he replied.

Quickly finding his rhythm on the narrow steel rungs, Tyburn soon reached the gallery floor. Not that he could see it – the smoke bombs had done such a good job, he could barely make out his hand in front of his face. Having memorised the gallery layout, he knew the exact number of steps from the foot of the ladder to any point in the room – and one point in particular.

He turned to his right, took three paces and stopped, then turned to his left and took another ten paces forward. He reached out his arms until his fingers brushed a small picture frame on the wall in front of him. There, barely visible through the gloom, were the vibrant brush strokes of blue and gold paint in Picasso's *Blue Roofs*, now almost opaque, as if surrounded by a thick Paris fog.

He grabbed the frame in both hands and ripped it from its mount, causing the tiny motion sensor on the wall to let off a shrill beeping sound. Ignoring it, he took the same route back to the foot of the ladder where a black canvas carry case was now hanging from a length of climber's rope. He laid the carry case on the floor, placed the Picasso inside and zipped it up. Giving two sharp tugs on the rope to let Danny know he was done; he watched the case rise up through the murk until it was out of sight.

Wasting no time, he clambered onto the ladder and laughed at the ease with which the museum had given up one of its treasures.

Before he'd even set foot on the third rung, there was a loud shout from the gallery next door: 'Gary, don't go in there.'

Tyburn stopped and looked over in the direction of the doorway. Although a security guard or two posed no problems, he knew the chances of them entering a smoke-filled gallery were extremely remote, as the museum's health and safety policy dictated that, under no circumstances should any member of staff tackle a blaze, directly. They must wait for the fire brigade to arrive, and only when the building had been declared safe, could staff re-enter. Even if a fire engine was available on such a busy night, it would take at least six minutes for them to get there, after the alarm had been raised – plenty of time for him to grab what they came for and get out of there.

As the smoke began to clear, Tyburn could just make out Danny waving furiously through the open skylight, and shouting something; but it was difficult to hear over the cacophony of alarm bells. Satisfied the guards were following procedure, he gave the rope ladder a reassuring tug and began to climb once more.

Then he felt something grab his ankle. He looked down to see a fresh-faced security guard clawing at his trouser leg. Tyburn lifted his other leg and brought his boot crashing down onto the young man's face, causing him to fall back, howling in pain. But the guard wasn't done yet. Coughing and spluttering, he got to his feet, took the nightstick from his belt, and launched himself at Tyburn, exacting a fierce blow to the back of his knee.

Tyburn yelled out, and tumbled to the floor; whereupon the guard grabbed him by the wrists and thrust his knee into the small of Tyburn's back, pinning him to the floor. 'Thought you'd got me there, didn't you?' he said, coughing up more blood from his broken nose.

Tyburn lay there, waiting. As the lad turned to see if his colleagues were watching from the adjoining gallery, he brought the heel of his boot up hard into the guard's spine, sending him sprawling across the floor. He calmly pulled his Glock from his jacket pocket, got up and went over to where the young man was writhing in agony.

'Not so cocky now, are ya, ya little shit?' said Tyburn, glancing over at the doorway, to see if the other museum guards were up for the fight. 'Looks like it's just you and me, then,' and he pushed the gun barrel into his temple.

The guard stared at the floor as he coughed up another gloop of congealed blood.

'Steady kid, I don't want you dyin' on me, just yet.'

Scared as he was, the young man wasn't the only one having an emotional crisis, for inside Tyburn's head, a battle was raging. The psychopath in him wanted nothing more than to top the little shit, cowering in front of him; but the left side of his brain kept reminding him, this was no ordinary job, and killing someone would risk blowing it all to hell. Unfortunately, keeping a lid on things wasn't Tyburn's forte. He looked at his watch – it was time to go.

He pushed the barrel of the Glock into the lad's skull until a small ring of blood began to form beneath the cold steel. Preparing to die, the young man curled up into a ball and started to whimper, quietly, which cut no ice with Tyburn; he'd wasted far better men than this, without a second thought. But the words of his boss kept calling out to him, "No fuck-ups Marcus, just in and out". His index finger tightened against the trigger. *To hell with that. Nobody tells me what to do.* Just one little squeeze and his bloodlust would be satisfied.

Suddenly, everything went deathly quiet, as the fire alarm stopped its incessant ringing.

'Are you gonna spend all night down there?' called a voice from above.

Tyburn looked up to see Danny peering through the skylight. He returned his icy glare to the security guard.

'Looks like it's your lucky day, son,' he said, sliding the gun back into his pocket.

As he started to walk back to the ladder, he quickly turned and kicked the guard in the jaw, sending teeth and bits of gum shooting from his mouth. With his ego duly restored, he stepped back onto the ladder and climbed up onto the gallery roof.

'What was all that about?' said Danny.

'Where's the picture?' growled Tyburn, in no mood for backchat.

Danny handed him the black canvas bag, which Tyburn duly looped over his shoulder so it hung across his back.

'As you managed to leave us fuckin' stranded up here, you'd better grab that rope ladder, hadn't you.'

Danny did as he was told, hooking it over the capping stones and down the side of the gallery wall.

Under the cover of bangs and whistles from a nearby fireworks display, the two men made their way back across the rooftop of the main museum building and down to the waiting Audi, parked nearby. Leaving Oxford under a smoke-filled sky, they joined the traffic on the A40 and headed back to London, ready to lie low with the night's takings.

*

A short while later, four members of the Oxfordshire Fire Service entered Gallery 55 in full breathing apparatus. Most of the smoke had dissipated, but it was still an eerie scene; the only sound being the Darth Vader-like hiss of air filtering through their respirators as they moved from room to room. Finally, the all-clear was given to the museum's head of security – there was no fire.

By 9.00 pm, most of the fireworks in Oxford had subsided, with just the occasional rocket and mine going off around the city. Gallery 55, however, was dark and quiet. The only sound – the splash of raindrops in a steadily growing puddle beneath the open skylight.

On the wall where the Picasso had once hung, a solitary red light clicked on and off in the darkness, signalling the loss of a great art treasure – likely, never to return.

Chapter Twenty-Two

Randolph Hotel, Oxford

5 November 1999

Resting against the padded headboard, with the remnants of her celestial dream still circling round in her head, Emily flicked through the TV channels using the remote. It was 8.10 pm. She was just about to close her eyes when the siren from an emergency vehicle came blaring past her window. Given the number of fire engines that had made their way up Beaumont Street in the last two hours, she duly ignored it. But when the blue flashing lights kept on flashing, curiosity got the better of her, hauling her off the bed to peer through a gap in the curtains. Parked in front of the Ashmolean were two large fire tenders and a whole host of firefighters getting ready for action. A shiver went down Emily's spine. Surely not a fire in one of the country's finest museums – that would be a catastrophe. She took a seat by the window and gazed through the rain-speckled glass as the drama unfolded.

She watched intently as what looked like the senior firefighter wandered over to the museum entrance to be greeted by two security guards. After a brief discussion, one of them looked up and pointed to the roof of the west wing. There didn't seem to be any sign of a fire, and she was beginning to wonder what all the fuss was about, when a plume of smoke puffed up from one of the skylights. She put her hand over her heart and watched with trepidation at the thought of all those precious artefacts being ravaged by the flames.

While three of the firefighters put on breathing apparatus and entered the building, others began unfurling fire hoses and preparing to remove ladders from the tenders. With their sirens blaring, a number of police cars arrived at either end of Beaumont Street, and quickly closed the road to all non-emergency vehicles.

The front of the museum soon became a chaotic scene of police, firefighters and museum officials coming and going, and pointing – there was a lot of talking and pointing, mostly in the direction of the smoking roof, where men with torches could be seen inspecting the skylights.

Another car, unmarked this time, made its way through the police cordon and pulled up outside the museum gates. A man got out. He was tall, slim and in his late fifties; and judging by his confident demeanour and dowdy-looking clothes, Emily surmised he was in charge. What most caught her eye, though, was his mane of shoulder-length silver hair and a rather impressive handlebar moustache. He flashed his badge at one of the uniformed police officers and walked over to talk to the firefighter wearing a white helmet. They both looked up at the skylight and, after a brief discussion, the silver-haired man strolled towards the entrance where two worried-looking museum officials had come out to meet him. They were none other than Julian Mountfield and Henry Faber.

After speaking with them for a minute or so, the silver-haired man turned round and looked up at the top floor of the Randolph Hotel, scanning from left to right until he got to Emily's window. To her horror, he pointed straight at her. She froze, as if she'd just been picked out in an identity parade. She desperately wanted to close the curtains, but that would be ridiculous, so she kept staring back. Finally, he turned round and walked inside the museum with the two curators.

She pulled the curtains shut and sat on the bed. *What on earth was that all about?* Then, a terrifying thought hit her – had Julian left the sketchbook in his office? Fire could spread so quickly; had her prize possession been destroyed in the blaze, or perhaps become drenched with water from the sprinklers or fire hoses? She tried desperately to recall where Julian's office was – she knew it was somewhere on the second floor, and from memory, not a million miles from where she'd seen smoke on the roof.

She suddenly came over all hot and bothered, and began pacing up and down the hotel room; spending the next twenty minutes going over every possible scenario, whilst curtain-twitching to see if the museum had, against all odds, burst into a raging fireball.

Having finally convinced herself that it was pretty unlikely, she was just getting ready for bed when she heard the sound of a diesel engine starting up outside. She pulled back the curtains to see one of the fire engines leaving. Not only that, but the police had reopened Beaumont Street where traffic was, once more, flowing past the front of the museum. Even the crowds of onlookers on St Giles' had lost interest and were heading back to their colleges and pubs.

She closed the curtains, and was about to head to the bathroom to brush her teeth, when the phone rang on the bedside table. Who the hell is that calling at this hour? she thought, and picked it up.

'Hello?'

'Miss Bradshaw, this is Philippe from reception. I'm sorry to trouble you, but there is a gentleman here who would like to speak with you.'

'Really? It's rather late. Who—' Before she could finish, another voice came on the line.

'Hello, Miss Bradshaw, my name is Detective Chief Inspector Cordell from Thames Valley Police. Would you mind if we had a brief chat?'

'Err ... what about, exactly?'

'I need to talk to you about an incident at the museum.'

'Oh yes, I saw the commotion from the window.'

'I'm sorry to trouble you, but I really need to see you right away. May I come on up?'

'Um ... I was just getting ready for bed, actually.' Then, curiosity took over. 'Okay, look, ... can you give me a few minutes and I'll meet you down in the bar.'

'That would be great, thank you.' Cordell replied.

'Err ... how will I know you?'

'Oh, don't worry, Miss Bradshaw, I'm sure we'll recognise each other,' he said, and hung up.

Emily's heart was pounding. No doubt, Cordell was the silver-haired man pointing up at her, earlier. But all she could think about was the fire, and whether her sketchbook was safe.

Five minutes later, she was dressed with a quick dash of make-up, and checking her hair in the lift mirror before arriving at the ground-floor lobby.

To a large proportion of the hotel's guests, the Morse Bar was the jewel in the Randolph's crown – its walls covered with oak panels, topped with an impressive vaulted ceiling, from which hung three large glass chandeliers – all designed to provide patrons with a relaxed atmosphere of understated grandeur.

Emily saw a man sitting at the bar and smiled to herself. The silver-white hair and handlebar moustache were a dead giveaway. Now she had a name to go with the face.

'Detective Chief Inspector Cordell?' she said, holding out her hand.

'Miss Bradshaw?' he said, getting to his feet and shaking it. 'Thank you for agreeing to see me.'

She declined his offer of a drink and joined him at a quiet table in the corner, watching intently as he folded his dark grey raincoat over the back of his chair and took a sip from his pint of draught ale. Obviously not averse to a drink on duty, she thought, as he wiped the froth from his moustache. His hair was much whiter under the lights of the bar, and the deeply drawn wrinkles in his face made him appear quite weather-beaten, as though he'd spent most of his life at sea.

'What did you want to ask me?' said Emily.

'I saw you looking out of your window, earlier. You must have had a good view of things from up there?'

'Yes, I suppose so. Did the fire do much damage?'

'I was wondering if you happened to spot anything unusual?' he said, ignoring the question.

'Such as?'

'Any activity on the museum roof?'

'No, I can't say that I did. When the fire engines turned up, I saw smoke coming from one of the skylights. That's about it.'

'You're certain? Nothing before then?'

'If I'd seen anything suspicious, I'd have been straight on the phone to the police,' she said, giving him a quizzical look. 'Why, has there been a break-in?'

He took another sip of his pint, as though thinking for a moment.

'Yes, to the third-floor gallery.'

Emily's interest suddenly piqued. 'My God, was anything taken?'

'I can't go into details, Miss Bradshaw. I'm sure you understand.'

'But what about the smoke?'

'The thieves used smoke bombs as a diversion. It must have looked quite dramatic from where you were standing.'

'It certainly did. So that's why Julian was looking concerned.'

'You know Julian Mountfield?'

'Yes, he's helping me with some research.'

Cordell nodded. 'And Henry Faber?'

Emily raised her eyebrows at the mention of that name. 'Err … well, let's just say, he introduced himself to me, earlier.'

Cordell's mobile phone started to ring.

'Excuse me while I take this,' he said, and walked over to the bar. Emily watched as he nodded a couple of times, hung up and returned to the table.

'I'm sorry, I'm needed back at the museum.'

'You haven't finished your beer.'

'It's fine,' said Cordell, reaching into his coat pocket. 'Here's my card. If you do happen to remember anything else, please give me a call.'

'Of course. Oh, by the way, how did you know which room I was in?'

'I counted the windows on the third floor, then asked reception if there was a young lady staying in the seventh room from the end,' he said, putting on his raincoat.

'Right, that explains it.'

After bidding the DCI good night, Emily took the lift back up to her room, sat on the bed and drained the last of the Prosecco. She was so glad there hadn't been a fire – that would have been a travesty; even more so, had Draper's sketchbook been reduced to a pile of ashes.

But a major robbery, just yards from where she was staying. And at the Ashmolean, of all places – now that would be headline news.

Chapter Twenty-Three

9 Pembroke Studios, Kensington, London
28 February 1896

With walking stick in hand, John Everett Millais stepped down, gingerly, from the horse-drawn carriage.

'Would you be kind enough to wait?' he said to the driver, in his distinctive gravelly whisper – the great man, now a slave to the throat cancer that had turned him into a ghost of his former self.

The driver cupped his hand to his ear. 'Sorry sir, I didn't quite catch that.'

'He said, would you mind waiting?' boomed a voice from behind the carriage.

Millais smiled on hearing his old friend's dulcet tones. 'William, it's good to see you.'

The two ageing Pre-Raphaelites embraced, then walked together down the gravel path, chatting casually as they approached the block of red-bricked artists' studios set back from the clamour of Kensington High Street.

'Congratulations on your recent investiture,' said Hunt. 'The Academy should count themselves fortunate to be able to appoint such a worthy successor to Lord Leighton's presidency.'

'That is very gracious of you, William.'

'Is the post yours for life?'

'It is, if I want it. Although, I fear my condition will only allow me to carry out my duties for a year or so.'

Hunt glanced solemnly at his brother in everything but blood. 'Mmm ... well, as long as it doesn't keep you from your painting. It would be a tragedy if the world were deprived of more of your great work.'

'I know the task will be irksome at times, but I have thought it over carefully and I fear the Academy would suffer greatly, were I to decline.'

'I fear you are right, my friend. By the way, did you hear of Lear's latest pun on the subject? ... that a new *Millais-nium* of art has finally come.'

Millais smiled, modestly, as they walked up to the red door of Studio 9.

'Come now, John, what is so important that I must abandon my work on such a bitterly cold morning?'

As with his acceptance speech at the Academy, a few days before, Millais chose his words carefully. 'Being confronted, as I am, by the impending onset of my mortality, I find myself harking back to the days of the Brotherhood. And never more so than today. We three had such great energy back then, such vision; and all driven by a common creed – to change the world with our art.'

'Halcyon days, indeed,' nodded Hunt. That said, one has to say that each of us has gone on to achieve a great deal, with respect to our own particular labours, don't you agree?'

'Why, yes, of course. And, no doubt, you will recall the commitment we made to produce the seven great works of enlightenment?'

'Naturally, brother – *The Lights of the World.*'

'Well, it occurred to me the other day that, although we each put forward what is arguably some of our finest work, the task remains unresolved.'

'John, I think it must have slipped your mind. You contributed two works, as did Rossetti, and I three. How did we fall short?'

'The seven works were a compendium for those who sought to undergo their own spiritual awakening. And yes, of course, we did our best to guide them along that path, signposting the seven wrathful powers that would confront them on their journey. Then it struck me, after all our noble endeavours, we failed to show them the prize that awaits, once enlightenment has been realised – peace for the soul, until the end of time.'

Hunt gave his long grey beard a thoughtful stroke and looked into the eyes of his old friend, knowing full well he was right.

'Are you volunteering for the task? If so, I'm sure that if you manage your presidential obligations wisely, then—'

'Alas, the medical experts do not share your optimism, William. We must face facts – my days of laying brush to canvas are all but over. And that is why I have asked you here today; so we might finish what we started.'

Hunt looked somewhat perplexed, but remained silent as Millais continued.

'This final work should act as a beacon of hope for the future – an icon for the dawning of a new century. Would it not be more fitting for a younger mind to complete the task on our behalf? One who shares our heartfelt values and beliefs?'

'And am I to suppose that such a man resides behind this red door?'

Millais put his hand on Hunt's shoulder. 'His name is Herbert Draper and he was the seventh born in his family – a Septimus child, William.'

'Go on.'

'He's always been a great admirer of the Brotherhood, and was highly thought of by his mentor, Lord Leighton. He has even attended some of my lectures at the Academy.'

Hunt frowned at the prospect of some young upstart deigning to consider himself worthy of comparison to the hallowed members of the PRB.

'I have seen his work, William – it is most accomplished. But I would like you to judge for yourself, if you have it in your heart to humour an old, dying friend?'

'Very well. Who am I to refuse the newly elected President of the Royal Academy, and a Knight of the Realm?'

'Quite,' said Millais, knocking gently on the front door with his stick.

A distinguished-looking young man with piercing green eyes and a tapered moustache, opened the door. He stood there, staring at the two eminent Pre-Raphaelites gracing his doorstep: Hunt, with his mass of bushy grey hair and matching beard, and Millais, frail and gaunt, leaning on his walking stick.

'Good morning, Herbert, please forgive us for calling unannounced,' said Millais, humbly.

Draper eventually found his voice. 'Err... yes, yes... gentlemen, please do come in.'

'I hope we are not interrupting your work,' said Hunt, waiting for Millais to enter before stepping inside.

'Not at all. I was just ... mixing up some oils for my next picture.'

'Herbert, may I introduce my learned friend, Mr Holman Hunt.'

'It is indeed an honour, sir,' said Draper, shaking his hand. 'I have been an admirer of your work for many years.'

William nodded, inspecting the studio with his critical gaze.

'And Sir John, may I extend my heartfelt congratulations on your recent appointment as President of the Academy?'

'Thank you,' said Millais. 'If I am able to fulfil my responsibilities even half as well as our beloved Lord Leighton, I shall consider myself most fortunate.'

'Of that, you can rest assured, sir. Now, gentlemen, can I get you some refreshments, tea perhaps?'

'No, thank you; we are rather pushed for time,' said Millais, noticing that Hunt was already snooping around some of Draper's works. 'Perhaps you would indulge us in a brief tour of your studio.'

'Why, of course.' Draper led them into a spacious room, bathed in light from a pair of two-storey windows overlooking a central courtyard. Against the walls stood a number of paintings and sketches in various stages of completion. And resting on an easel at the far end of the room was the finest of them all – a dramatic seascape depicting a group of fishermen who had, to their surprise, landed a frightened sea siren in their nets. Hunt and Millais stood in front of it, transfixed.

'When I received your letter, Sir John, asking if you could visit my studio, I immediately contacted Mr Huish – to whom I sold the painting – to ask if he would kindly loan me *The Sea Maiden* for a day or two. Naturally, when I told him the names of the two esteemed gentlemen coming to view the picture, he was more than delighted.'

Hunt could barely take his eyes off the powerful, flowing composition; from the clawing arms of the love-ravaged fishermen, to the pale naked flesh of the sea nymph, glaring desperately at her captors. He hated to admit it, but this young man had talent.

Millais made his way round the room, giving Hunt time to draw his own conclusions on Draper's work. He stopped by a small table and picked up an ink sketch of a Grecian girl feeding a caged bird in a clifftop garden.

'Something I did a few years ago – it's called *The Tame Partridge*,' said Draper.

'Exquisite,' Millais replied.

'I see you've had Miss Lloyd sit for you,' said Hunt.

'Yes, she is a great favourite of mine, as she was for Lord Leighton, I believe. When I saw her in his *Flaming June*, I felt quite impelled to paint her myself.'

'And what is the name of this piece?'

'It's called *The Youth of Ulysses*. Leighton much admired it when it was shown at the summer exhibition, last year.'

Millais looked over at Hunt to gauge his reaction, but the wily old master was giving nothing away.

Having completed the brief tour, Draper led the two elder statesmen upstairs to a galleried sitting area where they each took a seat.

In some pain, Millais cleared his throat and leaned forward in his chair. 'Herbert, I think it only appropriate that I explain the true nature of our visit.'

'Of course,' said Draper.

'As you know, I have been plying my trade for a good many years, and I fear my commitments to the Academy, as well as this damned illness, will prevent me from undertaking any more works of, … a serious nature.'

'Rubbish,' said Hunt.

'William, please. As you see, my old friend has a lot more faith in my restorative powers than I do. Unfortunately, time is not a commodity I possess a great deal of, …'

He began to cough violently.

'Are you alright, Sir John?' said Draper, looking concerned.

Millais held up his hand and nodded. 'I'm fine, I'm fine,' he said, sitting back in the chair to catch his breath.

Hunt continued, 'What the President of the Royal Academy is trying to say is, that we would like your help with a project that John, Gabriel and I have not had the opportunity to complete.'

With his composure restored, Millais smiled at his old friend. Just as he'd hoped, Draper had somehow managed to win over the cantankerous old maniac.

'But gentlemen, I would consider it an honour to be of whatever assistance I can.'

Millais continued, 'I'm afraid it is a little more than mere assistance we require of you, Herbert. We would like you to produce a painting to celebrate the dawning of a new century in British art – a brave new world, if you will.'

Hunt got to his feet and looked over the balcony to the studio below. 'Not just that. The work must also purvey a special meaning to those who view it – one of hope, enlightenment and spiritual peace. Do you consider yourself up to such a task, sir?'

Draper sat staring at the two patriarchs, desperately trying to take in the magnitude of their request.

'Yes ... yes, I think so.'

'You look a bit stunned,' said Millais.

'Forgive me, it is not every day that two of the greatest exponents of British art walk into your studio and request a special commission of you. I just hope I'm able to fulfil your expectations.'

'If your *Sea Maiden* is anything to go by, young man, you have nothing to worry about,' said Hunt. 'Now, I see the president is getting a little tired. Why don't we agree to meet again in a month's time. That should give you ample opportunity to develop your ideas, should it not?'

And with that, Draper thanked them both and showed them to the door.

'You came round to the idea sooner than expected,' said Millais, as he and Hunt walked back to the waiting carriages.

'There is little doubting the young man's talent,' said Hunt.

'Oh, come now, William. Surely Lord Leighton's tutelage was instrumental in bringing out more than just the man's God-given gifts.'

'If sir would let me finish. I was pondering, quite recently, whether there will ever be an artistic movement as bold and pure of heart as the Brotherhood we founded, all those years ago?'

Millais laughed. 'I very much doubt that, my old friend.'

'As did I, until a few moments ago, when I looked into the eyes of that young artist. I saw the passion and belief in him that used to form the bedrock of our, once-noble, school of thought. More understated perhaps, but it was there all the same. And do you know what else I saw?'

'What was that, brother?'

'Something of you, Johnny – something of you.'

Chapter Twenty-Four

The Randolph Hotel, Oxford

6 November 1999

Emily sat quietly finishing her toast and marmalade, and nursing the effects of a mild hangover. She'd surfaced a little later than planned and was sharing breakfast in the hotel's main dining room with, amongst others, an amorous young couple who could barely keep their hands off each other, a small group of Japanese tourists getting ready to enjoy the sights of Oxford, and an elderly American woman who looked like she'd had so many facelifts, she could barely open her mouth to eat.

Across the road, all signs of last night's drama at the Ashmolean were gone and coaches full of weekend visitors were now pulling up outside as though nothing had happened.

The break-in had occurred too late in the day to make the morning newspaper, but Emily searched for it anyway. She was just thinking whether to give Rosa a call when her mobile let out a ping on the tablecloth. It was a text from Julian Mountfield.

Can I join you for breakfast?

Oh my God, she thought, looking out of the window to see if she was being watched. She texted back. *Yes, sure.* Then took out a small mirror from her handbag to make sure she was presentable.

A few minutes later, Julian walked in through the double doors and strolled confidently over to her table.

'Good morning, Miss Bradshaw. I trust you're enjoying the Randolph's five-star hospitality.'

'Yes, I am, thank you,' she said, with as bright a smile as she could muster. 'How did you know I was here?'

'Ah well, I have the eagle-eyed DCI Cordell to thank for that,' he said, taking the chair opposite.

'Of course. I expect you've been busy, after the break-in last night.'

'I have indeed. In fact, I've got a security review meeting in an hour. So, as I was passing, I thought I'd pop in and see how you were doing.'

Emily smiled and looked at her empty plate. 'Can I order you some breakfast? The poached eggs are very good.'

Julian put up his hand. 'Thank you, but I managed to grab a bite before I left the house this morning. Ahh, what a damned mess,' he said, gazing out of the window at the museum.

'I know, it's awful. Did they take much?'

'In terms of quantity, no – a single painting. But to us, it was priceless.'

'Of course. Are you allowed to tell me which one?'

'I don't see why not. It was a beautiful Picasso called *Blue Roofs*, from his second visit to Paris. Do you know it?'

'I'm ashamed to say, I don't. Do the police have any leads?'

'Not as yet. Cordell thinks that, because they targeted the one painting, it may have been stolen to order. Personally, I have my doubts.'

'I met him last night. He came and questioned me about the robbery.'

'Really? What did he say?'

'Oh, he just asked if I'd seen anything suspicious from my bedroom window.'

'And had you?'

'No. The first I knew about it was when the emergency vehicles turned up. I thought there'd been a fire.'

'No, thank God. They dropped a smoke canister through the skylight to set off the alarms and trigger a call to the fire brigade. Obviously, it was just a cover for the break-in. Can you believe the nerve of these people?'

'Do you think there's a chance they can recover it?'

'It's a well-known work, so it's never going to appear on the open market. My guess is, it will be added to the Art Loss Register and that will be the end of it. I'd be surprised if we ever see it again.'

'Oh, don't say that. I'm sure the police inspector is hot on their trail.'

He looked down at the table. 'Maybe ...'

Emily felt like reaching over and touching his hand, but stopped herself – she barely knew the man.

Julian looked up and smiled. 'I wanted to let you know that, with all this going on, it may take me a little longer to get back to you on the sketchbook. I hope you don't mind.'

'Of course not. You've got far more important things to worry about.'

As she was biting into her last slice of cold toast, one of the hotel bellboys approached the table. 'Miss Bradshaw?'

'Yes?'

'I have a letter for you,' he said, holding out a silver tray.

'Oh, thank you.'

She took the small white envelope, addressed in printed italics to, Emily Bradshaw.

'Excuse me, when did this arrive?' she said, as the young man was walking away.

'A motorcycle courier dropped it off at reception a few minutes ago, miss.'

'Okay, thank you,' she said, staring at the envelope. 'That's bizarre.'

'How so?' said Julian.

'If someone needed to contact me, why didn't they just phone or text?'

She slit open the envelope with a clean butter knife and removed the folded sheet of paper inside.

'What the ... ?' she said, reading the typed note.

'Something wrong?' said Julian.

'Here, read it for yourself.'

He took the note and studied it carefully.

EMILY,

*YOU HAVE CLIMBED THE MOUNTAIN, NOW
FOLLOW YOUR HEART.*

*#8. The path to enlightenment guides those who seek
to banish the darkness of ignorance.*

THE SHEPHERD

'What on earth does that mean?' said Emily.

Julian scratched his chin. 'Well, if I was to hazard a guess, and I might be completely wrong here, I'd say they were referring to Draper's painting.'

'Which painting?'

'The one he was doing preparatory sketches for in your book.'

Emily scrunched up her face. 'How on earth did you get that from this?'

'I'm not sure about the number eight, but "banish the darkness", that could be talking about the light from *The Gates of Dawn*; and "the path to enlightenment", the rose-strewn path leading up to them. Or it might mean, now you've found the sketchbook, you're embarking on a journey of some kind.'

'A journey to where?'

'Emily, this is the first time I've seen it, just like you. I'm simply hypothesizing.'

'I know, I'm sorry,' she said, taking the note from Julian and studying it. 'This last bit, about "banishing the darkness of ignorance". I mean, it's not exactly making itself crystal clear, is it?'

'Mmm, ... perhaps we need to think a bit more, abstractly,' he said, pondering the rest of the message.

Emily was unsure whether to admire him, or be utterly infuriated by him. Then, just like a museum tour guide, he began to verbalise the logic behind his conclusion.

'The whole concept of *The Gates of Dawn* is the beauty and strength of the goddess Aurora – she, being the one who banished the darkness of night and brought forth the sun. Draper obviously conceived it as a symbol for the Victorians to welcome the dawning of a brave new world, banishing what some saw as the ignorance and drudgery of what had gone before, you see?'

'Yes, kind of.'

'That, and an expression of latent female sexual power, of course. But that's another story.'

Emily raised her eyebrows and was about to interject when Julian continued, 'So, if you ask me, the Shepherd, whoever that might be, is asking you to look further into the painting itself – to analyse it.'

'We don't know that for sure. I mean this Shepherd person could be any old nutter.'

'Yes, that is a possibility. Then again, he or she has managed to work out where you're staying. And you have to admit, the message is rather intriguing.'

He stood up, reached into his jacket pocket and took out his mobile phone. 'Would you excuse me – I need to make a call.' Without waiting for an answer, he wandered off in the direction of the reception desk, leaving Emily wondering what on earth was going on.

She scratched her head and tried to make sense of the bizarre train of events. She kept thinking back to the dream she'd had in the bath, last night – so vivid, so erotic. And here was a message talking about mountains and paths; it was as though someone was tapping into her brain. More importantly, just who the hell was this *Shepherd*? Was it the same person who'd left her the note in the Bristol Library? She didn't know what to think any more. She took a gulp of lukewarm coffee and put her head in her hands. It wasn't even 8.30 am and her headache was getting worse.

A few minutes later, Julian walked back in looking quite pleased with himself.

'Shouldn't you be getting back to the museum?' said Emily. 'I've taken up enough of your time.'

'Not at all. I've spent the last twelve hours thinking about nothing but that damned break-in, so talking to you is a welcome distraction, believe me.'

'Well, if you're sure.'

'Yes. Listen, I've just spoken to an old friend of mine who did some work for The Worshipful Company of Drapers in London, earlier this year.'

'Right,' said Emily, wondering where this was going.

'*The Gates of Dawn* painting hangs in the drawing room at Drapers' Hall. Apparently, it was hidden away for years under a darkened stairwell, until some discerning soul decided to resurrect it, and hang it in the large drawing room, where it still resides today.'

'That's very interesting, but I don't see what it has to do with this,' said Emily, waving the note in front of him.

'No, nor did I, until just now. The chap I've just been speaking to worked for the company who were commissioned to clean and, if required, restore the painting. He told me his colleague was working on it and came across a tiny symbol on the back of the picture frame.'

'What sort of symbol?'

'All he could tell me was that it was like a sun mark.'

'A sun mark?'

'That's what he said. His colleague didn't know what it meant, or when it was put there, but that's what he saw.'

'And you think this sun mark is what the note is referring to?'

'Well, it does kind of make sense. Perhaps that 'sun' is meant to banish the darkness of your ignorance.'

'Oh, ... thanks!' said Emily.

'No, I didn't mean it like that. Look, it's just a long shot, really.'

'I'm sorry; I was being flippant,' she said, with a smile. 'It would be kind of fun to check it out though, wouldn't it?'

'Well, I do know The Drapers' Company are extremely protective of the treasures in their collection. You can't just wander in off the street and ask to have a look round.'

Emily gave him a sideways look. 'Oh, it can't be that hard, surely.'

'Well, my friend did say that the archivist at Drapers' Hall conducts special guided tours at certain times throughout the year. I'm sure we could get you two in there, somehow.'

'Which two?'

'You and Rosa.'

Emily thought about it for a moment. To be honest, this did sound right up Rosa's street. 'Well, I guess she might be game for a bit of detective work.'

'Okay, I can make some enquiries and see if there's a tour coming up, if you like?'

Emily had to smile to herself. Julian now seemed more excited about investigating the sun mark than she was. 'Well, if it's not too much trouble?'

'No, not at all. One doesn't get to become a museum curator without being able to pull a few strings, you know.'

'No, I suppose not. But let's say Rosa and I do manage to wheedle our way into this drawing room – what are we supposed to do when we get there?'

'Well, try asking the archivist a few questions, for starters.'

'And if that doesn't work?'

'Well, I don't know, ... use your imagination.'

She stared at him, then shook her head and laughed. It would be fun to do some proper artistic research for a change.

'Leave it with me, Emily. I'll see when we can get you signed up to the next tour. Oh, it might be worth saying that you're from some fashion house, or textile association ... just to give it a bit of credence.'

'Okay, if you think it'll help. I'm sure we can come up with something.'

Julian got to his feet. 'Right, if you'd excuse me. I think I'd better get back to it. Poor old Henry will be tearing what's left of his hair out over there.'

'Oh, that reminds me,' said Emily, fishing in her handbag. 'I bumped into him over at the museum, yesterday; or should I say, he bumped into me.'

'What, our Henry?'

'Yes, the very same. He left me a rather strange message on his business card. Do you know what he's talking about?'

Julian took the card and read it. 'No ... I have absolutely no idea.'

'Me neither. I don't want to snitch on one of your colleagues, but he was the man bidding against me at the auction. He told me the whole thing was most unusual.'

'Well, he's right. But these discoveries do happen from time to time – the barn-finds of the art world, as it were.'

'Do you think you could have a chat with him? Perhaps the three of us could meet up and get this whole thing sorted out?'

'Yes, I'm sure he'd be happy to – once we've dealt with the fall-out from the robbery. I'll call you.' And with a captivating smile, he left Emily to her last mouthful of cold toast.

She sat back in her chair and tried to take it all in. Things were definitely getting weirder by the day. But foremost in her mind, and currently her biggest concern, just how the hell was she going to explain all this to Rosa?

Chapter Twenty-Five

Orchard Lane Farm, Wendover, Buckinghamshire

7 November 1999

Birch leaves and heavy rain pelted the Range Rover's windscreen as it crunched its way down the gravel track towards the converted farmhouse. Luke Waltham's three-year-old Weimaraner pricked its ears, sat up and barked a warning to its owner, who was sitting reading *The Times* at the kitchen table.

'What is it, Dorian – visitors?'

Since his divorce from Joanne, Luke had chosen a solitary life, with just a dozen chickens, some ducks and Dorian for company. Kate, now twenty-seven, was her own woman and adored her father in every respect, helping him to grow the business acquired with money from his father's estate. ArtScreen Limited were art restorers, as well as providers of specialist security staff and technology solutions to museums, galleries and wealthy private clients, worldwide; and she was their sales director.

Following the death of his father, the gap in Luke's life had been filled with two things – his daughter, and a substantial art collection secreted away in the bowels of the Berkshire farmhouse. Those who knew him well, and few did, would say he'd become a different man since George's death – darker, more introspective than his laid-back days as a college lecturer at the RCA. Perhaps the emotional rollercoaster with Joanne had hit him harder than he realised. Or was it some deep-seated affinity with his great-grandfather, James Waltham, whose attempt to steal back *The Blind Girl* had met with such spectacular failure?

Kate had been his focus, his fountain of strength in those desolate moments when he withdrew inside himself; for only she could bring him back. It never ceased to amaze him how much confidence and drive there was in one so young; a lucidity that, even as a child, had far outweighed her tender years. She'd blossomed into a beautiful young woman, whose friendship he valued more than anything in the world. Kate also shared his love of art, and Luke had taught her everything he knew – to appreciate both beauty and ugliness in all its forms, a familiarity with the creative influences and techniques he used to teach at the RCA; and finally, an in depth understanding of the history, philosophy and, most importantly, the politics of art – something which, in their business, one simply had to master to survive. Now she was the finished article; a vital component in his latest venture. He knew he could trust her, and in the dark, serpentine world in which they had become embroiled, that was a precious commodity, indeed.

As the four-by-four reached the house, Luke got up and gently put his hand under the dog's jaw.

'You're moonlight and chocolate, aren't you boy?' he said, kissing Dorian's head, and switched on the outside lights, illuminating the main courtyard.

Luke opened the kitchen door and watched as Tyburn and Danny carefully extracted a large black carrying case from the boot.

'Good evening gentlemen,' he said, ushering them both inside.

Dorian, unable to contain his excitement at having late-night visitors, jumped up at Danny.

'Get down!' said Luke, pulling the dog's chain-link collar. 'Don't worry, he'll calm down in a minute or two.'

Danny, not a fan of dogs, nervously patted Dorian on the head, while Tyburn laid the car keys and carrycase on the kitchen table. Luke unzipped the case and flipped back the cover. There in all its impressionist grandeur lay Picasso's *Blue Roofs*, a view over the Parisian rooftops from the artist's lodgings at 130 Boulevard de Clichy.

'Will you look at that; isn't it magnificent?' he said, lifting it up to gaze at it under the kitchen lights. 'I imagine you two mock those of us who pay such homage to a few daubs of old paint. But this is genius, gentlemen, pure artistic genius. It's such a shame it can't stay here with me.'

'You got a buyer?' said Tyburn.

'Yes, an American collector – he's big in pharmaceuticals and rare artworks, apparently. And, judging by his taste in Picassos, not too concerned about how he comes by them. Anyway, I spoke with his representative this morning – they should be here within the hour. I'd appreciate it if you two could stick around, just in case there's any … disagreement.'

'Huh, let 'em try,' said Danny.

Luke took a seat, barely able to keep his eyes off the painting. 'So, everything went to plan then, Marcus?'

Tyburn glanced at Danny. 'Yep, no bother.'

'Right. So not entirely, then? said Luke, sensing the tone.

'One of the security guards thought he'd be a have-a-go hero.'

'And?'

'And, nothin'. I just gave him a taste of my boot, that's all.'

'I hope you didn't go over the top, Marcus. You know I hate violence.'

'He's fine. He was lucky we were on the clock.'

'And where did you dump the Audi?' said Luke, realising that Tyburn's recent call, confirming everything had gone without a hitch, had been less than candid.

'The lake in Abingdon. Shame really, it was a nice motor. Still, that Range Rover's not a bad little run around.'

'Keep it,' said Luke, looking somewhat distracted.

'Don't mind if I do,' said Tyburn, grabbing the keys back off the kitchen table.

'Danny, would you mind taking Dorian for a walk?' said Luke. 'You'll find some boots and a torch in the utility room.'

'Err … yeah, okay.'

'Thank you. Don't go too far, I'll need you back here in fifteen minutes.'

When Danny had gone, Luke turned to Tyburn. 'You need to reign in that temper of yours. As I've told you before, this isn't just about tonight.'

'Alright, I hear ya. So, are you expectin' trouble from these yanks?'

Luke pursed his lips. 'Difficult to say. In my experience, you can never trust these corporate types. So I need you to be on your guard, just in case.'

'How much are you askin'?' said Tyburn, gesturing to the Picasso.

'It's been a while since something like this came to the market. We agreed four million over the phone. I'll put three back into ArtScreen and keep the rest aside for operating costs. Oh, that reminds me ...' said Luke, removing a brown paper package from the kitchen dresser, '... your fee, as agreed.'

Tyburn nodded, stuffing it inside his leather jacket.

Twenty minutes later, as Luke and Tyburn were discussing details of the long game, the kitchen door opened and Dorian came rushing in, followed by an out of breath Danny, panting harder than the dog.

'Looks like he's been takin' you for a walk,' smirked Tyburn.

'You're not wrong ... by Christ he can go,' said Danny, between wheezes. 'By the way, there's a car coming up the drive.'

'What sort?' said Luke.

'A dark-coloured Merc, from what I could make out.'

'That'll be the Americans. Danny, take the painting and put it on the dining-room table, just through there?'

Danny did as he was told, while Luke and Tyburn watched the shiny black Mercedes swing into the gravel courtyard and stop next to an old milk churn by the kitchen door. Tyburn stepped outside to get a look at the occupants, but could see nothing behind the blacked-out glass.

The car door swung open and out stepped a smartly dressed man in a sports jacket and roll-neck jumper, carrying an attaché case.

'Gregg, good to see you,' said Luke, extending his hand. 'Come on in out of this awful weather.'

The American returned the handshake, looking up at the rain-filled sky with contempt. Two burly men in dark suits accompanied Gregg Banks into the farmhouse, followed by a scholarly looking man with wire-framed glasses and huge bags under his eyes. Bringing up the rear was a scowling Marcus Tyburn, far from intimidated by the show of American muscle.

'Thank you for coming all this way,' said Luke.

'Hey, no problem. Normally, Mr Knox likes to do business in person, if possible. But his condition means he rarely leaves the house these days. So I'm afraid you're stuck with me.'

'Of course, of course,' nodded Luke. 'Now, gentlemen, can I get you a drink? A whisky perhaps?'

'No, I think we'll just press on, if that's okay?'

Luke showed them all into the dining room, where the Picasso was waiting for inspection on the table.

'I assume you've no objection to my colleague, here, casting his expert eye over the painting, Mr Waltham?'

'Be my guest. As you've no doubt seen from the headlines, Gregg, it was hanging in the Ashmolean, just two days ago.'

'Oh, I'm sure. But Mr Knox believes in taking every precaution, when dealing with people like you. No offence.'

Luke laughed. 'None taken.'

Watching from the doorway, Tyburn clearly had, and glared at Banks as the haggard-looking art expert walked over to the dining-room table and peered down at the painting. He removed a small silver magnifying glass from his pocket and proceeded to inspect every detail of Picasso's sweeping brush strokes – a curious blend of white-green clouds, dabs of chimneypots in brightest orange and roof tiles laid with smears of Prussian blue.

Finally, after careful analysis of the tell-tale signature and reverse side of the picture, he nodded to Banks, who'd been watching his every move.

'Okay, Mr Waltham, ...' said Banks, '... it seems we are dealing with the genuine article. Now, let's get down to business. As you know, Mr Knox is a knowledgeable collector and he has asked me to inform you that, after careful consideration, he wishes to scale down his previous offer, following what he considers to be, ... a significant slowing of the market.'

'That's fuckin' bollocks,' said Tyburn.

'Marcus, cool it!' said Luke.

But Tyburn had already drawn his gun and was pointing it straight at Banks.

The two bodyguards quickly responded, likewise, causing the art expert to dive for cover under the dining table. Not wishing to be left out, Danny drew his piece and aimed it at the smaller of the two henchmen.

'I knew you cheatin' bastards would try and screw us over,' said Tyburn.

'Gentlemen, gentlemen. Let's all just calm down, shall we?' said Luke.

Banks was about to respond, when a car pulled up outside the dining room window, followed by a roar from, what Luke recognised as a V12 e-type Jag.

'Expecting company?' said Banks.

'Yes, I am. Now can we all put the guns away, before someone gets hurt,' said Luke.

Tyburn kept his eyes on Banks, his Glock didn't move.

'Hello. Where is everyone?' called a voice from the hallway.

In walked Kate Waltham, wearing a bright red Chanel winter coat and clutching a Louis Vuitton overnight bag. She had her mother's good looks – short blonde hair in a pixie cut, high cheekbones and long dark eyelashes setting off a pair of dazzling green eyes.

'Oh dear, raised guns,' she said, walking straight past the armed men and kissing her father on the cheek. 'Have negotiations broken down already?'

'Hello, darling. Gregg was just informing us that Mr Knox has had a change of heart. Apparently, he doesn't think our wonderful Picasso is worth four million pounds.'

'Really? And why is that, Gregg?' said Kate, with a look of consternation.

'I was just telling your father, Miss Waltham – Mr Knox has had to reconsider his previous offer, due to a recent downturn in the art market, but he—'

Kate held up her hand. 'If Mr Knox is indeed the world-renowned collector we believe him to be, then he will be all too aware that the demand for Picasso's work is, in fact, stronger than ever. Can I respectfully suggest your men put down their guns, so we can continue this discussion like adults?'

Banks nodded to his two bodyguards to lower their weapons. With a gesture from Luke, Tyburn and Danny did the same.

'I think you're safe to come out now?' said Kate, peering beneath the dining-room table. The art expert lifted the tablecloth and reluctantly crawled out to join his party.

'Gregg, enlighten us? What is Mr Knox's revised offer?' said Luke.

'He is willing to pay, a more than generous, three million pounds.'

Luke shook his head. 'No, no. I'm afraid that isn't going to be enough. You see, we've gone to a great deal of trouble to obtain this painting, on the understanding that your employer and I had a gentleman's agreement. And, being an honourable businessman, I'm sure Mr Knox is not the sort to go back on his word.'

Banks shrugged. 'What can I say? Business is business, you know that.'

'Oh, absolutely. I quite understand.' Luke moved towards the door. 'Now, as we're not going to be able to conclude matters here tonight, I'm sure you won't mind if I ask you to be on your way. I need to contact the other buyer we have lined up for the *Blue Roofs*. She's waiting for my call, you see.'

Banks stared at Luke, trying to work out if he was bluffing.

Tyburn looked on, his palm resting on the butt of his Glock as he studied Banks' every movement, every expression – like a panther, ready to pounce on his quarry.

'You have another buyer? How very astute of you,' said Banks.

'Well, as we say here in England, if you want to avoid disappointment, don't put all your Picassos in one basket.'

Tyburn smirked.

Luke continued, 'Don't get me wrong, Gregg. We'd much rather do business with you. I mean, you're here, we're here – it's simple economics, really. And I can't imagine for one minute that Mr Knox would be happy for you to travel all this way, only to return empty-handed.'

Kate stepped forward and pulled a buff-coloured envelope from her handbag, handing it to her father.

'Oh, thank you darling, I almost forgot. Now, just in case your boss needs a little reminder of how I like to do business, he might be interested in this.' Luke removed the document inside, studied it for a moment, then handed it to Banks. 'My daughter and I are well-respected in the art world. We know a lot of people, who in turn, know things about a lot of people.'

As the American looked at the document, his face and neck became flushed; his expression growing more incensed by the second.

'It's a list of the paintings Mr Knox has managed to acquire for his very private collection – a number of which are, in fact, listed on Scotland Yard's index of stolen art treasures. We also have it on good authority that he stores these paintings in a secure underground vault in his private mansion in Lake Tahoe. Now, I don't want to pressure you, Gregg, but if we were able to successfully conclude our business here tonight, you have my personal guarantee that none of this information will find its way into the hands of the California State Police, or the FBI.'

Banks handed the list to the art expert, who carefully scanned it and nodded that it was accurate.

'If you'll excuse me, I need to make a call,' said Banks, marching out towards the empty kitchen.

As everyone waited, the atmosphere round the usually cordial dining-room table was electric. Tyburn grinned at the larger of the two American thugs, then turned his attention to Kate – watching intently as she removed her coat, placed it over the back of one of the dining chairs and sat down, crossing her legs as she waited for play to resume.

A few minutes later, Banks returned looking less than happy.

'If Mr Knox agrees to the asking price of four million pounds, he wants your absolute assurance that you will not release this information.'

'As one of my most valued clients, he has my personal guarantee to that effect. After all, we may want to do business again, someday; right Kate?'

'Oh, absolutely,' she said, with a conciliatory smile.

Banks reached for his attaché case. 'Alright Mr Waltham, we have a deal. You have an internet connection here, I assume?'

'Yes, my office is through here.'

Luke led the way across the hall to his study. Banks placed his attaché case on the desk and opened it, revealing a small metallic laptop computer. After obtaining a secure connection to Knox's bank in Switzerland, he prepared the real-time payment instruction for the agreed sum to another Swiss bank account number, supplied by Luke.

'Okay, four million pounds sterling.' Banks pressed the *Enter* key and waited a few seconds for the transaction to complete. He turned the display round so Luke could see the confirmatory message.

'I'm sure you won't mind if I check with my bank to ensure the money's gone over?' said Luke.

'Naturally,' nodded Banks.

After logging on to his own laptop and accessing his private bank account, Luke saw the balance had duly swollen by four million pounds. He logged off and with a business-like smile, got up from his desk and extended his hand to Gregg. 'How about a drink to celebrate?'

'Unfortunately, we have a flight to catch,' said Banks, walking straight past to collect the Picasso from the dining room.

The rain storm had moved on, leaving a starry sky and a distinct chill in the air as Luke, Kate, Tyburn and Danny watched the four men get into the Mercedes. Before it pulled away, the blacked-out window slid down, revealing Banks' sullen face.

'I'm sure I don't need to tell you what will happen to you and your lovely daughter, should that information fall into the wrong hands,' he said.

Tyburn lurched towards the car, but Luke held him back. 'As I said before, Gregg, you have my word.'

The American gave him one final glare, then disappeared behind the bulletproof glass as the car sped out of the courtyard and down the gravel track.

Kate turned to her father. 'Not a bad day's work. Four million pounds and a get-out-of-jail-free card from Mr Knox.'

'Which I'll be sure to cash in, at some point,' said Luke, putting his arm round her as they returned to the warmth of the farmhouse kitchen.

As Tyburn and Danny crowed about their faceoff with the Americans, and Kate poured everyone a glass of champagne, Luke couldn't help but think to himself – this wouldn't be the last time he'd cross paths with Willard Knox.

Chapter Twenty-Six

'We're members of the what, now?' said Rosa, staring at Emily as they strolled along Throgmorton Street toward Drapers' Hall.

Emily tried not to laugh. 'The West of England Wool Traders Association. If anyone asks, think sheep.'

'SHEEP! You have got to be kidding me,' said Rosa, shaking her head. 'And you're confident this is going to work, are you?'

'Yes, yes. I've talked it through with Julian and he thinks it'll be fine.'

'Oh well, that's easy for him to say. And, don't tell me – that's why you're wearing that ridiculous lamb's wool jumper, isn't it?'

'Come on, we don't want to be late,' said Emily, with a wry smile and carried on walking.

Arriving at a set of iron gates, topped with the Worshipful Company of Drapers' coat of arms and bearing the motto, UNTO GOD ONLY BE HONOUR AND GLORY, they headed along the private lane to the clerk's office, where a number of people were waiting outside. Moments later, there was a loud buzz, then a click as the grilled wooden door opened and a formal-looking doorman gestured everyone inside.

Emily and Rosa followed the others along a short corridor and into the small reception area, flanked by three marble arches on either side. A party of seven had already registered and were waiting patiently for the tour to start.

Having disposed of their coats and obtained a ticket from the cloakroom attendant, the two girls donned their best fake smiles and made small talk with others in the tour group, trying not to look like fraudulent interlopers.

It wasn't long before Emily got bored of the inane chat and began flicking through an information leaflet from the reception desk.

'Grand and yet classically understated, don't you think?' said Rosa, gazing round at the decor as she wandered over to join her.

'Looking at this, I don't think we've seen anything yet,' said Emily, showing her the leaflet.

At 11 am on the dot, a smartly dressed man entered and went over to talk to the receptionist. Satisfied that everyone had registered correctly, he walked into the centre of the room and introduced himself.

'Good morning, everybody and welcome to Drapers' Hall. My name is David Godstone, the company's archivist, and I will be taking you round the hall, today. Now, just so you know, the tour will take about an hour.'

There was a gentle murmur from the group of patrons.

'Don't worry, I won't bore you to death by talking the whole time. There will be ample opportunity to walk around and admire the magnificent courtrooms on the first floor, each of which contain their own unique blend of architecture, artworks and historical points of interest.'

Emily gave Rosa a look – one particular artwork was going to be attracting a great deal of interest, very shortly.

The archivist continued, 'This will be an informal tour, so please feel free to ask questions as we go. Oh, and there will be time for a quick comfort break. Now, if you'd care to follow me up the stairs to your right, we'll make a start.'

The group made their way up the oak-panelled staircase to a first-floor landing bathed in light from a large armorial stained glass window. With everyone gathered around and listening intently, the archivist began his spiel.

'As some of you may know, we are most commonly known as The Worshipful Company of Drapers of the City of London. What you probably didn't know is that our full title is – The Master and Wardens and Brethren and Sisters of the Guild or Fraternity of the Blessed Mary the Virgin of the Mystery of Drapers of the City of London.'

Standing beneath a dazzling 5,000-piece chandelier, Rosa leaned across to Emily and whispered, 'Bet that doesn't leave a lot of room on their business card.'

Emily chuckled quietly, but all she could think about was, when she was going to get a look at *The Gates of Dawn.*

'The word "mystery" makes us sound rather clandestine, but in fact it comes from the old Latin word *misterium*, meaning trade or skill. Founded over six hundred years ago, The Drapers' Company has always been a benevolent institution, helping any of its members who may have fallen into distress. Although its earlier involvement in the woollen cloth trade has ceased, the company continues to preserve its heritage, and maintain the traditions of friendship and hospitality.'

'Notice the carpet?' said Rosa.

Emily looked down at the huge expanse of red, white and blue weave covering the stairs and landing. 'I think it's by William Morris.'

Rosa nodded. 'You're right, it's got his trademark design style.'

'Now, if you'd all like to turn to your left, we'll make our way into the court dining room,' said the archivist.

The group moved into what was probably the most colourful room in the entire building. Dominated by a painted ceiling mural of Jason and the Golden Fleece, it boasted two giant silk tapestries depicting further scenes from Jason's quest. Everyone began to spread out across the room as the archivist continued to explain the history of what was originally called the Ladies' Chamber.

Emily grabbed Rosa's hand and led her over to one of the balcony windows overlooking the upper garden. 'Did you see it?'

'Did I see what?' said Rosa, checking her mobile signal.

'The painting.'

'No, where was it?'

'On the landing, there was a room to our right. When you looked through the double doors, you could see it, right there on the far wall.'

'Well, judging by the snail's pace this guy's going at, it'll be a while before we make it in there.'

'Or ...' said Emily, checking the room, '... I could nip out now and have a quick look.'

'Don't be ridiculous, someone will see you.'

'There's no one in there, it's the perfect time. You stay here with this lot and I'll catch up with you later.'

'Emily, ... Emily.'

But she was already making her way out onto the landing.

'Stick to the plan, Rosa. It'll be fine, Rosa,' she muttered, and walked over to join some of the party who were looking at a full-length portrait of the queen, hanging above the fireplace.

*

Grateful for the William Morris carpet masking her footsteps, Emily crossed the landing and entered the court drawing room. It was a stunning space with ornamental plaster, eight gilded wall mirrors and a coffered ceiling supporting a pair of enormous Victorian crystal chandeliers. But she only had eyes for one thing. At the far end, set against a red silk panel, was Draper's masterpiece – *The Gates of Dawn*, depicting Aurora gazing out across the room with imperious majesty.

'Oh shit,' said Emily, hearing the archivist's voice as the group filed across the landing, behind her. With nowhere to go, she crouched behind a cluster of aquamarine conversation sofas, ready to casually re-join them as they entered the room. But the archivist's voice gradually tailed off as the party moved into the court room on the other side of the landing.

Realising her reprieve was only temporary, she ran over to the back wall and looked up into Aurora's eyes. The goddess seemed so lifelike, as if she could step down from the canvas at any moment and seduce her with her omnipotent gaze.

Emily grabbed the corner of the picture frame and slowly eased it away from the wall. With just enough of a gap to squeeze her head behind, she looked up and down the back of the frame, searching for anything that might be described as a sun mark. Apart from a few scratches and a lot of dust and dirt, there was no sign of it. She tried looking higher up, but the top of the picture stretched way above her eyeline. With her arms and fingers beginning to ache, she gently eased the painting back against the wall.

This is hopeless, she thought, sitting on a nearby chair to consider her options. Drastic as it might seem, there was only one way she was going to get a good look at the back of that painting.

Stretching her neck and shoulders back and forth, as though readying herself for a session of free-weights at the gym, she sprang to her feet and approached the foot of the painting, with both arms outstretched.

154

Trying not to look as though she was engaged in some kind of subterfuge, Rosa lingered at the back of the tour group as they left the court room. She desperately wanted to see what Emily was up to, and briefly thought about sneaking off to join her; but the archivist would surely get suspicious if two of them suddenly went walkabout.

As they entered the livery hall, everyone, including Rosa, gazed in awe at the magnificent surroundings. Every single capital, balustrade, cornice and picture frame was dripping in gold leaf, to the extent that, a number of the party were wandering around with their mouths open.

'Yes, we get that reaction a lot,' said the archivist, hearing a few 'wows' at the sheer opulence of it all.

The enormous two-storey room boasted a total of twenty-eight green-and-red marble columns, all supporting a balcony that looked like it was made of solid gold. Set into the walls above were a series of arched mirrors, perfectly positioned to reflect the splendour of a painted ceiling that made all who saw it for the first time, stop and stare in wonder.

'If you look up, you'll find scenes from two of Shakespeare's masterpieces being played out above your heads. *The Tempest* in the centre oval, depicting Prospero calling to the deities and spirits of the elements. And to the north and south, two rectangular panels from *A Midsummer Night's Dream*, with Oberon, the king of the fairies riding his golden chariot of the dawn, and Titania, the fairy queen, sleeping while Puck flies overhead. It took the artist, Herbert James Draper, five years to complete all thirteen glorious panels, which he eventually did in nineteen o-eight. Now, if, like me, you're a fan of Draper, you'll be glad to know that we'll be seeing another of his great works, later.'

'Is this your first time?' whispered a voice next to Rosa.

She turned round to see a rather stocky man with short grey hair, peering over her shoulder.

'Err, ... yes, it is.'

'It's my third. I suppose you could say I'm a bit obsessed by this place.'

'I suppose you could.'

'You have to admire a man who can paint a ceiling like that, don't you? What I really came to see, though, is his magnum opus. Are you familiar with it?'

'No, I don't think I am,' said Rosa, suspecting what was coming.

'It's a painting called *The Gates of Dawn*. Shall we go and have a quick look, together? I know the way from here.'

'Oh no, we don't want to get in trouble, do we?' she said, looking round for something to distract him. 'Tell me more about this wonderful ceiling. Did he start in the middle and work outwards?'

As the man launched into his fact-filled monologue, Rosa discreetly checked her watch. Emily had been gone for twenty minutes. Surely she must have found what she was looking for by now?

*

No doubt, Herbert Draper would have turned in his grave, had he witnessed his beloved goddess, Aurora, lying face down on the drawing-room carpet. It had been a struggle, but with the aid of a nearby table and no small amount of cussing, Emily had eventually managed to lift the painting from its mount and was currently crouched on her knees, scanning every inch of the stretcher and frame for signs of a sun mark. She had no idea how big it was or even what it looked like, but one thing was becoming quite apparent – it's complete and utter absence from the back of the picture frame.

Having checked every scratch, knot and indentation she could find, she sat up and stretched her back. Julian's friend must have been mistaken. It simply wasn't there.

She was about to begin one final sweep when she heard voices, nearby. She checked her watch.

'Oh Jesus,' she said, realising she'd been looking for nearly half an hour, and the tour group, having nearly completed their circuit of the first floor, were headed straight for her.

She grabbed the painting and, using one of the padded chairs nearby, stepped up on to the side table below the red silk panel. With her arms straining, she lifted up the frame, trying desperately to loop the wire back onto the hook on the wall. Just as she thought she'd managed to catch it, she heard the sound of footsteps outside the door to her left. She froze and watched as it slowly swung open.

'What the hell are you doing?' said Rosa, poking her head round the door.

'Oh, thank God it's you,' said Emily. 'Now, give me a hand with this, will you; before I drop it.'

'Are you raving mad? They'll be here in a minute.'

'Well, the sooner you help me, the sooner we'll be out of here, won't we?'

Rosa closed the door and grabbed the bottom of the frame as Emily continued to try and hook the wire.

'Come on, hurry up,' said Rosa, looking over her shoulder.

'Yes, yes, don't rush me. It's nearly there. If I could just—'

Suddenly, the door handle turned and in walked the archivist, followed by the remaining members of the tour group.

'This room was designed and decorated by Herbert Williams and John G. Crace—' Then came a deafening silence. 'What the hell do you think you're doing?' said the archivist.

In the blink of an eye, Emily had become a bad person, the huge looking-glass mirrors encircling the room reflecting her shame as she searched for a plausible explanation. There was none.

'I, I was trying to—' She glared at Rosa in desperation, but Rosa just shrugged her shoulders, as if to say, *don't bother, mate – we're busted.*

'Would you both step away from the painting?' said the archivist.

Resting it carefully against the wall, they did as they were asked and, rather sheepishly, went and stood in the centre of the room.

'Your names?'

They looked at each other, then back to the archivist.

'I can get them from the register.'

'I'm Emily Bradshaw and this is Rosa Martell.'

Emily scanned the sullen faces of the tour group – their looks, rightly, judgemental. Now the defendants had a name. But there was no need for the jury to retire to consider this verdict – it was plain for all to see.

The stocky greyed-haired man walked over to Rosa. 'My obsession with Draper is nothing compared to yours,' he said sternly, and went and stood by the upturned painting.

'No, luckily for you,' Rosa replied, glaring at Emily.

The archivist pulled out a walkie-talkie from his jacket pocket and pressed the push-to-talk button. 'Hello, Steve, … David here. I'm in the drawing room. Could you get up here as soon as you can, please – we have a security breach.'

'I wasn't trying to steal it,' said Emily, a quiver of desperation in her voice. 'I just wanted to inspect the back of the frame, that's all,'

'It's true,' said Rosa. 'I mean, look at her, she's never stolen anything in her life.'

The archivist shook his head. 'Please, spare me the excuses. From what I can see, you've come in here to take the painting, or worse, to damage it for some God-forsaken reason.'

Emily threw her hands up in the air. 'We would never do that. We're both art lovers, for goodness sake.'

She opened her shoulder bag and pulled out the Draper sketchbook.

'My God, don't you go anywhere without that thing?' said Rosa.

Turning to the Aurora drawings, Emily walked up to the archivist and thrust the book into his hand.

'There, you see. They're Draper's own sketches for *The Gates of Dawn*. All I was doing was looking for some kind of sun mark he's supposed to have put on the back.'

The archivist stared at the drawings, then took Emily by the arm and ushered her to one side. 'This is an extremely valuable artwork that you've been … mishandling. You should have approached me through the proper channels.'

'I appreciate that, but aren't you even a little bit curious about all this?'

Just when she thought she saw a flicker of emotion in his eyes, two stern-looking security guards came marching into the drawing room.

'What's the problem, David?' said the elder of the two.

'Would you take these two young ladies down to my office. And make sure they stay there.'

'Shall we call the police?'

'No, no, leave that to me. I'll deal with it.'

Looking quite uncompromising, the two men escorted Emily and Rosa downstairs and into an oak-panelled office next to the reception desk. Having been told in no uncertain terms to stay put, the door was closed while the younger security guard stood watch outside.

'So, you didn't fancy just asking someone about this bloody sun mark, then?' said Rosa.

Emily paced up and down, nervously.

'I'll take that as a no, then, shall I?'

'Do you think he's going to let us go?' said Emily.

'How the hell should I know? What took you so long, anyway? Weren't you keeping an eye on the time?'

'I was, but I got so wrapped-up in looking for that damn thing, I forgot where I was.'

'If it's any consolation, you did the right thing showing him the sketchbook.'

'You think so?'

'No! Of course not. He probably thinks you were trying to bribe him, or something. I should never have let you talk me into this.'

Emily went and sat down behind a large mahogany desk that dominated the room. 'I definitely saw a glint in his eye when I showed him those drawings – he is a man of history, after all.'

'A man of history? For Christ's sake, Emily, he's probably reporting us to the police, right this minute,' said Rosa, and flumped down in a chair by the door, her arms folded across her chest.

After what seemed like an eternity, and a long, awkward silence, the door opened and in walked the archivist.

Emily stood up. 'We really are, very sorry—'

He raised his hand, dismissively. 'This way, please,' he said, and ushered them back into the reception area where two different men, dressed in plain clothes, were waiting for them. Without saying a word, the archivist led the small group back up the main staircase.

Rosa looked over and frowned at Emily. 'Where are we going?' she mouthed.

Emily shrugged.

At the top of the stairs, they turned right and entered the court drawing room, the scene of the crime, but with one slight difference – a large white dustsheet had been spread out on the carpet, directly beneath where *The Gates of Dawn* had been hanging.

'Gentlemen, if you please?' said the archivist.

The two plain-clothed men each reached into their jacket pockets, put on a pair of white cotton gloves and, after taking up a position on either side of the painting, carefully flipped it over onto its front and placed it face down on the dustsheet. Emily and Rosa stood there, trying to figure out what was going on.

'Thank you, gentlemen, I'll take it from here.'

The archivist took off his jacket, folded it in two and placed it on the side table Emily had been standing on, earlier.

'Miss Bradshaw. You said you were looking for a sun mark.'

'Err, yes. I couldn't find it anywhere.'

'Whoever told you it was here, was in fact, rather well informed,' he said, getting down on his knees to peer at the back of the dusty picture frame. Reaching into his pocket, he took out a penknife and teased out one of the stainless-steel blades, roughly two inches long. 'Although, ... I wouldn't have expected you to find it without knowing where to look.'

Emily watched as he slid the blade beneath a crusty old, brown paper label marked *W.A. Smith – Carver and Gilder*, at the top of the frame. With some gentle upward pressure and careful manoeuvring, he managed to loosen the backing to reveal a patch of light-coloured wood, beneath.

Emily looked on in amazement. It had never even occurred to her to look there, let alone attempt to prise off the label.

'There,' he said proudly. 'One sun mark.'

Emily got down on her knees and peered closely at the tiny symbol stamped into the wood.

8

'Oh my God, there it is.'

'Let me see,' said Rosa, kneeling beside her.

'So, when did you discover it?' said Emily.

'About a year ago, we had a visit from an art historian doing some research on Draper. Initially, he only seemed to be interested in the murals in the livery hall. Then, he asked if he could undertake a detailed inspection of *The Gates of Dawn*. So, having obtained permission from the master and wardens – on the strict understanding that I would oversee his work in the hall at all times – that's when we uncovered the sun mark.'

'Can you remember his name?' said Rosa.

'I have all the details in my office, downstairs.'

'I'm guessing he probably came here knowing what he was looking for?' said Emily.

'As a matter of fact, he did. He was working on a theory that *The Gates of Dawn* was the last in a series of eight paintings – which would perhaps explain the figure eight you can see here.'

'And all the paintings were done by Draper?'

'Well, here's the interesting thing. He thought the other seven were done by the three founding members of the Pre-Raphaelite Brotherhood.'

Emily frowned. 'Hunt, Millais and Rossetti – you're kidding?'

'Not at all.'

'But Draper wasn't part of the Brotherhood,' she said, recalling her research from the Bristol library.

'No, but he was thought to have been heavily influenced by them.'

Emily scratched her head. 'I still don't get it. Draper painted this in nineteen hundred. The Pre-Raphaelites were at their most prolific in the eighteen fifties and sixties. Why rope in another artist, after all that time?'

'An interesting question, ...' said the archivist. '... unfortunately, one to which I don't have an answer. Millais was elected President of the Royal Academy in eighteen ninety-six, after the death of Lord Leighton, and Draper attended the Upper Life School there, from eighteen eighty-five. So, perhaps the two met when Millais was giving some of his lectures.'

Emily gazed at the tiny stamp in the wood, trying desperately not to reach out and touch it. 'Look, I know it's a bit of a cheek, but would you mind if I made a drawing of the sun mark to take back with me?'

Rosa gave her a glare, as if to say, *For God's sake woman, let's just get out of here.*

'No need, Miss Bradshaw. We had some photographs taken when we first uncovered it. I can make you some copies, if you'd like.'

'Yes, that would be wonderful, thank you.' She smiled, hoping that his desire to share knowledge would also extend to forgoing pressing charges for theft, vandalism, and causing wilful damage to a valuable artwork.

'There is one thing I would like in return,' said the archivist, getting to his feet. 'I'd very much like to take some photos of the drawings in your sketchbook.'

'Yes, of course,' Rosa blurted out. 'That's alright, isn't it, Emily?'

She nodded. 'It's the least we can do, after all the trouble we've caused.'

With the impromptu inspection over, the archivist got back on his walkie-talkie and, within minutes, the men in white gloves were carefully re-elevating Aurora to once more gaze out across her earthly domain of sofas, chandeliers and mirrors, while Emily and Rosa accompanied the archivist back to his office.

'Thank you for being so understanding about all this,' said Emily. 'Could I ask, what made you change your mind ... about reporting us to the police?'

Rosa turned and glared at her.

'Miss Bradshaw, I've been a fan of Draper's work for many years. And, I have to admit, if it hadn't been for that sketchbook, you two would be explaining yourselves to the police, right now. But when you said you were trying to find the sun mark, I suppose you sparked my curiosity.'

'Well, I'm very glad that it did,' said Emily.

'Glad enough to make a small donation to the company's charitable works?' said the archivist, with an expectant look.

'Yes, we'd love to, wouldn't we, Rosa?'

Rosa looked at the archivist and smiled, with a hint of feigned enthusiasm.

'Oh, one more thing,' said Emily. 'That historian who came to see you last year – we'd very much like to speak to him, if we could.'

'Right, I'm sure I've got his name and contact details here, somewhere,' he said, rummaging in his desk drawer. 'Yes, ... here we are. It was actually January of this year that he came to see us. A charming old fellow, as I recall, and quite an expert on the Pre-Raphaelites. I'm no fool, but he did seem to talk in riddles, half the time and—'

'His name?' said Rosa, impatiently.

'Err, yes, of course ... it was Henry Faber.'

Chapter Twenty-Seven

Wickwar, near Bristol

8 November 1999

After a nearly three-hour journey back from central London, Emily opened the front door and was immediately confronted by the welcoming aroma of spaghetti bolognaise, with a touch of oregano and basil. She kicked off her shoes and flopped back onto the large red settee, exhausted.

'How did it go?' said Tom, walking in from the kitchen and handing her a large glass of Malbec.

'Drapers' Hall is pretty spectacular. Talk about opulent.'

'Those places often are. Did you find this thing you were after?'

'Yes, ... in a roundabout way.'

Tom looked at her, quizzically.

'Well, it didn't go quite as we'd planned,' she said, squirming in her seat.

'Oh Christ, you didn't break something?'

'No, no. We kind of ... got caught in the act.'

Tom's quizzical look turned to one of concern. 'Doing what, exactly?'

'Inspecting the painting.'

'What? Please tell me you got their permission.'

'Err ... no, not exactly.'

'Oh, for fuck's sake, Emily,' he said, looking up at the ceiling in disgust. 'How bloody stupid can you get?'

'Yes, I see that now.'

'So, what happened?'

'How can I put this, ... Rosa and I nearly got arrested for vandalising a valuable artwork.'

Tom put his face in his hands. 'I don't believe this.'

'Fortunately, the archivist is a big fan of Draper and I managed to win him over by showing him the sketchbook.'

Emily knew Tom adored her, despite her propensity for making life difficult for herself, at times. And yes, if there was a choice between straightforward and boring, and doing things the hard way, she would, on occasion, take the path less travelled. She'd always been that way, ever since she was a little girl. And, in his own strange way, he loved her for it, or so she hoped.

'Anyway, he ended up showing Rosa and I the sun mark – he knew all about it. And do you know the most curious thing?'

Tom could only shake his head.

'Henry Faber also visited Drapers' Hall, earlier this year.'

'Who?'

'The old guy – from the Ashmolean. The one who bid against me at the auction.'

'Right, okay.'

'Apparently he was looking for the sun mark, too. Don't you think that's strange?'

'Well, he does work for a museum. And correct me if I'm wrong, but he did actually ask for permission before he began rifling through their precious artefacts. So, actually, no, I don't think it's strange at all,' he said, and went back to his cooking duties in the kitchen.

Emily wanted to shout her objections, but found herself agreeing with him. 'Feed Bill, will you?' was all she could muster and took another mouthful of Malbec.

Hoping for a more empathetic response, she grabbed her mobile phone and clicked on Julian's number, expecting it to go to answerphone at this time of the evening.

'Hello, Emily,' came the response, after only two rings, 'How did it go at Drapers' Hall?'

'Pretty good, actually. We managed to find the sun mark, eventually.'

'Oh, that's great. Was it on the back of the frame, like the restorer chap said?'

This was more the reaction she was hoping for, and she curled her legs up on the settee.

'Kind of. We did have a bit of trouble locating it, though,' she said, crossing her fingers. 'The damned thing was hidden underneath an old label. But we got there in the end.'

'So, what did it look like?' said Julian, sounding genuinely excited.

'Like a little sun with the letter L in the centre, and the number eight underneath.'

'That is interesting.' There was a pause, as though he was mulling something over. 'Wasn't that cryptic message you received at the Randolph Hotel marked with the number eight?'

'Yes. And ... you're not going to believe this.'

'Go on.'

'Henry Faber was at Drapers' Hall, back in January; looking for the very same thing. Apparently, he thinks *The Gates of Dawn* was linked to seven other Pre-Raphaelite paintings, all of which had a sun mark on the back.'

'The archivist told you that?'

'Yes,' said Emily, hoping for a bit more surprise than that.

'Mmm, so how did the archivist know you were looking for it?'

'Err, well ...' This was probably the moment to come clean about the whole drawing room incident. 'Look, it's a bit of a long story. Why don't I tell you about it over lunch, tomorrow. My treat.'

'I am a little busy tomorrow. But hey, how could I refuse such a tempting offer. There's a wonderful French bistro round the corner from the museum. You can tell me everything over a bottle of Saint-Emilion.'

'Great, I'll meet you in the museum reception, say one o'clock?'

'Perfect,' he said.

'Oh, before you go,' said Emily, getting up off the settee. 'Would you ask Henry if he'd like to join us? I'd love to find out what he knows about all this.'

There was a brief silence on the end of the phone. 'I'm afraid Henry didn't show up for work today.'

'Oh. Is he okay?'

'Err, yes. He just seems to have taken the loss of the Picasso quite badly.'

'Right. I suppose I'd feel the same if someone had broken into our gallery. Look, not to worry; I'll see you tomorrow.'

She ended the call, picked up her wine glass and went to join Tom in the kitchen.

'Did I hear you say you're off to Oxford again, tomorrow?' he enquired.

'Yes, is that a problem?'

'No,' he said, shaking his head. 'By the way, there's a letter for you on the side.'

Emily tutted. 'More junk mail, I expect.'

'I don't think so – it's marked private and confidential.'

Emily stared at the envelope. There, in the same italic type as the previous note, was her name and address, this time beneath an Oxford postmark. She ripped it open and removed the small white sheet of paper.

EMILY,

YOUR JOURNEY HAS ONLY JUST BEGUN – USE THE ONE TRUE LIGHT TO FIND YOUR WAY.

#7. Wrath – eternal peace awaits those that cast off the bonds of oblivion, to follow the everlasting light.

THE SHEPHERD

'What is it?' said Tom.

'I'm not sure you'd believe me if I told you.'

'Please tell me it's not a court summons.'

'No, nothing like that. I received an anonymous note when I was staying at the Randolph the other day, telling me ... actually, I'm not sure what it was telling me. And this looks like another one.'

Tom held out his hand. 'Let me see.'

Emily handed it to him. He quickly read it and handed it back.

'Someone's having a laugh.'

'You think so?' Emily studied it again. 'When I showed the first one to Julian, he managed to work out what it meant.'

'Oh well, if Julian says it's real, then it must be.'

Emily looked down her nose at him.

'Perhaps you two could talk about it over lunch, tomorrow,' he said, stirring the Bolognese sauce with even more gusto.

'And what's that supposed to mean?'

Tom didn't respond.

Emily shook her head and stormed back into the lounge to look for Bill.

After a somewhat frosty dinner, without a single word passing between them, Emily made her excuses and went to bed; leaving Tom to read some papers he'd brought home from work.

Never go to sleep on an argument, Emily thought, as she lay in bed, staring at the ceiling. Those were her grandmother's words to her when she was an obstinate teenager; and sage words they were, too. Unfortunately, neither she nor Tom had heeded that particular advice on this occasion.

He really is a fucking idiot, sometimes; disliking someone he doesn't even know. He even thinks Julian's name is annoying, for Christ's sake! Well, if he cared for me at all, he'd realise, Julian is just trying to help me make sense of all this madness that's going on at the moment. There's nothing more to it than that. Not as far as I'm concerned, anyway. And if he doesn't fucking like it, then, well, ... perhaps he doesn't know me at all.

She tossed and turned for, she didn't know how long – growing more and more irritated – until, eventually, she closed her eyes and lost herself in a deep, dreamless sleep.

Chapter Twenty-Eight

Epsom Police House, Surrey

19 October 1851

'You're not going to believe this, sir.'

'Why don't you let me be the judge of that, constable?' said Sergeant Banwell, enjoying a slice of his wife's meat pie, washed down with a mug of hot tea.

'We've had a report come in from a mill worker over at Ewell Court. Reckons he's seen some kind of apparition down by the Hogsmill River.'

'Are you pulling my leg, Archer, because it's been a long day.'

'No, sir. God's honest truth. He was pretty shaken up by it, apparently.'

'And who reported this phantom, exactly?'

'Dunno their name, sir. It was one of Sir Henry Bridges' men – might be worth a look.'

'Yes, it might be.'

'Let me go, sir, and you can finish your tea,' said Archer, who had a passion for horses and liked nothing more than to take the station mare out for a gallop, when he got the chance.

Sergeant Banwell pondered for a moment. Ordinarily, he wouldn't think twice about sending one of his constables out on such a cold night; but the unusual nature of the incident, and its proximity to the gunpowder mill, troubled him.

'No, it's alright, Archer, I'll attend to it. Ready my horse, would you?' he said, and picked up his top hat and gloves.

'You'll be wanting these, sir,' said Archer, handing him his cutlass and pistol.

'Mmm, let's hope not, eh?'

But the constable was right to be cautious. Only last week, the London-to-Brighton stagecoach had been held up on the Epsom Road; and Lord knows what he was about to encounter down by the river.

Most knew the station sergeant to be a level-headed man, but as he mounted his chestnut mare and rode out of the side entrance to the small police house, he couldn't help thinking back to that harrowing summer, six years ago, when a spate of calamitous explosions rocked the nearby village.

Hopefully the apparition had been nothing more than a trick of the moonlight, or a drunken hallucination; but he had to be sure, and quick about it – it was a good ten-minute ride to Bourne Hall Lake, source of the Hogsmill. He gave the horse a swift kick and took off at a gallop towards Ewell.

With temperatures plummeting beneath the clear October sky, and patches of mist creeping along the riverbanks, the sergeant and his mare finally reached the turning off the Kingston Road. He pulled on the reins, steering the horse onto the well-trodden path that led through the narrow flood plain, or "wilderness" as the locals called it. They'd gone less than half a mile when they came to a small workers' hut with a tatty wooden sign nailed to the door: DANGER! KEEP OUT!

Banwell drew back the reins and stopped, looking left and right through the murk, but the only signs of life were the plumes of breath from himself and the mare, melting into the blanket of fog. With a click of his tongue, they continued along the leafy trail, past thickets of seasoned hawthorn and willow, bramble and thistle. A gentle breeze got up, rattling the dry autumn leaves and carrying with it the haunting call of a tawny owl from deep inside the wood.

As the soulless clank of hydraulic presses grew ever louder, Banwell tried to clear his mind of disasters past, and the fiery fingers of hell that ravaged the powder mill and its workers.

Then, something caught his eye. He tugged on the reins, causing the mare to stop and snort a great cloud of ghostly vapour as it looked round at its rider. He gave her a comforting pat on the neck and leaned forward to get a better view. There in the distance was a soft milky glow, radiating through the trees. He tried to focus, but it remained opaque and shapeless, its source growing brighter, then dimming as it merged into the gloom.

'Walk on,' he said, feeling for the butt of his pistol, preparing himself for whomever, or whatever, they were about to encounter. The path gradually opened into a clearing. They were close now. Banwell could see the light was coming from an old hut, down by the water's edge. He was about to dismount when the door began to open with a long, rusty creek.

'Show yourself. This is the police!' he shouted, drawing his pistol.

The tall silhouette of a man appeared out of the gloom and stopped a few yards in front of him, slowly raising his lantern to illuminate horse and rider. 'Is there a problem, sergeant?' he said.

'You don't look like a mill worker?' Banwell replied.

'No, far from it.'

'Then what the hell are you doing here?'

'Merely making some sketches of this old door. The wood is rotten, you see and—'

'You do know this is a gunpowder mill?' said Banwell, pointing to the distant buildings.

'Yes, of course.'

'Then put that bloody light out man, before you blow us all to kingdom come.'

The man opened the lantern door and gave a sharp blow, pitching them into a cold, swirling darkness.

'Who the hell are you?' said Banwell, rapidly losing patience.

'My name is William Holman Hunt – I am an artist.'

'Mr Hunt, this is private property. Do you have permission to be here?'

'Not what you might call permission, exactly. But rest assured, sergeant, I am not engaged in anything clandestine.'

'You sound more like a city gent, to me.'

'Hardly that, sir. I'm staying at Worcester Park Farm, up the hill, there. My friend and I came down from London a few weeks ago to study the landscape, as you can see.'

'If you're an artist, then show me your work.'

Hunt held up his sketchpad.

'Bring it closer man, do you expect me to see it from there?'

Hunt walked over and handed it to the sergeant. Barely visible on the thick white paper was a beautiful drawing of the old hut door, with its rusty hinges and tendrils of trailing ivy, but strangely, lacking its handle.

'Very well, Mr Hunt, I will let you off with a caution. But I must insist you accompany me back to the main road, immediately. This is no place to be wandering around with that,' he said, pointing to the lantern.

Hunt walked with Sergeant Banwell and his horse back along the riverbank and through the adjoining fields, until they reached the main road. After making him promise not to return to the mill or its grounds, the sergeant bid the artist goodnight and the two men went their separate ways.

*

Having arrived back at the Worcester Park farmhouse, Hunt placed the lantern on the hall table, hung up his coat and mopped his brow with his handkerchief, realising just how close he'd come to spending a night in gaol. He opened the door to the living room to see his friend, John Millais, sitting by the fire, writing up the day's events in his diary.

'You're back early,' said Millais.

'If you must know, I ran into a spot of bother with the local constabulary. Apparently, the mill is off-limits to local artisans.'

Millais laughed. 'What do you expect, taking a lantern into a gunpowder mill? You're lucky you didn't blow yourself to smithereens, and half the village with it.'

Hunt flopped down in his favourite armchair and gazed into the flames as the log fire hissed and spat like an old farm cat.

'Do you know, Johnny, the door of that old hut would be perfect for *The Light of the World*. It was as though the screeching owl and throbbing mill were crying out to me. *Me non praetermisso, Domine*. Lord, do not overlook me.'

'Most profound,' said Millais, knowing of Hunt's long and fruitless search for his first contribution to their moral crusade.

'Sadly, by the time I got there, the mist had descended, shrouding it from the moonlight. But I could still make out its rustic charm, decrepit and overgrown with ivy, its step choked with weeds, its hinges rusty and broken.'

'And how, exactly, did you manage to escape the clutches of the Epsom police?'

'If you must know, the kind-hearted sergeant let me off with a caution,' said Hunt, checking his pocket watch. 'Did Collins's train arrive from London?'

'A couple of hours ago. He walked through the door with his hair cropped shorter than an inmate from a house of correction.

172

Which is where you'd have ended up, had you blown up half of Surrey.'

There was a loud crack as a burning ember shot up the chimney, making Hunt jump.

'And where is our resident convict?'

'Charles has retired for the night. Apparently, the walk from the station left him quite exhausted.'

'Poor chap, he does so detest the country. And how goes the work on your beloved *Ophelia*?'

Millais shook his head. 'This dank weather hardly makes for good light on the riverbank. I'll try again tomorrow, assuming the wretched autumn gales don't blow me and my canvas into the water. Sometimes, I fear I should imitate poor Ophelia herself, as she sank to her muddy grave.'

'Take an umbrella, that's my advice.'

'At least that would allow me to shoo away the swans, who insist on parking themselves on the very spot where I wish to paint.'

Hunt couldn't help but smile at his friend's never-ending catalogue of trials and tribulations.

'Be patient, my good fellow. I'm sure it'll be worth it in the end.'

Millais nodded, wistfully. 'I do hope so - if only that Ophelia may touch the hearts of those who witness her tragic gaze, as she yearns to be free from the sorrow that imprisons her. "*When the body returns to nature and is resolved into its own roots, may the soul rise up, free from the bondage of man,*" he said, picturing Polonius' daughter clutching a posy of flowers to her chest, as the river enveloped her.

'I'm certain you will do her credit, Brother,' said Hunt.

'And what about you, William? Tell me of your visions for Christ and the lantern.'

Hunt sat forward. 'I shall put my best endeavours into *The Light of the World*. It was our good friend, Thomas Combe, who bade me to return to the Testaments for inspiration, and Revelation chapter three, verse twenty, that gave me pause.

> 'Behold, I stand at the door, and knock;
> If any man hear my voice, and open the door,

I will come in to him, and will sup with him,
and he with me.

'I am to embark on a personal journey,' Hunt continued. 'A quest for salvation. After my sad disregard for our great project, these past few years, this work shall act as a mirror to my soul. The judge and jury to my constant mood and purity. An image of such grace and portance, it will spare no hesitation in pronouncing my own weaknesses. As Christ stands knocking at the door with no handle, will I have the courage of heart to let him in?'

'And you are set on this being a moonlit landscape?' enquired Millais.

'A depiction of Christ's Holy Light, at the break of day, when the night is far spent and the day is at hand. Thy word is a lamp unto my feet and a light unto my path. For He, who, when in body, was the Light of the World, could not be unprovided when in the Spirit, with the means of guiding His followers when it was night.'

The small sitting room fell silent.

'Quite so, William. It will be a fitting icon for the seventh and final challenge of the soul, as it devours wrath and ascends to its final resting place. *"Eternal peace awaits those that cast off the bonds of oblivion, to follow the everlasting light."'*

'Indeed,' said Hunt, getting to his feet. 'Anyway, that's enough theology for one night. Have you fellows left me any supper?'

Chapter Twenty-Nine

Little Clarendon Street, Oxford

9 November 1999

Emily and Julian were seated at a table by the window in Pierre Victoire as the waitress handed them their menus.

'I like it here,' said Emily, admiring the light and airy French bistro, comprising wooden table furniture and bare brick walls. 'It has a kind of rustic charm, don't you think?'

Julian smiled. 'I come here a lot; and the food is wonderful.'

Having ordered and tasted a newly opened bottle of Saint-Emilion, Julian sat back in his chair, grinning like a naughty school boy.

'Come on, I can't wait any longer – tell me what happened at Drapers' Hall.'

'I can do better than that,' said Emily, fishing in her bag. 'I have photos.' She pulled out three close-up prints of the sun mark and handed them to Julian. One included a five pence coin placed next to the numbered symbol, to give an idea of scale – the coin being at least twice the size of the sun mark.

'My God, it's tiny,' exclaimed Julian.

'I know, it's no wonder we had trouble finding it. If you look, there are seven points on the sun, but we weren't certain what the 'L' in the centre, stood for.'

Julian stared at the photograph. 'Mmm, there's a line between each triangular point – why is that, do you think?'

'I don't know.' Emily took back one of the prints and looked at it. 'Aren't they just sunrays?'

'No, there's something else.'

She looked again. Then it came to her – like a magic-eye puzzle where the hidden image suddenly pops into focus.

'Oh my God, it's surrounded by Ws.'

Julian nodded. 'Seven of them, to be precise, encircling the L. And what else?'

'There is nothing else.'

'Come on, you're not trying.'

She continued analysing the sun mark, shaking her head. 'I can't see anything.'

Julian turned his copy round and pointed. 'The L has been placed in the centre of a letter O – you see? It reads, L-O-W.'

'Right, okay, ... so, what does that mean?'

'My God – I had no idea,' said Julian, staring out of the window. 'Now, I might be totally wrong here ...'

Emily sat waiting for him to finish the sentence; until, finally, she could wait no longer. 'Oh, for goodness' sake, what?'

'Right, ... sorry. After lunch, I'm going to show you a hidden treasure, not five minutes' walk from here.'

'Oh, you can't leave me hanging in mid-air like that.'

'Emily, I promise it will be worth the wait,' he said, laughing at her impatience.

'Fine, but if it's a big fat disappointment, I hold you entirely responsible.' She dipped into her handbag and pulled out an envelope. 'I, on the other hand,...' she grinned, '...am going to be completely up front with you. Look what I received in the post, yesterday.'

'You had another one?'

'I did. Unfortunately, I couldn't make head nor tail of this one, either.'

'May I?'

Emily handed him the cryptic note, which he duly studied.

EMILY,

YOUR JOURNEY HAS ONLY JUST BEGUN – USE
THE ONE TRUE LIGHT TO FIND YOUR WAY.

#7. Wrath – eternal peace awaits those that cast off
the bonds of oblivion, to follow the everlasting light.

THE SHEPHERD

Julian smiled, handing the note back to her. 'Well, that confirms it.'

'Confirms what?'

'What I'm going to show you, later.'

Just as Emily was about to try and prize the details out of him, the waitress arrived with their orders.

Forty or so minutes later, having both enjoyed a starter, followed by *plats principaux*, they settled the bill and Julian helped Emily on with her coat.

'What time is it?' he said.

Emily checked her watch. 'Just gone quarter past two.'

'Excellent, we have plenty of time. Come on, it's not far.'

'What isn't?' said Emily, trying to keep up as Julian marched out of the restaurant.

They headed back towards the Woodstock Road, through the small churchyard of St Giles' and into a tree-lined side street with university buildings on either side. Emily clocked the nearby street sign, Keble Road. It wasn't long before the intricate red-and-tan mosaic of Keble College – pinnacle of William Butterfield's Gothic vision, to give dignity to brick – loomed into sight. They turned onto Parks Road and entered the college's main gate through its imposing high stone arch.

'Give me a moment, will you?' said Julian, stopping at the porter's lodge.

Emily looked around the Liddon Quad, scanning the range of buildings bordering the sunken lawn. How bizarre, she thought, an island of dissident red brick in this, the bastion of collegiate gold limestone.

'Wonderful, isn't it?' said Julian, looking pleased with himself.

'This is what you wanted to show me?'

He laughed. 'Okay, let me ask you this. If you could visit just one of the buildings you see before you, which would it be?'

'That one,' she said, pointing to the huge brick-built chapel in the corner of the quadrangle.

'A fine choice. Come on, we don't want to keep the chaplain waiting.'

Following the quad's gravel path, they reached the doorway to the cloister, where a soberly dressed man in his late forties was waiting for them.

'Julian, how nice to see you.'

'You too, Peter. May I introduce a friend of mine, Emily Bradshaw. Emily, this is Peter O'Donnell, chaplain of Keble College.'

'Miss Bradshaw, welcome to Keble Chapel. Julian tells me you've come to see the painting.'

'Err, yes, that's right,' she said, not really knowing why.

O'Donnell led them up the cloister steps, along the covered passageway and into the main body of the church which towered over the other college buildings.

Emily gazed at the Victorian Gothic splendour around her. 'This is rather spectacular,' she said, not knowing where to look next.

'Yes, we're quite proud of William Butterfield's masterpiece. Apparently, the mosaics were inspired by many hours of study at St Mark's in Venice.'

They processed along the nave, paved in yellow, plum and sea-green floor tiles, with rows of quatrefoil-latticed pews on either side. Emily craned her neck to view the pastel-coloured ceiling, ribbed with a membrane of painted tiles, covering the entire vaulted span. But it was the chapel walls that really took her breath away. Along the base, ran a bold arcade of glazed plum-coloured brick and broader bands, set with stone flowers, suns and tendrils. Next, a series of mosaics depicting Old Testament scenes in a palette of suitably reverent colours – including alliterations to Christ, present. And finally, twelve, large, stained glass windows, each throwing great swathes of heavenly light onto any and all humble souls gathered below.

Julian smiled to himself as Emily dawdled along behind, remembering well the time he first laid eyes on Keble Chapel's idiosyncratic delights.

'Keep up,' he said, and disappeared through a small side door in the south wall, followed closely by the chaplain.

Moments later, Emily popped her head into the side chapel.

'Ah, here she is. Come and join us, Emily,' said O'Donnell, pointing to a small painting on the far wall.

Emily walked to the other end of the oblong-shaped room and gazed at the image in front of her. Illuminated by two spotlights was William Holman Hunt's nocturnal vision of Christ – his gentle enquiring eyes looking straight out at the viewer, full of love and forgiveness.

'Takes your breath away, doesn't it?' said Julian.

'Oh, it's ... majestic,' replied Emily, moving forward to get a better look.

'We've used one of the spotlights to emphasise Christ's lantern – the conservator of truth.'

'And the old door, what does that symbolise?' said Emily.

O'Donnell smiled to himself, hoping she would ask. 'The door represents the human soul. It cannot be opened from the outside. You'll notice there is no handle, and the hinges are rusted and overgrown with ivy – indicating this particular soul has never been receptive to the Divine Love of Christ. Love cannot enter where there is egoism, hate and envy, so the Lord simply waits to be asked inside.'

'His eyes do seem to look right into the heart of you,' she said.

'Yes, they do. You see that bright speck in the sky above Christ's head, that's Venus – the morning star, reflecting the dawn of a new day. And the tangle of old weeds and fallen apples represents the passing of time – the autumn of our lives.'

Julian moved a little closer and gazed at the faint glow in the skyline beyond the apple trees. 'Apparently, Hunt began the picture when he was only twenty-four years old, but didn't finish it until he was nearly twenty-seven,' he said.

'What took him so long?' said Emily.

'Well, various reasons, including his absolute determination to paint the perfect dawn sky. And also, to make the figure of Christ, mystic in aspect, and not suggesting any one person. Apparently, the face was a composite of various people, including J.L. Tupper, John Millais, Thomas Carlyle, Christina Rossetti, Lizzie Siddal; and even Hunt himself.'

Emily clutched her hands to her heart. 'I've seen old prints of it before, but none of them do it justice. I had no idea it was even here.'

'Oh, most people don't,' said O'Donnell. 'It was donated to the college in eighteen seventy-two by the widow of Thomas Combe, printer to the university, on the understanding it would hang in the main chapel building. Unfortunately, William Butterfield was opposed to the notion, and made no provision for it in his design. It hung in the library until the eighteen nineties, when another architect, J. T. Micklethwaite, was asked to design this side chapel to house it.'

Emily walked up to the small altar, where a security rope and wall-mounted motion sensor were positioned to prevent over-enthusiastic visitors getting too close.

'Isn't there another version of it, somewhere?'

'Yes, there is,' replied O'Donnell. 'Holman Hunt was so incensed at the treatment of his painting that he produced a duplicate, which hangs in St Paul's Cathedral. Theirs is far better known than the original here at Keble. And, to be perfectly honest, I prefer it that way.'

'They don't know what they're missing,' said Emily.

Julian stepped forward. 'Peter, would you mind if we took a closer look?'

'Of course not. Give me a hand, would you?'

Emily stood and watched as O'Donnell unhooked the rope and walked over to the ornate wooden case, housing the painting. Before she could say *The Light of the World*, the two men had unhooked the gilt frame from its mount and were laying the picture face down on the marble altar.

'Are you allowed to do that?' said Emily.

'Ha-ha, yes, we regularly take it out of its case, to make sure everything's as it should be.'

Emily turned to Julian. 'Is this one of the—'

He looked at her and quietly put his finger to his lips.

Oblivious, the chaplain took a cloth from his pocket and gave the back of the picture frame a gentle wipe.

'Of course, we don't normally go to such lengths for our visitors, but when Julian popped in a few minutes ago and said, how would I like to be the first to witness an incredible discovery, how could I refuse?'

They gathered round the painting and examined the back of the frame.

'So, what exactly am I looking for?' said O'Donnell.

'Emily and I refer to it as the sun mark, but in our experience, it's not that easy to spot,' replied Julian.

'There,' said Emily, as if to contradict him.

O'Donnell pushed his glasses up the bridge of his nose and peered at the grubby little indentation Emily was pointing to.

7

'Well I'm blowed. Do you know, I've been handling this picture for more years than I care to remember and I've never seen that before. What is it, exactly?'

'We think Hunt put it there, but we're not exactly sure why,' said Emily.

Julian looked at her. 'We do have a theory, but it's nothing more than a working hypothesis, at the moment.'

'Fascinating. Well, you must keep me posted,' said O'Donnell. 'I'd be very interested to find out what it signifies.'

After helping re-mount the painting in its casing, Emily and Julian thanked the chaplain for his time and walked back out into the fading afternoon light.

Seeing the grin on Julian's face, Emily tugged his arm. 'You'd already worked it out, hadn't you? When I showed you the photos from Drapers' Hall, earlier, you knew what it meant.'

'Oh look, I had a hunch that L-O-W stood for *Light of the World*, but I wasn't absolutely sure, until now. Emily, this is very exciting.'

'So, Hunt, Rossetti and Millais referred to each of the paintings as a "light of the world", and if Draper's *Gates of Dawn* was the last in the series, that means there are eight in total.'

'Yes, but what was the point of it all?' said Julian, looking back at the chapel. 'What were they up to?'

Emily gave a resigned smile. 'You know, there is a man who can help us with that.'

'Henry, yes, of course.'

'How is he? Did he come into work this morning?'

Julian shook his head. 'No. I called at his house last night, but he wasn't there. So I spoke to his sister – they share a house in Summertown – and she told me he hasn't been feeling himself for quite some time. This whole break-in business at the museum seems to have tipped him over the edge. Alice tried getting him to open up about it, but he just stormed off and locked himself in his study. That just doesn't sound like the Henry Faber I know.'

Emily thought back to that moment in the Barton & Cole car park and the look of terror on Henry's face as he was being driven away by that evil-looking man. Perhaps she had misjudged him, after all.

'Well, if he's missing, we should go to the police, surely,' she said.

'Mmm, ... my guess is, he's probably just gone somewhere to think things through. And he did seem quite enthusiastic, the other day, when we were discussing the refurbishment work we've got planned for the gallery.'

'The one that was broken into?'

'Yes. We've had a number of attempted break-ins, these past few years, and last Friday was the final straw for me. So, I dug out a bunch of plans Henry and I drafted a while ago, to redecorate the West Wing and install some new state-of-the-art security measures. It won't be cheap, but hopefully I can convince the Board of Visitors that we've got a good case.'

'Good luck with that. And do let me know if you see Henry. I'm desperate to find out more about the other paintings.'

'Yes, of course. I'm sure he'll come around when he's ready.'

Having escorted Emily back to her car, Julian turned to go, then stopped.

'By the way, you never did tell me how you managed to get hold of those photographs of the sun mark from Drapers' Hall.'

'Oh, didn't I?' she said, scrabbling in her bag for the car keys. 'Must have slipped my mind.'

Chapter Thirty

Parks Road, Oxford

9 November 1999

Henry Faber stood at the corner of the street and watched as Emily and Julian entered Keble College. After their first encounter at the auction house, his interest in Emily had now become one of concern. Why was she involved in all this? Was it happenstance, or was someone playing a sinister game with this captivating young woman? From their brief conversation at the Ashmolean, she seemed to be an innocent party, but he needed to be sure.

Having satisfied himself that they were going in to see *The Light of the World*, he made his way along Parks Road, marvelling at the tree-lined avenue of birch, elm and horse chestnut in deep autumn shed. Approaching the centre of town, he got the feeling someone was following him. He glanced over his shoulder and saw, not fifty yards behind him, the man he'd come to fear more than anyone else in the world. Dressed in black and smoking a cigarette, Marcus Tyburn maintained his distance, staring straight ahead with a look that chilled the blood in Henry's veins.

He passed the Kings Arms, busy with lunchtime drinkers, and kept on walking, trying desperately not to panic. Reaching the junction with Broad Street, he ran across the road, through the iron gates leading to the Sheldonian Theatre and into the quadrant of the Bodleian Library. Before he'd even had chance to enter the Proscholium, he looked back and saw Tyburn pushing past a group of school kids pouring through the North Range passageway. Like a hounded fugitive, Henry turned and ran as fast as he could, through the South Range and past the Radcliffe Camera in the direction of High Street. Then he saw it – divine refuge in the form of St Mary the Virgin and her University Church. Gasping for breath, he scurried through the front entrance towards the welcome glow of the gift shop.

'Good afternoon,' said the lady behind the counter.

Henry ignored her, bolting straight on past and heading for the nave. He quickly scanned the interior for somewhere to hide, spotting the large wooden pulpit towering above the rows of pews. He ran over, unclipped the red security cord and, ignoring the glares from a handful of bemused looking tourists, climbed the curving steps to the top. He opened the door and crouched down on the hexagonal wooden floor, curling up as tight as his arthritic joints would allow – waiting, listening for anything that sounded like approaching footsteps. But all he could hear was the musical chatter of a Japanese couple inspecting a gravestone in the church wall, nearby.

All of a sudden, everything went quite dark. He looked up at the leaded window above his head as the incessant *click-click-click* of hailstones hitting the stained glass gradually turned into a roar.

After waiting for what felt like an age, he slowly got to his knees and peered over the edge of the pulpit. There was no sign of his assailant. In fact, the nave was completely empty. Even the Japanese couple appeared to have moved on to their next historic attraction. As quickly as the hailstorm had come, the clouds parted revealing a beam of late afternoon sunlight shining in his eyes. He raised his hand to block out the glare and noticed the outline of a man sitting in the upper gallery. Suddenly, the nave began echoing with the sound of clapping as the man got to his feet.

'You need to try harder than that, old man,' said Tyburn.

Henry bowed his head in defeat – his race was run. 'What do you want?' he said, wishing the pulpit floor would somehow open up and transport him into the vaults below.

'To teach you a lesson.'

'I don't know what you're talking about.'

Tyburn made his way down from the gallery to the base of the pulpit and pulled the Glock from his jacket pocket.

'Why don't you and I take a walk up the tower? I hear the view can take your breath away.'

Like a condemned man, Henry descended the gently curving pulpit steps to face his aggressor.

'After you, old man,' said Tyburn, and with a shove sent Henry sprawling across the floor, straight into the base of a massive stone pillar. Taking a moment to gather his senses, he slowly reached up, his fingers gripping a small notch near the base of the column – the historical significance of which did not escape him, for this was the very pillar that had once supported the wooden stage for Thomas Cranmer's 1556 trial for heresy against the Catholic Church. As he got to his feet, Henry hoped he might display even but a fraction of Cranmer's remarkable courage, when faced with whatever ordeal he was about to endure.

With a sense of trepidation, he made his way over to the gift shop, with Tyburn following close behind.

'Two for the tower,' growled Tyburn.

'Have you been before?' said the woman behind the counter.

'No.'

'Well, here's a leaflet telling you all about it—'

'Yeah, yeah. Just give us the bloody tickets.'

The woman stared at Tyburn. 'That'll be three pounds, please.'

He handed her the cash, grabbed the tickets and ushered Henry through the small wooden door next to the till. After climbing some narrow stairs, they found themselves on a landing, facing the fourteenth-century library. To the right was a small office with the door open. A young man sitting at a desk, looked up and nodded.

Henry saw his opportunity. 'Good afternoon, would you be so kind as to—'

'Don't even think about it,' said Tyburn, discreetly jolting the gun into his left kidney. 'This way to the tower, mate?'

'Yes, up the stairs and keep on going,' said the man.

'There you go, pops, we gotta keep goin',' said Tyburn, guiding Henry towards the far wall and another set of wooden stairs.

Once at the top, they found themselves outside, perched on a steel gantry above the church roof. With the wind tugging at Henry's grey hair, they climbed the metal staircase at the base of the tower, into an old beamed room featuring whitewashed walls and crudely painted icons hung here and there. Built into the far wall was a Perspex window showing the workings of Thomas Paris' 1741 clock – it's huge brass cogs steadily counting down the remainder of Henry's time on earth.

In the centre of the room hung three corded bell ropes that disappeared through trapdoors in the ceiling, like hangman's nooses. Henry walked past them, pretending not to notice.

'Don't worry, not my style,' said Tyburn, caressing one of the ropes, before climbing the wooden stairs next to the clock. He peered through the doorway, up into the narrow stone stairwell. Unfortunately for Henry, all was quiet. 'Hope you ain't afraid of heights, old man,' he smirked.

Henry didn't answer, preferring to focus on the nigh impossible task of finding a way out of this nightmare, alive.

'Get up here,' said Tyburn, gesturing with his gun for Henry to go ahead of him.

Begrudgingly, he clambered up the crude wooden steps and through the small doorway to the foot of the spiral staircase. He craned his neck, looking up at the stone steps circling way above his head. If the fall from the top didn't kill him, the climb up the tower certainly would. Prompted by a shove in the back from Tyburn, he grabbed hold of the iron handrail attached to the central column, and began his ascent.

As predicted, the higher they climbed, the harder Henry found it; and after barely a minute, he came to a sudden halt, clutching his chest.

'I'm afraid I'm not as fit as I used to be,' he said, gasping for breath.

'Get a move on,' yelled Tyburn, jolting him in the small of the back with his Glock.

With his arthritic knees burning as if they were on fire, Henry resumed his climb; hauling himself up by the handrail, step by agonising step.

Then, like an epiphany, it came to him. The small notebook in his jacket pocket – if he could just get it out without Tyburn seeing. He stopped again, pretending to clutch his heart.

'I'm sorry, I need a break. Unless you want a dead body falling on your head.'

'Don't tempt me,' said Tyburn.

Henry leaned forward, his fingers feeling for the notebook and pencil tucked inside his jacket. Exaggerating his breathing, he glanced over his shoulder to see Tyburn's red face staring down at his shoes. This was his chance. With his left arm held across his stomach, and using the quarters of his jacket for cover, he took out the notebook, rested it on his forearm and opened it to a blank page. Sliding the tiny pencil into his fingers, he began to scribble something, anything, intelligible.

'Alright, that's enough. Get movin"
'Another minute, please.'
'I said fuckin' move it, old man!'

Grimacing with pain, Henry set off once more, his left hand gripping his belt buckle, the other blindly scrawling away as best he could.

'Hold it,' said Tyburn, grabbing his ankle. 'Did you hear voices?' Henry froze, praying someone was on their way down the tower. At first there was a stony silence. Then came a squeaky laugh from somewhere below, echoing round the circular wall. It was the most joyous sound he'd ever heard. While Tyburn was looking back down the stairwell, Henry tore out the scribbled page and tucked the notebook and pencil back in his pocket.

'Move! And not a sound, or I'll end you right here,' said Tyburn, shoving him in the back.

Eventually, daylight appeared above them in the shape of an open doorway. Red-faced and utterly exhausted, Henry stumbled out onto the viewing platform, gulping mouthfuls of fresh air into his lungs. He looked along the stone walkway, but any hopes of catching the attention of some windswept tourists were soon dashed – it was completely deserted.

'This way,' said Tyburn.

Henry put up his hand. 'Please, just give me a moment,' he said, leaning against the wall in front of him.

Then came the sound of voices from the stairwell, getting ever closer. Henry discreetly screwed the scribbled page into a ball, clasping it tightly in his hand. Moments later, two eager young faces appeared in the stairwell, squinting up at the daylight. It was the Japanese couple he'd seen earlier.

'The gallery's closed!' barked Tyburn, waving them back down the tower. They stood there, looking somewhat bemused.

Henry watched as Tyburn turned to unhook the heavy iron ring holding the door open. This was his chance. He stepped forward and threw the little ball of scrunched-up paper towards the young Japanese woman; then watched in horror as a gust of wind sent it ballooning over her head and tumbling down the tower steps, behind them.

With a loud bang, the door slammed shut. 'Fuckin' tourists,' said Tyburn, giving the door a sharp kick.

Henry's heart sank. His rescuers were gone. Had they seen the note, or would they just squash it under foot without a second thought? Even if they did find it, would they be able to make out his hurried scrawl? Either way, he was alone – left to meet his fate at the hands of this raging psychopath.

*

Disappointed at not being able to see the spectacular rooftop views described in the guidebook, Himiko, the young woman from Osaka looked down at her boyfriend and explained that they would have to turn back. As they trudged back down the corkscrew steps, Himiko felt something beneath her shoe. She stopped and picked up the little ball of paper, flattening it out in the palm of her hand.

'Kichiro, STOP!' she shouted. He turned and looked up at her, quizzically. 'Look at this,' she said, handing him the note.

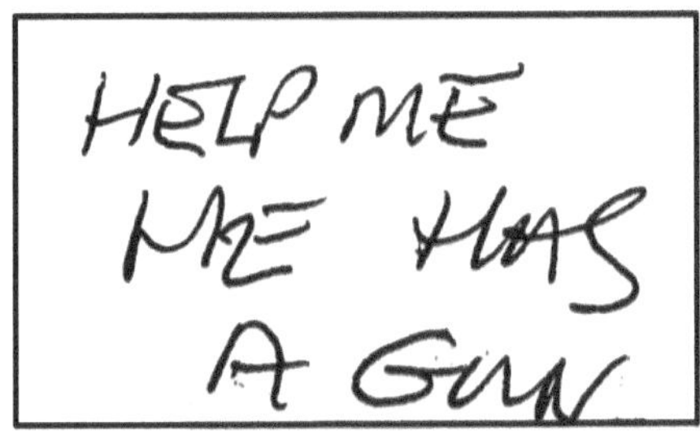

'Probably, just some kind of British joke,' he said, and went to throw it down the steps.

'No!' she screamed, causing him to stop in his tracks. She reached down and grabbed the note from his hand. Unbeknown to Henry, she'd seen the look of terror on his face, just before the door slammed shut, thinking it strange at the time. But this was proof – something was wrong. Having explained it to her boyfriend, they hurried back down the tower; the tiny, scribbled note, with its cry for help, clasped tightly in Himiko's hand.

*

With the door to the tower bolted shut behind them, Tyburn continued his reign of terror on poor Henry Faber.

188

'You know why I've brought you up here?' said Tyburn.

'No, I don't.'

'Well, it ain't the bloody view,' he said, waving his gun above the stone parapet. 'You've been stickin' your nose into other people's business.'

'I don't know what you mean.'

'You've been talkin' to that Emily girl, haven't you?'

'No, I haven't seen her since the auction.'

'Don't fuckin' lie to me,' Tyburn said, whipping the butt of his gun across Henry's face and sending him tumbling to the floor.

'I saw the two of you in the museum, havin' a nice little chat. Tellin' her all about that sketchbook, were you?'

'No, no, nothing like that,' said Henry, clutching his bruised cheek.

'Tryin' to warn her off? Make sure she didn't get caught up in somethin' she shouldn't?'

'You've got it all wrong. We were just chatting about Guy Fawkes' lantern. I thought it would interest her.'

'You know, for such a clever bloke, you're a lousy fuckin' liar. Now get up.'

Henry gripped the top of the stone parapet and hauled himself to his feet, only for Tyburn to give him another shove along the narrow walkway. After a few yards, they entered a tiny passageway cut through one of the huge stone pinnacles. The cold wind bit into Henry's face as he stepped out onto another viewing platform, this time facing east. He glanced up at the griffin-shaped gargoyle jutting out above his head. In legend, griffins not only mated for life, but if either partner died, the other would spend the rest of its days in respectful solitude – much as he himself had done, following the death of his beloved wife, Bonnie.

In one last desperate plea, Henry turned towards his captor. 'You have to believe me – Emily knows nothing about what she's involved in.'

'Yeah, but you do. And I can't risk you blabbin' to the police.'

'I won't tell them anything, you have my word.'

Tyburn laughed. 'You should've listened to me back in Bristol.' Reaching inside his jacket, he pulled out a silencer for the Glock. 'You went to one of these posh colleges, didn't you?' he said, screwing it to the barrel with icy composure.

'Yes, Magdalen ... just over there.'

'Well, take a good look, cos it's gonna be the last thing you ever see.'

Henry had somehow grown accustomed to the gun being shoved in his back every few minutes, but the sight of that hollow steel tube brought a sudden chill to his soul. He looked over to the eastern skyline for a final glimpse of his beloved Magdalen, where, as an undergraduate of the Ruskin School, he'd marvelled at the splendour of his surroundings, not least the small summerhouse on the banks of the River Cherwell that became his adopted studio. So long ago, those days of innocence, spent lazing with friends in the cool, green grass of the Deer Park, sketching the wild flowers in the purple river meadows. Finally, graduating with honours in 1950, he'd prided himself on maintaining friendships with fellows and tutors alike, eventually retiring as an Emeritus Fellow of the College he so dearly loved. But those days were long gone, and soon the college bells would be ringing in the dawn of a new millennium – one he would never live to see. Would man truly come of age in the twenty-first century? Somehow, he doubted it.

'Any last requests, old man?' said Tyburn.

'You'd be incapable of fulfilling any request of mine,' he replied, wistfully.

'In that case, let me put you out of your misery.'

Pressing the Glock against his temple, Tyburn ushered him to his knees. He was about to squeeze the trigger, when a chorus of police sirens came drifting up on the wind. Tyburn leaned over the stone balcony to check if the cavalry was headed his way. Three police cars came tearing along High Street, screeching to a halt outside the church, with blue lights flashing. He watched as the armed officers exited the vehicles and began swarming round the base of the church like ants.

'Fuck!' he said, banging his fist on the wall.

Buoyed by the flurry of activity, Henry peered over the parapet into Catte Street. Two armed officers were staring up at the viewing gallery. Dare he believe that there was a glimmer of hope? Not that this psycho would hesitate to snuff him out in a second.

Tyburn turned and glared at him. Henry could see the cogs whirring in his brain – should he kill the old man and risk a murder charge, or get out now, while he had the chance? Henry knew which option he preferred.

Tyburn pushed him back against the wall, and held the gun under his chin. 'Seems your luck's in, old man. But the next time you step outside, you'd better look over your shoulder, cos I'm gonna be there. And if you even breathe the name Emily Bradshaw to anyone, it'll be the last thing you ever do.'

And with that, he was gone.

Henry didn't know whether to laugh or cry. Once more, he peered over the balcony. Members of the Armed Response Unit were taking up positions around the tower, while handfuls of uniformed police officers began closing off the surrounding streets. He thought about the young Japanese couple who'd apparently found his note. If he ever saw them again, he'd make sure they knew – he was forever in their debt.

*

Taking two steps at a time, Tyburn tore down the spiral staircase until he reached the metal gantry at the foot of the tower. Without even thinking, he clambered over the guard rail and leapt feet first onto the roof of the Adam de Brome Chapel, then crept along the narrow strip of lead flashing running down the centre of the roof to the end wall. Knowing the police would be putting a surveillance ring round the building, he peered over the edge into the church garden, below. It was clear, but the drop was forty feet or more – too far to jump, even with the police on his tail.

He climbed over the crenellated wall and, crouching as low as he could, made his way along a narrow ledge that ran the length of the chapel. Spotting a hole in the guttering, he leaned over and saw what he'd been looking for – an old cast-iron drainpipe, channelling rainwater from the chapel roof. He knelt down and gripped the top of the pipe in both hands. Edging closer and praying the thing would stay put, he rolled himself off the ledge, clinging on for dear life as his knee scraped along the wall and hit the downpipe with a thud. Planting his feet against the wall, either side of the drainpipe, he took a moment to steady himself, then began clambering down – one hand below the other. He soon got up a rhythm and it wasn't long before his boots were touching the wet grass.

Seconds later, and with a major police incident unfolding behind him, he was off like a thief in the night, blending into the hustle and bustle of the old university town.

*

Henry looked out across the Oxford skyline, the weak November sun bathing the church tower in a golden glow. A rainbow arced across the charcoal sky, then another – a perfect pale reflection. He hadn't moved since Tyburn made his escape, preferring instead to savour his moment of liberation. Ignoring the police activity below, he began to look back on a life that, for the most part, had been peaceful and fulfilling. He'd never been blessed with the gift of progeny – the fellows and masters of Magdalen College were his family, as they had been to so many learned souls over the centuries.

And what of the future, he wondered. Would he ever come to know the true meaning of his existence? Perhaps this was it – the here and now on which he dwelt, searching for the perfect eulogy to sum up a life. Surely, it was quite simple – as the answers to such problems often were. He'd been blessed to share life's ups and downs with his beautiful wife, Bonnie, who had graced their marriage with warmth and tenderness for more than forty years, until cancer finally took her from him. And, not forgetting his sister, Alice, with whom he now shared a life and a home; and who doted on him more and more, as the years took their toll. But there was something else: his undying passion for art – an aesthetic love affair on which his whole life had been founded. Nurtured in the flower meadows of Magdalen College, and manifesting itself in his own raw, yet quietly accomplished works, its beauty, honesty, power and inspiration had dazzled him, ever since he was a boy. Even now, he never ceased to be amazed by its unerring ability to arouse and manifest the human spirit. But as time passed, his fascination lay more in the God-given talents of real artists such as Rembrandt, Turner, Vermeer and Van Gogh – creative geniuses who would forever hold a special place in his heart. And now, at the ripe old age of seventy, as his bones creaked and his mind dwelt more on the past than the future, he realised that he'd found his final resting place, nestling at the bosom of art and history in Oxford's very own cabinet of curiosities – the Ashmolean Museum. Although soon to retire, this was a place where he could happily see out his days, surrounded by artefacts that had been brought to life by some of the most talented and creative minds in the history of mankind. This too was love, as Henry Faber had come to know it.

And yet, he sensed there was something else – a hidden flame residing deep inside his intuition. One last existential question to be answered, perhaps.

He looked down into the corner of Radcliffe Square and saw DCI Cordell waving up at him.

'You okay?' shouted Cordell.

He gave a thumbs up and continued gazing up at the two perfect rainbows.

'Ah, who needs a pot of gold, anyway?' he said, his words quickly gathered up and taken off by the whispering wind.

Chapter Thirty-One

Luke Waltham stood at the office window, watching the rush-hour traffic crawl up and down Sloane Street. He turned and stared at Tyburn, conscious of the fact that if he wanted to maintain even the merest hint of composure, he'd better choose his next words, carefully. 'I'm sorry Marcus, you did what?'

'He was about to blow the whole thing. So I thought I'd put the wind up him – let him know we were onto him.'

'And you thought throwing an old man off a church roof would resolve things, did you?'

'I wasn't gonna do that. Just pop a cap in him, give him somethin' to think about, that's all.'

'Oh, for Christ's sake, what were you thinking?'

'I was thinkin', if he blabbed, we'd all be lookin' at a ten stretch.'

'And it didn't occur to you that, had you … popped a cap in him, as you put it, this place would be crawling with police by now?'

'Stop frettin'. I escaped, didn't I?'

'More by luck than judgement. Did anyone see you, besides Faber?'

'The gift shop woman, and some Japanese couple. But I got clean away before the coppers knew what was goin' on. It'll be fine, trust me.'

Luke sat down at his burr-walnut art deco desk, staring at Tyburn with a mixture of exasperation and contempt.

'Your antics could have set us back months, do you realise that?'

Tyburn scowled, fighting the urge to get up out of his chair and lamp Waltham, right where he sat.

'But, I do have to agree with you on one thing ...' Luke continued, '... Faber appears to have got this all worked out, somehow. And that's a bigger problem.'

'I thought my little chat with him, after the auction, had put him straight – obviously not.'

'Do you think he knew we left the sketchbook on top of the washstand for Emily to find?'

Tyburn nodded. 'He told me he was biddin' for it himself, but that's bullshit. He must have found out we were fishin' for the girl and hidden the book so she wouldn't find it. Fortunately for us, she did. Then, a few days later, I caught him talkin' to her at the museum.'

'Did you hear what they were saying?'

'No, as soon as the old man clocked me, he was out of there like a jackrabbit.'

Luke sat rubbing the back of his neck. 'So, he was trying to tip her off?'

'I'd lay money on it. Although, when we were up the tower, he said she didn't have a clue what she was involved in.'

'Mmm ... let's hope she's still none the wiser. And that your antics have put Faber off trying to contact her again.'

'If he knows what's good for him. I could always pay her a visit.'

'Christ, no! We can't risk spooking Miss Bradshaw, she's too important in all this. And as for Henry Faber, just leave him alone. In fact, leave them both alone – is that understood?'

Tyburn glared at Luke. 'Sure, you're the boss,' he said, getting up and wandering over to a row of bookshelves which ran the length of the office. Pretending he knew one end of a book from the other, he studied the volumes, then removed one that looked expensive.

'So, how are things at the museum?' he said, changing the subject.

'Fine,' said Luke, watching him, intently. 'The trustees have accepted our proposals, so, all that's left to do is finalise the design for the new security system and we'll have the installation team in there and ready to start work before Christmas.'

Unable to take the manhandling of one of his precious books a moment longer, Luke got up out of his seat, marched over to where Tyburn was standing and snatched the rare edition of the

Rubaiyat of Omar Khayyam from his hand – placing it carefully back in its rightful slot.

With a shake of his head, he returned to his desk. 'Of course, Kate handled the sales pitch, brilliantly. Although, with the figure we quoted, they'd have been crazy to go anywhere else. I'll need to use some cash from the Picasso to subsidise the work, but we got the contract, that's all that matters. I even offered to redecorate the gallery for them, as part of the deal.'

'I'd better take a fresh look at those floor plans,' said Tyburn.

'Yes, do that. Kate tells me the installation will take about eight to ten weeks – give or take – so, we should be ready to go by the first week in April.'

'You mentioned a while back about gettin' shot of the museum's head of security – Maynard, isn't it?'

'Yes.

'Want me to take care of it?' said Tyburn, bristling at the prospect.

'Good God, no. I'll get a specialist in to sort that out. Perhaps Maynard could get caught with one of the museum's rare coins in his pocket; or something of that nature. Anyway, we'll need our guy in there before we start work.'

'And who's that?'

'There's a Dutch chap I met in The Hague, a few years ago – Coos Van Leer. He's got just the right experience, and he's good with technology. I'm seeing him next week.'

'What about security guards? I've got a man who'd be up for it.'

Luke glowered at him. 'I normally leave that level of recruitment to Kate. Is he reliable?'

Tyburn nodded. 'Yeah, George and me go way back.'

'Alright, if he's any good and Kate likes him, we'll get him on the ArtScreen payroll. Set something up, would you?'

Tyburn nodded and headed for the door.

'Oh, and remember,' said Luke, not looking up from the papers on his desk, 'lay off Henry Faber ... and the girl.'

Tyburn snorted and closed the office door behind him.

Never a great one for conflict, Luke shook his head and went and stood by the window overlooking Cadogan Place Gardens. With a resigned sigh, he gazed across the road at a group of trees, dressed in their autumn colours.

His grand plan had been working perfectly, up to now; but he just got the sense that, following the events of yesterday, things were starting to unravel. Much as he hated delegating responsibility to anyone other than Kate, he'd always thought of himself as a pretty good judge of character, the ex-wife aside. Oh, no doubt, he'd done some pretty stupid things in his time; but to put his trust in a headcase like Marcus Tyburn – was just plain asking for trouble. Something had to be done.

Chapter Thirty-Two

The German Gallery, New Bond Street, London
5 February 1861

Ernest Gambart's German Gallery – a place where the hoi polloi could mix with the great and the good for the admission price of one shilling – was heaving with people wanting to see *The Finding of the Saviour in the Temple*. William Holman Hunt had spent four years trying to earn enough money to finish the painting, eventually succeeding in May 1860 when Gambart purchased it, and the copyright, for a total of £5,500 – a landmark figure.

Gambart had just finished speaking with the Chancellor of the Exchequer, William Gladstone, about the challenges facing newly elected U.S. president, Abraham Lincoln, when he spotted a noted dignitary making her way over to the painting.

'Lady Trevelyan, how lovely to see you.'

'Mr Gambart, ...' she said, extending her gloved hand, which he duly took and bowed, graciously. '... may I congratulate you on putting on such a wonderful exhibition. And with so many devotees on such a cold day.'

Gambart donned his most courteous smile. 'Why, thank you. And may I say how fortunate we are to count you among them, you being such an admirer of William's work?'

'Oh, very much so,' she said, gazing at the painting of the young boy Christ standing in the Holy Temple. 'In fact, William was kind enough to share some of his experiences of the Holy Land with me, when we last met. But I'm sure you don't want me boring you with such trivialities.'

'On the contrary, we would be delighted to hear them,' said Gambart, supported in his request by a handful of onlookers.

She laughed, coyly. 'Well, ... one story that I found particularly moving was his account of the approach to the Holy City with his friend and fellow traveller, Thomas Seddon. Apparently, whilst enduring a long, arduous journey through the rugged hills of central Palestine – the hot, stagnant air clawing at their minds with each jarring step of the mules – they were beginning to give up all hope of reaching civilisation before sundown. Each hilltop was approached with renewed expectation, only to be met by the disappointment of yet another deep valley, six or seven miles wide. Then suddenly, the mules stopped and the two men raised their heads, feasting their sore eyes on the great landscape before them. For there in the distance lay the holy city of Jerusalem – a vision of domes and minarets, surrounded by ancient walls and terraces, richly coloured in amethyst and amber by the setting sun. William tells me, he gazed at Temple Mount, looking resplendent amongst the cypress trees, and felt a wave of serenity wash over him as the soft, fragrant breeze kissed his face, and exalted the birds and windmills into a symphony of life. Poor Mr Seddon, normally such a jocular fellow by all accounts, could only sway back and forth in his saddle, with tears streaming down his cheeks – such was the euphoria that overcomes many a traveller when greeted by the vision of the City of Truth from the western approach.'

There was polite applause from the crowd that had gathered to hear Lady Pauline Trevelyan's eloquent narration.

'What a delightful picture you paint,' said Gambart. 'I'm sure William would be most honoured by your touching rendition.'

'Well, of course, it was Mr Hunt's personal recollections of that sacred place that touched me so deeply,' she said, turning to the painting. 'Now, tell me Mr Gambart, are you familiar with the picture's figurative meaning?'

'Why, yes. William was good enough to share some of his personal insights with me when I purchased it.'

'How exciting. I do find paintings that contain symbols and allegories to be the most fascinating. Perhaps you would be good enough to share them with me?'

'It would be my privilege,' he said, proudly standing next to Hunt's work. 'At first glance, William appears to have presented us with a scene of confrontation in the Temple, between the old and new dispensations. The seven rabbis are shown exemplifying the sins of pride, indolence, envy and conceit through their open hostility to the young Christ. Whereas Jesus himself is portrayed in the role of the reformer – a young boy in whom the unswerving devotion to duty is so great that he appears quite at ease debating dogma with the old doctors. And yet still obedient to his earthly parents.'

'Why yes, you can see Christ tightening his belt, as if to make ready for the great task that awaits him in later life,' said Lady Trevelyan.

Gambart nodded approvingly, causing a murmur of appreciation from the group of onlookers for her discerning eye. He continued. 'Now, ... here we have the blind rabbi holding the Torah, and the blind beggar seated outside the Temple. Now one might suppose William is not only making reference to the healing miracles that Christ would go on to perform, but also a comparison of the beggar's incapacity, with the physical and spiritual blindness of the old doctor. I also sense his desire to highlight the plight of the many destitute Jews in the Holy City, who continue to be neglected by the church elders, even to this day.'

'Yes, William did mention this to me. Most concerning,' said Lady Trevelyan.

'Quite so. My favourite cameo, however, is the little scene being played out in the background. You see here, the masons in the temple courtyard are shown measuring the headstone at the corner and are about to reject it, just as described in Psalm 118. Hunt has shrewdly created a counterpart to this, inside the Temple. The old priests reject Christ, who, as the Messiah, will become the cornerstone of the new church – once the common people, such as those in the courtyard, reject him and demand his crucifixion. If you look closely, you can see William has echoed this by placing two bound posts in the shape of a cross, where the cornerstone is to be erected.'

'How very preceptive of him,' said Lady Trevelyan, peering closely at the little courtyard scene.

Gambart continued, 'Now, hidden in the shadows at the back of the temple is a depiction of a paschal lamb being taken from the ewe by some money changers – reminding us of Christ's cleansing of the Temple, and perhaps echoing Mary's eventual distancing from her son.'

Lady Trevelyan nodded. 'Why, thank you, Mr Gambart, your commentary has been most illuminating,'

Looking a little flushed, she took out her handkerchief and gently dabbed her forehead. 'Although, I fear the air in here has become a little stuffy. Would you excuse me.'

'Of course,' he said, bowing courteously. When he could see she was out of earshot, he turned and headed straight for the main office. 'Where is that blasted superintendent? It's like a damned greenhouse in here.'

Meanwhile, crowds of admiring onlookers continued to amass around Hunt's historic scene – marvelling at his portrayal of scripture, melodrama and historical import, played out in Royal David's City – for it was the closest most of them would ever get.

*

Lady Trevelyan soon recovered her composure and was chatting to some of the cream of London society, when there was a loud scream.

'FIRE! FIRE!' someone shouted.

She looked round and, to her horror, saw that a velvet canopy, erected to prevent reflections in the glass of Hunt's painting, was on fire. Ignited by a row of gas lamps, nearby, the whole curtain was ablaze, sending clouds of smoke billowing up the walls. Moments later, the whole flaming structure came crashing to the ground.

Panic spread quickly. While most of the crowd ran screaming to the safety of the adjoining rooms, Lady Trevelyan remained rooted to the spot, her eyes fixed on a section of flaming material that had draped itself over the picture frame. With no consideration for her own safety, she pushed her way through the oncoming crowd towards Hunt's Temple, now on the verge of destruction.

'Water, water! Someone get water!' she cried.

Everyone ignored her, more concerned with saving themselves, than the fate of a painting. A gallery attendant carrying a bucket of cold water came rushing over and hurled it into the flames, to little or no effect.

'Is there any more?' shouted Lady Trevelyan.

'All the fire buckets are frozen. This is all I could find,' said the attendant, staring helplessly at the devastation.

'Here, take this,' she said, removing her valuable Indian shawl. 'Quickly man! Save it if you can.'

The attendant grabbed the shawl and went to work beating back the flames, as Hunt's picture smouldered at the edges. With some of the crowd looking on from a distance, other gallery attendants came running over to help, until finally, all that remained was a heap of fire ravaged material and charred wood.

The first attendant stood back, panting for breath and looking as if he didn't know whether to laugh or cry.

'Thank you, madam,' he said, turning to Lady Trevelyan. 'I reckon Mr Gambart owes you a debt of gratitude – not to mention a new shawl.'

'Is the painting quite damaged?' she said, trying to see through the veil of smoke.

'I'm no expert, but I'm hoping we may just have saved it.'

A round of applause broke out behind them, with shouts of 'Bravo! Bravo!' as dozens of onlookers cautiously re-entered the room to survey the pile of smouldering debris.

*

A week later, after Hunt had managed to restore the Temple painting to its former glory, it was back being re-hung in Gambart's German Gallery.

'You've worked miracles, William,' said Gambart, inspecting the fire-damaged area. 'How on earth did it manage to survive?'

Hunt stood back with arms crossed, gazing critically at his restoration work.

'Only by the grace of God, is my guess. Not to mention, several coats of varnish. Of course, there was some minor discolouration near the edges, but I think I've made the best of it.'

'You most certainly have. I can see no sign of injury at all. The public, and I, owe you a debt of gratitude, William.'

'Mmm ... I'm sure you'll give the spectators of London every opportunity to show their appreciation,' said Hunt, smirking at the more than savvy gallery owner. 'When do you re-open, tomorrow?'

'This afternoon, actually,' replied Gambart. 'There's no point in keeping an expectant public waiting, is there?'

Affording himself a knowing smile, he stood and watched as Hunt instructed the gallery attendants, relishing the prospect of increased ticket sales from this miracle of a painting – this veritable phoenix from the flames.

'I wonder if our brave heroine will grace us with her presence?' said Hunt, satisfied the picture was at last, hanging straight.

'Who can say,' Gambart replied. 'The insurance company tried desperately to find out who it was that assisted with the rescue, but to no avail – she simply disappeared.'

'Well, whoever she was, her courage and insight saved the Temple painting – were it not for her, my portrayal of the young Saviour would have been lost forever.'

Gambart placed his hand on Hunt's shoulder, then walked off to prepare for the afternoon's re-opening.

Having discharged the gallery attendants from their duties, Hunt stood alone, staring at one of the Brothers' seven sacred icons: *The Finding of the Saviour in the Temple* – portraying its message to all those with eyes to see.

#6. Folly of Man – learned we may be with another man's learning, only wise can we become with wisdom of our own.

Chapter Thirty-Three

There is something satisfying about the sound of gravel crunching underfoot, thought DCI Cordell, as he strolled up the garden path and brushed a fallen maple leaf from his shoulder. Autumn was well and truly underway in the pleasant suburban gardens of Summertown, and this particular frontage was better than most. The lawn still had pockmarks from its last hollow tine aeration and the herbaceous borders were pared back, ready for the onset of winter.

Lovingly tended by someone with time on their hands, he thought, approaching the red-brick porch. Not, perhaps, his best detective deduction, given that he knew the brother-and-sister occupants were well beyond normal retirement age. He walked up to the front door and pressed the brass doorbell, causing a loud chime to go off somewhere in the house.

A minute and two rings later, the door still hadn't been answered. 'Retired, and a little hard of hearing,' he surmised, standing on his tiptoes as he peered into the huge bay window.

Back-tracking up the front path, he spotted a wooden gate tucked round the side of the house and walked over to try the latch – it opened with a click.

'And, far too trusting, considering the events of yesterday,' he muttered to himself.

He followed the path round the back and spotted a grey-haired lady tending one of the borders.

'I hope you don't mind, but the gate was open,' he said, respectfully.

The woman carried on placing a handful of bulbs into a bucket-sized hole in the ground.

'Hello, my name is Detective Chief Inspector Cordell.'

She spun round, sharply.

'Who are you?' she said, wielding her garden trowel and looking anything but menacing.

'Detective Chief Inspector Cordell.'

'You'll have to shout. She won't hear a thing with that scarf on,' came a voice from the nearby greenhouse. Henry Faber took off his gloves and wandered over to where Cordell was standing. 'Unless she's got her hearing aid on full blast, which it won't be, she's as deaf as a post, poor girl.'

'Is this him, Henry? Is this the one who attacked you yesterday?' said Alice Faber, still brandishing her trowel.

'No, dear. This is Detective Chief Inspector Cordell – he's helping us with the break-in at the museum.'

Cordell held up his warrant card so Alice could see it.

'There's no need to shove it up my nose. I'm deaf, not blind,' she said, squinting at his ID.

'What can we do for you, Detective Chief Inspector?' said Henry. 'Have you got some news about the robbery?'

'Partly, yes. Perhaps we can talk inside?'

Alice removed her scarf and gloves, and reached behind her ear to turn the volume up on her hearing aid.

'I suppose you'd like some tea?' she said, and marched off towards the back door without waiting for an answer.

'You'll have to forgive my sister, we're not used to company. We tend to keep ourselves to ourselves, for the most part.'

Cordell smiled and followed them into the house. To his surprise, it had a modest, yet contemporary feel. Certainly not the decor one normally expects of an older suburban couple, or in this case, siblings – but what did he know?

Henry led the way into a large rectangular lounge with a set of French doors looking out onto the back garden. Cordell gazed admiringly at the patchwork of paintings and sketches on display, encompassing many different artists and genres, yet nothing looked out of place.

'I like this,' said Cordell, walking over to a small impressionist landscape of a river meadow – its confident dabs of amethyst, green and gold so vibrant, you could almost smell the cowslips. In the bottom-right corner was the artist's signature, hiding in the long grass – H. J. FABER.

'I didn't know you—'

'I used to dabble, in my younger days.'

'Oh, more than dabble, I'd say. Did you sell many?'

Henry laughed, nostalgically. 'No, no. I was never that prolific. In the end, I decided to dedicate my life to the study of those with immeasurably more talent than myself.'

'You do yourself a disservice, sir. This shows you had real flair, in my humble opinion.'

'You're very kind, Chief Inspector. And coming from someone who's seen as many artworks as you, I will take that as a compliment.'

A few minutes later, Alice arrived wheeling a small tea trolley laden with cups, saucers, plates, a pot of tea and a rather spectacular looking chocolate gateau. 'Do you like cake, Chief Inspector?'

'My wife tells me I've got to cut out the sweet stuff,' Cordell replied, taking a seat on the vintage tan leather sofa.

'Nonsense,' she said, with a wave of her hand. 'We all need to spoil ourselves, now and again. I defy you not to like this, it's my speciality,' and she cut him a large slice, handing it to him on a snazzy, sixties style plate.

'It's pointless resisting,' said Henry, parking himself next to Cordell. 'She'll wear you down in the end.'

'Well in that case, what's a man to do?' Cordell bit into the dark fluffy cake, spilling chocolate crumbs all over his trousers.

Having poured everyone tea, and handed Cordell a napkin, Alice sat in the leather armchair by the French doors and fiddled with her hearing aid.

'So, are you here to tell us you've found our Picasso?' said Henry, hopefully.

'It's early days yet. My guess is, the painting's being kept somewhere safe, probably waiting for a potential buyer.'

'You think it could still be in this country?'

Cordell looked pensive. 'It's difficult to say. If, as is sometimes the case, it was stolen to order, then it may already have left our shores and be tucked away in the vault of some foreign collector.'

Henry suddenly looked rather pale.

'I'm sorry, that's probably not what you wanted to hear.'

'It's alright. I've lived long enough to know that if the high rollers of this world want something badly enough, they'll stop at nothing to get it. The way things are going, institutions like the Ashmolean will count themselves fortunate to have even temporary custodianship of such treasures.'

'I wish I could say you were wrong, Mr Faber, but the spread of global wealth and corruption has brought great power to those with neither the grace nor intelligence to wield it responsibly. In some countries, the criminal classes have grown more affluent and influential than the governments meant to be running them. But look, as long as people like me are on their tail, there's always a chance we can recover what they've taken.'

'You must have made some progress by now, surely,' said Alice.

'Well,' – Cordell took a gulp of his tea – 'we know at least two men were involved, but they were wearing masks, so we don't have a description of them.'

'What about the security guard, ...' Alice continued, '... didn't he get a look at the man who attacked him?'

'Poor lad,' said Henry, shaking his head. 'He was pretty badly beaten up by those thugs.'

'I'm afraid all he could tell us was that the man was fairly tall, athletic build and had a strong London accent. Not much to go on, really.'

But Alice wasn't letting Cordell off the hook, that easily. 'I assume they had a getaway car – is there any trace of that?'

'Ah, now there we have had some luck. One of the residents near the museum said they saw a black Audi parked outside their house at the time of the break-in. Fortunately, they had the good sense to take the registration, and it turns out it was stolen from an address in Swindon, two weeks ago. We're trying to trace it, but my guess is it was dumped soon after the robbery.'

'Mmm ... it's a start, I suppose.' retorted Alice, looking distinctly unimpressed.

'I'm sure he's doing all he can, Sister,' said Henry, getting up to show him out.

'Actually, I do have a few more questions,' said Cordell. 'I wanted to talk to you about what happened at St Mary's, yesterday.'

'Ah, now I can save you some time, there, Chief Inspector,' said Henry, confidently. 'I've already given my statement of events to the Oxford police.'

'I know, I've read it. There's just one or two points I'm not quite clear on.'

'Your cup's empty, I'll make some more tea,' said Alice, prompting a stare from Henry.

Cordell raised his hand in thanks. 'I understand from Julian Mountfield, you haven't been into the museum this week, is that correct?'

'No, I've been feeling a little off-colour, recently; what with the break-in and everything,' said Henry, shifting nervously in his seat.

'Yes, of course. So, if we could just go back to the events of yesterday. What were you doing in the centre of Oxford, exactly?'

'Yes, okay, ... I remember I had a splitting headache, so I decided to go for a walk to see if I could clear it.'

'And when did you first become aware of this man following you?'

'Well, I was passing by St Mary's and thought I'd go in and have a sit down to rest my legs – it's quite a walk from here to the centre of town. Anyway, the next thing I know, this man grabs me by the arm, sticks a gun in my ribs and forces me to go up the tower with him.'

'And you'd never met or seen him, before yesterday?'

Henry shook his head. 'No, never.'

Cordell looked puzzled. 'Why do you think he went to such extraordinary lengths to get you up to the viewing gallery?'

'Chief Inspector, I have absolutely no idea.'

'Did he say anything?'

'No, not a word.'

'And all the time you were with him, he gave no clue as to why he was abducting you?'

'No, nothing. I didn't know where we were going until he took me over to the gift shop and bought two tickets to the tower. If it hadn't been for that lovely Japanese couple, I dread to think what would have happened. Of course, then the police arrived, and I guess he saw them and just panicked.'

'You don't think it might have had something to do with the break-in at the museum?'

'Oh, I doubt it. What could he possibly want with me in that respect?'

'I don't know, Mr Faber, you tell me.'

Henry began to fidget. 'No, no, I'm sure it was simply a case of him wanting to steal my wallet, or something of that nature.'

'Steal your wallet? Surely he could have done that in the church, instead of dragging you all the way up the tower.'

'You're probably right. I must confess, it has me stumped. As I'm sure you can appreciate, Chief Inspector, I'm just relieved to come out of this relatively unscathed,' he said, touching the plaster on his cheek, where Tyburn had pistol-whipped him.

'Yes, of course. Come to think of it, I didn't see any police outside when I arrived. Have Thames Valley offered to have somebody keep an eye on the house for you?'

'They did, but I declined. I'm sure it was an opportunistic crime.'

'Opportunistic enough to want to kill you.'

'No, it wouldn't have come to that, I'm sure.'

'If I recall, the note picked up by the Japanese couple said, "Help me, he has a gun". Surely you must have thought your life was in danger?'

'Well, ... come to think of it, I suppose I was beginning to wonder about his intentions.'

'His intentions? ... that's one way of putting it. Look, I've taken up enough of your time, Mr Faber. I'll be in contact if we make any progress on the painting.'

Henry escorted Cordell to the hallway.

'What about your tea?' said Alice, walking out of the kitchen with a freshly brewed pot.

'No thank you, Ms Faber, I have to get back to the station.'

As Cordell opened the front door, he stopped and turned around.

'There was one more thing, Mr Faber. Do you happen to know a young woman by the name of Emily Bradshaw?'

'No, not that I recall,' said Henry, staring at the DCI's lapel.

'Really? ... well, it seems she knows you. When I interviewed her on the night of the break-in, she told me she'd spoken to you in the museum, that afternoon.'

'I'm sorry, it doesn't ring any bells. I guess my head's still a little befuddled, what with everything that's been going on.'

'Alright, no matter. I'll be in touch,' said Cordell, and walked off down the gravel path with a somewhat cynical look on his face. He'd conducted hundreds of interviews in his time, and he had to profess that, on the scale of one-to-ten in terms of credible responses, Henry Faber's was complete and utter bullshit.

*

After Cordell had gone, Henry went back into the lounge to clear up the tea things.

'Why did you lie about knowing that girl?' said Alice, glaring from the doorway.

'It's nothing for you to worry about, Sister. Come on, you've got to finish planting those tulips, and I have some leaves to sweep up from last night's gales.'

'Don't patronise me. I can always tell when you're being economical with the truth. Perhaps we should get the police to keep an eye on the place. I didn't sleep at all last night.'

Henry gently took Alice's arm. 'Alright my dear, if you're worried, I'll give them a call later.'

After helping her tidy up in the kitchen, Henry put on his wax jacket and walked into the back garden. The sky looked cold and grey, and a light drizzle had started to fall. He held his rake upright like a trident, surveying the expanse of grass in front of him. But try as he might, he couldn't stop reflecting on his terrifying encounter at the top of the church tower. Up to now, he'd put a brave face on it, but Tyburn's actions were beginning to contaminate his spirit, just like the moss that had begun to ravage his beloved lawn. Everything seemed to be closing in on him, draining his willpower. Now, even the police were asking awkward questions. He'd never admit it, but Alice was right to be worried. Perhaps it was time to confront Emily and tell her exactly what was going on – before it was too late.

Tomorrow, he'd go back to work at the Ashmolean. Somehow, he felt safer there – in familiar surroundings. He could think more clearly and make preparations. And, most importantly, keep a close eye on the enemy within.

Chapter Thirty-Four

Wickwar, near Bristol

11 November 1999

It had just gone 8.00 am in the Old Cider House when there was a knock at the front door.

'Can you get that, Tom? I'm not decent,' shouted Emily from the spare bedroom.

The atmosphere in the cottage was still a little frosty, following the argument a couple of nights ago. Not helped by Emily having spent lunch with "him" at some "cosy little French bistro" that she "couldn't stop raving about". Needless to say, Tom was less than impressed by the attentions of Julian Mountfield, innocent or otherwise. Even Bill could sense something was wrong and was keeping a low profile under the spare bed until the storm had blown over.

'Tom, did you hear me?'

Then came another knock – more emphatic this time.

Tom necked the lukewarm remnants of his coffee and headed for the front door. Never the most affable of people, first thing in the morning, he could just about say 'hi' to the postie and feign a smile, if required. 'Don't you worry about it ... I'll get it,' he said, grabbing his coat and laptop on the way.

He opened the front door to be greeted by a smartly dressed man wearing a sports jacket and white shirt, unbuttoned at the neck.

'You must be, Tom.'

'Correct. And you are?' he said, struggling to put on his coat.

'I'm Doctor Julian Mountfield; no doubt Emily has mentioned me.'

'Err ... no, I don't think so.'

'Oh, ... well, I'm a curator at the Ashmolean Museum. Is she here? I wondered if I might have a quick word.'

Tom stepped aside, pointing the way into the living room. At that moment, the postman arrived and handed Tom a white envelope.

'Well, look at that, an Oxford postmark. It's not from you, is it?' said Tom, sarcastically. 'She won't be long, and I'm running late, so—'

'Yes, of course, Tom ... don't let me hold you up.'

Tom stared at him, smarting at the over-familiar use of his first name by someone he'd only just met. It shouldn't have bothered him, and if it had been anyone else saying it, it probably wouldn't; but it wasn't, and it did.

'Sure, make yourself at home, why don't you,' he said.

Julian reached out his hand. 'Would you like me to give her that?'

Tom ignored him, leaning the envelope against a picture frame on top of the piano. Then, without so much as a shout of goodbye to Emily, he marched out the front door, slamming it behind him.

*

Moments later, Emily walked down the stairs. 'Who was it?'

'Good morning.'

She span round. 'Julian, what are you doing here?'

'Hi. Sorry to drop in unannounced, but I'm just on my way to the Birmingham Art Gallery and wondered if you'd like to tag along?'

'Wickwar is hardly on the way from Oxford to Birmingham.'

'Actually, I live near Cirencester, so it's not that much of a detour. Are you free today?'

'Let me think. I've got to feed the cat, make breakfast and give Rosa a call to tell her how we got on in Oxford yesterday – that's it. That's my day.'

'Okay, that's settled then,' said Julian.

'And what is it you're taking me to see, exactly? Have you found another sun mark?'

'Well, they do have a wonderful Pre-Raphaelite collection; and I've a sneaking suspicion we might just find one or two more.'

Emily gave him a sceptical look. 'We can't just waltz in there and start ripping pictures off the walls. Believe me, it doesn't go down too well.'

'No, of course not. I've arranged for us to meet the assistant curator, Robert Green – he's a friend of mine, and has kindly agreed to shut the gallery for an hour while we conduct our search.'

'Does he know what we're looking for?'

'Not exactly. But knowing Robert, he'll be most intrigued by it all.'

'Okay, I'll make us some coffee, and we can get going.'

Then she noticed the white envelope resting on top of the piano. 'Is this what I think it is?'

'The postman handed it to Tom as he was on his way out,' said Julian.

Emily studied the now familiar italic type. It was marked

Private and confidential, F.A.O. Miss Emily Bradshaw

and had an Oxford postmark, dated 10 November 1999.

Julian peered over her shoulder. 'Looks familiar.'

'It does, doesn't it,' she said, tearing it open to reveal another cryptic note.

> *EMILY,*
>
> *BEWITCHING DEVILS WILL SEEK TO TEMPT YOU INTO THE DARKNESS. LISTEN TO YOUR HEART AND STICK TO THE PATH.*
>
> *#1. Darkness – blessed are they that harbour the beacon of hope, when all around them is desolation and despair.*
>
> *#6. Folly of Man – Learned we may be with another man's learning, only wise can we become with wisdom of our own.*
>
> *THE SHEPHERD*

'Ah, … two clues this time,' she said.

Julian nodded.

'What?' said Emily, noting the look on his face. 'Do you know these paintings?'

He shrugged, then broke into a knowing smile. 'Well, … let me put it this way, I think we're heading to the right place.'

Chapter Thirty-Five

Birmingham Museum and Art Gallery

11 November 1999

'We're a little early,' said Julian, as he and Emily climbed the grey marble steps leading to the first-floor atrium. Emily had never been to the BMAG and stopped to admire Joseph Southall's vibrant fresco of Corporation Street at the top of the staircase, while Julian announced their arrival at the reception desk.

'Robert's running a little late,' said the receptionist. 'He sends his apologies and says he'll meet you in Gallery Eighteen in half an hour.'

'That's fine. We wanted to have a look round, anyway,' said Julian.

'Do you know the way, sir?'

'Yes, yes, I'm no stranger to this place,' he said, and thanked the receptionist, before escorting Emily in the direction of the Round Room.

Having taken in Jacob Epstein's imposing statue of the archangel Lucifer, they made their way to the Feeney Picture Galleries, housing two important collections entitled Birmingham School of Art and The Pre-Raphaelites. As they entered the black marble doorway of Gallery 18, Emily stood and surveyed the impressive array of pictures on the blue-painted walls.

'So, which ones are we interested in?'

'You mean to say, you're not even going to try and work it out for yourself?' replied Julian, with a mischievous grin.

Emily looked at him. 'Yes, of course, ... I can do that.'

She took out the Shepherd's note from earlier that morning and began a visual sweep of the room, occasionally stopping to check the two clues. Having scrutinised the paintings in the first section, she wandered over to where Julian was admiring a nice Burne-Jones.

'I don't think it's any of these,' she said, hesitantly.

'Oh, you don't? Well, in that case, you'd better try the next room.'

Emily studied his expression to see if she'd missed something, then made her way into the adjoining section, leaving Julian to his own devices.

Perhaps a change of approach was called for. She stood in the centre of the room and, turning clockwise, quickly scanned each painting for its suitability. Just as she thought she was about to strike out once more, she stopped and gazed at a large religious picture by the doorway. She couldn't quite put her finger on it, but there was something about it that drew her in. She looked at the second clue.

> #6. Folly of Man – Learned we may be with another
> man's learning, only wise can we become with wisdom
> of our own.

She walked over to have a closer look. It was a large rectangular painting depicting Christ as a boy, standing in front of a large gathering of Jewish elders in Herod's Temple. Some were giving Jesus particularly disparaging looks, as if to say, *how can one so young possibly comprehend the importance and subtlety of holy doctrine, let alone debate such issues with temple priests, so advanced in their wisdom and experience?*

That was precisely the point of the clue. It was saying, according to the artist, even at that tender age of eleven or twelve, Jesus was not only capable of acquiring vast amounts of knowledge, but when it came to a deeper understanding – discerning the real message spoken by God – he possessed the innate ability to formulate his own doctrine, his own perceived wisdom for humankind. She'd read somewhere that, although the event in the Temple was recorded as occurring on Jesus's twelfth birthday – when Emperor Caesar Augustus had instituted a national census – in fact, it related to his designated twelfth year of birth into the Essene Community, when he was twenty-three or twenty-four years of age. All of which made his act of staying to debate his father's business with the Temple elders, much more likely. But, like so many things that captivated Emily's imagination, that was very much a fringe theory.

Anyway, this is it, she thought, standing back to admire her chosen painting – *The Finding of the Saviour in the Temple*, by William Holman Hunt. Feeling rather pleased with herself, she began her search for the next one. The Shepherd's clue read:

> #1. Darkness – blessed are they that harbour the
> beacon of hope, when all around them is desolation
> and despair.

Using her tried-and-tested method, she went back to the centre of the room and resumed her sweep of the walls. A few yards from Hunt's painting was a beautifully worked portrait of two young girls sat by a stream; the colours of which were so captivating, so vibrant, the picture seemed to emanate a kind of benevolent glow from the heart of the canvas. She wandered over and read the small information card, next to it.

John Everett Millais (1829–1896)

The Blind Girl, 1854–6

Oil on canvas

> Millais began by painting the landscape for *The Blind Girl* on a visit to Winchelsea in Sussex in 1854. The figures were then added in Perth, where he painted Matilda Proudfoot, a replacement for Effie Ruskin (later to become Millais's wife), who was the original model for the blind girl, and Isabella Nicol as her sister. The dazzling, sun-drenched cornfield forms an unforgettable backdrop to the light and colour denied to the main figure. The painting was seen by a number of contemporaries as an avant-garde treatment of a 'pathetic' or religious subject. Presented by the Rt. Hon. William Kenrick 1892.

Emily looked closely at the two figures and noticed that the girl with red hair had a small note pinned to her shawl – it said, *Pity the blind.* Judging by the state of their clothing, she and her sister were beggars, and she would play the battered concertina in her lap for pennies. Millais had painted the sky overhead with dark, angry clouds, signifying the deluge of misfortune that had befallen the two poor young souls. And yet, the beautiful double rainbow in the distance seemed to indicate a glimmer of hope – that perhaps someone, somewhere was looking out for them. It was a touching depiction of adversity, charity and optimism, and Emily knew that it fitted the Shepherd's clue, perfectly.

'Wonderful, isn't it?' said a voice next to her.

'I can't believe I've never seen it before. This has to be one of them, don't you think?'

'One of what?'

Emily looked round. 'Chief Inspector Cordell, what are you doing here?'

'A little bird told me Julian Mountfield was coming here today, so I thought, why not take the chance to get out of Oxford. What about you, Miss Bradshaw?'

'Actually, Julian called round and asked if I'd like to come and see the Pre-Raphaelite collection, so, here I am.'

As if summoned by the mention of his name, Julian appeared from the next room.

'Chief Inspector, you're a long way from Oxford,' he said, running his fingers through his hair.

'Yes. As are you,' replied Cordell.

'Stunning, isn't it?' said Julian, turning towards *The Blind Girl.* 'Apparently the critics in the Royal Academy slated Millais's use of crude brushstrokes in the meadow grass. Personally, I think it shows the genius of the man, encouraging the viewer's eye to focus on the important subject – the two beggar girls.'

Cordell nodded. 'Is this what you came to see?'

Julian looked at Emily. 'Yes, amongst other things.'

As if on cue, two museum attendants appeared and began quietly ushering the handful of other visitors out of the gallery.

'I'm very sorry, but we need to close for some essential maintenance,' said one. 'We'll be open again after lunch.'

The second positioned two large screens across the open doorway to shield the room and its occupants from prying eyes.

'What's going on? Surely they're not closing already?' said Cordell.

'Chief Inspector, perhaps we should go downstairs and talk there,' said Julian.

'No, it's alright, I'd like him to stay,' said Emily.

Cordell looked at them, somewhat confused.

'Ah, there they are,' came a voice from the main doorway. Robert Green, the assistant curator, parted the two screens and made his way over to where the others were standing.

'I'll explain later,' said Emily, touching Cordell's arm.

'Robert, great to see you,' said Julian, shaking his hand.

'I see Matilda and her sister are attracting a fair bit of attention,' said Green.

'And rightly so. Robert, may I introduce Miss Emily Bradshaw, a colleague of mine?'

Emily shook Green's hand, wondering quite how and when she'd been promoted to the role of Julian's "colleague".

'And this is Detective Chief Inspector Cordell from Scotland Yard.'

Green frowned. 'Right. Is there a problem?'

'No, no – he'll just be observing, if that's alright with you?'

'Yes, of course – the more the merrier.' Green checked his watch. 'Now, one point of order. As it's Armistice Day, we'll shortly be observing a few moments' silence at eleven o'clock. If that's okay with everyone?'

They all nodded.

With a humble smile, Green turned to Millais's painting. 'Now, who would have thought that a couple of innocent young girls, such as this, could have cost two men their lives?'

'Really, how so?' said Emily.

'I think I've heard this story,' said Cordell. 'Didn't someone try to steal it, many years ago?'

Green nodded. 'Quite correct, Chief Inspector. Fortunately, the perpetrators were caught red-handed. But not before two of them were shot and killed trying to get away.'

'Someone was obviously watching over them that day.'

They all turned to look at Emily.

'The two girls, I mean.'

'Yes, I suppose so,' said Green. 'Now, if you'd just tell me which paintings you want to look at, I'll get the porters to fetch them off the wall.'

Emily stepped forward. 'Okay. I'm sure Julian will correct me, but it's obviously this one – *The Blind Girl*, and then Holman Hunt's *The Finding of the Saviour in the Temple*. Right?'

'Fine by me,' said Julian.

'You have good taste, Miss Bradshaw,' said Green. 'Alright, give us a few minutes and we'll get underway.'

Emily and Julian watched as the porters got to work removing the paintings from the gallery walls.

Cordell wandered over to where Julian was standing. 'Could I have a quick word, Doctor Mountfield?' he said.

'Err, yes, of course,' said Julian.

Emily glanced over as the two men walked to the far side of the room. Perhaps they've found the Picasso, she thought, and returned her gaze to the two porters.

*

'Do you have some news about the robbery, Chief Inspector?' said Julian, hopefully.

'Not exactly. I just wanted to ask you about the skylight in the gallery at the Ashmolean.'

'Okay, what about it?'

'It seems that the pane removed by the burglars wasn't made of the standard security glass.'

Looking puzzled, Julian folded his arms across his chest. 'I'm sorry, you've lost me.'

'The thieves cut through it with a glass cutter.'

Just at that moment, Robert Green held up his hand. 'Everyone, it's eleven o'clock, so could I ask that we take a few moments to pay our respects to those who gave their lives or were wounded in service to this country's freedom – thank you.'

A solemn hush fell over the gallery. Heads bowed and eyes closed as the group took time to honour and remember.

Julian Mountfield, however, was somewhat distracted. Much as he wanted to stare at the floor and ponder reflective thoughts of red poppy fields and long-lost relatives, he found himself wondering where on earth Cordell was going with all these questions about the damned skylight. He glanced over at Emily as she stood quietly, with her head bowed and her hands clasped in front of her – she was a picture of under-stated beauty, as far as he was concerned. And, much as he knew he had to keep their relationship strictly professional, she was beginning to get under his skin, in the nicest possible way. If he didn't keep his wits about him, this was all going to get very complicated, very quickly. And DCI Cordell sticking his oar in, certainly wasn't helping matters. With his emotions working overtime, he finally closed his eyes, swallowed hard and succumbed to the solemnity of the moment.

'Thank you, everyone,' said Green, and wandered back over to the two porters, who had been respectfully standing next to *The Blind Girl* for the last two minutes.

'Sorry, where was I?' said Cordell.

'You were asking about the skylight,' Julian replied.

'Ah yes. I got the boys at the lab to take a look at it, and it appears the skylight was made of a standard six-millimetre pane with a coating on the outside to make it look like reinforced safety glass.'

'I – I can't believe it,' said Julian, pushing his glasses up the bridge of his nose.

'How long have those skylights been in place?' said Cordell.

'I'd need to check with our Building Services Department, but from memory, they were replaced a couple of years ago. Surely, you're not saying they were deliberately installed to allow for a break-in?'

Cordell shrugged. 'I'm just telling you what we know. But it does appear that someone has gone to great lengths to make it look like the skylight was secure, when in fact, it was anything but.'

'Perhaps the supplier was out to save money at our expense.'

'Maybe. Or perhaps they were laying the groundwork for something more lucrative. Can you remember the name of the contractors who did the work for you?'

Julian scratched his head. 'No, not off the top of my head.'

'Then, could I ask you to check when you get back to the museum. I'm sorry to have to come and hassle you when you're obviously very busy, but this is pretty important, as I'm sure you can appreciate.'

'No, that's fine. I'll get my secretary to email you the details in the morning. Ah, it looks like they're ready for us.' And with that, Julian strolled over to where the others had gathered.

*

Emily looked at him and smiled. 'Everything okay?'

'Absolutely, couldn't be better,' said Julian, running his fingers through his hair.

The two porters had carefully stood each of the paintings on the side of a felt-lined carrier trolley, ready for inspection.

'There we are,' said Green, rubbing his hands together. 'Two rather delightful Pre-Raphaelite paintings for your delectation. Now, what are we looking for, exactly?'

'Yes, what are you looking for?' said Cordell, joining the group.

'With luck, you'll find out soon enough,' said Julian, ushering Emily forward.

She knelt down and scanned the back of Hunt's *Saviour*, just as she'd done with the other two paintings in Drapers' Hall and Keble College.

'The frame's a little black in places,' she said, resisting the urge to lick her finger and give it a good rub.

Green nodded. 'Yes, the picture caught fire in Ernest Gambart's German Gallery in eighteen sixty-one. Luckily, the damage wasn't too serious and Hunt managed to repair it. I suppose we're fortunate to have it here it all.'

But Emily wasn't listening, concentrating all her efforts on finding the sun mark – her hazel brown eyes darting up and down the picture frame, looking for any tiny nick or scrape that could be a candidate. Then she spotted it.

'There,' she said, pointing at the small round O surrounded by seven flaring Ws.

Cordell leaned forward, straining to see what she'd found. 'What is it?'

'It's a sun mark,' she said, proudly.

'May I see it?' said Green, who had been patiently waiting to one side. He took out a small magnifying glass from his pocket and crouched down to inspect the tiny impression stamped into the wood.

'Good God, I've never seen that before. And, if I'm not mistaken, ... it has the number six beneath it.'

'Let's have a look at *The Blind Girl*, shall we?' said Emily.

Green nodded to the two porters, who carefully turned the trolley round to reveal the back of Millais's painting to the inspection committee.

Now he knew what to look for, Green took great delight in joining the search. But as the minutes ticked by, it soon became apparent that Matilda and Isabella weren't ready to give up their secret, quite so easily.

'I can't see it,' Green said, puffing out his cheeks in exasperation. 'Are you sure this is the right painting?'

'Positive,' said Julian. 'Emily, you don't think it could be—?'

'Exactly what I was thinking,' she said, with a resigned nod. 'Robert, do you have a knife?'

'Oh, no. I'm afraid I couldn't possibly let you do that.'

'No, you don't understand,' said Emily. 'It might be hidden underneath that old Christie's label.'

Cordell stepped forward and presented Emily with a Swiss army knife from his pocket. 'You know what they say, a copper should always be prepared.'

'I thought that was the scouts,' said Green, looking far from happy.

'Actually, we did find one under a label on another painting. So, if we're really careful, I'm sure it'll be worth it,' said Emily, flashing her eyes at the assistant curator.

'Alright,' he said begrudgingly. 'But if anyone's going to attack the back of this incredibly important artwork with a pocket knife, it's going to be me.'

She smiled and gave him the knife, like an army nurse handing a scalpel to a field surgeon.

Green rolled up his shirt sleeves, blinked a few times to clear his vision, and ever so slowly slid the edge of the knife along the top right-hand corner of the label – searching for the tiniest gap between paper and wood. The others looked on, transfixed, as the gleaming steel blade slid millimetre by millimetre beneath the thin brown paper, piercing the micro-thin layer of dried glue. The tension in the air was palpable as label and frame slowly relinquished their one-hundred-and-thirteen year bond, until finally, only one small corner remained attached. Being as gentle as he could, Green lifted the label to reveal a small square of lightened wood. And there it was – a tiny sun-shaped imprint with the number one stamped underneath.

'Well, I'm blowed,' said Green, relieved to have completed the delicate operation without killing the patient.

'What a place to put a label,' said Cordell.

'Robert, would you mind if I took a few pictures?' said Emily, fishing a camera out of her bag.

'Be my guest,' said Green, wiping the sweat from his brow. 'I have to ask – do you have any idea what these marks signify?'

'It's difficult to say,' said Julian, stepping forward to inspect it. 'But they certainly suggest some sort of connection between the paintings.'

'I think there was a reason the Pre-Raphaelite Brotherhood put them there,' said Emily, snapping away with her camera. 'They were into their codes and symbols, weren't they? Perhaps they were trying to tell us something.'

Julian frowned. 'We don't know that for sure, Emily. We're not even certain it was the Brotherhood who put them there in the first place. It could have been one of the art dealers, for instance.'

'Gambart, perhaps?' said Green, closing the pocket knife and handing it back to the DCI.

'Well, thank you for letting me in on your discovery,' said Cordell, '... whatever it is. But I have to be getting back to Oxford.' And with that he walked over to the marble doorway and slipped between the two partitions blocking the gallery entrance.

'Oh, by the way, ...'

Julian looked up to see Cordell peering between the screens.

'... don't forget to send me those details about the skylight, will you?'

Julian smiled and gave him a confirmatory wave.

'What was all that about?' said Emily.

'Oh, just something about the break-in. I'm sure it's nothing.'

Emily couldn't help but notice the anxious look on his face, before she returned to photographing the back of the paintings.

After thanking the assistant curator for all his help, and having promised to keep him updated on their research into the sun marks, Emily and Julian left the museum and made their way back to Chamberlain Square, now busy with lunchtime crowds. As they passed by the statue of Queen Victoria, Emily stopped and grabbed Julian's arm.

'Listen, 'I've just realised something.'

He turned to look at her.

'I've been taking up far too much of your time with all this sun mark business. You've helped me find four, and if there are more to discover, then I'm sure the Shepherd will give me all the clues

I need. So I've made up by mind – from now on, I'm going to do this alone.'

'What? No, don't be silly.'

'Julian, you've been very kind, arranging tours of Drapers' Hall and Keble College, and this place. I think it's time I let you go back to your day job, don't you?'

'Well ... there is a lot going on at the Ashmolean. And, to be honest, I am quite concerned about Henry. Apparently, a couple of days ago, he was attacked in the centre of Oxford.'

Emily put her hand to her mouth. 'Oh my God, is he alright?'

'I think so. I spoke to his sister last night and she said he was in good spirits.'

'Poor fella. Did they catch the attacker?'

'No, I'm afraid he's still on the loose. But Henry did manage to give the police a good description.'

Emily shook her head. 'First, the museum break-in, then this. Do you know, when I first came across Henry at the auction, I really didn't like him. But now, I'm starting to feel quite sorry for the guy.'

Julian looked her in the eye. 'I've known Henry a long time and I can tell you for a fact, there's not a nasty bone in that man's body. I know it's going to happen at some point, but when he does finally decide to retire, I'll be lost without him.'

'Yes, I'm sure you will. Look, I was wondering, ... do you think he'd mind if I paid him a visit, just to ask him what he knows about the sun marks?'

Julian looked at her, pensively. 'Tell you what, give it a few days, then I'll call him and set something up. How does that sound?'

'Thank you. I appreciate that.'

They walked back to the car in silence, Emily's mind racing at the thought of undiscovered sun marks and a mountain of questions for Henry Faber.

*

Back in Wickwar, Julian watched Emily get out of the car and open the front door to the Old Cider House – it's windows glowing warmly in the failing light. He gave her a friendly wave and pulled out onto the deserted high street. With his head a maelstrom of emotions, his parting smile began to fade. Emily was right – much as it pained him, the apron strings would have to be cut. From now on, she'd have to make the rest of the journey, alone.

As he headed back home through the long and winding roads of the Cotswolds, he felt an acrid taste rising in his throat. For deep inside the normally unflappable Julian Mountfield, someone had pressed the panic button – and that someone was DCI Cordell.

Chapter Thirty-Six

Woodbine Villa, St John's Wood, London
30 September 1853

'Frederick Stephens, what sort o' place is this to bring a young lady?' chuckled Annie, as she knocked on the door of the ground-floor apartment – knowing full well, she was about as far from being a lady as it was possible to get.

The question to her gentleman chaperone, however, was a valid one. Woodbine Villa had the dubious reputation of being one of North London's finest courtesan houses; a place where wealthy Victorian gentlemen would keep their mistresses hidden away from their family residences on the other side of Hyde Park. But on this occasion, the meeting was one of artistic endeavour, not adultery. William Holman Hunt opened the door with great gusto, as he did with most things in life.

'Miss Miller, please come in,' he said, ignoring Fred completely, and leading Annie into the furnished parlour. Fred followed on in silence, well used to being neglected by his artist friends when alluring female company was present.

'What a lovely apartment,' she said, admiring the gaudy decor and brand-new Rococo-style furniture. Unused to such refinements, she flounced around the room and giggled, playfully. 'I do 'ope your intentions are 'onourable, Mr 'unt? If I didn't know you better, I'd say you brought me 'ere to take advantage of me.'

Fred jumped in. 'Annie, please, I'm sure William wouldn't dream of—'

'It's alright, Fred. I'm sure Miss Miller well recalls the purpose of her coming here today. Now, Annie, if you'd kindly go into the other room, you'll see I've laid out some clothes and accessories for you to wear. Hurry along now, I'd like to get started while the light is still good.'

Annie winked at Fred and did as she was told.

'I see you've been busy adding some finishing touches to the place,' said Fred, searching the room for clues on Hunt's latest work.

'I've spent all morning getting things just the way I want them, so please, sit down over there, there's a good fellow.'

The Awakening Conscience was to be a counterpart to Hunt's other great work of spiritual enlightenment, *The Light of the World*, depicting the pursuit of social realism in a touching portrayal of prostitution and the fallen woman – quite a departure for this sensitive and spiritual young artist, despite his bullish nature. In a rare snapshot of Victorian life that, although hotly debated, was seldom represented in such graphic terms, Hunt's latest painting would portray a real human story: the moment of self-awakening for a young woman, trapped in a world of fantasy and deceit – one from which escape seemed all but impossible. As was typical of the Brothers' early work, the viewer would be confronted with a subtle blend of authenticity and symbolism, showing how the still small voice could reach out and speak to the human soul, whilst deeply entangled in the turmoil of life.

'William – is that a dead bird on the carpet?' said Fred, as he was making himself comfortable.

'Yes, yes. I'll explain later,' Hunt replied, getting more and more agitated as he waited for his model. 'Don't just sit there, Fred, give me a hand with these curtains.'

A warm breeze blew through the French window, rustling the sheet music on the upright piano; and there in the doorway stood Annie, wearing a white petticoat and paisley shawl, with a large pink bow tied round her neck.

Both men stopped what they were doing, and found themselves secretly contemplating the very act of impropriety Hunt wished to condemn in his picture.

'Is this what you 'ad in mind – me posin' as a kept woman?' said Annie, with her hands on her hips.

'Perfect,' said Hunt. 'Just one final touch.' He reached into his pocket and took out three bejewelled gold rings which he placed on the fingers of her left hand, all except for her ring finger – making it clear that her lot in life was solely that of a gentleman's mistress.

Annie looked at the rings, then at Hunt. 'And there's me thinkin' you were about to make an 'onest woman of me.'

'Now, if you would come and stand over here, by the piano,' said Hunt, quickly changing the subject.

In truth, he was completely smitten with Annie. He'd first laid eyes on her, some years before, when she was working as a skivvy in the Cross Keys, Chelsea. Then only fifteen, she had a vibrant, bubbly character and knew how to laugh and joke with men. A creature of the slums, she lived in poverty with her sister at their uncle's house, behind the pub. But Hunt saw past the unwashed hair of a vermin-covered wretch, whose mouth was as coarse as the men she served; recognising, instead, the essence of a conventional beauty, embodied in her perfect bone structure, elegant aquiline nose and thick blonde hair, the combination of which was too much to resist for a knight-errant of the PRB. The fact that she was from an impoverished background made her an ideal candidate for redemption – a girl, who, without the right support and guidance, could easily end up on the streets.

Meeting at his studio for preliminary sketches, Annie had been modelling as his *fallen woman* for two weeks, when Hunt found himself deliberating a moral dilemma of his own. How could he reconcile painting a picture about the abuse and subjugation of young women, when he was effectively propagating the same sort of relationship with her, albeit as a sitter? The hypocrisy was all too apparent. The proper and obvious solution was marriage, but that was out of the question – for the moment anyway. Many of the girls who sat for the Pre-Raphaelite Brothers made advances towards the three eligible bachelors, seeing an easy path to marriage, respectability and most important of all, security. Like Millais and Rossetti, Hunt had been careful not to get himself trapped in an unwanted arrangement, preferring instead to wait for the right girl to come along. But the very idea of turning Annie into a respectable young lady, fit for Victorian society, was hard to resist.

'Imagine that your lover is sat playing the piano, with you on his lap,' said Hunt. 'Fred, come here; you can be the philanderer.'

Fred gave him a stern look. 'William, I don't think that would be at all appropriate.'

'Rubbish. Come on, I haven't got all day.'

Fred reluctantly took up his position at the piano, readying himself to act out playing Hunt's chosen sheet music, whilst pretending to sing along at the top of his voice.

As Annie went over to join him in the pose, she bent down to pick up a cream-coloured glove on the floor.

'No, leave it,' said Hunt, sharply.

Annie dropped it, somewhat taken aback.

'It's symbolic, and must be placed ... just so.'

'And why, pray, is that?' asked Fred, still far from happy about playing the debaucher.

'You see the shaft of sunlight on the carpet, there? I placed the glove at the girl's feet to represent the psychological barrier between her and her freedom. Redemption is possible, but only if she can take the final step from darkness into light – breaking free from the mastery that her lover holds over her.'

'You 'ave thought this through, 'ain't you?' said Annie, and parked herself firmly on Fred's lap, wiggling her bottom back and forth in the process.

'Annie, I want you to imagine that, on hearing the words of the song Fred is playing, and seeing the sunlit leaves through the open window, you jump up from his lap and clasp your hands together in a moment of epiphany.'

'Epi ... what?' said Annie.

'An awakening. You realise you're trapped in this clandestine relationship and, if you don't escape soon, your destiny is sure to be one of rejection, shame and most likely, the workhouse.'

She turned round and scowled at Fred, playfully. But there was a hint of comprehension in her eyes – that Hunt could easily be describing a girl like her, were she to let opportunities like this pass her by.

Hunt pressed the point still further. 'She thinks back to when she was a little girl, playing outside her childhood home, when she realises, by stark comparison, what a dark and shameful existence she now leads. The lover, meanwhile, will share none of the evils of his wrongdoing, and sings on blissfully; serving only to intensify her desire to break free from the gilded cage in which she finds herself.'

His articulation complete, Hunt made a few adjustments to Annie's shawl, then went over to the canvas to capture his muse. She played the part beautifully – a vision of seduction, with her wavy blonde hair cascading loosely down her back, and a look that portrayed a young woman close to tears as she faced the bleakness of her future.

Fred, realising he was the supporting actor in this scene, continued his casual observations of the room. A vase of Convolvulus, symbolising deceit, had been placed on top of the piano. On the wall above it hung an engraving called *Cross Purposes*, emphasising the growing polarity between the two lovers. Fred's eye returned to the dead bird, its wings outspread on the carpet, as if Hunt had designs to later paint in a cat sat beneath the table, playing with its catch – like the adulterer toying with his mistress.

He returned to the piano he was supposedly playing and, reading the sheet music in front of him, began to silently recite the words of Thomas Moore's *Oft, in the Stilly Night*.

> Oft, in the stilly night,
> Ere slumber's chain has bound me,
> Fond memory brings the light
> Of other days around me;
> The smiles, the tears
> Of boyhood's years,
> The words of love then spoken;
> The eyes that shone,
> Now dimm'd and gone,
> The cheerful hearts now broken!

After an hour of crouching in the same position, Annie cricked her neck and turned round. 'Your clock's stopped, William. What time is it?'

Hunt sighed and put down his brush and pallet, resigned to the fact that minds were wandering.

'I set it to just before midday, which is said to be the time when one's concentration achieves greatest clarity,' he said, ironically.

Annie stretched her back and walked over to the open window for some air.

'Fred, be a good fellow and ask Mrs Ford to make us a jug of lemonade, will you?' said Hunt, mopping his brow as he watched the sunlight catch Annie's hair.

She turned around and seductively ran her fingers through her long golden locks, her ample bosom swelling the front of her nightgown to bursting point. Hunt tried desperately not to stare, but found himself taking desirous glances at her voluptuous curves. His sister, Sarah, had warned him about Annie's attire being too shocking for the viewing public – for they could not fail to be distracted by the thought of her nakedness, beneath. And here he was, consumed by the self-same desire – his own sexual morals no better, in fact, than those of the rake in the chair.

Annie caught sight of his wandering eye. 'What is it, William? Am I not posin' right for you?' she said, playfully.

'No, no. You were sitting perfectly, my dear.'

He looked somewhat distracted for a moment. 'Annie, I hope you don't think it too forward of me, but I have observed, these past few weeks, a certain ... chemistry between us.'

'Well, now you mention it. I 'ave noticed you doin' quite a lot of ... observin', when my back's turned,' she giggled.

'Yes, well. Since we've been working together, it occurs to me that I should, perhaps, face up to my responsibilities and take certain steps to ensure your future well-being.'

'That's mighty noble of you, William, but I'm quite capable of takin' care of myself, you know.'

'Yes, I'm sure. However, you'll forgive me for saying, but you hardly come from the most privileged of backgrounds.'

'So, ... what of it?'

'Annie, during our previous conversations, you made it known to me that perhaps, one day, you have aspirations to become a lady of good standing.'

'Well, yeah. Wouldn't any gal in my position? Assumin' o' course, I could find the right sort of gentleman. One who wouldn't take advantage of my trustin' nature – if you get my meanin'.'

'In that case, it would give me great pleasure, if you would agree to—'

'William, are you sayin' what I think you're sayin'?'

'Annie, please let me finish. If you would agree to me ... funding your education and personal advancement.'

Annie looked crestfallen and turned towards the French window.

'An education, personal advancement. Why, that's very generous of you, William.'

'Excellent. Now, I shall shortly be travelling to the Middle East, so we should start right away. And, if you work hard and complete your training, as agreed, then perhaps, … we could discuss a date for marriage on my return.'

Annie's dejected look turned to a joyful smile and she threw her arms around Hunt, kissing him on the cheek. It had been her long-held ambition to read and write, but rarely did life present such a golden opportunity for a girl of the slums.

'That would be most acceptable,' she said, beaming from ear to ear.

At that moment there was a clinking of glasses and in walked Fred, closely followed by Mrs Ford carrying a tray of drinks.

'Fred, I have some news,' said Hunt, and proceeded to explain his plans for Annie's advancement.

'This is most exciting, don't you think, Annie?' said Fred.

'It's bloody wonderful, is what it is, make no mistake.'

'My landlady's daughter is a former governess,' said Hunt. 'I shall ask her to begin your tuition in reading and writing at the earliest opportunity.'

Fred picked up the top hat – purposely placed on the table to indicate the rake's fleeting visit – and popped it on his head with a gentle tap.

'William, I've been thinking. An old medical student friend of mine has a wealthy aunt who gives lessons in etiquette and deportment. If you wish, I could enquire if she would be willing to provide some training for Annie?'

Hunt looked at Fred, and Annie looked at Hunt.

'A fine idea, Fred. I'll leave it to you to make the necessary arrangements?'

'I shall write to Mrs Bramah, this very evening.'

Annie clapped her hands and stamped her feet. Her path to a better life was being laid out, right before her eyes.

*

With the light fading, Annie and Fred took a cab back to Chelsea, leaving Hunt to watch the late evening sun disappear over the North London skyline. This had been a good day. Hunt, the artist, had his muse. Not only that, Hunt, the redeemer, was about to prevent a young woman from entering a lifetime of fornication and depravity. What better way in which to illustrate the second of the Brothers' works of enlightenment.

> #2. Desire – A man's lust is his eternal shame, for the
> appetite of a licentious man will never be fulfilled.

Feeling at ease with himself, he went back to the canvas and, with only the soft glow of candlelight to work by, painted the black book with a gutta-percha cover lying on the table. A recent purchase from a bookshop on the King's Road, he knew one day it would be the perfect gift for Annie – *The Origin and Progress of the Art of Writing*.

Now, he could journey to Jerusalem, secure in the knowledge that Annie was in the safe hands of Fred's loyal guardianship. And, if all went to plan, he would return a successful artist and gentleman, with a newly educated fiancée waiting in the wings.

If only Hunt had paid a little more attention to the wallpaper hanging in the boudoir of Woodbine Villa, and its symbolic warning of the need for vigilance. A regret he would later reflect on in a pamphlet to accompany the public showing of *The Awakening Conscience*. It read simply:

> The corn and vine are left unguarded by the
> slumbering cupid watchers and the fruit is left
> to be preyed upon by the thievish birds.

Chapter Thirty-Seven

Julian Mountfield sat staring at the telephone, a glass of single malt cupped in his hands as he pondered something that he should have foreseen, but hadn't. Cordell's discovery of the false skylight had placed him in a real quandary. Should he make the call or not?

No, don't be ridiculous, you can handle this. That's what they're paying you for, isn't it?

On the other hand, just one quick call and he could get it off his chest. Perhaps offset some of the blame, if he was lucky. Racked with indecision, he shifted in his seat. Not even the scream of a fox in the nearby woods could divert his attention from this latest bombshell.

He got up and walked over to the fireplace, resting his arm on the Cotswold-stone chimney breast as he stared into the flames. It had been a long day, but an enjoyable one. In fact, any day spent with Emily Bradshaw was a delight, as far as he was concerned.

Hearing a creak in the floorboards upstairs, he sighed and stared forlornly at the wedding ring on his finger. If he was a single man and ten years younger, Emily Bradshaw wouldn't stand a chance. He gulped down the last of the scotch and picked up the cream-coloured receiver. His wife detested the old GPO-style telephone and the time it took to dial even the simplest of numbers. Julian, however, found it strangely reassuring in this age of BlackBerrys, Apples and other digital fruit. He loved the comforting sound of the mechanical whirr as the dial spun back to the start, then stopped with a click. He dialled the number and waited for it to connect.

'Luke, it's Julian. I hope I'm not disturbing you? ... Good, good. It's just a quick call to let you know about something that happened today. It's probably nothing to worry about, but I thought I'd better just— ... Yes, right, sorry ... Well, it's Cordell, he came to see me at the museum today, in Birmingham. ... No, I wasn't expecting him, he just turned up, unannounced. One minute Emily and I are looking at some paintings; the next thing I know, he's stood there talking to her. ... Well, apparently, they've discovered that the security glass in the skylight was fake and want to know who installed it. ... Yes. ... So, what do I tell them? ... ArtScreen? ... But that'll lead them right to your door. ... Well, I don't know, I could try and stall them, or maybe tell them it was another company that did the installation? ... Okay, if you're sure. I mean, what if—? ... Right, right. ... No, that's fine. ... Emily? She's got four more paintings to uncover. ... Oh, absolutely – hook, line and sinker. Don't get me wrong, she's a smart cookie, but she's completely wrapped up in all this. ... By Christmas? ... Yes, I don't see why not. ... Luke, there is one other thing. She's asked me to set up a meeting with Henry Faber. ... Well, she wants to pick his brains, I guess. ... Oh, she says she's taking up too much of my time, and— ... Yes. ... Of course, of course. ... By the way, did you know that Henry was abducted in Oxford, the other day? ... I'm not sure, but he was pretty shaken up. ... Yes, I know. ... Okay, I'll keep an eye on him. ... Right, right. ... Luke, I was just wondering— ... Luke? ... Hello?— ...'

Julian slowly replaced the receiver and went to pick up his glass, it was empty. He walked over to the drinks' cabinet, slid back the wooden door and reached inside for his favourite bottle of Glen Garioch, usually reserved for special occasions. But not tonight. He unscrewed the top and smelt the open bottle – hints of butterscotch and sweet, white chocolate filled his nostrils. He poured himself a decent measure and took a gulp of the smooth amber liquid, tilting his head back and closing his eyes as the dry notes of barley and apples warmed his throat.

After a few distracted moments, he didn't know how long, he opened his eyes and gazed at his reflection in the mirror. The tired-looking man staring back at him, seemed to be asking just one question.

How the fuck did you get yourself mixed up in all this?

Chapter Thirty-Eight

Abingdon, Oxfordshire

12 November 1999

'They've found it, sir. Could be a while before they get it to the surface, though.'

'Alright. I'm going for a look round,' said Cordell, pulling up his coat collar as he set off to inspect the perimeter of the lake.

The sky above Abingdon was crisp and clear, but the path was still wet from last night's rain, and it wasn't long before his black leather shoes were caked in mud. With his hands in his pockets, he gazed out across the surface of the water, thinking back to the call he'd received earlier that morning. It was Julian Mountfield's secretary with details of the contractor who'd installed the faulty skylight – a company called ArtScreen, apparently. He'd got some distant recollection of them and asked one of the junior CID officers to give them a quick background check. Needless to say, it came back clean and above board, and Cordell was straight on the phone to their managing director, Luke Waltham, to quiz him about the work they'd done at the Ashmolean. Waltham was aware of the break-in, but quite shocked to hear the robbers had broken in through one of their skylights, promising a thorough investigation into the matter – although, he did recall they'd been experiencing some quality issues with one of their Scandinavian suppliers, around the time of the installation.

It was exactly a week since the Picasso had been stolen and, with no concrete leads, Cordell was starting to get that horrible feeling of yet another trail gone cold. Having taken statements from everyone in and around the museum that night, all he could say with absolute certainty was that the two men were clinical, no doubt professionals, and had targeted one particular painting. Was it an inside job? Possibly – the Ashmolean had certainly had more than its fair share of break-ins over the last ten years. Unsurprisingly, this one too had made the national headlines – 'Picasso Piracy at Top Museum' proclaimed one of the tabloids; 'Bonfire Night Bonanza' read another – each taking great delight in telling the world how thieves had gained access to the roof of the museum, then broken in through one of the skylights and simply lifted the Picasso off the wall, as fire engines and emergency vehicles went sailing past, on their way to various out-of-control bonfires. In his experience, publicity like that only served to light fires under the Force's intelligentsia, or add fuel to those already lit. And now, certain influential members of Oxford's academia were exerting huge pressure on Thames Valley Police to find the culprits and return the missing Picasso. Unfortunately for Cordell, all that Masonic bluster had worked its way down to him, via the ancient and well-practised art of delegation, or, as he liked to call it, 'accountability displacement'.

Then came some news that had significantly brightened his mood. No sooner had he arrived at work that morning, than he was summoned upstairs to see Detective Chief Superintendent Alexander McHardy to give an update on progress, or rather, the lack of it. He was on his way there when one of the case officers informed him that an anonymous caller had witnessed a black Audi being dumped in a lake, south of Oxford – he was there in a flash. It might be nothing, but as the low autumn sun sparkled through the trees onto the rippling black water, instinct told him otherwise.

As the crane driver lowered the cradle into the water, guided by two police frogmen, Cordell noticed someone watching the recovery team through a gap in the trees.

'Excuse me, sir,' he said, striding over to the man, who looked to be in his late fifties, wearing a shabby wax jacket, combat trousers and walking boots, and clasping the lead of a golden Labrador sitting patiently by his side. A gust of wind tugged at the man's mass of tangled grey-brown hair, that looked like it hadn't seen a brush in weeks.

'Do you walk him here every day?' said Cordell.

'I do, and she's a bitch,' said the man, not taking his eyes off the two frogmen about to submerge for the second time.

'Right.'

'Every mornin' and again at night. Loves the water, see. Can't get 'er outta there, sometimes.'

'I don't suppose you were here when the car was being dumped, were you?' said Cordell.

'Yeah, I saw it. That's why I came down 'ere; to see 'ow long it'd take you lot to fish 'im out.'

'You were the one who called the station, this morning?'

The Lab whined and looked up at her master to be let off the lead.

'Aye ... that were me,' said the man, stroking the dog's head.

'You rang off before the desk sergeant could get your details.'

The man shrugged his shoulders. 'I couldn't be doin' with all that nonsense. I just told 'em what I saw, an' left 'em to it.'

'Then perhaps you wouldn't mind answering a few questions for me?'

'Suppose not. Ain't got nuthin' to rush back for, now the wife's gone.'

'Ah, sorry to hear that, Mr ...?'

'Addison, Brian Addison.'

'Mr Addison, my name is Detective Chief Inspector Cordell. So, when did you see the car being dumped, exactly?'

'Bonfire night. She don't like fireworks, as a rule. But for some reason, she were barkin' an' scratchin' at the kitchen door, goin' crazy to be let out. So I thought I'd better take 'er.'

'What time was that?'

''bout eight-ish. There was a few bangs an' whistles, but nuthin' too bad. Must 'ave been the rain ... put people off. Anyway, we walked down the lane and over to the lake. Got 'ere 'bout ten past, I reckon.'

'It was dark, then?'

'Oh, aye, ... I carry's a torch, see.' Addison pulled a Maglite out of his pocket. 'We'd only been 'ere a few minutes, when I saw some 'eadlights over the far side. I thought it were a van, deliverin' to one of the ware'ouses. But it kept gettin' closer to the water – then I saw it were a car.'

The Labrador let out a loud bark. 'What happened then?' said Cordell, crouching down and giving the Lab a stroke, before Addison lost his thread.

'When the car stopped by the lake, I 'ung back and watched 'em. She were on the lead, so they hadn't spotted us.'

'Them?' said Cordell.

'There was two of 'em, with torches. They wasn't 'angin' about, neither.'

'How far away were you?'

''bout where we're stood, now. I saw 'em unload some stuff from the boot – a couple of rucksacks and a big square bag o' some sort. That's when I knew.'

'Knew what?'

'They was up to no good. No fishin' rods, see. Normal blokes don't go unloadin' a car on the edge of a lake in the pitch black, unless 'em-s doin' a bit of night fishin', right?'

'No, I suppose not.'

'Next thing, they was pushin' the bloody car into the lake, the deepest part too.'

'You think they knew that?'

'Oh yeah, 'undred yards to the left, an' that thing would 'ave been stuck there with its arse in the air.'

'Right. Now, I know it was dark, but did you manage to get a look at them?'

Addison shook his head. 'Nah, definitely two of 'em, though. An' not from round 'ere, neither.'

'What makes you say that?'

'One kept shoutin' at the other. Usin' some pretty tasty language an' all. A Londoner, I reckon, judgin' by 'is accent.'

'Did you hear anything specific? Names, places, anything like that?'

'Nope.'

'And then what happened?'

'We follows 'em to the industrial estate. Course, I was 'angin' back a bit. By the time we got there, they was leavin' in another car.'

'What sort of car?'

'Range Rover, from what I could make out. Didn't get the reg, before you ask.'

'Okay, thank you, Mr Addison. It's a shame you didn't call us sooner.'

'Yeah, well ... you're 'ere now, ain't ya?' he smirked.

The two men looked over to where the frogmen were diving, just as the boot of the Audi A4 broke the surface. The crane lifted the vehicle high into the air, spouting torrents of water in all directions, like a giant automotive fountain.

'Reckon it's got summat to do with that break-in?' enquired Addison.

'Which break-in?'

'The one at that museum in Oxford, a week or so back. They said on the news you was lookin' for a black Audi. Looks like you' got yourselves one.'

'I'd better get over there. Can I take your number, Mr Addison, just in case we need to speak to you again?'

'I ain't got a phone – got cut off a few months back. As I said, I only lives up the lane – last 'ouse on the left, before the main road.'

Cordell thanked him for his time and marched off to join the recovery team, just as one of the Crime Scene Officers opened the passenger door, spewing gallons of fetid water onto the bank.

'Here you go, sir. Want to take a look inside?'

'Give me a torch, will you?' said Cordell, pulling on a pair of forensic gloves and flicking the boot release. On inspection, it contained nothing but the stench of fish and blanket weed. He lifted up the carpet to reveal the spare wheel, a small jack and a mass of green slime.

'Great,' he said, slamming the boot lid shut.

He walked round to the passenger door and peered inside. The interior had been stained brown by seven days of accumulated mud and silt. He flipped open the glove box and used the torch to check inside; it was empty, as were the door wells and centre console. If he was honest, he didn't expect to find anything. These guys were professionals and no doubt would have checked the car over before sending it to the bottom of the lake.

More in hope than expectation, he slid the passenger seat forward and, with the aid of the torchlight, peered underneath. Something glinted on the floor next to the seat runner. He reached forward and picked up the small cylindrical object – a cheap disposable lighter that had somehow managed to elude its owner. Holding it carefully at each end, he brought it out into the open and inspected it closely. Made of red plastic, it was plain on one side, with the other containing the monogram of a snake coiled round a gemstone – below which were the words *The Ruby Viper* in gilded lettering.

The Ruby Viper

He was no expert, but it sounded like the name of a club, a London club, perhaps; but certainly not one he recognised. He placed it in an evidence bag and tucked it into his pocket.

After removing his forensic gloves, he took out his mobile phone and scrolled down the list of contacts until he came to a number for Scotland Yard. There wasn't much of a signal out here, so he made a mental note. The minute he got back to the office, he'd be straight on the phone to renew an old acquaintance – in Vice Squad.

Chapter Thirty-Nine

The Pitt Rivers Museum, Oxford

12 November 1999

Emily looked down on the glass cabinets of the Pitt Rivers Collection, each one painted black and stuffed with strange objects and curios from the four corners of the earth. Compared to the light and airy Oxford Museum of Natural History next door, this was a dark and mysterious place, full of shrunken heads and scare devils. It reminded her of the huge private collection amassed by newspaper magnate, Charles Foster Kane, in Orson Welles' cinematic masterpiece, *Citizen Kane*. But, instead of being secreted away in some vast private warehouse, stuffed full of wooden crates, here the exhibits were displayed to intoxicate, fascinate, bewitch and beguile, and in some cases, curdle the blood with their magic spells and barbarous intent.

At the far end of the display hall stood a giant totem pole made by the Haida people from Graham Island, British Columbia – part of the Wabanaki nation, meaning People of the Dawn. At more than eleven metres tall, its towering carved figures cast a protective eye over the kingdom of antiquities, ready to launch a booming voice at any small child who dared to leave so much as a fingerprint on one of the glass display cases.

It was pretty much as Emily remembered it, from when she came here as a little girl. *The Top Five* had been a list of her favourite items in the collection. She'd laboured over it for hours in the car on the way home. Each item had to meet certain criteria. Nothing too large that wouldn't fit in her bedroom; that ruled out the totem pole. And nothing too creepy. Although she was completely fascinated by the "witch in a bottle" and other exhibits in the Treatment of Dead Enemies cabinet, they were excluded on the basis that she didn't fancy waking up one night to find they'd suddenly come to life and were lined up at the bottom of her bed, ready to devour her. No, *The Top Five* was reserved for beautiful things; items she would never grow tired of. Now, what were they?

She was about to take a retrospective tour of the first-floor cabinets when a voice called out behind her.

'Welcome to the realm of the arcane, Miss Bradshaw.'

She turned round. 'My God, you frightened the life out of me,' she said, clutching her chest.

Henry Faber gave her one of his enigmatic smiles. 'Rekindling some childhood memories?'

'Yes, how did you know?'

'Oh, I get the same feeling whenever I come here. I was seven when my parents first brought me to see the collection.'

'I was eight, and loved every last inch of the place. Still do. Anyway, thanks for agreeing to meet me, Mr Faber,' she said, feeling a little guilty that she'd jumped the gun on Julian's recommendation to wait a few days, and rang him the moment she'd got back from their Birmingham visit.

'Please, it's Henry. And you're welcome, my dear. You said on the phone you had something to show me?'

'Yes, you might be interested in this.' She reached into her bag and placed the Draper sketchbook on the glass cabinet in front of her.

'Oh my,' said Henry, retrieving a pair of wire-framed reading glasses from his jacket pocket.

He opened the front cover and, like those before him, began carefully turning each page to take in the masterful drawings. Watching him marvel at its contents, Emily got the impression this was more of a re-acquaintance than a new encounter. She decided to test the water.

'Thinking back to the auction – what I could never understand is, why someone would hide such a wonderful thing at the bottom of a box of old prints.'

'Ah yes, I'm afraid that was my fault,' he said.

'Sorry, how was it your fault?'

'When I first saw it, it was lying on top of a washstand – heaven knows why the auction house had left it there. In my experience, something this rare and valuable should have been kept in a glass case. Anyway, I saw you coming over, and quickly stuffed it in a box, so you wouldn't find it; or so I thought.'

'Well that was a bit sneaky.'

'Yes, I suppose it was,' he chuckled. 'And for that I apologise. My interest was predominantly an academic one – in particular, these wonderful sketches at the back.'

'You mean Aurora?'

'Yes, they're a prelude to the majestic vision Draper was about to create in *The Gates of Dawn*.'

'I've seen it, ... in Drapers' Hall.'

He looked up. 'You have?'

'You were the one who discovered its secret, weren't you?'

He closed the sketchbook and took off his glasses. 'That's not strictly true.'

'So, there are eight paintings with sun marks, right?'

'Yes ... how did you know?'

'Julian and I found four – *The Light of the World*, *The Finding of the Saviour in the Temple*, *The Blind Girl* and *The Gates of Dawn*.'

Henry grabbed the hand rail, looking somewhat taken aback. 'My word – you have been busy.'

'I say "we" found them – we did have a lot of help from a certain mysterious benefactor. You wouldn't happen to know anything about that, would you, Henry?'

'Benefactor? No, I'm afraid I don't.'

'Oh come on, the cryptic clues from someone called the Shepherd?'

'Honestly, I have no idea what you're talking about.'

Emily reached into her coat pocket and handed him the three letters. He studied them carefully; his expression becoming graver by the second.

'Emily, I can assure you, I have never seen these before.'

'Well, if you're not the Shepherd, who is?'

'I don't know, and I'm not about to speculate.'

'Then, at least tell me the names of the other four paintings.'

He gazed at her with a look of resignation. 'Very well. They're in the Tate Gallery in London. Firstly, there is Rossetti's *The Girlhood of Mary Virgin*, painted in eighteen forty-nine. Then, *The Awakening Conscience* by Holman Hunt, completed in eighteen fifty-three, which he altered on at least four occasions. Next, Millais's *Ophelia*, eighteen fifty-two – my personal favourite. And finally, what Rossetti referred to as his "most

poetic work" – the haunting memorial to his beloved wife Lizzie,
– *Beata Beatrix*, completed in eighteen seventy'

'And have you seen them – the sun marks I mean?'

'Yes.'

'And they're all individually numbered?'

'They are.'

'That's incredible,' said Emily, looking out across the huge room. 'There must have been a purpose to it all, surely?'

'Oh, I'm certain of it. Did you know that the Brothers referred to the collection as *The Lights of the World*?'

But Emily wasn't listening, as she stared over the balcony towards the far end of the room.

'What is it?' said Henry, following her gaze to the ground floor.

Emily didn't know his name, merely the black leather jacket, the dark swarthy complexion and the evil look he'd given her, after nearly mowing her down in the auction house car park.

'Forgive me, I have to go,' said Henry, grabbing her arm. 'If you value your life, Emily, go back to Bristol and stay there, please!'

Before she could ask what he meant, he was scurrying off towards the staircase leading to the ground floor. She peered over the balustrade to see the madman running at full pelt to intercept him from the opposite direction. A few moments later, Henry appeared on the floor below, rushing towards the exit.

'Look out, he's coming for you!' shouted Emily, but it was too late. The stranger threw himself at the old curator, knocking him to the floor. Visitors nearby looked on in shock, trying to work out what on earth was happening.

Henry began to crawl under a nearby cabinet of carved Buddhas, but the assailant grabbed him by his ankle and hauled him back into the open space. Emily watched, helpless, as Henry kicked and writhed to try and free himself from the man's clutches.

One of the museum staff ran over to try and help.

'Fuck off!' said the thug, pulling a gun from his pocket and pointing it straight at the young attendant.

'Oh my God,' said Emily, putting her hands to her face.

'No, no, don't shoot.' pleaded the lad, quickly backing away with his hands in the air.

Screams began to echo round the hall as the sight of a gun sent panic-stricken visitors rushing for the exit, dragging small children, pushchairs and each other towards the comparative safety of the Natural History Museum, next door.

*

Relishing the pandemonium he was causing, Marcus Tyburn dragged Henry by his ankle all the way to the back of the hall, propping him up against the glass cabinet at the base of the huge totem pole.

While Henry looked up at his captor, a loud bang echoed through the display hall as the doors at the far end slammed shut. His heart sank as, once again, he found himself alone with this madman.

'What's up, Prof, surprised to see me?' said Tyburn.

'On the contrary ... vermin like you have a habit of reappearing out of darkened corners.'

Tyburn pushed his face up close to Henry's. 'You know, for a smart man, you're pretty fuckin' dumb. I told you what would happen if I caught you talkin' to her again, didn't I?'

He clenched the old man's throat and pressed down hard. Henry grabbed his thick muscular wrist, desperately trying to yank it away as he kicked and gurgled, fighting for every breath.

With his grip on Henry's windpipe growing ever tighter, Tyburn glanced at the tattoo on the back of his own hand – a man hanging by a noose from a three-legged gallows, and the words *TYBURN TREE* inscribed below. It was like a talisman of death – a reminder of the power he wielded over the ignorant and the weak.

One by one, Henry's fingers relinquished their feeble grasp on the sleeve of his captor's leather jacket, as he slowly but surely began to lose consciousness.

*

'Stop it!' screamed Emily, looking down from the gallery above, but the man ignored her, seemingly hell bent on extinguishing poor Henry's life.

'I said leave him alone, you evil bastard!' she yelled, her voice quivering with rage.

The man slowly turned and glared up at her.

247

Then it hit her – with all the other visitors having fled, she was the only witness. She watched as the assailant got to his feet, his eyes fixed firmly on her as he made his way over to the first-floor stairway.

Her mind was scrambled; which way to run? Then, as if raised up by some dark elevator, the madman appeared in the doorway, not twenty yards from her. She turned and sprinted back along the first-floor balcony, looking left and right for a way out.

Blocking the exit, the man leaned against the doorway and let out a throaty laugh. 'Keep runnin', bitch. Cos I'm comin' for you.'

With nowhere to go, Emily climbed over the balcony at the far end of the hall and reached out to grab the side of the giant totem pole. Holding her breath, and beseeching whatever gods she was about to offend to spare her miserable little life, she leapt from the ledge, clinging as tightly as she could to the shoulder of a black-eyed bear, as the huge wooden structure rocked back and forth. Fortunately, the gods were in benevolent mood and creaking under the weight of its human fugitive, the totem pole suddenly righted itself beneath her feet.

She peered down at the floor – a drop of about twenty-feet. If she landed awkwardly or broke her ankle, she was as good as dead. Just as she was about to turn round and place her trainer in an inviting-looking foothold, a hand grabbed her by the shoulder. She screamed. The man's face was just inches away, glaring over the balcony. She sank her teeth into the back of his hand and bit down hard. He roared with agony, letting go to nurse the gaping wound.

Facing no other option but to trust in the gods once more, Emily jumped from the bear's shoulder, her eyes wide as the floor came rushing towards her. Just missing the glass cabinet at the bottom, she hit the floor tiles and rolled over onto her side. With two sore feet and no broken bones, she picked herself up and rushed over to where Henry was lying, pale and lifeless. She put her fingers to his neck and felt for signs of a pulse. Somehow, he was still clinging to life – just.

Too frightened to even think about her assailant's whereabouts, she turned and ran towards the main entrance, weaving in and out of the display cabinets like a slalom skier. Reaching the stone steps at the far end, she leapt them two at a time and banged on the arched doors for all she was worth.

'Let me out! Let me out – please!' she shouted.

There was no response.

Expecting a crushing blow from behind at any moment, she steeled herself and spun round, only to see the madman still grappling with the top of the totem pole. She watched as he attempted to ram the toe of his boot into a dusty crevice between the pair of mischievous-looking bear cubs. Looking strangely ill at ease, he missed the foothold completely and fell crashing to the floor. For a moment, Emily's heart rose – watching as the fallen psycho stumbled around, looking dazed and confused.

'Thank you,' she said, in praise of the Haida ancestors, who'd apparently taken great offence at this second intruder and his attempt to desecrate their sacred monument with his deep-seated malevolence and dark energy.

But her hopes were short-lived – the man steadied himself against a glass cabinet and slowly raised his head in Emily's direction. She turned and banged on the door once more. 'Please, let me out!' she screamed. 'He's going to kill me!'

Just as she'd given up hope, there was a click of the latch and the door opened. The arm of a security guard reached out and grabbed her, yanking her inside the Natural History hall, before quickly slamming the door shut and locking it. Seconds later, something fast and heavy clattered into the other side, making the whole door frame shudder.

Emily staggered into the cloister-like corridor, her heart pounding like a drum. She turned and glared at the security guard.

'Why wouldn't you open the fucking door?'

'Sorry, miss, I was under strict orders – nobody in or out. But when I heard you screaming, I thought, sod that. I'm not leaving her in there to die.'

'You do know there's someone still in there, don't you? We have to get him out.'

'I can't, miss. You saw what sort of nutter we're dealing with. You were lucky he didn't take a shot at you. Anyway, the police will be here any minute – they'll take care of it.'

Resting against one of the wooden display cabinets, Emily sank to the floor in tears, racked with guilt at leaving poor Henry at the mercy of that lunatic. She was just about to ask the guard if he'd rung for an ambulance, when there was a loud crash from the display hall, next door.

'What was that?' she said, getting to her feet.

The guard put his ear to the door. 'Sounded like breaking glass.'

'You've got to go in there.'

'Miss, he has a gun. And, well ... I don't.'

'He could be about to kill him.'

'I'm sorry, I really am.'

Of course, he was right. The anger she was feeling was just a symptom of her own helplessness and remorse. There was nothing else to do but sit tight and wait.

*

After what, to Emily, felt like an eternity, an Armed Response Unit arrived to secure the perimeter of the building and escort everyone to a place of safety. Although, to her untrained eye, their whole strategy seemed to be more one of cautious abeyance, than urgent action.

Despite the paramedics' continued suggestions that she go to hospital to get checked out, Emily insisted on waiting for Henry, no matter what the outcome. Thirty minutes later, the all-clear was given and the Specialist Firearms team began making their way back to the control checkpoint. With a thermal blanket draped over her shoulders, she walked over to one of the uniformed police officers patrolling the cordon.

'What's happening, have they caught the gunman?'

'Sorry, miss, I can't give you any information – this is a crime scene.'

'I know it is, I was the one he was trying to kill.'

The constable looked over his shoulder, then moved closer to whisper in her ear. 'He's gone, miss.'

'What? He can't have.'

'They searched the place from top to bottom, there's no sign of him.'

'But, he couldn't have just disappeared into thin air?'

'Well ... maybe he got out through the side exit.'

'Side exit?' she said, wondering how the hell she'd missed that. 'And what about the old man – is he still alive?'

'Barely. The paramedics are seeing to him now. Do you know him?'

Without answering, she quickly ducked under the police tape and ran as fast as she could towards the entrance to the Natural History Museum.

'Miss, miss ... you can't go back in there!' shouted the constable.

Emily sprinted through the entrance hall, past the watchful statues of Aristotle and Francis Bacon, beyond the giant casts of Iguanodon and Tyrannosaurus Rex, and over to the arched doors of the Pitt Rivers Collection. From the top of the steps she could see a team of paramedics huddled in the centre of the hall.

Fearing the worst, she walked towards display case number 122, worryingly titled *Treatment of the Dead*. Suddenly, she felt the crunch of broken glass beneath her feet. She looked to her right and saw that one of the display cases had been broken into and robbed of an exhibit. She clutched her chest, bracing herself for the horror of what she was about to encounter.

One of the paramedics stood up and walked over to her with his arms raised. 'Sorry miss, you have to leave,' he said, steering her away from the scene, his face kind and compassionate.

'It's okay, he's a friend. I just want to—'

'You really don't want to see this. The poor guy's been subjected to a horrific attack.'

'But, he was fine when I left him. I checked his pulse.'

As she spoke the words, she saw the pool of blood next to where Henry was lying. Then she saw what had caused it – the roughly carved handle of a tribal axe was sticking up out of his left thigh.

'Oh my God!' she said, placing her hand over her mouth.

'Come on, he's in good hands. We're about to get him off to hospital.'

'Will he be okay?'

'It's touch and go – as you can see, he's lost a lot of blood.'

Emily stood to one side and watched as the team strapped Henry into the stretcher. With a line of adrenalin hanging from his arm and an oxygen mask over his nose and mouth, they wheeled him out to the waiting ambulance – the axe still protruding from his leg at a forty-five-degree angle, and being carefully supported by one of the emergency responders. Emily followed on behind, her head bowed in shock, wondering how an act of such barbarity could be perpetrated against another human being.

As she approached the exit, her foot kicked something on the floor, sending it scooting under one of the display cabinets. She bent down to pick it up and saw that it was a silver jeweller's loupe, with the initials H.J.F. engraved on the cover.

There and then, she made herself a solemn promise – if Henry was lucky enough to make it through this whole ghastly episode, she would give him the Draper sketchbook. After all, he was the one who found it. For her to have even played a part in unlocking the Pre-Raphaelite's secret was a privilege in itself. No, the badge of honour belonged to him.

She just hoped he would live long enough to enjoy it.

Chapter Forty

Thames Valley Police Station, Kidlington, Oxford

12 November 1999

DCI Cordell walked out of the lift and over to the temporary desk assigned to him by the local CID. It was older and grubbier than the suite of workstations recently installed for the permanent staffers at Kidlington, but Cordell didn't care; as long as it had a phone, a chair and a network cable for his laptop, he didn't mind where he sat – so accustomed was he to hot-desking at various police stations across the length and breadth of Europe, these past ten years. Such was the life of a DCI in the Met's Art and Antiques Squad, based out of Scotland Yard.

'Been out for a spot of fishing, 'ave we, Francis?' said one of the more arrogant members of Thames Valley CID.

Cordell shook his head with disdain as he waited for the vending machine to dispense his cup of coffee, then went and hung up his coat next to one of the pillars bisecting the office.

The cocky detective, sporting a suit that wouldn't have looked out of place in an MTV pop video, wandered over, sensing he'd got Cordell on the ropes.

'So, I hear the trail's gone cold on the stolen Picasso?'

'Sorry Ogden, what was that?'

'It's Owen. Detective Inspector Owen.'

'Right, Owen. Well, as you asked, I think I may have just landed my first proper lead,' said Cordell, removing the evidence bag from his coat pocket and lobbing it onto his desk.

'Oh, that's lucky,' Owen smirked.

'You make your own luck in this world,' said Cordell, and sat down to ponder his latest find.

'Yeah well, it's not like it's a serious crime, is it?'

Cordell looked up at him. 'Tell you what, if ever I need some old clichés digging up from the archives, I'll give you a shout, alright? Now, haven't you got some stolen bicycles to be tracking down, or something?'

One of the constables sitting nearby sniggered.

'He'd better have a bloody sight more than that in his in-tray,' said DCS McHardy, as he entered the office.

Owen glowered and sloped off back to his desk.

'Did you find anything at the lake?' enquired McHardy.

'Nothing that directly links the car to the robbery. But I'm hopeful this might turn out to be something,' Cordell replied, holding up the evidence bag.

'Mmm, doesn't look much. Any prints on it?'

'Doubtful, after all that time in the water. I'll get it over to forensics, just in case.'

'And what about your contacts in the art world – surely one of them must have heard some chatter about who did this?'

'No, nothing, it's all gone spookily quiet since the break-in.'

'Perhaps it's time for you to start shaking things up a little. As I said to you this morning, some powerful people want this thing resolved quickly, before every villain from here to Glasgow starts thinking Oxford's an easy target.'

'I'm doing my best, sir.'

'Well, call me old-fashioned, Cordell, but I'd like a damned sight more than just your best,' said McHardy, and headed off in the direction of his office.

Cordell scratched his head and took a sip of the acrid brown sludge the vending machine had the nerve to call "finest Brazilian dark roast". He picked up the phone and dialled the Scotland Yard number he'd looked up by the lake, earlier. As he waited for the connection, he gazed at the little red lighter.

'Reynolds,' a voice answered.

'Pete. It's Francis Cordell.'

'Francis. How's life in the world of missing masterpieces?'

'Oh, you know … some you win, some you never see again.'

'Ha-ha, yes, I'm sure. Anyway, what can I do for you, my friend?'

'I'm over in Oxford, trying to get a lead on this break-in at the Ashmolean.'

'Oh yes, I heard about that. Took a Picasso, didn't they?'

'Yes – *Blue Roofs*. Fabulous little thing. And, to add insult to injury, the buggers have left me naff all to go on, apart from a broken skylight. Anyway, it's a bit of a longshot, but I've just stumbled across something you might be able to help me with.'

'Okay.'

'Earlier this morning, we pulled what we think could be the getaway car out of a lake near Abingdon. Apart from a load of green slime, it was totally clean. But I did come across a disposable lighter under the passenger seat.'

Reynolds laughed. 'Well, that'll narrow it down to a few thousand possible suspects.'

'Yes, yes, listen ... on one side, there's a monogram of what sounds like a night club – The Ruby Viper – do you know it?'

'Yeah, I know it.'

Cordell gave himself a self-congratulatory fist pump. 'Okay ... so, what is it, some sort of private members' club or something?'

'You could say that. Certainly not the sort of place you'd frequent, Francis. It's a high-class sex club in town, owned by a bloke called Jackie Forgan.'

'Never heard of him. Is he the type to get mixed up in something like this, Pete?'

'Mmm, to be honest, the whole family are up to their necks in racketeering – everything from gambling to prostitution and people-trafficking. You name it, they've got a finger up its arse. Although, I wouldn't have said art theft was their thing.'

Cordell was silent for a moment.

'You still there, Francis?'

'Yes, yes. So, how good is your memory, Pete?'

'Good enough to remember you still owe me a case of scotch for a certain favour I did you – three bloody years ago. It would have been maturing nicely by now.'

'Ah, okay, ... tell you what, let's make it two cases. I'm in a hole here, Pete.'

'Go on, what do you need?'

'I need you to sanction a raid on the place. You know the sort of thing – look for drugs, check out the books, get me the tapes from their security cameras for the last three months, that sort of thing.'

'Christ! How am I going to swing a warrant for that little lot?'

'Oh, you'll think of something. You said yourself, they're into all sorts of dodgy shit.'

Reynolds let out a sigh. 'My God, you don't want much, do you?'

'You asked me what I needed – there it is,' said Cordell.

'Alright. Give me a few days and I'll see what I can come up with.'

'Thanks, Pete. I really appreciate this.'

'You'd better, my friend.'

With that, Cordell hung up the phone and sat back in his chair. Perhaps the ice-cold trail of the missing Picasso was about to start warming up a little.

Chapter Forty-One

Kelmscott Manor, Oxfordshire

27 July 1871

Kelmscott Manor is a mellow old place – a haven of pastoral peace and tranquillity in the river meadows of the south Cotswolds. Built from local limestone, it exudes rural charm, with its mullioned windows, high pointed gables and a stone-tiled roof, dappled with golden lichen – the perfect tonic to calm the nerves. It also provided artistic inspiration for a certain member of the Pre-Raphaelite Brotherhood, for whom the creative juices had all but ceased to flow.

As the early morning sun hit the top of the old Mulberry tree outside the dining-room window, Dante Gabriel Rossetti sipped his breakfast tea and felt a renewed sense of well-being envelope him for the first time in years. A mood not lost on the young woman sitting next to him – Jane Morris, wife of fellow artist and friend, William Morris, in whose house he was now staying.

Shortly after having moved into Kelmscott, William had, remarkably, made his excuses and left for Iceland, in order to indulge his passion for Nordic folklore and literature. Bidding farewell to his wife and two young daughters, he simply said, 'Be well and happy,' and left them in the care of Jane's lover – an exceedingly grateful Rossetti.

'Do you like eggs, Mr Rossetti?' said Jenny, Jane's eldest daughter.

Her younger sister, May, chuckled to herself as she waited for a response from her mother's curious friend.

'I do, as a matter of fact,' said Gabriel. 'Can either of you guess how many I'm going to have this morning?'

'I can, I can!' said May. 'Two.'

'Two? No, I don't think that's going to be nearly enough.'

'My turn. I think you're going to have three eggs,' Jenny said, smugly.

'Three? Now, that is a lot,' said Gabriel, patting his belly. 'But I am feeling particularly hungry, so—'

'No? You're not having four eggs?' said May.

'Yes, yes, I think so. Four eggs it is for me, this morning,' said Gabriel, bringing fits of giggles from the two sisters.

'Alright, get along now, both of you,' said Jane, putting on her serious face for the girls. 'You don't want to keep the governess waiting.'

'Oh, Mother, can't we go and watch them build hay stacks in the cornfield?' said Jenny.

'After your lessons, perhaps. First, you have to tell me all about the Emperor Hadrian and what he had his legions build in the North of England.'

The two Morris sisters, each wearing plain medieval dresses with a string of coloured beads round their necks, got down from the table and trudged into the panelled White Room to begin their schooling. Or, as far as May was concerned, gazing out of the window at the chuckling blackbirds feasting among the gooseberry bushes.

Alone with his love, Gabriel took Jane's hand and smiled a contented smile.

'Janey, this house and its surroundings are the loveliest haunt of ancient peace that can be imagined. An earthly paradise. And in it, I have you.'

He kissed her on the cheek, as he did every morning when William was away, and went upstairs to his makeshift studio – the Tapestry Room, adorned with four seventeenth-century wall-hangings, all mellowed with age.

Not one for great swathes of faded indigo and yellow-brown wool, from which he took no inspiration, Gabriel walked over to the easel supporting his latest painting, *Beata Beatrix*, the image of a young woman with rust-brown hair and a face as white as ash, with whom he'd become completely obsessed. Looking ghostly and serene, she sat with her eyes closed, her head tilted towards heaven and hands cupped in her lap, ready to receive a poppy from the beak of a dove perched nearby. The message was clear – death would soon become her.

As with all Gabriel's works, this replica of an earlier painting was steeped in symbolism, and mirrored the death of Dante Alighieri's beloved muse, Beatrice, in thirteenth-century

Florence, with the tragic passing of his own wife, Lizzie Siddal, some nine years before. Even Beatrice's flame-red hair was an obvious reflection of Lizzie's own russet-coloured locks, whilst her green tunic and purple-grey dress embodied the essence of hope and sorrow, life and death. And, as if to underline the point still further, there in the background stood the figure of Love – dressed in red, and holding up Beatrice's waning life as a flickering flame.

However, Gabriel saw this haunting yet powerful image as emulating, not so much the end of life, but the moment of spiritual transfiguration to a higher place, where he hoped Lizzie's soul was now at rest. Such was the inspiration for his second and final contribution to the Brothers' seven works of enlightenment:

> #4. Lust for death – all must dissolve into their
> beginnings, but only those with love in their
> heart may ascend the heavenly realms.

The passing of time had, for the most part, helped to soothe his feelings of loss, and spending the summer at Kelmscott with Jane was a welcome distraction. But he would often find himself prone to the direst attacks of guilt and betrayal, bubbling up from the depths of his subconscious and darkening his mood like a thick London fog.

He walked over to the open window and rested his hands on the stone sill, breathing in the fresh morning air to clear his mind. Past the dovecote and neighbouring barn were a row of elm trees flanking the Radcot Cut – an artificial stream lined with yellow flags and willow trees, their branches dancing in and out of the lazy brown waters channelled from the River Thames.

All was peaceful and quiet, except for the *coo-cooing* of a dove perched high on a nearby chimney pot. With a clap of its wings, it swooped down and smashed into the window next to where Gabriel was standing. He stumbled backwards, sending the easel and Lizzie's picture, crashing to the floor.

Seeing her lying there, banished and helpless, sent his mood spiralling downwards, as if the whole world was suddenly conspiring against him. Even the deep azure sky had become sullied with dark angry clouds, playing on his superstition and melancholy.

He picked her up and gently placed her back on the easel, blowing the specks of dust and dirt from her face. Gazing upon her lips of fire, he began to lose himself in the serenity of her sickly pale skin, her aura glowing like the Magdalene's – full of compassion and wisdom in the moment of her glorious rebirth; seeing beyond closed eyes, he who is blessed throughout all the ages.

But for every ray of light in a tortured mind, there is shade – reflected in this instance by the sundial on the wall, drawing death to her, pointing like a phallus, as if to say, the love you gave was fated, barren from the start. Gabriel sank to his knees, pawing at Lizzie's soulful image, his conscience racked with guilt. Could it really be ... that he loved her more in death than in life?

As the dove, stunned by its collision with the window, took to the air once more, Gabriel recited the words of his sonnet, *Without Her*:

> 'What of her glass without her? The blank grey
> There where the pool is blind of the moon's face.
> Her dress without her? The tossed empty space
> Of cloud-rack whence the moon has passed away.
> Her paths without her? Day's appointed sway
> Usurped by desolate night. Her pillowed place
> Without her? Tears, ah me! for love's good grace,
> And cold forgetfulness of night or day.'

Wiping the tears from his eyes, he raised himself up and sat on the windowsill, watching Jane as she walked in the garden below, her long, dark hair shining like silk. Pausing to smell one of the fragrant roses lining the path, she appeared so serene, so at peace with her surroundings. And for that, he envied her. If only there was a way to lay his ghosts to rest, to stem the feelings of conflict and remorse that plagued him, constantly. How he longed to reignite the passion in which he and Jane had wrapped themselves when they first met. He squinted at the brightening sun, still low in the summer sky – had it been there all along? He couldn't tell. For a moment, he felt his spirits rise from the ashes of despair, like the phoenix bird – resolute and pure of heart.

*

Later that morning, having spent a couple of fruitless hours on the painting, Gabriel accompanied Jane for a leisurely stroll along the riverbank, not far from the manor house. Approaching the water, they stopped to admire the bumblebees popping in and out of the pink Himalayan balsam; whilst overhead, willow branches swayed in the warm summer breeze, sending a family of blue tits chattering into the air.

'Look!' said Gabriel, pointing as a kingfisher darted across the water in a flash of turquoise and copper. And he remembered why he loved this place.

'When I am done with Beatrice, I would very much like to paint you, here – framed in a garland of willow,' he said.

With little more than a gentle smile, Jane touched his cheek and they carried on walking to the bend in the river.

'You recall the collection of poems I had published last year, Janey,' said Gabriel, tugging nervously at the bottom of his waistcoat.

'Yes, my darling. What of them?'

'There is something I've been meaning to tell you about them.'

'Oh Gabriel, please don't keep punishing yourself about that unfortunate business. The criticisms levelled at you were those of ignorant fools – men who could never even conceive of creating something as beautiful as your anthology, even were the Lord God to grant them the rest of eternity in which to do it.'

'That's very sweet of you, my love. But as you know, the judgement meted out by my detractors has caused me great torment. And, much as it pains me, I have come to realise that it was not the quality of the sonnets to which they objected – more the circumstances of their resurrection.'

'Gabriel, let's not speak of such things on such a lovely morning.'

'Janey, I must, ... for art was the only thing for which poor Lizzie felt a true calling. Were it up to her, she would have left the book of poems on my pillow, I am certain of it. And, were she to know of the desperate choice I had to make, I have no doubt she would have opened the coffin lid herself and laid the folio on the gravestone, so that no other hand were needed. Yet, no matter how hard I try to put those nightmarish visions to rest, they rise up like spectres to haunt me when I least expect it. It would lift my resolve to the heavens if you would allow me to unburden this heavy heart, one last time.'

She put her hand on his. 'Of course.'

Having found them a pleasant spot near the river's edge, Gabriel sat and gazed into the gently flowing waters of the Thames, his thoughts transported downstream to London, the fountainhead of his transgression and home to all his guilt.

'Janey, I hope you will not think less of me for unburdening my pain, but I was utterly inconsolable after Lizzie's passing. Not even my work gave me comfort. Then, after years of inexplicable emptiness, I suddenly found myself able to spout forth the most deep-seated reflections – like some prosodic wellspring, fed by the very elixir of life. My sonnets were ghosts who would keep their shrouds down, tolerably close and creek enough themselves to render a piano unnecessary. As their own vacated graves serve them to dance on, there is no danger of disturbing the lodgers beneath.'

Jane sat listening as Gabriel poured forth the years of anxiety and regret he'd only ever managed to articulate in his poetry. Although from humble beginnings, she was a remarkably intelligent woman, benefiting from a private education through her marriage to William Morris, which in turn gifted her with a passion for reading, embroidery and playing the piano. All of which meant that Gabriel's words were certainly not lost on this sensitive young consort.

Heartened by her kindness and understanding, he continued. 'One day, I was discussing the lost manuscript with my friend, Charles Howell. I must have set forth such a tide of despair because, in no time at all, he had planted the seed of an idea so spellbinding, it had all but consumed me – I must retrieve the book of poems from Lizzie's grave. After a great deal of rumination, I instructed him to recover the manuscript, granting him power to act on my behalf in all matters, as he thought best, and ensuring the utmost discretion of everyone involved. He wrote to the Rt. Hon. Henry Bruce, then Home Secretary, asking him to authorise the exhumation order, which, incredibly, he did. And there it was, the plans were laid. All I had to do was wait.

'Come that fateful evening, I found myself in the company of Charles' wife, Kitty, as we waited for events to unfold. There was little conversation between us, and as the minutes passed by so slowly, all I could do was stare blankly at the mantel clock. I do believe poor Mrs Howell was more nervous than I. In an effort to distract myself from the woeful chain of events I had set in motion, I tried to recount the sonnets, soon to be given new life. Alas, my thoughts continually fell on poor Lizzie, lying there blissfully unaware that the tranquillity of her final resting place was about to be so rudely and unceremoniously shattered.'

*

Highgate Cemetery, London
5 October 1869

'Here, this way,' said Howell, shining his lantern on a collection of graves, set in a quiet corner of the cemetery.

'You're sure it's here?' said Tebbs, Rossetti's friend and lawyer, reluctant to leave the sanctuary of the gravel path.

'Yes, this is the one.' Howell shone the light onto a tall headstone, capped with a large quatrefoil denoting the Rossetti family plot.

'Look, it's marked I-H-S ... the three Greek letters of Jesus's name, just as Gabriel described it.'

He knelt down over the horizontal gravestone and brushed away the moss to reveal the inscription.

ALSO TO THE MEMORY OF

ELIZABETH ELEANOR

WIFE OF THEIR ELDER SON
DANTE GABRIEL ROSSETTI
WHO DIED FEBRUARY 11TH 1862
AGED 30 YEARS.

'Mr Tebbs, would you care to confirm?' said Howell.

The lawyer adjusted his spectacles and squinted at the carved lettering.

'Yes, I can confirm – this is the grave of Elizabeth Eleanor Rossetti,' he said, removing his hat in respect.

With that, the two gravediggers from the Funeral Company of London began building a fire by which to work. But if Howell and Tebbs thought they were going to stand idly by, watching the other men toil, they were sadly mistaken. Before long, they were straining every last muscle to help lift the stone slab guarding Lizzie's grave, and Rossetti's precious manuscript. After a lot of huffing and puffing, the gravestone was eventually laid to one side, revealing a similarly shaped area of compacted soil.

The two gravediggers looked at Howell. 'You sure, guv?' said the older man.

Howell glanced at Tebbs, then nodded, returning to the warmth of the fire as the first shovel broke the earth.

'There's no turning back now,' said Tebbs, stomping his feet to get some feeling back into his toes. 'Tell me honestly, Charles, do you think Gabriel is justified in retrieving these poems?'

'I do, sir. Surely, it would be more of a crime to deprive the world of his words than to ... remove a little dirt from God's hallowed ground. Anyway, it makes no difference to Lizzie now.'

Tebbs looked into the dancing flames, his brow furrowed with concern.

'You do not agree?' asked Howell.

Tebbs remained silent, not wanting to anger his client's representative.

Howell continued, 'No doubt Gabriel thought it a noble action to place the book inside her coffin, that day; but after seven years, I believe it just as reasonable for him to give up this prolonged bout of self-denial, in the same way one would ... return a mourning suit. I have spoken with a number of Gabriel's friends and they, like me, consider his so-called act of devotion to have been a most foolish gesture. In which case, would he not merely be persisting in his wrongdoing to let his poems rot away to nothing?'

'I suppose when you put it that way, one can see the merit in it,' said Tebbs.

The nearby bell of St Michael's church struck the hour and still the men dug, each casually discarded spade of earth adding to the growing spoil heap. Suddenly, one of the steel blades hit the top of the casket with a thud. A watching barn owl let out a ghost-like screech, as if to mark the moment. Howell and Tebbs rushed over and peered into the gaping hole, watching intently as the two gravediggers carefully removed the remaining subsoil to reveal the coffin lid.

'There, what's that?' said Tebbs, pointing to a greenish brown oblong peeking out of the mud.

The young lad crouched down and brushed away the earth with his bony fingers, revealing a dulled brass plate bearing Lizzie's name.

'Let's get her out, shall we?' said Howell.

The old man raised his hand in the air. 'Give us a minute, sir,' he said, wheezing heavily as he rested his forehead on his spade handle.

After a brief respite, and a warming slug of whisky, the two men threaded a length of rope through the brass handles and, with the help of Howell and Tebbs, hauled the casket up until it rested at the graveside.

Anxious to proceed, Howell grabbed a crowbar and hammer and attacked the seal of the coffin lid, working his way round with a succession of blows, as the others looked on, respectfully. With just a single stubborn screw remaining, he readied himself and gave the crowbar one final heave.

Suddenly, the coffin burst open, expelling a rush of fetid air, as if some ghostly spirit had been loosed from years of interment. Holding a lantern over the casket, Tebbs peered down at the gruesome contents. No sooner had the rank stench hit his nostrils than he turned away and was violently sick in a nearby shrub. Howell, however, had come prepared, placing a handkerchief soaked in camphor over his nose. He bent down to pick up the small book resting on Lizzie's chest, then stopped – recalling that a treasured personal Bible had also been placed on the body. Having returned the holy book to where he found it, he brought the lantern closer.

Then he saw it. Wedged down the side of the coffin, next to Lizzie's head, was a dark-coloured book. He carefully lifted it out, bringing with it great strands of matted red hair – an indication that perhaps Mrs Rossetti was not quite as willing to relinquish her husband's loving tribute, as had been imagined.

From Gabriel's description, Howell recalled the poems were bound in a rough, grey calfskin with pages edged in red. The pitiful-looking object in his hand bore little resemblance to that – its cover stained and discoloured, the pages sopping wet and stuck together with what looked like wormholes puncturing the paper.

'Is that it?' said Tebbs, looking pale and holding a handkerchief to his mouth.

Howell nodded. 'It appears we have what we came for.'

'Oh, my – is it legible?'

'It's certainly not in the best condition. Hopefully, my friend, Doctor Llewellyn Williams, will be able to lend his considerable expertise to its restoration. By the time we return it to Gabriel, it will look as good as new, I'm sure.'

Far from convinced, Tebbs turned away as Howell pulled another clump of Lizzie's hair from between the sorry pages.

'Charles, I'm sure you recall how much poor Gabriel cherishes the image of his young wife in her flowering. It would break his heart to think of her in anything but a state of unblemished serenity.'

'Why yes, of course. If he asks, I will tell him she was a vision of radiance, looking quite at peace by the glow of the fire.'

With that, Howell tipped the gravediggers two shillings and left them to re-bury the coffin, for the most part, as they'd found it.

The following day, Howell handed the badly decayed portfolio to Doctor Williams, in some vain hope that it could be brought back to life, and the tale of its unceremonious resurrection masked from all but the enlightened few. Yet somehow, he doubted it.

*

Kelmscott – by the Thames, Oxfordshire
27 July 1871

Lost in the swirl of emotions of that haunting day, Rossetti stared forlornly at his shoes.

'After a further ten days, I eventually received the manuscript from Doctor Williams.'

Jane, already familiar with the lion's share of the sorry tale, gave his hand a gentle squeeze.

'Can you imagine my alarm, when, despite them being expertly dried and disinfected, I found the pages to be in a state of complete and utter degradation? The poem, *Jenny*, had a wormhole right through the middle of it.'

Jane nodded, supportively. It was all she could do.

'Although, my spirits were raised when Charles informed me that, by some miracle, Lizzie's body had remained in an almost perfect state of preservation. So much so, that when they opened the coffin, she looked as beautiful and youthful as she ever had in life. And her copper-coloured hair had, by all accounts, continued to grow, so that it practically filled the casket. It was a vision that still gives me great comfort, to this day. And yet there is a part of my soul that deeply regrets the whole sorry incident.'

Jane reached up to kiss his cheek. 'You did what you thought to be right. And as for those cruel, cruel people who spoke of Lizzie casting you down with some vile spell of retribution, well, they are nothing more than heartless imbeciles.'

He turned to look at her.

'I think deep in my heart, I know that now,' he said, the tears streaming down his cheeks.

Then, before Jane knew what was happening, he was removing his shoes and socks, rolling up his trouser legs and stepping out into the shallow water off the small river-beach, sending hundreds of tiny fry flitting in all directions.

'Gabriel, what on earth are you doing?' said Jane, as he cupped his hands and plunged them into the river.

'I am cleansing myself with the waters of the Isis,' he said, letting it cascade over his head. 'To my great shame, my creative powers have become sullied by a secret that I have kept from you for far too long.'

He turned towards the riverbank and stretched out his arms towards her. 'In truth, I wanted my poems to breathe new life, so that they might once again fill the air with love. Don't you see, Janey? It was all for you.'

'Gabriel, I'm flattered, truly, but please come out of there, before you catch your death of cold.'

Overcome and shaking with emotion, his mind could not help but conjure up the damsel-like figure of Beatrice, so artfully portrayed by his late friend, the sculptor, John Hancock.

He placed both hands on his heart, and in joyous tones spoke the words of the great Florentine poet, Dante Alighieri, from his book, *La Vita Nuova*:

'In that book which is
My memory ...
On the first page
That is the chapter when
I first met you
Appear the words ...
Here begins a new life'

Chapter Forty-Two

Emily sat on the settee, her knees tucked up under her chin, sipping a mug of tea that Tom had just made her – the dark bags under her eyes a clue to her state of exhaustion. After tossing and turning for over two hours last night, she'd taken herself off to the spare bedroom where she'd got precisely no sleep at all. The horrific events at the Pitt Rivers Museum kept playing over and over in her mind, not to mention Henry's last words to her before he was brutally attacked: "If you value your life, Emily, go back to Bristol and stay there." Well, here she was, and she felt anything but safe.

Truth be known, Tom was feeling just as anxious, although Emily could see he was doing his best to hide it. Having received a call from the police the previous afternoon, explaining that Emily had been involved in a serious incident, he'd jumped in his car and driven like a madman to Kidlington Police Station, where she was giving a statement to Thames Valley CID. Walking back to the car park, she'd burst into tears and spent the next few minutes wrapped in Tom's arms, sobbing quietly. All the tension and petty squabbling of the last few days was gone.

'Did I put sugar in it, babe?' said Tom.

With a nod, she placed the mug on the coffee table and bent down to pick up Bill, who'd been sitting, staring at her for some time. She gently stroked his back as he wandered up and down her lap, eventually curling himself up in a ball with his nose tucked into his tail. She smiled and wished she felt as safe and secure.

Tom sat down beside her and put his hand on her knee, staring blankly at some inane Saturday morning TV show.

'You can't go back to work on Monday, not after all this,' he said, eventually.

'What? No, I'll be fine. It'll take my mind off it.'

'Do the police want to see you again?'

'No. I gave them a description and told them all I could.'

Tom looked at her and gave her knee a squeeze. 'I'm sure they've got their best people on it.'

'I hope they catch that fucker and string him up by his balls, after what he did to Henry.'

'He's in the Radcliffe, isn't he? Do you want me to give them a call and see how he's doing?'

Emily shook her head. 'No, I'll ring them later.'

There was another long silence. Suddenly, the letter box flipped open, then slammed shut with a clang. Tom got up and walked over to retrieve the small white envelope lying on the carpet. He turned it over and looked at the postmark. 'Oh, you're joking.'

'Is that—?' said Emily, spotting the italic type.

'Afraid so. Do you want me to open it?'

'No. Just put it in the bin,' she said, lifting Bill up and placing him gently on the settee beside her. They can go to hell as far as I'm concerned.'

'Fair enough,' said Tom, frowning at the envelope.

Emily got up and switched off the TV. 'I'm going upstairs to get my work stuff together. Why don't you go down the pub or something?'

'I'm not in the mood, to be honest.'

'Alright. I won't be long,' she said, grabbing her mug of tea.

It was a couple of hours before Emily finally made her way back downstairs. She'd only put her head down on the bed for a few seconds, then found herself waking from a deep, dreamless sleep. The house was quiet. Bill was still curled up on the settee and there was no sign of Tom. Perhaps he'd gone down the pub, after all. She rubbed her eyes and was thinking about getting herself a restorative glass of wine when she noticed the envelope on the coffee table. Hadn't Tom put it in the bin, earlier? She couldn't remember. Ignoring it, she walked into the kitchen, poured herself a glass of Malbec from a half-empty bottle on the side and returned to the comfort of the settee. Bill lifted his head and looked at her with sleepy eyes.

'What? I'm not opening it,' she said, taking a sip of wine and switching on the TV with the remote. She sat watching *Top of the Pops 2* with feigned interest while Bill barely moved a whisker.

'Oh, who am I kidding?' she said, reaching over and grabbing the envelope. She slid her finger under the flap and ripped it open, annoyed by her complete lack of willpower.

The fourth note from the Shepherd was laid out as before:

EMILY,

YOUR JOURNEY OF DISCOVERY IS ALL BUT AT AN END.

#2. Desire – A man's lust is his eternal shame, for the appetite of a licentious man will never be fulfilled.

#3. Ignorance – the mind is not merely a vessel to be filled, but a vine to be nurtured for the most precious of fruit.

#4. Lust for Death – all must dissolve into their beginnings, but only those with love in their heart may ascend the heavenly realms.

#5. Kingdom of Flesh – when the body returns to nature and is resolved into its own roots, may the soul rise up, free from the bondage of man.

THE SHEPHERD

She sat back and closed her eyes, feeling utterly drained. The initial enthusiasm of the last two weeks had left her. She couldn't even be bothered to work out whether the clues matched the final four paintings Henry had described. All she could think about was that poor man, lying in a hospital bed and fighting for his life. She screwed up the note and hurled it across the room.

'Leave me alone!' she shouted, her eyes filled with tears.

*

When Tom returned from the supermarket, he found Emily sound asleep on the settee, still clutching an empty wine glass. He picked up the screwed-up paper ball that had come to rest at the foot of the stairs and dropped it nonchalantly into the wastepaper bin. After gently prising the wine glass from her fingers, he bent down and kissed her on the forehead.

'No more adventures for you, my girl,' he whispered, and went into the kitchen to start preparing dinner.

Chapter Forty-Three

Orchard Lane Farm, Wendover, Bucks

13 November 1999

Rarely in his life had Luke Waltham been so angry. When the news of Marcus Tyburn's unprovoked axe attack on Henry Faber reached him later that morning, he stormed out of his office, cursing like a trooper – much to the surprise of the ArtScreen staff doing some weekend work, most of whom had never heard him raise his voice before, let alone lose his rag completely. He got into his Aston Martin DB7 and tore up the A40 towards the farm at Wendover, where Tyburn had been told to meet him. Of course, being 'told' to do anything didn't sit well with Tyburn, but he reluctantly agreed.

Forty-five minutes later, Luke arrived at the farm, still seething as he marched over to the Range Rover where Tyburn was sitting smoking a cigarette. He grabbed the handle and yanked the car door open.

'Do you remember the conversation we had three days ago?' said Luke.

Tyburn glanced at him with a look of disdain. 'What's your problem? I did you a favour.'

'Really? And how do you work that out?'

'That old fucker was gonna tell the girl everythin'. So I taught him a lesson,' said Tyburn, barely able to keep the grin off his face.

'Well, I'm glad you think it's funny.'

'What are you frettin' about?'

'I'll tell you what I'm fretting about. Every copper within a three hundred mile radius is going to be looking for you. Not only that – you've probably scared the crap out of Emily, to the point where she'll never want to see another Pre-Raphaelite painting as long as she lives.'

'I don't see it like that.'

'Oh, you don't. Well, shall I tell you how I see it? This job is pretty much screwed, thanks to you.'

'Rubbish. We carry on as planned. The old man's in a coma, so the police won't get anythin' out of him. And Mountfield will soon sweet-talk the girl round. Before you know it, she'll be right back where we want her. Then all we have to do is—'

'You just don't get it, do you?' said Luke, shaking his head. 'You've compromised everything. Emily will have been interviewed by the police and no doubt given them a detailed description of you. They may even know your name, by now. Cordell is probably issuing an all-ports warning for your arrest, as we speak.'

'Fine. I'll lay low for a while.'

'Damned right, you will. I don't want you stepping foot outside this farmhouse until we know how much damage you've caused. You can stay in the cellar until things calm down.'

'Fuck that! I'm not stayin' cooped up in some dingy fuckin' basement.'

'If you want to remain part of this team, you'll do exactly as I say. Now get inside, before somebody sees you.'

The scowl on Tyburn's face told Luke all he needed to know, as if he wasn't already aware – Tyburn despised him and all he stood for.

He got out of the Range Rover and slammed the door. 'Alright, where is it, then?'

Luke led the way into the farmhouse, through to a solid oak door leading off the main hallway. He opened it and flicked the light switch, revealing a set of concrete steps. 'After you,' he said.

The two men descended into a large rectangular space running virtually the entire length of the building. Far from being cold and damp, the fully furnished cellar comprised of grey stone walls, restored oak beams and under-floor heating, making it all quite homely. This was Luke's quiet space.

Tyburn slumped into one of the leather armchairs, flicked on the widescreen TV and stretched out his legs. 'Maybe this won't be so bad, after all,' he said, clocking the fully stocked wine rack in the far corner.

'Just keep the noise down, and I'm sure we'll get along fine.'

'Don't worry, you won't hear a peep out of me. What's in there?' said Tyburn, pointing to a thick steel door in the far wall.

'None of your fucking business, now give me your car keys,' said Luke.

Tyburn frowned. 'What do you want them for?'

'I need to park it in the barn. I don't want my nosey neighbours knowing you're here.'

Tyburn fished in his pocket and threw him the keys.

'I'll get Danny to get you a change of clothes and help you move the sofa-bed from upstairs.'

'Tell him to bring me some smokes, while he's at it,' barked Tyburn.

Luke gave him a disparaging look.

'... and a couple of ashtrays.'

'I won't be long. And don't even think about touching those,' said Luke, pointing to the wine rack. 'That stuff's far too good for the likes of you.'

Luke climbed the stone steps, closed the cellar door and walked into the kitchen. Resting both hands on the work top, he looked out of the kitchen window and let out a deep, calming sigh. Having Tyburn in the house was the last thing he wanted, but at least he could keep an eye on him for a while – take him *off grid*, as far as the police were concerned. But how do you control a wild animal without chains and a gun – a caged one at that? The simple truth is, you can't. There was too much at stake to get rid of him now. Marcus Tyburn had become, a necessary evil.

Chapter Forty-Four

It was the week before Christmas and DCI Cordell was feeling anything but festive. Investigations into the gruesome attack on Henry Faber had proved fruitless, with no leads as to the identity of the perpetrator, or his motive. Even the CCTV footage from the Pitt Rivers Museum was inconclusive, showing little of the man who'd been savvy enough to keep his face turned away from the cameras.

And here was Cordell, holed up in a small office in Scotland Yard, clutching two remote controls and gazing at a pair of portable TV screens perched on the corner of DCI Reynolds' desk. This was not his idea of fun.

Vice Squad's raid on The Ruby Viper, appropriately code-named Operation Gallery, had gone perfectly, enabling Reynolds to confiscate over a thousand hours of footage from the club's six wall-mounted security cameras. The most useful of which was positioned in the corner of the grand foyer, catching everyone as they entered the club and made their way up the sweeping staircase to the sumptuous lounge, bar and private rooms on the first-floor.

But, for Reynolds, the real icing on the cake was finding the five Eastern-European girls found locked in a room on the top floor. Drugged, beaten and abducted from their hometown near the Romanian/Bulgarian border; they'd been illegally trafficked into the country and were working as sex slaves to pleasure the club's wealthy patrons, including bankers, company executives and a handful of professional footballers – all of whom regularly visited the club for their fix of young female flesh.

Unfortunately for Cordell, ploughing through hours and hours of video wasn't the sort of task he could delegate to one of his junior colleagues. It required an experienced eye to spot just the right sort of villain. The trouble was, he didn't exactly know who or what he was looking for as he scanned the faces entering the club and making their way upstairs. If he observed someone of interest, he had to switch to the next monitor to follow them through to the lounge area, where cameras were discreetly hidden behind flower arrangements and decorative wall mirrors. It was tiring work and even a slight lapse in concentration caused him to have to rewind the footage and re-check it for a second or third time.

Three hours in and he was about to call it a day, when Reynolds wandered in with two mugs of fresh coffee.

'How's it going?'

Cordell sneered and chucked the remote control across the desk.

'That good, eh?'

'There's a couple of familiar faces, but no one with enough nous to break into the Ashmolean and nick a multi-million-pound painting.'

'Sounds to me like you admire them.'

'Who?'

'The blokes you're after.'

'You're kidding. In my book, they're every bit as bad as the pimps and pushers you go after. It may sound a bit prosaic, but you'd be surprised how the victims of art theft can become emotionally traumatised when something they've loved for a number of years is taken from them – it's like losing a member of the family.'

Reynolds let out a snort of derision. 'Come on, Francis, ... really?'

'It's true. Any honest collector worth their salt, knows that they're just temporary custodians of these treasures, so they can be passed on to others after they're gone. But someone who steals an artwork doesn't deserve to feel pleasured by it, to have the honour of owning it. They're an affront to human creativity in my book. So no, I don't admire them, or think they're not worth bothering with, just because they've nicked a piece of art!'

'Okay, okay. You've made your point.'

'Right, then park your backside down there and give me a hand, will you?'

Reynolds pulled up a chair and fished through the large cardboard box of DVDs on his desk.

'Okay, what have we got here? *Stair cam – November fourth.* That was the day before the break-in, wasn't it? I doubt they'd have been in the club that night.'

Cordell twisted the end of his moustache between his fingers. 'You're probably right. But let's take a quick look, anyway.'

Ten minutes in, Reynolds sat back in his chair and rubbed his eyes. 'Francis, I'm popping out for a quick fag. My vision's starting to go blurry.'

'Call yourself a detective, … bloody lightweight,' said Cordell, still glued to the TV monitors. 'Anyway, I thought you were trying to give up.'

'I do, every New Year's Eve. Then, after a week or two in this place, I'm back on forty a day.'

'Right, well grab me a ham sandwich on your way back, will you? And a KitKat, if they've got one.'

'Do you want white or—' Reynolds suddenly grabbed the remote and pressed the *PAUSE* button.

'What? … what is it?' said Cordell.

Reynolds pointed to the screen. 'I know that guy. That's Danny Forgan.'

'Okay, what's so unusual about that? Didn't you say his dad owns the club?'

'Yes, yes, but who's that with him?'

Cordell stared at the frozen image. 'I can't see, he's looking away from the camera. Check the box for the next DVD; we might be able to catch him going through to the lounge.'

Reynolds scrabbled around and found another disc labelled *Lounge Cam 2* from the same date.

'Here,' said Reynolds, handing it to Cordell.

He opened the tray, removed the old DVD and dropped in the new one, pushing it back in, impatiently.

'Fast forward to nine thirty-seven pm, will you?' said Reynolds.

'Alright, give me chance.'

'There they are, heading for the bar. They've got their backs to us again.'

They watched closely as the two men ordered drinks, then made small talk with two scantily clad bargirls.

'There – the tall one's turned round,' said Reynolds.

There was a pause as they both leaned in to get a better view.

Reynolds smiled when he saw the man's face. 'You know who that is, don't you?'

Cordell twirled the end of his moustache and grinned.

'Marcus Tyburn,' they said, in unison.

Chapter Forty-Five

Emily sat transfixed by the two naked figures of Satyr and Hermaphrodite, locked in an erotic entanglement – their white-plaster bodies writhing like snakes against the blood-red walls of the Randolph Gallery.

What on earth she was doing back in Oxford, she couldn't quite fathom. After the Pitt Rivers attack, she'd vowed never to set foot in the city again, and as for *The Lights of the World* paintings, all that would have to remain a secret for someone else to uncover. On receiving Henry Faber's information about the last four paintings, she'd texted the details to Julian Mountfield and made it quite clear that, as far as she was concerned, she wanted nothing else to do with it. Then came the phone call. Julian was his usual charming self and couldn't begin to understand how upsetting this whole thing must have been for her. After giving her an update on Henry's remarkable progress in hospital, he subtly turned the topic of discussion to the paintings. She was about to end the call when he played his trump card – an invitation – 'the chance of a lifetime', as he put it, and would she at least think about coming to the Ashmolean so he could discuss it with her? It was difficult, minus the details, but after sleeping on it for a few nights, she'd talked it over with Rosa and Tom, who had wildly differing views on the subject. Rosa had wisely laid out a few pros and cons, but in the end said, '... just hear him out; what harm can it do?' Tom, on the other hand, accused her of delusion bordering on insanity for even considering it – which she hadn't taken kindly to, but knew he was just trying to protect her in his own particular way.

In the end, it was her decision. And so, here she was, staring at a steamy and yet curiously hypnotic Roman sculpture. Although the female-looking Hermaphrodite appeared to be the victim of the piece, pushing the Satyr away with her right hand, on closer inspection she also had her foot hooked over his ankle, thereby preventing his escape. And if there was any doubt as to her true intentions, one only had to see the amorous expression on her face to realise she was every bit as intent on their sexual union as her lover. It took the sound of a nearby phone ringing to tear her away from the *scena d'amore*. She looked over to the front desk by the main entrance.

'Yes Julian, she's sat here waiting for you,' said the receptionist, glancing in Emily's direction.

Emily felt a flush of embarrassment in her cheeks. Why had she come here, again? After what had happened to Henry, the very idea of opening up the whole Shepherd's clue thing repulsed her. And yet, somehow, the enigma of the Pre-Raphaelites kept drawing her back – like a muse, flattered by the scrutiny of the artist's gaze. She knew this was a love affair doomed to failure, but the temptation was too great – the advances of the Satyr too strong, too alluring.

As she stood up to head for the exit, a familiar voice called out from down the hall.

'Beguiling, aren't they?' said Julian, strolling towards her.

'Err, yes. You could say that.'

He leaned over and kissed her on the cheek. 'How have you been?'

'Oh, okay, … considering,' she said, a little shocked at the informality. It had only been a few weeks since they last met, but a lot had changed in that time; in her mind, anyway.

'Of course, of course. It must have been difficult for you. Why don't we go upstairs? There's something I want to show you.'

'Okay,' she said, putting on an uncharacteristically nervous smile. What the hell am I doing? she thought, as they got into the lift.

Julian pressed the button for the second floor. 'How's Tom?' he said, sensing her unease.

'Fine. He's been really supportive.' Emily looked up at the floor numbers, watching as each one lit up.

'And how does he feel about you coming back to Oxford?'

She paused. 'Oh, he's fine with it. In fact, it was him who persuaded me to come', she said, lying through her teeth.

Julian nodded and smiled.

Having reached the second floor, they exited the lift and walked along a short corridor, past a large cabinet of medieval glass and into the room containing the Ashmolean's Pre-Raphaelite collection – Gallery 55. She remembered it from her visit with Rosa, a few months before, although the decor was different and there was the faint smell of fresh paint in the air. A handful of visitors were milling around, but it was still early, not even 10.15 am.

'I'm so glad you came,' said Julian, parking himself on one of the benches in the middle of the room. 'I know this can't have been easy for you.'

'It wasn't,' she said, sitting down next to him. 'So, what was it you wanted to show me?'

Julian raised his hands in the air. 'This,' he said, referencing the gallery.

Emily took another look around the room. Gone were the dowdy green walls and shabby paintwork, replaced with vibrant red wallpaper, fresh white skirting boards and silver-grey emulsion on the upper walls and ceiling. A new parquet floor provided the finishing touch to the *à la mode* look. Remembering that the thieves had broken in through the skylight, she looked up. It was as good as new.

'I like what you've done with the place.'

He laughed. 'Thanks. The thing is Emily, after I got your text, I paid a visit to the Tate Gallery and managed to persuade them to check the back of the last four paintings. Each one has a sun mark, just like the others. Henry was spot on.'

'Great, so you've found them all.'

'You found them, Emily, this is your discovery.'

'Hardly. It was Henry who put the pieces together. And I still think he was behind the whole Shepherd thing. Although, he denied it when I put it to him.'

'Of course he would. That's just like him, modest to the last.'

Emily looked at him. 'He's not dead, is he?'

'No, no, that's not what I meant. But I'm afraid the attack will have taken its toll on the poor chap. Apparently, the wound in his leg was so severe at one point, they thought they might have to amputate.'

'And did they?'

'No, no. Luckily, they managed to stop the infection in time. But it was touch and go for a while.'

'Blimey,' she said, shaking her head.

'I know. I just don't get why someone would want to do that to an innocent old man?' said Julian, putting his hand on Emily's arm. 'Look, I've worked with Henry long enough to know that he would want us to do something with this discovery. Not keep it hushed up like some secret for the privileged few. He'd be desperate for the public to see it.'

'And he told you that, did he?'

'In as many words, yes.'

'Okay, so ... ?'

'Emily, I have a proposal. I'd like you to help me put on an exhibition.'

She looked at him with a mix of trepidation and curiosity. 'An exhibition? ... of what?'

'The eight paintings – here in Henry's gallery.'

'You're kidding?'

'Not at all. What better way to honour his discovery, and yours, than with an exhibition celebrating the genius of the three Pre-Raphaelite Brothers? We could call it *The Lights of the World*.'

Emily gazed at the far wall. Her conscience detested the very idea of a "celebration", when Henry was going through such emotional and physical trauma. And yet, perversely, there was a part of her that couldn't help but be excited by it.

'It's your gallery, Julian, you don't need to ask my permission,' she said, standing up to go.

'Oh, but I do – if I want you to manage it.'

She turned and stared at him. 'What?'

Julian got to his feet and faced her. 'Why not? You've got the experience. And if it wasn't for you, I wouldn't be here talking about it. What do you say?'

She looked him in the eyes, visions of the wrestling Satyr and Hermaphrodite raging in her head. It was everything she'd ever dreamed of, to work for a great institution like the Ashmolean. And Julian was right, it would be a fitting testimony to Henry's work. But what about her job? Not to mention travelling to Oxford every day.

'No, I can't. There are too many obstacles.'

'What, your job in Bristol?'

'Well yes, there is that—'

'You don't have to worry on that score. I'll talk to Richard and we'll come to some arrangement, I'm sure. And you don't even need to commute to Oxford every day. We can put you up at The Randolph, while you're working with us.'

'Ha, right. I'm sure Tom would love that.'

'Emily, it's a fantastic opportunity for you. I've seen some of your work at the Royal West of England Academy – you're perfect for it. And I'm not just saying that.'

She couldn't quite believe what was happening. All the barriers and moral challenges seemed to be falling away. Of course, Tom would be far from happy, but she could work on him.

'Well, I mean ... you couldn't just base it on the eight paintings, you'd have to include a lot of background material, artist sketches, that kind of thing,' she said.

'Fine, we'll do the research, scour the world for anything related to the paintings. There's the Draper sketchbook for a start, we could have a whole section on that. And think of it, Emily, it would be the first time that all eight paintings have been seen together.'

'Yes, that would be quite something.'

'It'll be a new discovery for a new millennium – precisely why *The Gates of Dawn* was painted in the first place.'

'What about the other places?' said Emily. 'You'd have to get permission from Drapers' Hall, Keble College, Birmingham Museum and the Tate—'

Julian laughed. 'Don't worry about them. I'm sure they'll be only too happy to contribute, once they understand the importance of it. This is ground-breaking stuff, Emily, it really is.'

She nodded. No doubt Julian could convince even the most fortress-like institutions to loan out their treasures, if he put his mind to it.

'So, you'll do it?'

She let out a sigh and looked at him. 'For Henry, ... of course I'll do it.'

Chapter Forty-Six

Scotland Yard, London
27 March 2000

DCI Cordell stood at the vending machine, pondering which particular type of homogenised sludge he should choose to kick-start his morning. He stared blankly at the list of beverages: coffee, tea, chocolate, soup and even sparkling orange, apparently. He inserted a 20p coin and waited for the machine to dispense a hot chocolate. As he reached down to extract the ludicrously small plastic cup, a voice called out down the corridor.

'You're not actually going to drink that, are you?' said DCI Reynolds.

Cordell looked at the frothy red-brown contents and gave it a sniff. 'No, I don't think I am,' he said, and poured it back in the slops' tray.

'What are you doing in, this early? I didn't think you Art and Antiques boys surfaced before midday,' said Reynolds, smirking as he took a puff of his cigarette.

'Keep talking like that and those two cases of Scotland's finest might just turn into a batch of Asian knock-off.'

Reynolds laughed. 'Anyway, can you spare a few minutes? I've got something that might just cheer you up, you miserable bugger.'

Cordell found another 20p in his pocket, put it in the slot and hit the button for a cup of sparkling orange. 'Go on, I'm listening.'

'One of our Met. colleagues took a call this morning from a girl who works at The Ruby Viper. She's worried about her flatmate who's gone missing, a girl called Candice who also works at the club – real name, Alisha Cross.'

'Okay, what's that got to do with me?'

'Apparently, the night before Alisha went missing, she was beaten up by Danny Forgan.'

'That still doesn't tie him to the robbery.'

'Yeah, yeah, hold your horses. The girl also said Alisha overheard Danny and another guy talking about a job they were working on. And I thought, I know a bloke who might be interested in a bit of information like that.'

'What's her name – the girl who called?'

'Brandi Burrows. She's a dancer at the club. One of my officers is with her, now. Do you want to sit in on the interview?'

'Err, did Van Gogh cut off his own earlobe?'

'Okay, ... I'll take that as a yes. Come on, she's downstairs.'

Cordell reached down, took one look at the cup of bubbling orange liquid, that looked more like car radiator fluid than a 'refreshing fruit drink', and tipped it in the slops' tray.

*

The two DCIs entered Interview Room 2 and sat down at the table. The young, dark-haired woman sitting opposite was cheaply dressed in a lilac top, black imitation-fur coat and jeans, with large purple earrings and a matching plastic bangle that kept banging on the table, every time she finished taking a drag of her cigarette.

'Hello Brandi, I'm Detective Chief Inspector Pete Reynolds and this is DCI Francis Cordell. I know you've already spoken to one of my colleagues, but would you mind filling us in on some of the details? You're worried about the whereabouts of your flatmate, Alisha Cross, is that right?'

'Yeah, that's right,' said Brandi, her left arm held tightly against her chest. 'She's not been home for a couple of days, and that's not like her. She always rings me if she's ... staying out for the night.'

'When did you last see Miss Cross?' said Reynolds.

'Saturday afternoon. I left her in the flat. She was beaten up pretty bad, in the face an' that. She wasn't in no state to be working at the club, poor babe, so I left her on the settee with a bottle of wine and went to work. When I got home, about four am, she'd gone. No note, no nothing.'

'And you didn't report her missing, then?'

'No, not straight away. I thought she might have gone to one of the local hospitals, so I rang them all, later that morning; but none of them had seen her. I left it the rest of Sunday, but when there was no sign of her this morning, I got really worried. That's when I rang you lot.'

'You said Alisha was with Danny Forgan on Friday night, when she was beaten up?'

'Yeah, cocky little shit. His father owns the club. But you already know that, right?'

Reynolds smiled, knowing she was referring to the raid on the club, back in December.

'After a couple of drinks, Alisha and Danny went back to one of the private suites.'

'Alone?'

She paused. 'No, there was another bloke with them – a real nasty piece of work.'

'Do you know his name?'

'I think she said his name was Marcus. I've seen him at the club a couple of times.'

'Last name?' said Cordell, taking over the questioning.

She shook her head. 'Not sure I want to know, neither.'

'Why's that?'

'He's got that look – a real psycho. The less you know about someone like that, the better.'

'Okay. So, what happened to Alisha?'

'I was chatting to a gentleman in the lounge when I heard this screaming. She comes running in with her dress all ripped and blood on her face. She was pretty hysterical. We tried to calm her down, but she kept shouting that she was going to tell the police about what Danny had done. I mean, you can't threaten these people like that.'

'But that didn't stop you calling us,' said Cordell.

'She's my friend, what do you expect? Those bastards have taken her, I'm sure of it.'

'Alright, Miss Burrows, ...' said Reynolds, offering her another cigarette, which she took – her hand shaking slightly as she gripped his and approached the flame of his lighter. '... so, what happened to Danny and Marcus?'

'One of the security guys went back to look for them, but they'd gone.'

'You told my officer that Alisha overheard them talking. What about, exactly?'

'Danny was stoned. He kept going on about some big job he was working on. I think that's why this Marcus guy was with him, to stop him shooting his mouth off.'

'Did Alisha say what sort of job it was?' said Cordell.

'No. Just that it was a big pay-off and would set Danny up for life, if he played his cards right. She could see Marcus was getting pretty angry. Then, Danny said something to him and that's when it all kicked off.'

'What did he say?'

She shook her head. 'I might not have this right. I mean, she was pretty shaken up.'

'Okay, take your time – tell us what you remember.'

'It was something like, "Fuck you, Marcus, it'll be payday soon. Then I won't have to take any more of your shit."'

Reynolds looked at Cordell. 'What happened then?'

'Alisha said, Marcus went berserk at Danny, pushing him around, saying his big mouth was going to get him killed, one day. Then Danny just flipped, blaming it all on Alisha – accusing her of snooping around, listening to their conversations. She tried to make him see sense, but he was off his head and started hitting her and ripping her clothes. Then Marcus wades in and pulls him off her; and that's when things really got scary.'

'What do you mean?' said Reynolds.

'He got right up in her face and said, if she breathed a word of what she'd heard, he would cut her into little pieces.'

'That sounds like Tyburn,' said Cordell, under his breath.

'Alright, Miss Burrows. Look, I know you're worried about Alisha, but she's probably just gone to stay with her mum and dad. They live in Southend, right?' said Reynolds, referring to the printed notes from her call.

'Her mum does. Apparently, she's shacked up with some young fella over that way. Her dad fucked off years ago.'

'Right, well I'll get the uniform boys over there to check it out.'

Brandi nodded, disconsolately. 'I don't get why Alisha would just up and go without saying anything.'

'Probably scared out of her wits. Don't worry, we'll find her.'

While Reynolds showed Brandi out, Cordell sat thinking about the potential lead. *It'll be payday soon ...* What the hell did that mean? He checked the date on his watch. The attack on Alisha had taken place on Friday 24 March, just three days ago.

Was the Picasso going to be sold, or were they planning another hit – something bigger, perhaps? Either way, it was beginning to look like Marcus Tyburn and Danny Forgan were candidates for the Ashmolean robbery. In which case, if there was another big robbery on the cards, he was now playing catch-up.

Chapter Forty-Seven

Ashmolean Museum, Oxford

29 March 2000

In the darkness of Gallery 55, the newly installed motion sensors detected a sudden rise in room temperature. The hour was late and the sound of footfall from the museum's visitors had long since faded to silence. Two men dressed in dark blue overalls entered the gallery and made straight for the floor-standing radiators in the centre of the room. The first, pushing a trolley containing two large gas cylinders, looked up at the security camera and watched as it slowly panned, tracking their every move. The second man, a heating engineer carrying a tool box and metal flight case, waited until the gallery doors had been locked, then began removing a selection of tools, placing them neatly on the floor in front of him.

Safe in the knowledge that the imminent operation was being monitored by *friendly* eyes, the engineer picked up a large spanner and began loosening one of the coupling-nuts on the side of the radiator. Instead of the usual hiss of air and black water that should have spewed forth, it remained silent – having already been drained of its contents, and the water supply capped at both ends. He then loosened the second nut and separated the radiator valve from the copper pipe running down into the floor. He opened the flight case and prised a replacement valve body from the foam layer inside. Custom-built to replicate the originals, right down to the specks of dirt and grime on the outer casing, these valves had a particularly unique feature – each was fitted with a nozzle in the top, fed by a metal tube inside the valve head, and supplied from the radiator's outflow drain. He offered the new valve unit up to the screw thread of the radiator and wiped some silicon sealant round the joint, before tightening the new coupling nut, taking care not to strip it. He then removed a new replacement lockshield valve from the flight case – in this instance, modified to contain a small battery powered pump – and proceeded to do the same at the other end of the radiator.

After repeating the whole procedure on the second radiator, he packed up his tools and gave his partner the nod.

The next part of the operation certainly wouldn't be found in any heating engineer's technical manual. The two men each put on a gas mask, ensuring their breathing and vision was clear. The 'gas man' then fitted a rubber hose from one of the cylinders onto the drain-off pipe of the new valve, making sure it was clamped and sealed tightly. Carefully monitoring the pressure gauge and flow meter on top of the cylinder, he turned the nozzle to the open position and waited for the radiator to fill with its newly pressurised contents. After a few minutes, the flow rate dropped, indicating the cylinder was empty and the precisely calculated volume of substance had been dispensed. Having closed the drain-off pipe, he turned his attention to the second radiator and repeated the process. Once complete, he moved the gas cylinders to one side and held a specially designed gas detector next to each of the four replacement valves to check for leaks. With everything confirmed as airtight, he gave the engineer a final thumbs up.

While the security camera maintained its silent watch, the two men removed their gas masks and breathed a welcome sigh of relief – both radiators in the centre of Gallery 55 had been safely converted. This just left the engineer to fit one small but vital component. He returned to his flight case and gently teased out a small, black, magnetised transponder from the moulded foam. Lying on his side, he reached under the first radiator and attached it securely to one of the cast-iron fins. Having flicked a switch on the side of the box, he peered into the narrow gap. There, shining back at him out of the darkness, was a tiny red light – the device was armed. After doing the same to the second radiator, he closed the flight case, picked up his tools and walked over to the gallery door where Coos Van Leer was waiting for them.

As the three men strolled along the second floor corridor to the lift, the engineer took out a mobile phone from his pocket, selected the only number pre-set into it and waited.

After a few seconds the call was answered.

'It's done,' said the engineer, and hung up.

Chapter Forty-Eight

Ashmolean Museum, Oxford

30 March 2000

Emily rested her hand on the radiator in the centre of the room and felt the tingle of cold metal beneath her fingers. Three phone calls and they still hadn't fixed the bloody thing. But to be honest, she couldn't have cared less as she stood admiring Herbert Draper's magical depiction of Aurora, hanging on the wall in front of her. The goddess looked resplendent, otherworldly – the queen of the unique amphitheatre Emily had created for her and her seven luminaries.

With the exception of the wall containing *The Gates of Dawn*, the rest of Gallery 55 was completely bare, ready for the companion pictures to be hung in their designated spaces. Six packing crates were already positioned at strategic points around the room, whilst in the gallery next door, museum staff were busy arranging drawings, painted sketches and other exhibits that would serve as an introduction to the first ever *The Lights of the World* exhibition.

'Is it me, or are we missing one?' said Julian, walking over to where Emily was standing.

'We're still waiting for Hunt's picture to arrive from Keble College.'

'You're kidding. The one picture that resides here in Oxford and that's the one that's late. I'll give the chaplain a call and see what's holding it up.'

'No need,' said Emily, raising her hand. 'He's promised me, faithfully, it'll be ready for collection this afternoon.'

'My apologies. I keep forgetting what a master of organisation you are.'

'That is why you hired me, isn't it? Now stop worrying. Everything will be where it needs to be for the grand opening on Monday night.'

'Excellent. So, remind me, ... what's going where?'

'Okay, when people enter the room, the first thing they'll see to their left is *The Light of the World*. I thought long and hard about this, and I think it deserves a wall to itself. It's not the earliest of the initial seven works, but let's face it, it is rather special.'

'Oh, I agree,' said Julian.

'Then along this side wall we'll hang *The Blind Girl, The Awakening Conscience* and *The Girlhood of Mary Virgin*. And facing them on the opposite wall will be *Beata Beatrix, Ophelia* and *The Finding of the Saviour in the Temple*. That just leaves ... her.'

Julian turned to face *The Gates of Dawn* at the head of the room. 'Why, of course.'

Emily continued. 'Next to each painting will be a display card giving its history and an explanation of its symbolism. Oh, not forgetting its underlying doctrine, as supplied by the Shepherd.' She gave Julian a sideways glance.

'What was that look for?' he said.

'Well, I've been wondering. You don't think we're being a bit impetuous, referencing the Shepherd's doctrines in the exhibition? I mean, we've not been able to substantiate them, or even confirm their true source.'

'No, I don't think so. We're just telling the public what we know, that's all. I mean, we've used the same source to validate the sun marks and they were spot on.'

'Mmm, ... I just wish they had some provenance to them.'

'Stop worrying,' said Julian, with a wave of his hand. 'It's going to be spectacular. How's the merchandising coming along?'

'The catalogues are due to arrive from the printers tomorrow, and the new souvenirs for the gift shop will be on the shelves first thing Monday morning.'

'I have to say, you've worked wonders to get this ready in time.'

'Thanks. I'm pleased, ... very pleased,' she said, with a slightly soulful tone, as she looked up at Aurora.

Julian put his hand on her shoulder. 'Everything okay?'

'Oh yes, it's just ... I wish Henry could be here to see it.'

'Emily, he would be so proud of what you've achieved. Have you been to see him since he's come out of his coma?'

'No, I thought I'd pop over to the hospital tomorrow. I spoke to the ward sister last night and she said he's still very weak. Apparently, he doesn't remember anything about the attack.'

'I'm not surprised. He's probably blocked it all out.'

Emily shook her head. 'I can't imagine how he must be feeling. Some nights, I wake up in a cold sweat from thinking about that day.'

'I know it's difficult, but that's all behind you now.'

'Is it?' she said, looking him in the eye. 'You weren't there, you don't know what it was like, being in the same room as that—'

'No, no. I'm sorry, I—'

'Every day, I think about how that could have been me lying in that hospital bed. And just when I think I've put it to the back of my mind, those words come back to haunt me.'

'Words?'

'Just before the attack, Henry warned me to go back to Bristol and stay there. Well, I sure as hell heeded that advice, didn't I. And correct me if I'm wrong, but they still haven't caught that fucking psychopath, have they?'

'Err, no ... not as yet.'

Emily's sudden outburst prompted one of the exhibition team to pop their head round the door. 'Everything okay?'

'It's alright, Phoebe, we're fine,' said Julian, and led Emily over to the bench in the centre of the room.

She sat down with her hands in her lap, staring at the crate containing Rossetti's *Beata Beatrix*.

'Do you know, I thought it was Henry sending me those clues, but now, I'm not so sure. Doesn't it ever strike you that this whole thing could have been ... engineered, somehow?'

Julian looked taken aback, then laughed. 'What? No, not for a minute. The sun marks are real enough, and the paintings all seem to fit the descriptions, don't you think?'

'No – I mean ... Oh, I don't know what I mean,' she said, putting her head in her hands.

'Emily, let's put things in perspective. It looks like Henry's on the road to recovery, thank goodness. And here we are, about to open the most important exhibition of British art in the last hundred years. Why don't you just focus on that? Believe me, you'll feel much better when you see thousands of people coming through those doors and marvelling at what you and Henry have made possible.'

She nodded. 'Maybe you're right.'

'I am. And imagine what Messrs Rossetti, Millais and Hunt would have made of it all. Seeing some of their most beloved artworks displayed together for the first time, and all at the dawning of the twenty-first century – they would scarcely have believed it.'

'Oh, I think they would, somehow,' she said, with a smile. 'Let's face it, they were never short on ego, were they?'

It was an incredible thought, to imagine the three founding members of the Pre-Raphaelite Brotherhood and Herbert Draper, wandering around Gallery 55, proudly showing off the fruits of their labour to an admiring audience from the future.

Emily stood up and gave herself a gentle pat on the cheeks. 'Okay, panic over. I'm fine.'

'Sure?' said Julian.

'Absolutely. Go on, you must have a stack of things to be getting on with. And I've got some pictures to hang.'

Julian gave her hand a squeeze and left her examining a large packing crate labelled: Property of BMAG – *The Blind Girl*.

*

As he made his way over to the gallery entrance, Julian glanced up at the CCTV camera and puffed out his cheeks. That was a close one, he thought, and took out his mobile phone to call Luke Waltham with the good news.

The scene was set. The opening of *The Lights of the World* exhibition was on schedule for Monday, 3 April 2000 – when, for the first time in history, the Brothers' seven sacred works would be shown, together. And all spearheaded by Draper's consummate masterpiece of hope and optimism for a brighter future. What a wonderful spectacle was in store for the people of Oxford.

THE LIGHTS OF THE WORLD

#1 – *The Blind Girl* (John Everett Millais – 1856)
Darkness – blessed are they that harbour the beacon of hope, when all around them is desolation and despair.

#2 – *The Awakening Conscience* (William Holman Hunt – 1853)
Desire – A man's lust is his eternal shame, for the appetite of a licentious man will never be fulfilled.

#3 – *The Girlhood of Mary Virgin* (Dante Gabriel Rossetti – 1849)
Ignorance – the mind is not merely a vessel to be filled, but a vine to be nurtured for the most precious of fruit.

#4 – *Beata Beatrix* (Dante Gabriel Rossetti – 1870)
Lust for Death – all must dissolve into their beginnings, but only those with love in their heart may ascend the heavenly realms.

#5 – *Ophelia* (John Everett Millais – 1852)
Kingdom of Flesh – when the body returns to nature and is resolved into its own roots, may the soul rise up, free from the bondage of man.

#6 – *The Finding of the Saviour in the Temple* (William Holman Hunt – 1860)
Folly of Man – learned we may be with another man's learning, only wise can we become with wisdom of our own.

#7 – *The Light of the World* (William Holman Hunt – 1853)
Wrath – eternal peace awaits those that cast off the bonds of oblivion, to follow the everlasting light.

#8 – *The Gates of Dawn* (Herbert James Draper – 1900)
The path to enlightenment guides those who seek to banish the darkness of ignorance.

Chapter Forty-Nine

John Radcliffe Hospital, Oxford

31 March 2000

Having just tail-gated an attractive young doctor through the door to the Neurological Intensive Care Unit, Emily made her way along the corridor, looking for a list of patients and bed numbers. But this was no ordinary hospital ward. All the patients were lying flat on their backs and had tubes protruding from each nostril. Some had bandages round their heads, a sign of the recent neurosurgery from which they were recovering. Her pulse quickened at the awful prospect of what she was about to encounter.

'Can I help you?' called a voice from the nearby nurses' station.

'Yes, I'm looking for Henry Faber?'

'Certainly, and you are?'

'A friend. Emily Bradshaw.'

'Okay Emily, follow me, please,' said one of the staff nurses. 'The last time I checked, he was asleep, but you might be lucky.'

Emily followed her past a row of beds, each one separated by folded blue curtains hanging from a rail on the ceiling.

'How's he been, since coming out of the coma?'

'Oh, this type of condition is never black and white. Patients can go through different levels of consciousness and responsiveness, depending on how much of the brain is functioning and how this changes over time. All we can do is keep monitoring his condition and provide the treatment and stimulation he needs to reinstate whatever brain function remains.'

This came as a bit of shock to Emily. She'd assumed that once Henry woke up, he would soon be back to his old cryptic self. Of course, in reality, things were never that straightforward.

'Was there any brain damage?'

'It's possible. The attack starved his brain of oxygen for several minutes, so he's lucky to be alive.'

'I was also told, he may have to have his leg amputated, is that right?'

'It did look that way, at one point, yes. But he's a fighter and the doctors managed to save it. There may be some long term mobility issues, but we'll just have to wait and see.'

'Right, of course.'

'The poor chap's had a lot to deal with. But these things take time – he just needs to take each day as it comes. Here we are,' said the nurse, standing by the last bed in a row of six. 'It looks like he's asleep at the moment. Have a seat – he could wake up at any time.'

Emily stared at the plethora of wires and sensors protruding from Henry's body.

'Has his sister been in to see him today, do you know?'

'Not yet. She usually comes in around midday.'

Emily nodded, relieved she would have some time alone with him. Not that she knew what to expect or even the level of response to hope for. 'Is he able to talk?'

'Yes, a little. It'll be good for him to have someone new to engage with. We need to provide him with as much mental stimulus as we can during these early stages of recovery.'

'Okay, thank you,' said Emily, and the staff nurse returned to her duties.

Emily sat down on a plastic chair next to the bedside cabinet, being careful not to wake him. She looked up at the array of readouts above the bed, all constantly monitoring different aspects of Henry's bodily functions, literally keeping him alive. The largest screen belonged to a physiologic monitoring system showing his vital signs, including respiration rate, blood pressure, body temperature, cardiac output and electrical activity, the amount of oxygen and carbon dioxide in his blood, and, in Henry's case, the amount of cerebral pressure and blood flow to the brain. All of which, she guessed, were being fed through to the central nurses' station so that, should any of his measurements fall outside certain pre-set parameters, an alarm would be triggered and they could react immediately.

She couldn't help but notice the blood pressure reading – 157/85 with a pulse rate of 74 bpm. *Seems a little high. Perhaps that's normal for someone of Henry's age.* Then it struck her. How old was Henry Faber? When she'd first seen him at the auction, she'd reckoned he was in his late sixties or early seventies. But the person lying next to her now, with his pale, blotchy face and long grey whiskers, looked more like an old man of eighty or more.

She thought about giving him a gentle nudge, but decided against it – not wanting to set alarm bells ringing, having only just got there.

She looked down at the carrier bag she'd been clutching the whole time. 'I've brought you a little present, Henry,' she whispered, removing it from the bag. 'I think you'll like it. I'll put it up here by your water jug.'

She walked round to the other side of the bed and placed the small gilt picture frame containing a colour postcard of *The Gates of Dawn* on top of the cabinet. She was about to sit down when she felt a warm, clammy hand grab her arm.

'Can you ... get me some water?' croaked Henry.

'Yes, of course,' she said, and poured a small amount into a plastic beaker on the cabinet next to his bed.

'Would you like me to ...?'

He nodded.

Placing her hand behind his head, she gently tilted it forward and poured a few drops into his mouth, repeating the process until he'd had enough.

'I hope you don't mind. I thought I'd come and see how you were doing,' she said.

Feeling for the remote control by his side, Henry pressed one of the buttons and raised the bedhead so he could see her better.

'That's kind of you,' he said, blinking repeatedly to clear his vision.

In that moment, she was glad she came. It hadn't been an easy decision, given her inherent loathing of hospitals – formed as a child during the many visits to see her sick father in an old Victorian TB hospital in Gloucestershire, a place that reeked of malady and despair. In stark contrast, the clean, modern facility of John Radcliffe's ICU was a million light years away from that old sanatorium. How times had changed.

She smiled at him, pleased that he remembered her.

'How are you feeling?'

'Oh ... I've felt better.'

'I've brought you something to brighten the place up a bit,' she said, pointing to the picture frame.

Henry turned his head. 'Bless you. Isn't she radiant?'

'You used to call me Aurora, do you remember?'

Henry blinked and smiled to himself. 'It was your eyes. So much passion ... and hope for the future.'

'Oh, I don't know—'

'It's still there. I can see it,' he said. 'Not like me ... a stupid, frightened old man.'

'You mustn't say that, Henry.'

He patted the bed softly. 'They almost took my leg, you know.'

'Yes, I heard. But they saved it, didn't they. And you'll soon be up and about again. You've just got to take it easy and get plenty of rest.'

'Well, ... we'll see,' he said, lost in his own thoughts.

'Oh, I have some news for you,' she said, breaking the silence. 'We're putting on an exhibition at the Ashmolean.'

Suddenly, his face went a deep shade of red, his eyes full of concern. 'An exhibition?'

'Yes. We're calling it *The Lights of the World*. We've contacted the various galleries and institutions, and they've all agreed to loan us their pictures – isn't that fantastic?'

He grabbed hold of her arm. 'Emily, you don't know what you've done. You have to stop it. You have to.'

'Why? I – I don't understand.'

Suddenly, an alarm went off above the bed. The nurse who'd walked her in rushed over and pulled back the curtain to see what was wrong, joined shortly after by the on-duty doctor.

'BP is up, two-ten over ninety-eight; and his pulse is racing,' said the nurse, looking up at the monitor. 'I'm sorry, but I'm going to have to ask you to leave.'

'Oh God, is he alright?'

'Madam, ... please—'

Fighting all attempts to calm him down, Henry sat up and tried to push the doctor aside, so he could see Emily.

'Talk to Alice, ... find the Millais letter,' he said, and fell back on the bed, exhausted.

'But, where do I—' she said, before being cut off by the swish of the privacy curtain being drawn in front of her.

Unsure whether to stay or go, she eventually left the ward and made her way over to the Radcliffe's main block. She called Tom, then sat in the cafeteria for over an hour, before heading back to the NICU to check on Henry's condition.

Having learned he was now stable and resting, she made a much-relieved walk back to the car, before taking a slow and contemplative drive back into Oxford – the whole journey spent wondering, what exactly was the Millais letter? And, more importantly, why on earth did Henry want her to cancel *The Lights of the World* exhibition?

Chapter Fifty

Summertown, Oxford

31 March 2000

The Friday afternoon rush hour was well underway as Emily drew up outside Henry Faber's house in Summertown. She loved this part of Oxford, with its leafy suburban streets and expensive detached houses – a large number of which were built as homes for college fellows like Faber. Notable residents, so she'd been told, had included J.R.R. Tolkien, Colin Dexter, Desmond Morris, Iris Murdoch and Thom Yorke of Radiohead.

She'd first met Henry's sister, Alice, a few weeks ago, calling in to check on Henry's progress; and, despite her somewhat abrupt demeanour, had warmed to her straight away. She stood inside the front porch and pressed the brass bell push. Some time, and a couple of hard raps on the front door later, it opened to reveal Alice Faber, dressed in a thick woollen jumper, slacks and a pair of stout gardening shoes.

'Hello, Miss Faber, I hope you don't mind me calling in on you, unannounced.'

'Of course not, dear. And I believe I told you last time, do call me Alice.'

Emily smiled and followed her through to the kitchen at the back of the house.

'You're lucky you caught me. I was about to pop into the greenhouse for an hour, before it got dark. Do sit down, dear,' Alice said, pointing to one of the chairs at the kitchen table. 'Now, what can I do for you?'

'Well, I went to see Henry this morning, and—'

'I'm sorry, what was that?' said Alice, adjusting her hearing aid.

'I said, I went to see Henry this morning.'

'Yes, I know, dear, he told me. And he said to thank you for the lovely picture. He barely took his eyes off it, the whole time I was there.'

'Oh, I'm glad he liked it. I'm afraid he had a bit of a bad turn during my visit. Is he alright now?'

'Yes, he's fine. He'll be pleased when I tell him you called.'

'Good. Anyway, the reason I wanted to speak to you, is ... he told me something rather strange and, to be honest, I'm not sure what to make of it. He said I should ask you about the Millais letter. Does that mean anything to you?'

'Well, put it this way; when he woke up from his little post-lunch nap, this afternoon, he didn't stop going on about you and that damned letter. I didn't know what he was talking about, but apparently, it's hidden in a copy of Millais's original biography. Tell you what, dear, why don't you go on through to the library while I make us some tea, and we can look for it together?'

Eager to see Henry's collection of books, Emily entered the beautifully appointed library comprising two full walls of white-painted bookshelves with ribbed classical columns dividing each section. The most eye-catching feature in the room, however, was hanging above the mantelpiece – a picture of a young Breton girl, gazing up at streams of multi-coloured light pouring through a stained glass window. She was just about to inspect the artist's signature, when Alice came in carrying two mugs of tea, and thrust one in her direction.

'I've put two sugars in it, dear. You look like you could do with fattening up a bit.' Emily laughed and took the mug, grateful for what she hoped was a backhanded compliment.

'I've seen this painting before, when I was doing some research into Herbert Draper. It's called the *Trailing Clouds of Glory*, isn't it?'

'That's right.'

'I never knew Henry owned this.'

'He doesn't. He bought it for me,' said Alice proudly. 'Although in truth, I think he adores it just as much as I do.'

Emily wondered if it was just coincidence that this very painting was derived from the first series of drawings in Draper's sketchbook – the sketchbook Henry had found at the auction and then hidden from her, so she couldn't bid on it. Perhaps she'd been wrong all along; perhaps it was Henry who'd roped her into this whole thing. Could he be the one who'd put the book up for sale? But that made no sense – why would he bid on his own book? The auction house would never allow that, surely.

While she was pondering the events of the last few months, Alice was busy hunting through the rows of bookshelves.

'Henry told me the letter was tucked inside a copy of Millais's biography, which, if I recall correctly, is in two volumes and has gilded lettering on the spine.'

'Okay, that shouldn't be too hard to find. I'll look over here,' said Emily, approaching the shelves nearest the door.

'If this was one of mine, I'd be able to lay my hands on it in no time,' Alice laughed, shaking her head.

If it wasn't for a dinner date in Bristol with some of Tom's friends, later that evening, Emily could have happily spent all evening browsing through Henry's fabulous literary collection. The range of subjects was impressive, covering everything from art, ceramics, music, history, theology, philosophy, flora and fauna, and photography, to a superb collection of fictional literature and poetry spanning the twentieth century, together with some earlier works by Wordsworth, Coleridge, Tennyson, Blake and John Donne.

'This must have taken him years to put together,' said Emily.

'What, dear? Oh yes, he's loved books ever since he was a child,' said Alice, getting down on her knees to inspect the bottom shelf.

Emily's eyes fell on a pair of navy-blue books with gilded lettering and what looked like stylised grapes on the spine.

'Here, I think I've got it – *The Life and Letters of Sir John E. Millais*.'

'Bring them over here, dear. We'll see them better in the natural light.'

Taking care not to pull them out by the top of the spine, Emily removed the two heavy volumes – compiled by the artist's son, J.G. Millais, in 1899 – and took them over to a small desk by the window.

Alice opened the first one. 'Mmm, a little spotted, but a nice copy,' she said, admiring a sepia-toned photograph of the Pre-Raphaelite co-founder, holding an artist's palette and brushes. 'Now, what is it we're looking for?'

'I wish I knew,' said Emily. 'All Henry said was, to look for the Millais letter. Hopefully, we'll know it when we see it.'

'Oh, he is a silly old fool,' said Alice, shaking her head. 'There could be hundreds of letters in here. Why don't you look for it, dear; your eyes are better than mine.'

With Alice looking on, Emily turned the first few glossy pages, carefully examining each of Millais's correspondence for anything remotely related to *The Lights of the World*.

The minutes passed by and nothing had leapt out at them as an obvious candidate. Emily was just about to suggest that Alice start looking through the other volume, when she came across two uncut pages with the leading edges joined together. Appearing weightier than the others, Emily pushed down on the V-shaped edge with her fingers, causing the hidden space between to pop open.

'There's something in here,' she said, peering inside. Reaching in with her thumb and forefinger, she gently extracted a small brown envelope.

'That looks like Henry's writing on the front,' said Alice, adjusting her glasses to get a better look. 'It says, Meeting of the principle PRBs – ninth of December, eighteen forty-eight, eighty-three Gower Street, London.'

Emily lifted the flap and removed the photocopied sheet of paper inside. At the top, almost like a family crest, was a symbol she knew all too well, but seeing it here in its original form, took her breath away.

'Well, what does it say?' said Alice.

'Sorry, let me read it to you.

'Dearest John, Dearest Gabriel,

'At a meeting on this ninth day of December, 1848, we the undersigned, being the three principle founding members of the PRB, do hereby agree to produce a series of seven painted works, henceforth known as The Lights of the World.

'Devout adherence to the sacred doctrines, portrayed therein, will empower man to discover the true nature

'And, ... they've listed the seven original doctrines behind *The Lights of the World* paintings.'

She looked at Alice, shaking her head in disbelief. Finally, after all these months of doubt and uncertainty, searching for the real meaning behind the Shepherd's tantalising clues, and here it was – tangible proof from the very artists themselves. And she was holding it in her hands; or a photocopy of it, at least.

'This is incredible,' said Emily, handing the letter to Alice. 'Did Henry ever mention he had this in his possession?'

'Oh, he can be quite secretive when he wants to be. Tell me, do you know what this symbol at the top represents?'

'Yes, we call it the sun mark. The Brothers used it to stamp the back of the seven paintings.'

'Really? How very cryptic of them.'

Emily peered into the gap between the un-trimmed sheets. 'I wonder why Henry chose these particular pages to conceal it?'

'Well, there's only one way to find out,' said Alice, opening the desk drawer and producing a silver letter knife.

'Oh no, I didn't mean—'

But, it was too late. Alice had already grabbed the book and was mercilessly slicing through the uncut pages. Emily leaned in closer to see what printed text had lain hidden there, all those years.

'There we go,' said Alice, and placed the book on the desk so they could both see.

The newly revealed page 219 contained a pencil drawing of Effie Ruskin, *née* Gray, later to become Millais's wife. The page opposite, however, referred to a letter Millais had written to his friend, Mr Thomas Combe. As soon as Emily read it, she knew exactly why Henry had chosen this as his hiding place.

'Alice, I know it's a bit of a cheek, ...' said Emily, waving the photocopy in her hand, ' ... but would you mind if I took this back to the museum, so they can do some proper research on it?'

'Yes, dear, of course you may. Henry wanted you to have it.'

After thanking her for the tea, Emily sat in the car and stared at the small brown envelope. It was just gone 7.30 pm, which had definitely put paid to dinner with Tom and his friends. But none of that mattered. What she held in her hand was simply astonishing, and Henry had led her straight to it.

For some reason, her mind kept going back to the painting above the fireplace – the *Trailing Clouds of Glory*. Could Henry really be the one who had planted the sketchbook at the auction; and then drip-fed her clues so she could piece it all together? But that didn't make any sense. The Shepherd's final letter had arrived in Wickwar on the Saturday morning when Henry was in hospital. Was the postmark first or second class? She couldn't remember. Whichever way she looked at it, Henry was the common denominator.

She placed the envelope on the passenger seat, turned the ignition key and, leaving a plume of grey-white exhaust smoke hanging beneath the street lights, headed for the Woodstock Road. Ignoring the ring road, she went back through the centre of town, craving the hustle and bustle of traffic and people. Realising she could see her breath inside the car, she switched on the heater and looked down at the handwriting on the envelope beside her. Something told her it was the contents of the Millais letter that had nearly gotten Henry killed, that day. And, having blatantly ignored all his warnings to stay away, here she was in possession of his very own copy. A shiver went down her spine. With the Pitt Rivers madman still on the loose, and Henry only just recovering from his near-fatal injuries, she'd be a fool to ignore the possibility that – she could now be a target.

It was time to seek help – to take up an offer she'd been given some months ago; and happily ignored, until now.

Chapter Fifty-One

Wickwar, near Bristol

2 April 2000

The stolen Citroen ZX parked in the high street may as well have been invisible – the type of vehicle no one notices; not even with the driver sitting inside, patiently watching, waiting; his eyes fixed firmly on the pub, a hundred yards away. The girl and her bloke were regulars on a Sunday lunchtime, but the arrival of the man with long silver-coloured hair – that was a surprise.

Marcus Tyburn maintained his gaze until all three had gone inside, then lit a cigarette and pushed the button to wind down the driver's window an inch or two. He exhaled a plume of smoke and cast his mind back twenty years to a job that had left a deep scar on his subconscious. He'd been the getaway driver for a hit on a large country house in Derbyshire – a move into the big league for the young, up-and-coming villain. Thousands of pounds worth of antiques and jewellery had been taken, most of which were going to a fence with buyers in mainland Europe and the Far East. But Special Branch had been tipped off and were waiting for them in the lanes outside the house. Three of the gang, including Tyburn, escaped, but only after having shot a police officer in the process. The fence, however, did not get away, and after thirty-six hours of intense interrogation and sleep deprivation – tactics that would certainly not be tolerated in today's modern policing – he was made an offer he couldn't refuse. Either shop the rest of the gang, or go to prison for the next ten years. As far as the fence was concerned, it was a no-brainer. The remaining gang members were duly named, tracked down and captured within a matter of days. Tyburn was only twenty-two and served a reduced sentence of seven years for a first offence. After a few months in one of Her Majesty's open prisons, the fence had something of a moral epiphany and switched sides to work with the police, using his extensive knowledge of the art world's dark corners and dubious characters. The Met's hit rate went through the roof and artworks that were thought lost forever were suddenly being recovered from their unscrupulous owners. So successful was he that a special role was created for him, much to the disgust of some senior officers who knew about his criminal past. Like it or not, he had a knack for getting results where others had failed; and, as the years went by, his hit rate grew, together with his reputation.

Having had plenty of time to dwell on it, Tyburn had no problem picturing his face – the pock-marked complexion with steel-grey eyes and long, sand-coloured hair running down over his shoulders. Francis Cordell – the ex-fence, was obviously older now; the sand-coloured hair almost silver, and a handlebar moustache that made him look like an ageing Wyatt Earp. But it was him alright – Detective Chief Inspector Francis Cordell, no less. Definitely a case of poacher-turned-gamekeeper. Tyburn had another word for him.

Checking the safety catch was on, he stepped out of the car and tucked the Glock down the back of his trousers, before taking a quick look up and down the high street. All was quiet, not that Wickwar could ever be described as busy. He crossed the road and walked up to the front of the Old Cider House. To the left was a gated passageway cutting through to the back of the property. Checking the coast was clear, he took a large pair of bolt cutters from inside his coat, sheared the small padlock and slipped inside, closing the tall iron gates behind him. Along one side of the passage ran the grey stone wall of the old Wickwar Antiques Centre, a disused three-storey warehouse whose dark shuttered windows looked down over the back gardens of the neighbouring high-street cottages.

Tyburn emerged into the sunlight and saw his target – the curved brick wall surrounding the rear of Emily and Tom's property. He tried the gate; it was bolted from the inside. Using a gap in the mortar as a foothold, he hauled himself up over the wall and into the tiny cottage garden, before making his way over to the back of the house. Both the kitchen door and window were locked. He clenched his fist and with a sharp jab of his elbow, broke the pane, sending a shower of glass onto the kitchen floor. Moments later he was inside. He didn't really know what he was looking for, just something, anything to confirm Emily had worked out what they were up to. But with her and Cordell meeting up the day before the exhibition was due to open – that was proof enough for him. The question was, how much did she know?

He walked down the curving passageway and into the dining room, clocking the open laptop on the dining table. No sooner had he pressed *Enter*, than the Windows' login screen appeared, asking for a password. He didn't really do technology. Perhaps one of Luke Waltham's ArtScreen geeks could have a look at it. After removing the cables and closing it to collect on his way out, he began flicking through some papers stacked on a shelf unit behind him. Then he noticed a book with something sticking out of it. He tipped it forward and pulled out the small brown envelope. The photocopied sheet inside was of an old letter with a name at the top. Only a few weeks ago, he'd overheard Waltham and Mountfield harping on about some "Millais letter", that had been handed down through Waltham's family. Tyburn had switched off, until the point in the conversation where they started debating how on earth Henry Faber had got hold of a copy. That meant someone outside the gang knew about the paintings, and that was a problem.

It seemed the old man had passed it on to the girl, after all. If only he'd finished him off in the church tower, when he had the chance. Now the girl was a problem, too – no doubt blabbing everything she knew to Cordell over a bloody pub lunch. He'd given up telling Waltham she should be taken out of the equation. What did they need her for, anyway? Mountfield was their inside man; he could easily have pulled the exhibition together. But Waltham wouldn't hear of it, insisting she still had a role to play, and people would get suspicious if she suddenly went missing.

Well, the days of jumping to Waltham's tune were over. He didn't trust him as far as he could throw him. And the same went for that bitch of a daughter of his, Kate. No matter – he'd got his own game plan to think about, now.

But, first things first – dear sweet little Emily Bradshaw had to be silenced; and from where he was standing, there was no time like the present.

Chapter Fifty-Two

The Buthay Inn, Wickwar, near Bristol
2 April 2000

Sunday lunch in Wickwar's only remaining public house was an event enjoyed by both villagers and townies alike – aided in no small part by the local draught ale, brewed not half a mile down the road. Seated in the spacious dining area, Emily, Tom and DCI Cordell raised their glasses to celebrate the forthcoming *The Lights of the World* exhibition at the Ashmolean Museum.

'So Tom, as we're sat in The Buthay Inn, what exactly is a Buthay, when it's at home?' enquired Cordell.

'It's a reference to a nearby field where the medieval longbowmen used to practise their archery during the Hundred Years' War.'

'Right, well, I'm glad you cleared that up. And may I say, thank you, to you both for asking me to join you for Sunday lunch. I don't come over to Gloucestershire very often; and, well … I've definitely been missing out.'

'That's okay,' said Tom. 'Emily's been so busy in Oxford these past few weeks, it'll be a chance for both of us to catch up with her.'

'Do forgive my partner, Chief Inspector, he is prone to exaggerate on occasions,' she said, giving Tom a swift kick under the table.

Cordell laughed. 'Now, Emily, what's all this about a letter belonging to Henry Faber?'

'Before I get to that, perhaps I'd better tell you where we are with the exhibition. We found eight paintings with the sun mark on the back, like the ones you saw in Birmingham, yes?'

'Okay,' said Cordell.

'And, as you know, those eight paintings form the basis of the exhibition, which the museum has spared no expense in publicising, given the international importance of the discovery. They've done a full press launch including newspaper articles,

TV and radio adverts, posters, you name it. We're even doing an interview with the BBC local news, next week. Julian's asked me to do it – God knows why.'

'Cos he's got a face for radio, that's why.'

'Tom!' Emily snapped.

'Sorry, …' he said, raising both hands in the air, '… but he has.'

'You're not a fan of Julian Mountfield, then, Tom?'

'You could say that. I've only met the guy once, but I just don't trust him. There's something about him that feels … fake.'

Emily huffed. 'That happens to be my boss, you're talking about.'

'I know it is, but you know me, I speak as I find.'

'Anyway, as I was saying, …' continued Emily, '… the exhibition starts with a big launch party, tomorrow evening.'

'That all sounds very exciting,' said Cordell. 'So, what's bothering you, exactly?'

'I went to see Alice Faber a couple of days ago, and we found this hidden in Henry's library.' She handed Cordell the photocopy of the Millais letter. 'It details the seven challenges the soul will face on the path to spiritual awakening.'

'Sorry, … I'm not sure I understand.'

'The point is, I've never seen this before, nor has Julian. And each of these doctrines, as they call them, correspond to one of *The Lights of The World* paintings. Henry knew it and so did the Shepherd – the person who kept sending me those strange clues in the post. Anyway, when I told Henry we were putting on an exhibition, he was horrified. He virtually begged me to put a stop to it, then nearly had a heart attack before he could tell me why.'

'You think Henry is the Shepherd?'

'Well, I did wonder about that, but he flatly denied it when I asked him about it. In which case, there's someone else out there who's known about these paintings, all along. If it hadn't been for the Shepherd leading me to the next painting, I'd just be the proud owner of a lovely sketchbook by Herbert Draper, and that's it.'

Cordell scratched his head. 'I'm still not quite following.'

'My point is, why was someone so keen for me to figure all this out? It's almost as if this whole thing was engineered to bring these paintings together in one place. And the only person who tried to stop it, Henry Faber, damn near got himself killed in the process. Don't you think that's a bit strange?'

'Well, I suppose, when you put it like that,' he said, playing with his moustache.

'And that's why I called you.'

'Right. Actually, while we're talking about Henry, we think we're very close to tracking down the perpetrator.'

'That's great. So, who is it?'

'I'm sorry, I can't—'

'Really, not even after that bastard tried to kill me?'

'Okay, his name is Marcus Tyburn, do you know him?'

'No, and I'm not sure I want to.'

Cordell laid his palms on the table. 'We also believe he was one of the men who broke into the Ashmolean, back in November.'

'My God! He took the Picasso?'

'Quite likely, yes. There could also be another robbery in the pipeline, but we don't know when or where.'

Emily took a large gulp of wine. 'You don't think he's going to hit the Ashmolean again, do you?'

Cordell shook his head. 'No, I don't imagine so. Not with all the hype and extra security around the exhibition.'

'Okay, now I'm worried. Can't you put out one of those all-points bulletins on him, or something?'

'Already done – but no luck, I'm afraid. Look, there's nothing for you to be concerned about, Emily.'

'You think?'

Only half listening to the conversation, Tom began scrabbling around in his pockets. 'Bugger!' he said. 'I think I've left my wallet at home. Have you got any cash, Emily?'

'No, I thought you had some.'

'Don't worry, I'll pay and we can sort it out later,' said Cordell.

'No, no. It'll take me two minutes to pop back home and get it.' And before Cordell could even think about protesting, Tom was up out of his seat and heading for the door.

Cordell looked at Emily. 'I wouldn't have minded.'

'It's fine. He won't be long.'

Cordell took another sip of his pint and sat back in his chair. 'There is something else I wanted to ask you, Emily. Have you heard of a company called ArtScreen?'

'Yes, they're the contractor that did the re-fit of the galleries at the Ashmolean.'

'Right, and what constitutes a re-fit, in this instance?'

'Well, lights, air-conditioning, security systems, everything.'

'And were any other companies invited to tender for the contract?'

'Oh, for sure. The Board of Directors would have insisted on it. To be honest, Julian handled it all before I joined.'

'You said they installed the security system?'

'Yes, and supplied the staff. And, from what I've seen, they're very professional. Julian certainly rates them.'

'And did he have a hand in securing the contract with them?'

Emily gave him a quizzical look. 'I guess so. I know he's pretty friendly with their managing director, Luke Waltham.'

'Really? I didn't know that ...' said Cordell, giving the end of his moustache an insightful twirl.

*

Having crossed the road from the pub, Tom opened the front door to the Old Cider House and stepped into the lounge. As he stood there scanning the room, everything appeared just as they'd left it, twenty minutes ago; but something wasn't quite right. Unable to explain it, he shook his head and began hunting for his wallet.

'Where the fuck is it?' he said, drawing a blank in all the obvious places. 'I bet she's put it somewhere safe.'

He walked through to the dining room and was about to check the dining table when he saw something move out of the corner of his eye. He spun round, just in time to see a dark shadow launch itself at him. Before he knew what was happening, he felt a sharp blow to the head and crashed backwards into the dining room table, landing in a heap on the floor. Dazed and streaming with blood, he looked up and saw the outline of a man standing over him, his fist raised.

Then came the second punch – savage, brutal – like the blow from a sledgehammer.

With his will power crushed, Tom finally gave in to the unstoppable force of his attacker and blacked out.

*

Tyburn picked up the laptop and small brown envelope that had fallen from the dining table and stepped over Tom's prostrate body. He was about to make his way out to the kitchen, when the sound of a ringtone broke the silence. He bent down, reached inside Tom's coat pocket and fished out the mobile phone – the display read *Emily*. As he stared at her name on the tiny screen, a wicked grin spread across his face.

He clicked the little green button and lifted the phone to his ear.

'Hello bitch!'

Chapter Fifty-Three

The Buthay Inn, Wickwar, near Bristol

2 April 2000

'Tom, have you found—?' Emily stopped in her tracks, her face frozen like a death mask as she tried to process the disparaging voice on the other end of the phone.

'What is it?' said Cordell.

She just looked at him. Without saying a word, she ended the call and put the phone down on the table.

'Emily, talk to me.'

'He's got Tom,' she said, with tears welling up in her eyes.

'What? Who's got Tom?'

But she wasn't listening. She stood up, grabbed her coat and ran towards the door.

Cordell quickly reached for his jacket and went after her. 'Sorry, we have to go,' he said to the young waitress approaching the table with their menus.

He ran out onto the pavement and gripped Emily's arm as she was about to cross the road.

'Emily, look at me. Who's got Tom?'

'He said if I ever want to see him again, I have to go over to the house, right now.'

'Was it him, was it Tyburn?'

'I don't know, I think so.'

'I'm calling for backup,' said Cordell, reaching for his phone.

'No! If you do that, he'll kill him. Come on, we've got less than a minute.'

Cordell pulled her back. 'Look, if this is him, he'll have no hesitation in carrying out his threats.'

'Let go of me then,' she said, trying to shake him off.

'Alright, but let me do the talking, until we find out exactly what he wants.'

Emily nodded, nervously.

'I'll go in first, and you stay behind me. Have you got the front door key?'

She reached in her pocket and gave it to him, her hand shaking. As they approached the front of the house, she noticed the living room curtains had been drawn. Desperately trying to keep it together, she closed her eyes, steeling herself for whatever horrors were going on inside there.

With key in hand, Cordell walked up to the front door. 'Remember, follow my lead and be strong for Tom's sake. Everything's going to be fine.'

She so wanted that to be true, but deep in her heart, she knew they were about to confront something truly evil.

Cordell took a deep breath and pressed down on the door handle – it was unlocked. He pushed it slowly until a small crack appeared. From what he could see, the front room appeared dark and quiet. He pushed some more.

'Get in here, Cordell,' came a voice from inside.

They walked into the lounge and were immediately confronted by the sight of Tom, gagged and bound to a chair in the centre of the room. He looked drowsy with his head bowed. Next to him stood Tyburn, his gun pointed squarely at Tom's temple.

'Oh my God – are you alright, Tom?' said Emily, seeing the stream of darkened blood running down his face.

He looked up, his anxious eyes pleading with her to do what the man wanted.

Cordell calmly closed the front door and turned to face his old adversary. 'Marcus. It's been a long time.'

'Shut up, Cordell. We'll get to that later. Both of you, out the back, now,' said Tyburn, waving his Glock in the direction of the kitchen.

As she walked past, Emily ran her shaking hand against Tom's cheek. 'Be strong, baby,' she said, with as much bravery as she could muster.

Watching them closely, Tyburn bent down and whispered in Tom's ear. 'Not a sound, or I'll waste your girlfriend, got it?'

Tom nodded, then closed his eyes in hopeful solitude.

Cordell led the way through the dining room, down the narrow curving passageway and into the kitchen, closely followed by Emily, with Tyburn's gun nudging her in the back.

'What now, Marcus?' said Cordell, 'Are we going to do some gardening?'

'Shut up, smart arse. Take off your coats and leave your phones on the side.'

They did so, while Tyburn opened the back door. 'Move it,' he said, shoving them both outside.

As they crossed the small patio and approached the gate in the garden wall, Cordell noticed a small axe lying on a pile of logs, nearby.

'Go on Cordell, I fuckin' dare you,' said Tyburn, and grabbed it on his way past.

Cordell opened the gate and walked out into a small, gravelled courtyard. To the left was the covered passageway and the main road. To the right, the bulk of the courtyard, backing onto the antiques' warehouse and a row of stone-built houses.

'Where now?' he said, hoping for a better chance of escape on the main road.

'Over there,' said Tyburn, waving his gun towards the back door of the warehouse.

Emily glanced up at the three stories of crumbling red brick and rotting window frames towering above them. In all the years she'd been living next door, she'd never seen anyone at those windows. Maybe today. *Oh please, let it be today.*

'You know it's occupied,' she said.

'Nice try, love. I looked in the shop window when I walked past – the place has been empty for years. Now break it down,' said Tyburn, pointing to the door, and handing the axe to Cordell.

'What?'

'I said, break it down. Even a pussy like you should be able to manage that.'

The old wooden door looked like it hadn't been opened in decades, with its flaking red paint and hinges pitted with rust.

'Come on, I haven't got all day.'

Emily willed Cordell to catch him off guard and bury the axe in his skull, but Tyburn looked to be no slouch, and would probably blow his brains out before he'd even raised his arm.

Turning to face the door, Cordell picked his spot and began dealing a succession of blows on one of the door panels.

'Put your back into it,' said Tyburn.

'Tell you what, ... give me the gun, and you can have a go?' retorted Cordell.

Conscious of poor Tom sitting next door, tied up and bleeding, Emily grabbed the axe from Cordell, and with a couple of angry blows, made a more than sizeable hole.

'What did I tell you,' Tyburn cackled. 'Now, stick your hand in and unlock it.'

Emily threw the axe on the ground and reached inside, feeling for the lock on the other side. Her heart sank – the key was there. She turned it and pulled down on the handle, causing the door to swing open with a discontented groan.

'Inside, both of you,' said Tyburn, giving them both a shove.

The smell of dust and dry rot hit them instantly. The room was small and looked like it had been used as some sort of packing area. Apart from some metal shelving, a long wooden bench and a roll of parcel stickers marked FRAGILE, it was completely empty. The floorboards were bare and covered in fallen ceiling plaster, and the only adornment to the grey painted walls was an Autosport racing calendar from 1994, hanging from a rusty nail.

'Through there,' said Tyburn, pointing to an open doorway in the far corner, then locking the back door.

Emily and Cordell made their way into a huge open space that occupied the rest of the ground floor, right through to the shop-front windows on the high street. At the back of the room was a large metal container, about three-feet high and ten feet in diameter, with a flat circular stone in the centre. Another larger millstone, blackened with use, stood on its side, supported by two solid oak beams projecting from a central pillar. The sight of the old horse-powered apple crusher filled Emily with dread as she wondered just what horrors Tyburn had in store for them.

'Keep walkin',' he said, directing them to a flight of stairs on the far wall.

Taking a firm grip of the handrail, Emily and Cordell climbed the wooden stairs, each step bringing a concerning creak from the ageing timbers. The first floor had a different appearance altogether, with a row of glazed shop fronts running down either side. Of course, the antique dealers were long gone, and the shelves held nothing but a thick layer of dust and the odd discarded price tag.

Tyburn kept herding his two captives upwards until they reached the top floor – another open space, divided by two rows of red cast-iron pillars running down the centre of the room. They'd reached the end of the line.

He grabbed Emily and shoved her towards the nearest pillar; then came back for Cordell and dragged him over to the neighbouring one, twenty feet away.

'Take off your clothes.'

The horror of those words hit them like a gun shot.

'What?' said Cordell.

'You heard me – strip.'

'Look, just tell us what you want and we'll—'

'I said, take your fuckin' clothes off!' and he whipped the butt of his gun across Cordell's face, sending him stumbling backwards.

'You too, bitch.'

Emily stared at Cordell in horror, wishing she could somehow wake up from this living nightmare.

'Do it!' shouted Tyburn.

With her hands trembling, she began to undo the laces of her trainers. Tyburn stood watching, his focus mainly on Emily, occasionally glancing over at Cordell to make sure he, too, was disrobing. Having removed her knitted jumper and jeans, she stood next to the cold iron pillar, looking utterly vulnerable in her bra and pants, her feet together and hands clutched under her chin. Avoiding Tyburn's gaze, she glanced over at Cordell, who was now down to his pants and socks.

They both heard a tiny click as Tyburn removed the safety catch on the Glock and pointed it at Emily.

'Now the rest.'

'Please, we'll do whatever you want.'

'Just do it.'

Realising she had no choice, she reached round and undid the clasp of her bra, then slowly pulled the shoulder straps down one by one. Covering her breasts with her right arm, she let it fall to the floor. With tears in her eyes, she gradually pulled down her pants with her left hand and stepped out of them, placing her hand between her legs. Tyburn looked her up and down, and smiled to himself, then turned to face Cordell, who was already naked with both hands covering his genitals.

'Sit down with your backs to the pillar.'

They both complied, watching nervously as Tyburn reached into his pocket and removed two plastic cable ties, taken from Emily's kitchen drawer.

'Hands behind the pillar, both of you.'

Cordell reluctantly took his hands away from his groin and tried to calm himself as Tyburn walked round behind him.

'What do you expect to achieve, keeping us here?' he said, wincing as the tie dug into his wrists.

There was no answer. Tyburn walked over to Emily. She drew her legs up under her chin, trying to make herself as small as possible. He grabbed her arms and pulled them round behind her, stroking the smooth pale skin of her forearm with one hand while gripping her hands tightly with the other. Biting her lip, she closed her eyes, desperately trying to quell the revulsion welling up inside her. Without warning, Tyburn looped the tie around her wrists and yanked as hard as he could. She howled with agony as the thin plastic cut into her flesh.

'You want to keep us out of the way, is that it?' said Cordell, trying to distract him. 'So we don't spoil your plans?'

Tyburn marched over and stood astride Cordell's outstretched legs.

'I wouldn't be shootin' my mouth off, if I was you. It just gives me an excuse to hurt you more.'

Cordell saw the fist coming, but could do nothing about it. There was a loud crack as his nose fractured and the back of his head hit the iron pillar. He turned his head from side to side and groaned with agony as blood streamed from his nostrils, down through his moustache and onto his bare chest.

'Why? Why did you do that?' screamed Emily.

Tyburn laughed. 'That's nothin', love. Me and him have got a lot more makin' up to do, yet.'

Having born witness to so much cruelty at the hands of this psychopath, fear turned to anger. 'You're a fucking animal!' she yelled.

Tyburn walked over to where she was sitting, gripped the plastic cord round her wrists and yanked it skyward, making her squeal with pain.

'Unless you fancy some of what he's gonna get, I suggest you shut your fuckin' mouth.'

Ignoring her cries, he hooked the cable tie over a metal bolt sticking out from the back of the pillar, forcing her shoulders forward, and her wrists and elbows to be contorted at an angle. She shrieked with anguish – her upper body burning as if it was on fire. Tyburn crouched down, his face inches from hers.

'You think that hurts, just give it a couple of hours.'

He calmly reached into his pocket and pulled out the brown envelope containing the photocopy of the Millais letter.

'Tell me where you got this and I'll unhook you.'

She raised her head and looked at it, briefly. 'I've never seen it before.'

He slapped her across the face. 'Don't lie to me. I found it in your house. Where did you get it?'

'Leave her ... alone,' spluttered Cordell, as a big glob of congealed blood ran down his throat. 'I'm the one you've got a beef with ... not her.'

Ignoring him, Tyburn took out a flick knife from his trouser pocket and held it up to Emily's face. With her eyes glaring at the silver button on the handle, he tapped it with his thumb, sending the steel blade shooting out from the hilt.

'I'll ask you one more time,' he said, moving the cutting edge up to her throat. 'Where did you get the letter?'

She closed her eyes, her heart racing. 'It came in the post – weeks ago. Someone sent it to me.'

He pushed the tip of the blade onto her smooth white neck, almost drawing blood.

'You're lyin'.'

'No, ... I'm not.'

'Tell you what, why don't I pay your boyfriend a visit and we'll see how he feels about losin' some fingers?'

'No, no! This has nothing to do with him,' she cried, her mind a jumble as she desperately tried to think of an explanation, any explanation, but the real one.

'Alright, the truth is ... my boss gave it to me.'

'What?' said Tyburn, looking taken aback. 'Mountfield gave you this?'

'Yes. One day, we were talking about the exhibition and he showed me the letter. I asked him where he got it and he said it had been sent to him from someone called, the Shepherd. We thought it would make an interesting exhibit and he let me take it home, so I could study it.'

'You wouldn't be makin' shit up to protect that old fart, Faber, would you?'

Emily shook her head. 'Henry had nothing to do with it. He was in hospital in a coma – thanks to you.'

As soon as she said it, she knew it was a mistake. Tyburn's eyes grew wild – the look that crazed men get when presented with the object of their desire. He pushed the tip of the blade into her skin until a tiny drop of blood appeared on her neck. She froze, staring straight ahead, too frightened to move or even breathe.

He glared down at her naked body. 'Up close, you've got better tits than some of those Soho whores,' he said, tilting his head to get a better look. 'Ever thought of strippin' for a livin'? Nah, course you ain't, posh tart like you.'

He turned the blade so the back edge was touching her skin, then ran the tip slowly down her neck, tracing a line between her breasts and over her belly. Licking his lips, he gently placed the knife on the floor and grabbed her knees with both hands.

'Please don't – I beg you,' she sobbed.

'You're not goin' to deny me a little fun, are you?'

Emily closed her eyes, her body quivering at the touch of this evil creature. He was about to reach between her legs, when a police siren sounded outside. He stopped and looked over to the nearest window. Emily did the same, praying the car would come to a screeching halt and unload an elite team of armed police officers to burst in and rescue them. But the siren kept on going, its pitch changing as it went past the window and slowly faded into the distance.

Tyburn turned back and leered at Emily, coarsely running his fingers up between her thighs.

'Please, I'll tell you everything,' she whimpered, seeing he was intent on just one thing.

'I know what you're planning, ...' said Cordell, '...you're going to steal those eight paintings from the Ashmolean.'

Tyburn froze. Clenching his fist, he got to his feet and walked over to Cordell. 'And where the fuck did you get that idea?'

'I've had my suspicions for a while.'

Tyburn laughed. 'You don't know shit.'

'We know you and Danny Forgan stole the Picasso. You dumped the getaway car in a lake near Abingdon. But you were sloppy – you didn't clean up after yourselves. The night before the robbery, you and Danny went to a club in London – The Ruby Viper.'

Cordell stopped to cough up more blood from his battered nose.

Emily looked up at the ceiling. *Keep talking, Francis – please, just keep talking.*

'Then, there's ArtScreen getting the security contract at the museum. What were you lot up to, I asked myself? That's when I learnt about the paintings from Julian. Eight works by the Pre-Raphaelite Brotherhood, all extremely valuable and being brought together in an exhibition at the Ashmolean. The same museum you and Danny broke into, five months ago. Coincidence, Marcus?'

Tyburn stared down at Cordell, trying to work out if the DCI really had something, or was just trying to distract him from his little bit of captive female flesh. 'The way I see it, Cordell, you came here to see her because you didn't know jack.'

'You don't get it, do you? I told the boys at the Met about you. They've had you under surveillance for weeks. Now, they're just biding their time, waiting for you to make your move.'

'In that case, they'll be comin' up those stairs any minute now, to save your sorry arse.'

'That's right, they will,' said Cordell.

Tyburn stood there, scratching his chin. 'See, now there's a little voice chirpin' away in my head, sayin' – he knows everythin', and he's told all his mates at Scotland Yard. And that's put me in a bit of a quandary. So, I'm afraid I will need you to tell me the truth; or I am goin' to have to kill you both.'

Tyburn pushed the blade of the flick knife slowly into Cordell's neck – generating yet more blood.

'One last time, did you know about the raid tomorrow night?'

'Yes, I told you—'

'And I said, don't fuckin' lie to me or I will end you, right now!'

'I'm telling you the truth—' said Cordell, pushing his head back against the pillar.

'Let's see, shall we?'

Tyburn turned and grabbed Cordell's shirt off the floor, using the knife to cut off one of the sleeves. He then walked over to Emily, stretched it across her mouth and tied it behind her head. She sat there, wide-eyed, wondering what fresh horror was about to befall her, as Cordell looked on nervously. Neither knew what was coming.

Tyburn moved round behind her and began gently caressing her fingers. He then reached into his jacket pocket and took out a stainless steel cigar cutter.

'Marcus, for fuck's sake, be reasonable,' said Cordell.

Emily let out a muffled cry beneath the gag, dreading the thought of what Tyburn was doing behind her back.

'Which finger shall we start with – the little one? No, wait, I've got a better idea,' he said, gripping her hand and sliding one of her slender fingers into the hole between the steel cutters.

'I can just imagine you and blokey next door, in church on your weddin' day. He takes your hand, weddin' ring at the ready, and guess what? No ring finger; just a tiny little stump.'

Emily let out a muffled scream, shaking her head in terror. With his thumb and forefinger poised to squeeze the blades together, Tyburn looked over at Cordell.

'Tell me the truth or the bitch loses a digit?'

'Alright, alright. I was lying,' said Cordell. 'I'm the only one who knows what you're planning.'

'So, tomorrow ... we're good to go?'

Cordell nodded.

'Sorry, I didn't catch that.'

'Yes, yes! You're not under surveillance. We didn't even know where you were, before today. Please, just let her go.'

Tyburn smiled and pulled the cigar cutter from Emily's finger. Her head sank forward and she burst into tears.

'That's good news for me, and for her. But not for you, Detective Chief Inspector – we still have some unfinished business.'

Cordell looked at him, apprehensively. 'Come on now, ... that was years ago.'

Tyburn took his knife and ripped the remaining sleeve from Cordell's shirt.

'All those years inside gave me plenty of time to think about what I was goin' to do to you. And, believe me when I tell you, this is gonna hurt.'

After stuffing the sleeve into Cordell's mouth and tying the gag good and tight, he circled the pillar, like a shark that had just caught the smell of blood.

'What's it gonna be? Tongue, nose, a little circumcision, maybe?'

Before Cordell could answer, Tyburn grabbed the little finger of his left hand and shoved it into the cigar cutter. 'Tell you what, you give me one finger for each year I spent inside. That's seven fingers.'

Suddenly, Cordell felt a searing bolt of pain as the blades of the guillotine shut, and his finger fell to the floor. He let out a muffled scream, expelling air through his nose in pulses of gut-wrenching agony. Emily turned away, her heart pounding with revulsion.

'Come on, Francis, don't be such a baby. We've only just got started,' said Tyburn, circling the pillar. Cordell's eyes bulged as his interrogator disappeared behind him once more. Suddenly, he felt his middle finger being grabbed and encircled by steel. Then came another agonising jolt as the blade cleaved flesh and bone. His muffled screams echoed around the walls – for longer this time, his head shaking from side to side as he tried to nullify the pain; to no avail.

Suddenly, Cordell's wails were interrupted by the faint sound of heavy metal music. Tyburn reached inside his jacket and pulled out a mobile phone.

'What!? ... Where am I? ... What the fuck's that got to do with you? ... What, now? ... Okay, okay, I'll be there in an hour.'

He put the phone back in his pocket and walked over to Cordell, whose face was tilted to one side, looking like he would pass out at any moment.

'Lucky for you, I've got to go and see a man about some pictures,' said Tyburn, crouching down to meet the DCI's trauma-addled gaze. 'But don't forget, matey – you still owe me five fingers.'

He reached round behind the pillar. 'Tell you what, I'll put these here as a reminder,' he said, placing the two severed digits on the floor at Cordell's feet.

His resistance spent and his body mutilated, Cordell closed his eyes and threw up into his gagged mouth.

Tyburn laughed and made his way towards the top of the stairs. 'Oh, by the way, bitch,' he said, turning to Emily. 'Any messages you want me to pass on to that boyfriend of yours, before I go?'

'NO! Please—' she screamed, through her gag. But Tyburn was gone.

A short while later, the door on the ground floor slammed shut – they were alone. Emily stared blankly at the wall, too frightened to move, or even dare to hope that the reign of terror was finally over. She thought about Tom, next door; praying he wasn't going through the same agonising hell, they'd just had to endure.

Having finally convinced herself he was still alive, she looked over at her fellow captive, eventually managing to catch his eye. 'Alright?' she mumbled.

Cordell gently nodded, wincing as another wave of pain shot through the remains of his left hand, then returned his anguished gaze to the dusty floorboards.

Emily stared at him for a moment, then looked back down at her own pale, naked legs, and started to sob.

*

Later, much later, when she was all cried out, and her head and shoulders ached so much, it felt like her body might explode, Emily let out an exhausted, stuttering sigh and looked over to the window. The sun would be setting soon. Then they would be truly alone, trapped in this cold, dusty void; probably the last place anyone would ever think to look for them. Was this it – the culmination of her life? Was this really the time and place she was actually going to die?

As the light faded and the surroundings lost their definition, her ears became her eyes, picking out noises and vibrations that would normally have passed her by. Everything seemed amplified, like a divergent orchestra playing a symphony of random sounds, filled with new meaning. The cars at the traffic lights, revving their engines – like mechanical outbursts of human emotion. Playful screams from children in nearby gardens – expressions of hope, happiness and freedom. A blackbird beginning its evensong outside the window – the sound of nature's aria, full of expression and life, and the fight for survival.

It was getting cold and before long, the comfort of daylight had all but vanished into the ether. She stared forlornly at the goosebumps all over her body, shivering as a gust of wind rattled the window pane. Then came a different noise – remote at first, then closer. Something clawing, grating all around her – in every dark corner, above and below. She daren't think about those creatures, with their sharp teeth, twitching whiskers and long worm-like tails. No, no; not here, not now.

Suddenly, she felt alone. So very naked and very alone. Tied up and gagged with a man she hardly knew, a man who was probably going to die right in front of her. He hadn't said a word in ages – he may already be dead. Then, all she'd have for company would be her nightmares and the cold, gnawing darkness of the oncoming night.

Chapter Fifty-Four

Orchard Lane Farm, Wendover, Bucks
2 April 2000

It was the final briefing. The hand-picked gang of thieves had been told to be at the farm for 3.00 pm and included two recent recruits – a conman by the name of George Yates, acting as a security guard in the Ashmolean's all-important west wing, and Coos Van Leer, ArtScreen's new head of security. Luke Waltham held court over proceedings, focusing on a set of architectural plans, maps and diagrams for each stage of the job, carefully annotated and laid out on the old farmhouse table. Marcus Tyburn was running late.

Kate poured herself some freshly brewed coffee from the percolator, as Julian casually wandered over to join her.

'And where did you two disappear off to, earlier?' he whispered.

'Sorry, what?'

'You and your dad, you were gone for ages after lunch. You must have had a lot to talk about.'

'Oh, nothing really – we just took the dog for a walk to clear our heads.'

'Right. Only I couldn't help but notice, Luke looked a little worried when you came back. Is everything alright?'

'Yes. Why wouldn't it be?'

'No reason. I was just curious.'

Kate looked at her father. 'He has got a lot on his mind at the moment. I'm sure you can understand that.'

'Oh sure, – haven't we all?'

'Anyway, how are things with you and Emily? I assume you're all set for tomorrow?' enquired Kate.

'Absolutely. She's worked wonders to get everything ready on time. I think under normal circumstances, this would have been one of the most successful exhibitions we've ever staged – if you know what I mean.'

Kate looked at him and smiled. 'Creating the perfect illusion is so important.'

'Yes, I suppose you're right.'

'I am. Come on, I think Dad's ready to make a start.'

After a brief pep talk, Luke began walking through the various stages of the operation.

'Julian, the main entrance to the museum – opens at seven pm sharp, yes?'

'That's right; if not a little bit before. Emily and I will be in the Randolph Gallery to greet the guests as they arrive. We're expecting around a hundred people, so it should be quite a turnout. At seven-forty pm, after a bit of chit-chat over champagne and canapés, we'll start to make our way upstairs. George will follow on behind and pick up any stragglers.'

'You will be polite, won't you, George?' said Kate. 'We don't want people to think they're being herded about like sheep.'

'Yeah, yeah, I'll treat 'em like royalty, don't you worry,' said George.

'Right, so when George gives me the nod that everyone is present, we'll get started with the speeches.'

Luke looked up from the plans. 'Good, good. Make sure you keep it short and snappy, Julian, we can't afford any delays.'

'I'll do my best, assuming the mayor doesn't ramble on for too long. I'd allow five minutes, … six at the most.'

'Okay. George, what's your cue?'

'When I see Julian take the mayor over to cut the ribbon, I'll close the gallery doors and lock everyone inside. Of course, before all that, I will have turned on my little device, here.' George placed a small black box on the table. It was about the size of a mobile phone and had three antennae sticking out of the top.

'What on earth is that?' said Julian.

'It's a mobile phone jammer. It blocks a range of frequencies between the cell and the base station. I simply push this button, here, and lay it on the display cabinet at the top of the stairs. Anyone in the gallery who tries to call for help will find they can't get a signal.'

'Does it work?' said Kate, picking up her phone.

George flicked the switch on top of the device. 'Try and make a call.'

Kate looked at the display on her phone. 'I can't, it's saying I've got no network.'

'Nor I,' said Julian.

'What about the walkie-talkies?' said Van Leer.

'They should work fine, they're on a completely different wavelength,' said George.

Luke nodded. 'Excellent. Now, Coos, you'll be up in the control centre, keeping an eye on things.'

'Yes, me and my team will be watching the monitors. When I see George close the outer doors, I'll turn off the alarms in Gallery fifty-five, so the eight paintings can be removed from the walls. All but one of the guards on duty that evening is 'in the know', so there shouldn't be any resistance from that quarter.'

Luke was about to turn to Danny Forgan when the kitchen door opened and in walked Tyburn.

'Thought you'd honour us with your presence, did you?' said Kate.

'Shut it, little girl. I don't answer to you.'

'No, you answer to me,' said Luke. 'Where the hell have you been?'

'In Wickwar, clearin' up your mess.'

'What are you talking about?'

Tyburn sat down and tossed the brown envelope containing the photocopy of the Millais letter onto the kitchen table.

Julian reached over and opened it. 'Where did you get this?'

'I found it in your girlfriend's house.'

'What? ... what were you doing there?' he asked, nervously combing his fingers through his hair.

Luke glared at Tyburn. 'I told you to stay on the farm, not go parading around the countryside and breaking into people's houses, for Christ's sake!'

'Right,' said Tyburn. 'So, you won't be interested to know that Cordell and the girl had lunch, this afternoon? Or that she was given that letter by Mountfield, here.'

'What? Don't be ridiculous,' said Julian.

Tyburn continued, 'Cordell's been on our tail for weeks, tryin' to put all the pieces together. Luckily for us, they hit a brick wall.'

Luke put his head in his hands. 'How can you possibly know that?'

'It took a little persuasion, but he eventually admitted it.'

'And where are they now?' said Kate.

'Where's who?'

'Emily and the detective, where are they?'

Tyburn leaned back on his chair and grabbed a chicken sandwich from a plate behind him. 'They won't be botherin' us, if that's what you're worried about.'

'Oh my God, you haven't—' said Julian.

'What, ... killed your girlfriend? That would smart a bit, wouldn't it.'

Luke thumped his fist on the table. 'I told you, no more violence.'

'Oh, calm the fuck down, they're fine. They're tied up in a warehouse next to her gaff.'

On hearing of Emily's abduction, Julian launched himself at Tyburn, his face red with rage. Tyburn stood up and grabbed him by the arm, twisting it behind his back.

'Do that again and I'll rip your fuckin' head off,' he said, throwing him back into his seat.

Julian sat there, quietly rubbing his shoulder.

'You're a fucking animal,' said Kate.

Tyburn looked at her and laughed. 'You're the second person to call me that, today.'

'Alright everybody, let's just calm down,' said Luke, raising his hands in the air. 'If, as Marcus says, CID are in the dark and Cordell is ... out of harm's way, then it looks like we could still be on for tomorrow. There is, however, the small matter of the boyfriend. He'll have reported her missing by now.'

Tyburn shook his head. 'He's tied up too. I told you, I took care of it.'

'What about Emily? I need her for the launch party,' said Julian.

'Who's runnin' that fuckin' museum, you or her?' growled Tyburn.

Luke scratched his chin. 'You'll have to improvise, Julian. Say she's been taken ill, or something.'

Julian got up and stormed out of the kitchen. Kate went to go after him.

'Leave him, sweetheart,' said Luke, grabbing her arm. 'He'll be back when he's cooled down.'

Kate nodded and went and stood by the kitchen window, quietly fuming at Tyburn's antics. She knew he was a loose cannon, but this time, he'd really excelled himself.

'Okay, let's focus our minds back on the task at hand, shall we?' said Luke, taking a deep breath and laying his palms flat on the table.

'So, by seven-ten pm, Marcus, Danny and I will be hidden in the anteroom at the far end of Gallery fifty-five. The doors will be locked, so we won't be disturbed. We'll wait there until the speeches have finished and Coos has de-activated the alarms. At around seven forty-seven pm, when the guests have begun to move into the main exhibition area, Coos will give us the signal to storm in.'

'And what will that be?' enquired George.

'We need to maintain radio silence, except for emergencies, so the walkie-talkies are out. There's a painting in the anteroom called *Danae and the Brazen Tower*. When we see the alarm indicator light next to the painting go off, in we go. That'll be your job, Danny, to watch that light.'

'Fine by me.'

'Marcus, once we go in, I need you and Danny to take control of that room as quickly as possible.'

Tyburn's eyes widened – taking control was his speciality. 'Right. I'll let off a few shots, then the lad, here, can round up all the punters and get 'em lyin' face down on the floor, where I can keep an eye on 'em. Anyone who misbehaves gets a clout. They'll soon learn we're not there to fuck around.'

Luke pointed his finger at Tyburn. 'Remember what I said, no violence and no shooting the guests, is that clear?'

Tyburn just glared at him. 'Sure.'

'Danny, once you've closed the connecting doors, you and I will start removing the paintings and loading them, carefully, into the wooden packing crate. And I do mean, carefully.'

Danny nodded.

'When we're all packed up and ready to go, George will let us out of the west wing, re-lock the doors and escort us to the elevator at the top of the stairs.'

Julian walked back into the kitchen and stood next to Kate; his arms folded tightly across his chest.

'Apparently, we're takin' you hostage, Mountfield,' said Tyburn, fixing him with a grin. 'So, you'd better behave, or I might just have to give you a clout.'

Julian ignored him, staring blankly at the floor.

'On a serious note, Julian, ...' said Luke, '... we do need to get you out without anyone suspecting your involvement. So just do what the other guests do, and don't forget – look terrified.'

'Don't worry, I'll play my part.'

'I know you will,' smiled Luke. 'Now, once we've moved the trolley down to the ground floor, we—'

'Yeah, yeah, ...' interrupted Tyburn, '... we head for the loadin' bay, put the crate in the van, and sweet-cheeks here drives us all off into the sunset, right?'

'Wrong!' said Kate, walking over to stand next to her father. 'I'm afraid there's been a slight change of plan.'

There was stunned silence round the kitchen table.

'What the fuck's she talkin' about?' said Tyburn.

'We're not going out the back way. We're leaving via the main entrance at the front of the building,' said Luke.

'What? That's crazy,' said Danny.

Tyburn just sat and laughed.

Luke held up his hand. 'Let me explain. Over the past few weeks, I've had my suspicions that Cordell and his team were getting too close. So I decided we needed a little, ... insurance. Something that will guarantee we can walk out of the museum without any interference from the police.'

'And how the hell are we gonna do that?' said Tyburn.

'A few days ago, I had a radio-controlled device installed in Gallery fifty-five.'

There were more confused looks around the table.

'What sort of device?' said Julian.

'I guess you could call it a chemical bomb, of sorts. It's infused with a contaminant called ricin, hidden in the two radiators in the centre of the room.'

Again, Tyburn burst out laughing. 'Now I get it. This is a wind-up, right? Because, for a second there, it sounded like you'd turned this whole fuckin' job into some kind of terrorist attack.'

'I'm not joking, Marcus. This gives us back the control we need to get those paintings out of there. Trust me, it will work.'

Julian shook his head in disbelief. 'I can't believe you've planted a chemical weapon in my museum, Luke. We have hundreds of people walking around that building every day. Kids, for goodness sake. Are you mad?'

'Julian, hear me out for a second. It's quite safe until it's primed.'

'Oh, well, that makes it perfectly alright, then!'

'Okay, now listen, ... once we get to the ground floor, we move the crate over to the main entrance and walk out onto Beaumont Street, where Kate will be waiting with the van.'

George Yates threw his hands up in the air. 'You don't seriously think they're gonna just let us walk out the front door with a bunch of priceless paintings, do you?'

'That's precisely what they'll do, George. You see, at seven forty-five pm, before we enter the gallery, Kate will have put a call in to the Oxford police, informing them that a robbery is in progress at the Ashmolean, and one hundred guests have been taken hostage in the process. She will explain that, unless the robbers are allowed to leave freely and are not challenged in any way, a large quantity of ricin gas will be discharged into the gallery, killing everyone inside. She will insist that all roads within four square miles of the museum are completely clear of police and emergency services. And that will provide us with the perfect escape route.'

'What about police marksmen? We'll be like sitting ducks, walking out onto a busy main road,' said Danny.

'No, that's a fair point. Kate will make it quite clear in her call that, if there is any sign of marksmen on the rooftops, or if any shots are fired, we will release the ricin gas and one hundred innocent people will die.'

'We just walk out the front door and drive away?' said Van Leer.

'That's it.'

'You've lost your fuckin' mind,' said Tyburn.

Luke calmly got to his feet, walked over to a whisky bottle sitting on the dresser, and poured himself a shot.

'Look – I know you think Cordell's team are in the dark about tomorrow, but how can we know that, for sure? At least this way, we have a chance of getting out of there – a good chance. And, just so they understand we mean business, we'll take a hostage with us. That's you,' he said, pointing to Julian.

For once, Tyburn said nothing.

Van Leer smiled and shook his head. 'It's so fucking crazy, it might just work.'

'What happens then?' said Julian.

'Once we've loaded up the van outside the museum, we turn left into St Giles' and head north along the Woodstock Road. The police will be told that if we spot anyone attempting to follow us by road or helicopter, we will activate the weapon. The van will make its way to the cricket ground opposite St Edward's School, where we stop and unload the paintings.'

'Unload onto what, a bloody magic carpet?' said Tyburn.

'In a manner of speaking. I've arranged for a helicopter to be waiting at the cricket ground, ready to fly us to a remote farmhouse in Suffolk.'

'It had better be a big one if it's going to take the seven of us and the paintings,' said Van Leer.

'It's a Bell four-thirty, so there'll be plenty of room. If all goes to plan, we should be at the farmhouse by nine pm. There'll be a car with false plates for each of us, so we can go our separate ways and lie low for a bit.'

'And what about the pictures?' asked Tyburn.

'Oh, they'll be kept safe and sound, until our buyers have been contacted and the money exchanged. Once the financial transactions are complete, the money will be wired to your designated bank accounts, as agreed.'

Tyburn shook his head. 'Well, that all sounds fuckin' peachy.'

'That's the plan, Marcus, take it or leave it.'

'You're seriously tellin' me, if some copper with an itchy trigger finger lets off a few rounds while we're ... paradin' about outside the museum, you're gonna flip a switch and kill all those punters?'

Everyone looked at Luke, except for Kate – she didn't need to. She already knew the answer to that question.

Chapter Fifty-Five

Wickwar, near Bristol

2 April 2000

Somewhat reluctantly, Tom came to. Like someone rousing too quickly from their dreams, he tried desperately to suppress the relentless waves of reality washing over him; but the pain in the back of his head soon put pay to that – sharp, jabbing sensations, telling him that it was – *time to wake up, motherfucker!*

He opened his sleep-encrusted eyes to see the word *HYSTERIA* staring back at him through the gloom. He went to move his arms, ... nothing happened. Was he paralysed? Had he been drugged? Then, it hit him – the unavoidable truth – he'd been gagged, bound and tied to a chair with his hands behind his back, a prisoner in his own living room. He gazed down at his chest, once more. *Hysteria? You have to be kidding me – if only I felt that alive!* he thought, groaning at the muzziness in his head.

Looking around, he remembered his attacker had positioned him towards the far end of the lounge, at right angles to the huge sandstone fireplace – the grate still full of wood ash from two nights ago. Without being able to see his watch, and the old clock on the mantelpiece not having been wound in days, he tried to figure how long he'd been out for. It could have been an hour; it could have been ten. He looked at the faint glow through the curtains. The street light was on, but was it morning or evening? Judging by the lack of car noise on the high street, it felt like the early hours. In truth, he had no idea.

One good thing, at least that psycho hadn't come back to finish him off. But where was Emily? Was she dead? No, he couldn't let himself think that. She was strong – a survivor. And he loved her more than he cared to admit. Tears began to well up in his eyes.

Come on Tom, pull yourself together, for fuck's sake. She could walk in here, any minute, and you wouldn't want her to see you like this, would you.

Having regained his composure, he tried once more to move his arms and legs, but they were firmly anchored to the chair – tied with, what appeared to be, lengths of red satin chord.

Emily's going to be so pissed off when she finds out what's happened to her precious tiebacks, he laughed. Then wished he hadn't, as the dull stabbing pain resumed its assault on the back of his skull.

He blinked a few times to clear his vision, then noticed the red light on the answer machine. He'd not heard any messages; they must have called when he was unconscious. He watched it blinking, rhythmically, like a tiny beacon of hope. Perhaps it was the psycho, ringing to say he'd taken Emily hostage? Or maybe Emily herself, phoning to say her last goodbyes. Either way, friend or foe, it was contact with the outside world, and sitting there alone in the half-light, it was all he had. Somehow, someway, he had to get over there.

Ignoring the dull ache in his brain, he began shuffling the dining chair from side to side, inching himself forward. Having eventually managed to clear the side of the coffee table, he anchored his feet into the carpet, and pushed himself sideways, gradually rotating the chair through ninety degrees until he was facing the television. He could just about make out his reflection in the glass. *My God, what the hell do you look like?*

After a few moments spent psyching himself up for the next stage, he continued his tacking movements down the length of the lounge. Just as he was getting up a head of steam, one of the chair legs dug into the carpet. He quickly threw his weight backwards and somehow managed to stop himself toppling head first onto the floor. 'For fuck's sake, concentrate!' he said, sitting back in the chair.

Having gathered himself once more, he pushed out his shoulders and set off in the direction of the front door. This was it, the home stretch. He'd only gone a yard or so when he had to stop from the pain of the wooden back posts digging into his forearms. He closed his eyes and let out a muffled yell, biting down hard on the gag until he was ready to go again. This time, he rocked his body in time to each jerking motion, left then right, building up a steady rhythm until, at last, he drew level with a small wooden table under the stairs. He turned and stared at the *PLAY* button on the answer machine. If he could just lean over, and—

There was a loud crack as one of the chair legs gave way, sending him crashing into the low table to his right. The phone's handset and base unit took off in different directions, landing somewhere in the tangle of cables behind the TV. Still anchored to the chair and lying on his side, Tom blinked rapidly – blood from a fresh cut trickling down his forehead. He lay quietly for a few seconds, then let out a muted scream of frustration – but no one heard, no one came. A few feet away, the base unit lay upside down, its red light flashing in the darkness, taunting him – *message waiting, message waiting ...*

He shook his head. He'd given it his best shot, but it was time to call it a day; to drift off back to Xanadu and the warm, dreamy pleasure dome of oblivion he'd come to call home. He gazed at the *HYSTERIA* logo on his Def Leppard T-shirt, closed his eyes and thought about Emily – hoping with all his heart that she was safe and well. It was all he could do.

As he was about to lose consciousness, he thought he felt something warm and furry nudge his chin, followed by a strangely familiar purring sound. Then the purring stopped and everything went a mildly comforting shade of black.

Chapter Fifty-Six

Orchard Lane Farm, Wendover, Bucks
2 April 2000

It was late, and all the head-scratching and debate in Luke's final planning meeting was over. Tyburn and Danny were having a quiet smoke outside, while everyone else had gone to bed; apart from Julian, who was sitting alone in the library, trying to enjoy some of Luke's fine single malt, and failing miserably. Every time he tried to run through his opening speech for the exhibition, his thoughts would wander back to the plight of poor Emily – was she lying hurt, somewhere? Was she bleeding to death? When he'd tried to push Tyburn about it, he became violent, saying it was better for him to keep his effing nose out. Then there was this whole ricin business. He couldn't believe Luke had done that; not least, kept him in the dark about it.

His mind went back to the first time he'd met Luke Waltham, five years ago. Julian had only recently joined the Ashmolean as head of the Western Art department, when, one morning, his worst fears as a curator were realised in quite spectacular fashion. While working in his office, he got a call from one of the on-duty attendants saying there'd been a serious incident in one of the picture galleries. He rushed downstairs to find the west wing completely sealed off and a handful of museum staff, including Henry Faber, carefully inspecting a beautiful and valuable garden scene by Pierre-Auguste Renoir. It took a few moments to register what was wrong. Then he noticed the shards of glass on the floor and, to his horror, six steel nails protruding from the canvas. Apparently, a young man dressed in a hooded top and jeans, and clutching a nail gun, had calmly walked up to the painting and proceeded to fire half a dozen nails straight through the glass. Two security staff had bravely given chase but lost him in the city centre crowds.

The museum's problems didn't end there. The painting was due to be loaned out to New York's Metropolitan Museum of Art in a matter of weeks, as part of an exhibition on late French impressionism. Fearing the Ashmolean's restoration team would never be able to fix it in time, he was contacted out of the blue by a man named Luke Waltham. Apparently, he'd heard about the unfortunate incident and wondered whether his company, ArtScreen, could be of assistance. A month later, the restoration work was complete and the painting was being packed up, ready to be shipped across the pond. Within a year of their first meeting, Julian and Luke had become firm friends, finding common interests in art, literature and most of all, collecting. The kindred flame was well and truly lit when Julian was invited over to the farm to view something "quite intriguing". When he first laid eyes on the Draper sketchbook, he knew it was a remarkable find, but it took on a whole new perspective when Luke revealed the contents of William Holman Hunt's letter to Millais and Rossetti.

Soon, Luke had him eating out of his hand; and, within a few months, he'd managed to persuade Julian to betray the very museum he loved, all for a share in the proceeds of the theft of eight Pre-Raphaelite paintings. Initially, the prospect repulsed Julian; but Luke knew that, given time and the right encouragement, even the very idea of participating in such a daring scheme, would pander to his every desire and weakness.

Julian pulled back the curtains and looked out into the darkness. All he could see was the weight of his own judgement staring back at him. Of course, he loved his work, and took his responsibilities as a curator very seriously; for there was a duty of care that came with looking after some of the world's most extraordinary treasures, and he relished every minute of it. So why on earth had he forsaken all the values he held so dear? Had he been blackmailed? Was his life in danger? Had there been threatening calls to his wife and children? No – the sad fact was, everyone had their price, even him; Luke had simply made him an offer he couldn't refuse. He wasn't proud of his deceit, far from it. In fact, the thought of his museum being contaminated with deadly ricin gas made him feel physically sick. And here he was, the night before the robbery, having severe misgivings about the whole thing. What with Emily's kidnapping, Luke changing the escape route, and now the lives of good, honest citizens being threatened, everything seemed to have turned to madness. It was time to decide exactly where his loyalties lay – with good or evil, conservation or subversion, honour or disgrace.

As he knocked back the last mouthful of single malt, his head swimming with conflict and self-doubt, there was only one thing in this whole sorry mess that he did know for sure – heaven wasn't at the bottom of this glass.

*

Danny watched as Tyburn took a long, slow drag of his cigarette, then flicked the butt high into the air, sending a flash of orange sparks spiralling into the darkness.

'Not sure I like the sound of this, Marcus,' he said, his arms folded, leaning against the door of the old barn.

Tyburn frowned. 'Mmm ... what the fuck is Waltham playin' at?'

'Beats me,'

'I don't trust him – he's up to somethin'.'

'Yeah, but what?' said Danny, scratching his head.

'I reckon he's lookin' to cut us out.'

'What? You think he'd do that?'

'You don't make a last-minute change, like that, for no reason.'

'Well, he does think the filth are onto us.'

'No, there's somethin' else.'

'You don't think he knows we're working for Willard Knox, do you?'

Tyburn turned and grabbed Danny by his hoodie, forcing him up against the barn door. 'You dumb fuck, I told you not to mention that name down here.'

Danny grimaced as one of the rusty hinges dug into the back of his skull.

'They've all gone to bed, they can't hear us out here.'

'You've been shootin' your mouth off again, haven't ya?'

'What? No, I ain't said a word.'

'Who was it this time? The new guy, Van Leer – tryin' to impress him, were ya?'

'No, for fuck's sake, Marcus. I need this pay out as much as you do. You know you can trust me.'

Tyburn stared into his eyes and with a final shove, dropped Danny to the ground; then took out another cigarette and lit it.

Danny rubbed his head, watching as Tyburn walked into the centre of the courtyard.

'Tomorrow, in the gallery, when I give the signal, you take out Mountfield and leave Waltham to me,' said Tyburn.

'What, we're gonna kill 'em?'

'You got a problem with that?'

Danny shook his head. 'No … course not. Just seems a bit drastic, that's all.'

'No one screws with me and gets away with it. We'll grab the pictures and leave out the back way, like we planned.'

'What if he sets off this bloody … ricin thing?'

'Ha, – do you really think he has the guts to kill all those people? Bollocks! George will let us know if Waltham puts a foot wrong, don't you worry.'

'Yeah, that was genius, getting him on board.'

Tyburn took a drag of his cigarette and blew a huge plume of smoke into the cool night air.

'Me and George go back a long way. He's a pro, like me – he goes where the money is. As soon as I told him I'd struck a deal with Knox on the eight pictures, he nearly bit my hand off. And, let's face it, a three-way cut is a damned sight better than seven.'

Danny nodded at his so-called partner. 'Damned right.'

Truth be known, he wouldn't trust Tyburn for all the beer in Belgium; and he certainly wouldn't put it past him to try and cut him out of the deal, altogether.

It was time to pick a side. And, for his sake, it had better be the right one.

Chapter Fifty-Seven

Wickwar, near Bristol

2 April 2000

DCI Cordell was lost in a sea of hopelessness. Naked and bleeding, the pain in his hand so intense, he barely felt the overnight temperatures plummeting in the old abandoned warehouse. He sat quietly, his legs outstretched, supported by the very pillar holding him captive. With eyelids heavy through a lack of sleep, he'd somehow managed to endure the monotony of the early hours, moving in and out of consciousness, like a shaman trying to conjure up benevolent beings from a higher plane of existence. Anything to escape this dark, desolate place, with its blacked-out windows and atmosphere of neglect. He didn't know Wickwar, but could imagine this Victorian relic had long been forgotten, and even those who lived within sight of its towering brick walls, barely gave it a second glance. It felt like they'd been sucked into a black hole, where time and space were contorted beyond all recognition. And the top floor was the event horizon – not even waves of light could escape its all-consuming grasp.

Cordell moved his head to the left and could just make out the contours of Emily's naked body. He thought about trying to call out, but what was the point? Even without the gag, what would he say? He had no escape plan, no words of comfort. It was as though Tyburn had emasculated him, robbing him of all his self-esteem and rational thinking. Better to stay quiet and keep his suffering to himself.

He was just thinking about closing his eyes again, when something scuttled across the floor in front of him. He glared into the darkness, straining to see what it was. He'd heard strange noises during the night and paid no attention to them, convincing himself that the building was old and falling apart; it could have been anything. But this was different, closer, and very much alive. Then came another sharp burst of pitter-patter to his right. He turned his head, his eyes wide with panic, searching the blackness for it. Then he saw it, dark and squat – a few feet away. The rat rose up on its haunches, sniffing the stale air that had become enriched with traces of blood, sweat and bone. Its whiskers bristled, sensing the danger of an active human presence. Yet still it drew closer, lured by the prospect of edible matter. Cordell could feel the terror rising in his chest – each shallow breath filled with fear. Covering the wounds with his good hand, in a futile attempt to conceal them from the creature's bloodlust, he watched it's every move, powerless to resist.

Suddenly, the rat came scuttling towards him. Cordell yelped, drawing his legs up to his chest, but it had seen its target and clamped its teeth into one of the severed fingers, scurrying off back to its lair with it. Cordell leaned back against the pillar, trying not to dwell on the fact that part of him was being devoured by a wild animal. He moved his foot next to the remaining finger and flicked it over to where the rat had disappeared off to, just in case it felt like coming back for seconds.

The emotion of it all suddenly overcame him and his eyes filled with tears. Here he was, naked, disfigured and possibly bleeding to death. He'd failed to stop poor Emily and Tom from getting kidnapped, and if that wasn't enough, in less than twenty-four hours, some of Britain's most iconic paintings would be snatched from under his nose – very likely, never to be seen again. And the thing that hurt the most, there was absolutely nothing he could do about it.

*

The early morning sun peered over the rooftops, illuminating the dust in a tiny slither of light across the warehouse floor. Emily was lost in a dream of much-needed sleep – a chance to escape the torment for a while.

At some point, long after Tyburn's departure, she'd been able to unhook her wrists from the bolt protruding from the other side of the pillar, allowing her to lean back and rest her hands on the floor. The sense of relief in her upper body was beyond words.

Disregarding the cold, she'd somehow managed to escape to a dreamworld, where times were happier and people kinder. It started with her and Tom, sitting in their tiny cottage garden, drinking local cider, and talking about the time they first met, in the Three Sugar Loaves – an old Bristol pub, at the foot of Christmas Steps. She'd been standing at the bar, waiting to be served, when the chap next to her turned round, knocking virtually a whole pint of beer down her front. Tom was embarrassed, charming and strangely attractive. She was calm, charismatic and surprisingly forgiving, considering she'd been showered with pale ale. They chatted and swapped numbers, on the pretence that she would send him the dry-cleaning bill. A day later, despite endless ribbings from his workmates, he called her up and asked her for a date. And that was the start of their journey, together.

She was just about to kiss Tom goodnight for the first time, when a car backfired on the high street, waking her with a jolt. Seeing the golden spears of light piercing the window glass, she glanced over at the neighbouring pillar – Cordell was staring at her.

'Okay?' she asked, in muffled tone.

He blinked, then nodded a few times, as if he was trying to tell her something.

She shook her head and shrugged. *Sorry, I don't understand.*

He repeated the strange action. What on earth was he doing? She turned her head, looking down at the space between them.

'What is it?' she said, not that he could understand her, either.

He waggled his bloodied fingers and seemed to be pointing at something. She turned her head as far as it would go, but the pillar was blocking her view. She looked back at Cordell. Again, he tilted his head and pointed his fingers to the space behind her. Seeing no other option, she drew her knees up to her chest and gradually shuffled round on her bottom to the other side of the pillar, savouring the change of aspect; only to realise, it was much the same as the one she'd been staring at for the last seventeen hours.

Cordell started grunting at her, gesticulating with his upper body. There was obviously something he was desperate for her to see, but what? She humoured him with one last look around in front of her. No, ... there was nothing. Clearly, the loss of blood was making him delusional.

Exasperated, she shook her head. 'Where? I just can't—'

Then she saw it. Barely visible through the layers of dust and grime was a flat rectangular object, lying just a few feet away. Somehow, Cordell had seen it. As she looked over to him, he gave her a final confirmatory nod and leaned back against the pillar – his work was done, the rest was up to her.

Feeling the gritty floor beneath her skin, she pushed out both legs as far as they would go, but still couldn't quite reach it. This wasn't going to be easy. She shuffled forward on her bottom and, keeping her body as low to the ground as possible, stretched herself out until she could just about touch it. Straining every muscle, she pushed her right foot a few more inches and finally managed to grip the top of it with her heel. With her wrists pressed tight against the back of the pillar, she began to drag the object back towards her; praying it wouldn't get snagged on the floor boards. Having gotten it to within a few feet, Cordell began grunting and nodding enthusiastically, egging her on as best he could.

At first glance, it looked like a small metal advertising sign, and judging by the rust around the edges, an old one at that. God knows how anyone had missed it when the warehouse was being cleared. But none of that mattered, it was hers now – all she had to do was land it.

Using both heels together, she pulled the sign towards her until it came to rest beneath her thighs. After taking a few moments to catch her breath, she edged herself back round the bottom of the pillar, until she was facing in the opposite direction. Now came the tricky bit. Working completely blind, she reached out with her fingers and dragged the sign up to the pillar base. Then, placing her finger nails beneath the rusted edge, she carefully tilted the sign up through ninety degrees until it was resting vertically between her hands. Feeling quite pleased with herself, she moved her fingertips up the sides of the cool steel. Just as she got to the top, it slipped from her grasp – hitting the floor with a slap, and sending a cloud of dust into the air.

'Fuck!' said Emily, looking over at Cordell.

He glared back at her, then motioned with his head, as if to say, *Go again, go again.*

She readied herself once more, took a deep breath through her nose, and set her fingers searching for the rusted edge. Having located it, she slid her nails beneath the thin sheet metal and slowly raised it into an upright position, gripping it as tightly as she could. Then, walking her fingers up the sides of the sign, she rested the cable tie across the top edge. With one hand clasped on either side, she began to move them slowly back and forth, pushing the narrow strip of plastic down onto the jagged metal in between. Once she'd got used to the motion, she went a little faster, trying not to slash her wrists in the process. With her hands behind her, she could only manage small movements, taking a break every thirty seconds, or so, to rest her arms.

After several nerve-racking minutes, wondering if the plastic cable-tie would ever break, it finally snapped, freeing her arms in a moment of glorious liberation. Her whole body seemed to exhale, revelling in the joy of unencumbered movement.

She quickly untied her gag, then massaged her arms and shoulders to restore the circulation, gazing at the filthy green sign that had given her, her freedom – it said, *Norton Motorcycles – Parts & Service.* For a moment, she thought about using it to free Cordell, but her kitchen scissors would do the job in a fraction of the time.

Having quickly put on her clothes and trainers, she walked over to Cordell, untied his vomit-covered gag and wrapped his discarded jacket round his shoulders.

'I'm going to call for an ambulance. I'll be back in two minutes to cut you free, okay?'

'Thank you,' he said, his voice barely audible.

She ran down the two flights of stairs and through the old shopfront to the packing room at the back. The battered side door was locked and the key had gone. She poked her head through the hole in the upper panel, savouring the fresh morning air, but there was no way she was going to squeeze through there. She looked around for Tom's hand axe, but that was gone, too.

Her head dropped in disappointment - so close, and yet so far.

She ran back into the other room and saw the old apple crusher looming large. The wooden beam hanging over the edge of the metal container would make an ideal battering ram, but how would she get it out? Checking the joint at the top, she couldn't believe her luck – the nut that should have secured it to the central post was missing. She grabbed the end of the beam and pulled – the bolt slid out of its hole like a knife through butter.

Using all her remaining strength, she hauled the beam back to the packing room and prepared for the final assault. Standing in the doorway, she tucked the length of wood under her arm and ran as fast as she could towards the back door. It didn't stand a chance. The end of the beam went crashing through the central panel, sending bits of wood flying into the courtyard. She backed up and inspected the damage, but the hole was still too small to clamber through. Girding herself once more, she picked up the beam, took a few steps back and with a battle-cry Queen Boudica would have been proud of, charged at the door. The top half exploded outwards, as if it had been hit by a cannon ball. She dropped the beam and clambered out into the yard. The feeling of freedom and warm spring sunshine on her face almost brought her to tears. But, all she could think about was Tom – was he okay? Was he alive?

She unlatched the back gate, ran through the garden and opened the back door into the kitchen. Ignoring the chaotic scene in the dining room, she burst into the front room and saw Tom's body lying on the floor.

'Tom, Tom!' she screamed, kneeling down and patting his cheek. There was no response. She felt his neck for a pulse and noticed the bloody gash to the back of his head. After searching frantically for the landline phone, she finally found it behind the TV and dialled 999.

Having called for an ambulance, she found a pair of scissors in the kitchen drawer and went straight back to the top floor of the warehouse to free a very grateful, but very weak, DCI Cordell.

Thirty minutes later, a fleet of police cars and ambulances were on site, caring for the three victims and scouring the various crime scenes.

With an emergency blanket wrapped round her, Emily walked up to the ambulance in which Cordell was now lying with an IV line feeding much-needed blood into his arm.

'Is it okay if I have a quick word?' she said to the young paramedic, who was carefully bandaging Cordell's mutilated hand.

'Sure, but keep it brief.'

'How are you?' she said, crouching down to meet the DCI's gaze.

'I'm alright,' he said, wincing as the paramedic dabbed one of his stumps with an antiseptic wipe. 'Thank you for getting us out of there, by the way.'

'I can't take all the credit. If you hadn't seen that sign, we'd still be sitting there, now.'

'Maybe,' said Cordell, with half a smile.

Emily nodded, not really knowing what to say. 'Well, at least we've still got a few hours to lock down the museum and stop them stealing the paintings.'

'Yes, ... or we could try and catch them in the act.'

Emily looked at him, somewhat bemused. 'Surely we have to protect the artworks.'

'Yes, of course. But sometimes, it takes a thief to catch a thief.'

'Miss, we have to go,' said the paramedic.

She nodded and stood up. 'Take it easy,' she said, kissing Cordell on the forehead, convinced he must still be delirious from the ordeal.

She stepped down and walked over to join Tom, who was now conscious and about to be whisked off to hospital in another ambulance.

'I'm going to follow on behind, babe,' she said, squeezing his hand.

'Are you sure you're okay to drive?'

'Absolutely, I'll see you there, shortly.'

He nodded and closed his eyes.

Harbouring every drop of strength she possessed, she climbed into her beloved Alpine, and with both hands clamped firmly on the steering wheel, followed the two ambulances as they made their way along Wickwar High Street, towards the outskirts of Bristol.

She'd been through hell in the last twenty four hours, and much as she longed to relax and savour her new found freedom, there was one more battle left to fight in this war of good against evil – and it lay seventy miles away, in the centre of Oxford.

Chapter Fifty-Eight

Ashmolean Museum, Oxford

3 April 2000

Julian Mountfield ended the call and placed the mobile phone on his desk. He stared at it for a while, then scanned the room. Had they bugged his office? Were there hidden cameras watching his every move? He glared at the door as if, any second, ArtScreen security guards were going to burst in and haul him off to face Luke Waltham and the rest of them, for what he'd just done.

He walked over to the sideboard and poured himself a scotch – its warm caress providing little comfort as he gulped it down. He looked pale and tired. The bags under his eyes a sign of the sleepless night he'd had, worrying about Emily. He'd lost count of the times he'd been asked about her, that morning. Had he heard from her? Was she ill? Would she still make it to the launch party? He wanted to scream at them: *I don't know where she is! She could be dead, for all I know.* But of course, he'd kept his cool, responding: 'Apparently, she's got a tummy bug and been throwing up all night. I'm sure she'll try and make the launch, if she can.' That was enough to placate most people, for now, anyway.

Just as he was pouring himself another glass, there was a knock at the door. He spun round, quickly, spilling some of the whisky on the carpet.

'Who is it?' he said, trying to sound calm.

There was no response. He placed the glass on the desk and walked over to the door, pausing for a second before opening it. There stood Kate Waltham, looking cool and elegant, as always.

'Hello,' she said, with a confident smile.

'Kate, what a nice surprise,' he said, running his fingers through his hair. 'Please, come in.'

'I thought I'd pop by and ... Julian, are you alright, you look terrible?'

'Yes, I'm fine. I didn't get much sleep last night, what with all these last minute changes.'

'Oh, you mustn't worry. Dad's got it all worked out. Just concentrate on what you've got to do and the rest will take care of itself.'

'Yes, but what about Emily? It turns my stomach when I think what that bastard might have done to her.'

'Oh, stop fretting. She'll be fine.'

'How can you be so sure? She could be lying there, dead, for all we know.'

Kate perched herself on the corner of the desk and folded her arms.

'My, my, she really has gotten under your skin, hasn't she?'

'What? No, I wouldn't say that. I'm just worried about her, that's all.'

'Okay, listen. Dad had a word with Marcus last night, and he promised he'd left her completely unharmed.'

'Well, believe that if you like. Personally, I wouldn't trust a single word that comes out of that nutter's mouth.'

'Look, as soon as the job's over, I'll personally see to it that the police are told where to find her. By tomorrow night, she'll be sitting at home with her feet up.'

Julian nodded. 'If you're sure?'

'I am,' she said, putting her hand on his cheek. 'Now, tell me honestly – is everything set for tonight?'

'Yes, as far as it can be.'

'Good. Now remember, we'll be taking you hostage, so I'm afraid Dad will be pointing a gun at you when we leave the front entrance. But don't worry, it won't be loaded.'

No doubt under instruction from her father, Kate continued trying to put Julian's mind at rest, but his attention was focussed on another beautiful young woman – one who seemed to be occupying his thoughts more and more, these days. The mere mention of her name was enough to intoxicate him. All the things that used to be important in his life – the museum, the university, fundraising for local charities – seemed to have fallen by the wayside. He'd virtually made his mind up; if Emily felt the same way, he would leave his wife and family, and start a new life with her. Yes, she was ten years younger, but that didn't matter; not to him anyway. There was a chemistry between them, an intellectual symbiosis; not to mention the work that had drawn them together, these past few months. But her abduction was destroying him, and the thought of never seeing her again clawed at his very soul. No, he was glad he'd made the call. And when he saw her again, he would tell her exactly how he felt.

When Kate finally stopped talking, he opened the door to his office and escorted her upstairs to Gallery 55, where the eight *Lights of the World* were all on display.

As he showed her round, he gazed upon them with renewed affection; hoping to God that, just as for his beloved Emily, his remedial actions had not come too late.

Chapter Fifty-Nine

Frenchay Hospital, near Bristol

3 April 2000

From his bed in the trauma unit, DCI Cordell stared blankly at the white polystyrene ceiling tiles as the transfusion gradually worked its way into his bloodstream. Trying desperately to relax, and failing miserably, he leaned over to the bedside cabinet and checked his watch. Beneath the cracked glass, the hands had stopped at five minutes past two. I must have smashed it against the pillar, he thought, and sighed. He was not even close to coming to terms with losing two of his fingers, but the opioids were doing wonders for the pain. That, and helping to provide a slightly more rose-tinted outlook on reality.

He took a sip of the electrolyte drink he'd been given to aid rehydration, and recalled the brief conversation he'd had with the police officers in Wickwar. Hopefully, they'd done as he asked and passed on details of the imminent Ashmolean robbery to his colleagues at Kidlington. He placed the drink back on the side and being careful not to knock the IV line, lay back on the pillow.

Just as he was about to close his eyes, he heard footsteps approaching the cubicle. With a sudden swish, the curtain drew back and there stood Emily.

'Hello, Francis, how are you feeling?' she said, looking casually at the bandages on his hand and cheek.

'Okay. The nurses and doctors did a great job of patching me up. Mind you, if they give me any more painkillers, I'm going to be floating around the ceiling. Anyway, what about you?'

'I'm fine,' she said, rubbing the back of her neck.

'And Tom?'

'He has a mild concussion and a nasty gash on the head. They've done some scans and want to keep him in overnight, for observation.'

Cordell nodded. 'Oh, did you hear? Apparently, someone phoned the police and left an anonymous tip-off, telling them exactly where we were?'

'Not from him, surely?'

'Tyburn? God no, he doesn't do compassion. But it sounds like someone in that band of thieves has a conscience.'

'Apparently so,' said Emily, lost in thought for a moment.

'He also gave them a pretty detailed account of how they plan to hijack the opening ceremony. I'm sure the boys and girls at Kidlington will get on it straight away.'

Cordell saw the worried look on Emily's face. 'What is it – what's wrong?'

'Nothing. Look, I'd better get back and see how Tom's doing.'

'Sure. What time is it?'

'Just gone quarter past five.'

Cordell gave her a concerned look. 'Please tell me you're not thinking of going to the opening ceremony.'

She checked her watch again. 'I should be able to make it, if I leave now.'

'So, not, in fact, going to see how Tom's doing, then?'

She smiled. 'I'll pop in to say goodnight, before I go.'

'Look, there's no need to put yourself at risk, Emily. Thames Valley Police are all over it.'

'I have to be there, Francis. Those eight beautiful paintings are my responsibility.'

'No, they're not. And I won't let you walk into another dangerous situation, like that. If you get hurt, I'd never be able to forgive myself.'

'That's very sweet of you, but I can't just sit back and do nothing. I can't.'

Cordell shook his head. 'Then I want you to promise me that you'll stop off at Kidlington CID, first, and speak to DS Lloyd. He'll brief you on what's going on.'

'Okay, I will.'

'And please, please be careful.'

She touched his arm with a reassuring nod, and left the cubicle to go and say goodbye to Tom.

*

The rush-hour traffic was getting heavy as Emily joined the ring road in North Bristol. Sitting in a queue for the motorway, she dabbed the accelerator pedal, bringing a roar from the Alpine's engine. Patience had never been her strong point and the sooner she was on the motorway, the better.

Fifteen minutes later, she'd made it to the M4 and was heading east with the windscreen wipers doing their best to fend off some persistent drizzle. Relaxing into the old red leather driving seat, she felt utterly exhausted – physically and emotionally. Her life seemed to be a complete farce at the moment. Only yesterday, she was enjoying a nice Sunday lunch and looking forward to one of the most momentous days of her life, when, a little over twenty-four hours later, she'd been kidnapped, assaulted with a knife, and her partner was lying in a hospital bed with a serious head injury.

And now, here she was – an army of one – on her way to Oxford to confront a gang of dangerous criminals intent on committing armed robbery, and God knows what else. Had she completely lost her mind?

She nodded, resignedly. *Yes, obviously.*

Chapter Sixty

Ashmolean Museum, Oxford

3 April 2000

The evening rush hour should have abated by now, but as Tyburn and Danny approached the rear of the museum, the traffic in Beaumont Street was at a complete standstill.

'What's going on out there? It's total gridlock,' said Danny.

But Tyburn wasn't listening. He banged his fist on the security door labelled: *STAFF ONLY* and waited. 'Where the fuck's Waltham? He told us he'd be here at seven.'

'Probably stuck in traffic.'

'Well, I'm not waitin' for him.'

Tyburn glanced at the long line of stationary cars queuing in St John Street. 'And that'd better clear soon, or we're screwed.'

He knocked again, louder this time. The door opened and there stood Coos Van Leer in his security guard uniform.

'This way, gents,' he said, waving them inside.

Dressed in black and carrying large holdalls, Tyburn and Danny followed Van Leer silently through the maze of dark corridors and galleries until they reached the second floor of the west wing.

Waiting for them at the top of the stairs was Julian Mountfield, looking suitably anxious. Next to him, hanging from the ceiling, was a large banner depicting the bust of Aurora from Draper's painting – an iconic image used extensively by the museum to publicise the upcoming exhibition. It read:

Become enlightened!

Welcome to

THE LIGHTS OF THE WORLD exhibition

at the Ashmolean Museum

'Where's, Waltham?' snapped Tyburn.

Julian shrugged. 'I assumed he was with you.'

Tyburn marched off through the two exhibition galleries to the double doors at the far end, followed by Julian and Danny. Finding the anteroom locked, he banged on the door with his fist – there was no response.

'I'll need to let you in,' said Julian, fumbling for his keys. No other space in the entire museum was being guarded more closely than the small end gallery adjoining Gallery 55.

Tyburn looked at him with a face like thunder. 'Come on, we haven't got all day.'

'Remember, everyone will be on their way upstairs at seven forty pm, so please, be as quiet as you can,' said Julian.

Danny laughed. 'Why don't you fuck off and leave the work to us real men.'

Julian glared at him, unlocked the door, then marched back downstairs to await the arrival of the invited guests.

Tyburn slung his two bags on the floor where they came to rest at the foot of a huge wooden crate in the centre of the room.

'Well, thanks a fuckin' bunch, Waltham. You could 'ave told us you were gettin' here early,' said Tyburn.

'I just wanted to make sure everything was ready. We don't want any last-minute surprises now, do we?' he said, straightening the black balaclava covering his mop of blonde hair.

'Yeah, well. Let's stick to what we agreed from now on, eh?'

Tyburn unzipped one of the holdalls and removed a Kalashnikov assault rifle.

'You'd better get your gear on,' he said to Danny. 'It'll be showtime, soon.'

After checking the rifle one last time, Tyburn strapped it over his shoulder and put on his gloves and balaclava. Danny did the same, then went and sat down in a chair that Van Leer had purposely placed next to a small, brightly coloured oil on panel by Edward Burne-Jones, entitled *Danae and the Brazen Tower*.

'Just cos it's got his name on it, thinks he owns the fuckin' thing,' smirked Tyburn.

After studying it for a time, Danny soon got bored and turned his attention to the tiny red security light behind the painting.

With his chin resting in the palm of his hand, he sat there, as instructed, patiently waiting for it to go out.

For that was the sign for all hell to break loose; and the fear of God to be put into one hundred poor unsuspecting party guests, who were about to wish they'd never left the house that evening.

Chapter Sixty-One

Kidlington, Oxford

3 April 2000

The twin engine Eurocopter hovered for a few seconds, then touched down gently on the edge of the football pitch, sending two teams of under twelves and a rather disgruntled referee scurrying to the sidelines. DCI Cordell removed his headphones and thanked the pilot, before making his way across the wet grass to an unmarked police car.

'I wish they'd build a bloody helipad for this place,' said Cordell, wiping his shoe on the grass to remove a clump of mud.

'No room, sir,' said the driver. 'Unless they dig up the sports field. And that'd make us even more popular with the local kids.'

Cordell tutted, then stopped as he went to open the car door.

'Are you alright, sir?' said the driver, seeing him bent double.

Cordell put up his hand. 'I'm fine, just give me a moment.'

It wasn't so much the impromptu helicopter ride from Filton airfield that had left him feeling ill; more that he'd discharged himself from hospital, shortly after having received a full blood transfusion – much to the dismay of Frenchay's on-duty medical staff. And, judging by the contents of the sick bag he'd been clutching for most of the flight, they were right to be concerned.

A couple of minutes later, having been helped into and out of the police car, Cordell arrived outside the offices of Thames Valley CID – Kidlington, where Detective Sergeant Lloyd was waiting to accompany him to the first-floor briefing room.

'What's happening then, sergeant?' said Cordell.

'The briefing's just started, sir. DCS McHardy and DI Rodenby have taken charge in your absence.'

'Get someone to grab me a cup of tea, will you, before I keel over?'

'Yes, sir,' said Lloyd, and duly passed the request onto one of the junior officers.

Cordell and Lloyd entered the briefing room to find Detective Chief Superintendent McHardy in full flow.

'Francis. My God, man, shouldn't you be in hospital?' said McHardy, spotting the pale-looking DCI enter the room.

At least twenty plain-clothed and uniformed officers turned round and watched as Cordell, looking like he'd just returned from a war zone, made his way to the front of the room.

'I'm fine, sir. I couldn't just lie there and do nothing.'

'Someone get him a seat, before he collapses.'

One of the DCs stood up and offered his chair, to whom Cordell gave a grateful nod.

Satisfied he was, hopefully, not going to collapse on the briefing room floor, DCS McHardy continued, 'Right, as I was saying, we've put a lot of resources into this operation at short notice, so I hope the tip-off we received isn't someone playing silly buggers?' he said, looking at Cordell.

'No sir. It corroborates the information I received from one of the gang members, Marcus Tyburn, a little over twenty four hours ago.'

'Alright Francis. Perhaps, you could fill us in on some of the background; then DI Rodenby will take us through the operational details. And for goodness sake, stay seated man.'

As DCS McHardy stood aside, Cordell took a sip from the cup of tea he'd just been handed and prepared to address the room. He glanced over at the clock. It was 6.35 pm.

'Thank you sir. Okay, just to put this in context for everyone; we've got less than an hour to prevent what will, in my estimation, be the most audacious art robbery of the modern age.'

A buzz of chatter went around the room.

'And you're certain it's tonight?' asked DI Rodenby.

'Quite certain. We know from our investigations that the gang has been planning this robbery for the last two years, so it goes without saying that they're well prepared. The leader is this man, Luke Waltham,' he said, pointing to a photo on the board behind him. 'Managing director of ArtScreen Limited, a company of art restorers and security consultants, based in Sloane Street, London. They were asked by the Ashmolean, some months ago, to install a new state-of-the-art security system which is monitored from a purpose-built control centre on the first floor of the museum. Not only that, ArtScreen are responsible for all of the on-site security staff and gallery attendants.'

'Are any of the original museum staff working for them?' came a voice from the back of the room.

'One or two perhaps, but we don't know who they are. Probably best to assume all five of the on-duty security staff in that part of the museum are hostile, for now. Let's move on to the target. We believe they're planning to remove eight Pre-Raphaelite paintings that form the basis of *The Lights of the World* exhibition, the opening ceremony for which starts in precisely ... twenty-four minutes. In attendance will be one hundred guests, including university dignitaries, Friends of the museum, members of the press. And not forgetting, the mayor and his wife.'

'Why are they planning to steal the paintings tonight, with all those people around?' asked DS Lloyd. 'Surely it would be far easier to break in when the museum is closed?'

'Mmm, ... I must admit, I've been asking myself that question. They've gone to an awful lot of trouble to put this job together, right down to engineering the discovery of the eight paintings as a unique collection. They must have their reasons.'

'And what about the gang themselves?' said McHardy. 'What do we know about them?'

'In addition to the main man, Luke Waltham, there's his daughter, Kate, who he relies on for most of the day-to-day organisation. Then, we have Marcus Tyburn, a real nasty piece of work, for those of you unfamiliar with him. He's already got armed robbery, kidnapping, GBH and attempted murder on his latest RAP sheet, and that's just for starters. Then there's Danny Forgan – he helped Tyburn steal the missing Picasso from the Ashmolean in November, last year. I'm pretty certain he'll be involved. As to the others, I'm not sure. Possibly one or two insiders from the museum itself. Unfortunately, that's all we know, which does leave us on the back foot, somewhat.'

Yet more mumblings went round the room.

'Alright, pipe down,' said McHardy.

'In our favour, ...' Cordell continued, '... we do have the element of surprise. As DCS McHardy has probably told you, a Miss Emily Bradshaw – the exhibition organiser – and I, were held captive in a building, just outside Bristol, until earlier this morning. And as far as we know, they know nothing of our escape.'

'What about the tip-off? That must have come from someone inside the gang, surely?' asked Rodenby.

'Very likely, yes. But my guess is, whoever it was, probably had a change of heart. And the last thing they'd want is for the other gang members to find out they've been ratted on.'

'Sir, we've had a listen to that call, ...' said one of the local DCs, '... and, although the voice appears to have been disguised – somewhat badly, I might say – one of the lads thinks he recognises it as Julian Mountfield, Miss Bradshaw's boss at the museum.'

'That's interesting,' said Cordell, stroking the end of his moustache. 'In which case, we may have a friend on the inside.'

'Do we know how they're planning to get the paintings out of there?' enquired McHardy.

'No, sir. I can't imagine for one minute they're going to walk out the front door with them. We need to keep a close eye on the roof and the rear exit in Pusey Place.'

'Agreed. Sean from SO19 will cover that in a minute,' McHardy replied.

One of the uniformed officers at the back of the room put up his hand. 'What about the guests, sir? Judging by the way Tyburn treated you and Miss Bradshaw, they're not going to think twice about shooting anyone who gets in their way.'

'No, and you're right to be concerned,' replied Cordell. 'Marcus Tyburn and Danny Forgan are dangerous men, particularly Tyburn. I can testify to that.' He looked down at his left hand. 'I'm sure DI Rodenby will cover all that in his operational briefing. Alan, do you want to ...?'

Rodenby got up, and stood front and centre. 'Thank you, Francis. As soon as we got your information from the boys at Avon and Somerset, this morning, we threw a surveillance ring around the Ashmolean.'

He walked over to the large whiteboard, on which was an aerial plan of the museum buildings and surrounding streets.

'Mark, you've had a couple of your plain-clothes team patrolling the area for the last few hours. Anything to report, so far?'

'Not at this point, guv,' said DS Wilson. 'But I'd like to propose we increase the number of officers to five, so we can provide an even spread from the bottom of St Giles', all the way up Beaumont Street, and round the back in St John Street and Pusey Place.'

'Do it now,' said McHardy. 'Make sure you keep in constant radio contact, and if you spot any suspicious activity or vehicles pulling up outside the museum, radio in straight away.'

'Of course, sir,' said Wilson.

Rodenby continued, turning to DS Lloyd. 'Gary, I want you to be the eyes and ears inside the museum. We've managed to get you in as a waiter serving champagne at the welcome party.'

A chorus of cheers went up in the room.

'Yes, yes ... thank you,' said Rodenby, waving his hands to restore order. 'Make sure you keep a low profile, and if you do get chance to have a quick scout round, keep an eye out for the security guards.'

'Shouldn't we have someone up on the second floor, where the exhibition is?' said Cordell.

'We're one step ahead of you there, Francis. DC Hyams and DC Nash have volunteered to go in as undercover guests at the opening ceremony.' Rodenby walked up to the pair of young officers who were sitting nearby. 'Here are your tickets, and for Pete's sake, Nash, put on something smart. You do own a jacket and tie, don't you?'

'Of course, sir,' said Nash, smirking as a ripple of laughter went around the room. 'What do you want us to do, once we're in there?'

'What do you think – mingle, chat with the guests, that sort of thing. And try to show some interest in the bloody paintings; you're meant to be Friends of the Ashmolean.'

'Don't worry, sir, I'll keep an eye on him,' said DC Hyams, with a sideways glance at her younger colleague.

'Good, because I need you both to be on your metal as soon as you enter the museum. You'll be armed and wearing a wire, so go easy – these guys don't muck about.'

Nash's expression suddenly became more serious.

'Only use your firearms if there's a danger to life, and you've got a clear shot. You know the drill. Anything could happen in there, and I want you to be ready for it.'

'We will be, sir,' said Hyams.

'Right. As soon as you see the gang take possession of the paintings, say the go-code "Aurora" into your mic. That will be our signal to move in.'

DCS McHardy interjected, 'Hang on – let's be clear, here. We can't make a move inside the building. Not when they've got a hundred potential hostages at their mercy. We need to be ready to go, the moment they leave the museum. They'll see we've got them surrounded and, if they've got any sense, they'll surrender their weapons.'

'And if they don't, sir?' said Cordell.

'That leaves them with two options. They either make a run for it, or they try to shoot their way out.'

Cordell took a sip of his lukewarm tea and stared at the floor, as DCS McHardy re-took control of the meeting.

'Bob, we'll need your uniformed boys to put a cordon round the entire museum, from nineteen hundred hours. That means closing off Beaumont Street, St John Street and St Giles'. How many officers can you spare?'

'It's a bit short notice, sir ...' said the chief inspector, '... but I can let you have a couple of dozen on foot and four armed response vehicles – each with three armed officers. I assume you'll need them standing by?'

'Yes. I want all routes to and from the museum covered, so if they do make a run for it, we can track them, immediately.'

'Okay, but I wouldn't want any of my beat officers getting caught in the middle of a gun battle.'

'No, of course not,' said McHardy, glancing over to the six men wearing flak jackets, standing at the back of the room. 'Sean, I hope it doesn't come to it, but if things do kick off, we'll need your guys in position to take them out.'

Sean Ellis-Smith, troop leader of the Force Firearms Unit (SO19), walked to the front of the room and inspected the street map.

'In which case, can I suggest we put marksmen at four strategic points. Two to cover the museum's main entrance from the Randolph Hotel, here and ... here. Two, top-floor rooms will give us the best view onto Beaumont Street, if you can arrange that?'

McHardy waved at Sergeant Lloyd. 'Get onto the hotel manager.'

'And if all the rooms are booked, sir?' said Lloyd.

'Get them moved, man. We don't have time to fuck about. Sorry, Sean, what else?'

'What's this here?' he said, pointing to a row of buildings in Magdalen Street East.

'That's Balliol College.'

'Okay, one man in there to cover the east side. And this building at the back here, is that part of the museum?'

'No, that's the Oriental Institute.'

'I need one man on the top floor, and another in this apartment block, next to it. That should give us sight of the rear entrance and alleyway behind the main building.'

'Fine. Alan, get one of your team on that straight away.'

'Sir,' said Rodenby.

McHardy turned to Cordell. 'Francis, normally I'd have put you in charge of all this. But judging by the state of you, I can't imagine you feel up to that—'

'No, no, sir ... I'll be fine,' said Cordell, getting to his feet.

'Are you sure? I can just as easily get Rodenby, here, to call the shots.'

'Honestly, let me finish my tea and I'll be right as rain.'

'Alright,' he said, not looking at all convinced. 'Now Sean, no one fires without DCI Cordell's authority, is that clear?'

'Absolutely. My men will maintain an open dialogue with DCI Cordell at all times. Only when they receive a clear instruction from him, will they proceed to engage the target. If I could just ask, Chief Inspector, where will you be?' said Ellis-Smith, looking at Cordell.

'I'll be up in a helicopter over the museum – the eye in the sky. Is that alright with you, sir?' he said, looking at McHardy.

'Well, ... yes, I suppose we can stretch to that. Get onto RAF Benson, will you, Alan?'

'Right, sir,' said Rodenby, looking slightly aggrieved that he wasn't taking charge of the operation.

Cordell looked at the clock. 'Okay, it's just gone eighteen forty two, let's get moving. Good luck everybody.'

As everyone got up to leave, DCS McHardy took Cordell to one side.

'Francis, are you sure you're well enough to handle this? You've only just got out of hospital and, to be honest, you look like shit!'

'Honestly, sir, I'll be fine.'

'Alright, it's your call. I'll put DI Rodenby on the ground, so you've got coverage there. Now there are some bloody important people at the museum tonight, and I'm sure I don't need to tell you how vital it is they be kept safe. If it was down to me, the whole bloody event would be cancelled, but I'm afraid that decision was taken out of my hands.'

Cordell nodded, sensing McHardy was probably talking about some *high-ups* at Scotland Yard, wielding a big stick.

'Now, keep me posted, and for Christ's sake, Francis, ... don't fuck it up.'

'Sir.'

Walking as quickly as he could, and accompanied by DS Lloyd, Cordell made his way down to the lobby, where a car was waiting to take him to Kidlington airfield and a Chiltern Air Support Unit helicopter that had been despatched from nearby RAF Benson. He was hoping to just jump in the same aircraft he'd arrived in, but that had been called back to a serious incident on the M5.

'Are you ready for this, sergeant?' said Cordell, as the driver opened the car door.

'As I'll ever be, sir,' said Lloyd.

'Once you've been on to the Randolph Hotel, I want you to get over to the museum as quickly as you can. I'll keep the chopper out of sight over the other side of the city, until we know the gang are definitely in the museum building – we don't want to frighten them off. Now listen, sergeant, I need you to keep me updated on what's happening in there, understood?'

'Right, sir, you'll be the first to know.'

'Oh, one last thing, Lloyd, could you lend me your watch?'

'My watch, sir?'

'Yes, mine took a whack, earlier.' Cordell showed him the broken glass.

'Err ... yes, of course,' said Lloyd, removing the TAG Heuer his wife had given him for his fortieth birthday.

'Thank you, sergeant – nice,' said Cordell, and left Lloyd watching him and his watch, drive off into the night.

Having made the short journey to Kidlington airfield, Cordell climbed into the waiting helicopter and strapped himself in using his good hand. He was about to look for the sick bags when the pilot turned to him.

'Sir, I've got Detective Sergeant Lloyd on the radio for you. I'll patch him through to your headset.'

'Okay,' said Cordell, somewhat mystified.

'Sir, it's Lloyd here.'

'Yes, what is it, sergeant? I haven't even taken off yet.'

'We've just been informed by Traffic that there's been an incident in the centre of town.'

Cordell looked at the pilot. 'Incident? What incident?'

Chapter Sixty-Two

Reaching the outskirts of Oxford, an hour and twenty-five minutes after leaving Bristol, Emily realised something was wrong – the Botley Road was nose-to-tail with queuing traffic. Understandable at the height of rush hour, but not at 7.00 pm in the evening. She puffed out her cheeks and tapped her fingers on the steering wheel in a futile attempt to remain calm.

'Come on, come on,' she said, gesticulating with her hand, then winding down the window and sticking her head out to try and see what was going on. The line of queuing cars stretched way into the distance, while the outbound lane next to her was running freely.

As the sun got lower, bringing a warm dusky glow to the avenue of trees on either side of the road, she thought about the plan she'd hatched, if you could call it that. She would park near the museum, then sneak in the backway and try to contact one of the guards she knew could be trusted. They could lock the gallery doors and secure the area before the robbers got in. That should buy the police enough time to enter the building and catch them red-handed. It sounded simple when she ran it through in her head, but it would all come to nothing unless she could find a way to beat this bloody traffic.

As the white Sunbeam Alpine crawled towards the centre of town, she noticed the water-temperature gauge starting to climb, as it always did when she got stuck in a queue.

'Shit, that's all I need,' she said, thumping the steering wheel.

Then came the sound of distant sirens. She looked in the rear-view mirror and saw the cars behind pulling over to the kerb. Emily followed suit. Moments later, there was a rush of air as a police car and ambulance sped past, their blue lights flashing, until somewhere up ahead in the distance, they took a right turn and disappeared from view.

After countless stop-starts, she eventually came to a halt not far from the railway station entrance. Two women were stood talking on the pavement. She leaned over, wound down the passenger window and was about to ask if they knew what was happening, when there was a loud toot from the car behind. Emily turned round and glared at the driver.

'Where can I go?' she said, waving her arms in frustration.

The man mouthed something back, but before he could finish his moronic tirade, Emily revved the engine and pulled up all of five yards to the car in front.

It was 7.22 pm. Having taken more than twenty minutes to travel a little over half a mile, she finally decided enough was enough and slammed the car into gear, taking a sharp left into the railway station entrance. Although cars were queuing to get out, the way *in* was completely clear, and with the Alpine in low gear, she sped past the buses and taxis waiting outside the station building, only to meet another queue of vehicles waiting to enter the short-stay car park. Obviously other drivers had had the same idea. Exasperated, she let out a growl of frustration and rested her forehead on the steering wheel.

She didn't need this, not now. She looked in the rear-view mirror and saw another car coming up behind. Without thinking, she slammed the Alpine into reverse and pulled back from the car in front, wincing at the sudden screech of brakes from the approaching car. Not looking back to see who she'd upset, she turned the steering wheel and hit the accelerator, fighting the Alpine for control as she sped off towards the station exit. At the last minute, and with no thought for the consequences, she swung the car hard to the right, going completely the wrong way, straight into the station's bus lane, where bus drivers and pedestrians looked on in disbelief. Having ground to a halt in the waiting zone, marked *Bus – Standing*, she applied the handbrake and turned off the engine.

'Sorry baby,' she said, patting the steering wheel. 'I've got to love you and leave you.'

She jumped out, locked the door and, ignoring the heckles from angry bus drivers, ran as fast as she could, back to the Botley Road.

Passing the glass canopy of the Saïd Business School and sand-coloured facade of the Royal Oxford Hotel, she kept on running, filled with adrenalin and desperation as she overtook car after car, their occupants glaring jealously as she made her way towards the centre of town.

As she crossed the Hythe Bridge, the glow of tail lights and exhaust fumes snaked in all directions, accompanied by the endless drone of idling engines. Somewhere in the distance, a helicopter hovered above the stricken city, like a dragonfly observing the chaos below.

Red-faced and gasping for breath, she eventually turned into Worcester Street, following the meandering stone wall of Worcester College. I really need to go the gym, she thought, stopping for a breather outside the gate to the porter's lodge. Bent over, and with her hands on her knees, she looked up at the stream of stationary vehicles stretching all the way along Beaumont Street. She'd definitely done the right thing, abandoning her beloved Alpine when she did. Some people had even switched off their engines and were out of their cars, discussing the pandemonium with other drivers. The strange thing was, there didn't seem to be any reason for it – nothing she could see, anyway; just the eerie sound of distant sirens reverberating around the city streets.

'Are you alright?' came a voice behind her.

She turned round to see a young man staring at her – a college student, judging by the bagful of books slung over his shoulder.

'Err, yes. A bit out of breath, that's all.'

'Okay, it's just that – your nose is bleeding.'

Emily put her fingers up to her nose. 'Oh my God, so it is.'

'Here,' he said, handing her a tissue. 'Don't worry, it's clean.'

'Thank you. I've just run all the way from the station,' she said, dabbing her nostril.

'Oh, were you caught in the traffic?'

'Yes, do you know what's going on?'

The student looked almost excited to have been asked. 'Apparently, they've found three car bombs.'

'You're kidding. Where?'

'They say they're in St Thomas' Street, St Clement's Street and another off the Woodstock Road.'

'Oh my God, is anybody hurt?'

'No, the bomb squad are still trying to diffuse them.'

Suddenly, it all made sense – the gridlocked streets, the constant sound of sirens, the police helicopter.

'Has anyone claimed responsibility?' said Emily.

'Not yet. According to the BBC website, an anonymous call was made to the *Oxford Mail* about an hour ago. There are rumours that it's some sort of chemical weapon, can you believe it?'

Emily's mind was racing. Was the museum closed? Would they still go ahead with the opening ceremony? She had to get in there and find out.

'Listen, thank you so much, but I have to go,' she said, ignoring the somewhat disappointed look on the young lad's face, and ran off in the direction of the museum.

As she approached the stone balustrade of the Ashmolean's west wing, she slowed to a walking pace. Not knowing what she would encounter, she went up to the iron gates and peered over to the main entrance. A number of smartly dressed guests were about to go inside and undergo the recently implemented security checks. It was 7.28 pm. If nothing else, she'd made it on time.

Trying not to think about how her car was probably being hauled away by a council tow-truck, she headed down St John Street and into Pusey Place, her heart racing as she stood on the corner and surveyed the back of the museum. Apart from the nearby drone of queuing cars waiting to join Beaumont Street, all was quiet. Perhaps the robbery wasn't happening tonight, after all.

She approached the wooden hoarding blocking off the rear entrance and looked around to make sure no one was watching. Standing on her tip-toes, she reached up and grabbed the top of the gate with both hands – ignoring her sore neck and back, courtesy of Marcus Tyburn – and eventually managed to haul herself up on top. After sitting there for a few moments to catch her breath, she swung her legs over and jumped down onto the sloping tarmac.

The small courtyard was completely dark, save for the glow of the access control pad by the back door. She took out her security pass and ran the metallic strip down the slot in the keypad. There was a tiny click as the light turned green – she was in.

The vast majority of employees had gone home for the night, but her greatest fear was the security staff. In her mind, these now fell into two camps – the old guard who, although few in number, were trustworthy and loved working at the Ashmolean. Then there were the interlopers – the new intake of ArtScreen gallery attendants and security guards, who, from what she'd been told, couldn't be trusted to water a houseplant, let alone protect a museum.

The passageway leading off the small reception area was dark and quiet, the low drone of the air-conditioning her only companion as she walked towards the fire doors at the end of the corridor. Feeling a bit like an intruder, she pulled on the handle – it opened with a long metallic creak, making her wince at the broken silence. She closed it gently behind her, and turned round to check the way ahead. To the right was the museum's photographic studio – a narrow sliver of light shone from under the door. Someone's working late, she thought, and carried on down the corridor.

Ascending a set of steps, she turned the corner into a small foyer containing the lifts to the upper floors – one for staff, the other a goods lift for moving exhibits and artefacts. She pressed the button for the passenger lift, which had stopped on the first floor. Suddenly, she heard a door close behind her, followed by the sound of footsteps approaching along the corridor. She looked up anxiously at the floor numbers, and tap-tap-tapped the *CALL* button, willing the lift to start moving. The footsteps got closer and closer, finally coming to a stop behind her. With her heart pounding, she looked round to see one of the security guards, smiling at her.

'Oh, Harry, thank God it's you.'

'Hello, Miss Bradshaw. What are you doing back here? Aren't you meant to be at the posh do, upstairs?'

'I am, but I need to nip up to the exhibition gallery, first. I don't suppose you'd come with me, would you?'

'Yes. Is everything alright, you seem a little edgy?'

'God, where do I start? Listen, there's going to be a robbery here, this evening.'

He screwed up his face. 'A robbery? Oh, very funny, miss.'

'I'm serious, Harry. We have to get up to Gallery fifty-five and secure the paintings.'

'Well, if you say so. Let's go and take a look.'

There was a ping and the lift doors opened. They both got in and Harry pressed the button.

'We need to be careful,' said Emily. 'For all we know, the robbers could be up there right now.'

'Don't you worry, I'll be straight on the radio if we spot anything.' Harry watched as the numbers above the door lit up. 'You don't think that bloody ArtScreen lot are behind it, do you?' he said.

'I think they might be, actually.'

'Mmm ... I never liked the look of them, from the moment they arrived.'

She was about to tell Harry how her and DCI Cordell had been kidnapped, when the lift doors opened. She walked out, then realised they were on the first floor.

'Harry, you hit the wrong button. We want the second floor.'

He just looked at her.

'Harry, I said we want the—'

She watched as he drew his nightstick from its holster, flicked it out to its full twenty-one, bone-crushing inches and slowly walked towards her. Jovial old Harry was gone, and Emily suddenly found herself confronted by the enemy.

'Turn to your left, Miss Bradshaw,' he said, waving his nightstick.

'Harry, I can't believe this – you're one of them?'

'Shut up and walk.'

Emily turned and began to make her way down the corridor. 'Where are we going?'

He gave no response, calmly ushering her through a series of small galleries.

'You don't have to do this, Harry. How long have you been here, ten, twelve years?'

Still no reply.

'I bet it's at least that long. That's a lot of good service you've given to the Ashmolean. How did they turn you? Money, was that it?'

'Don't pretend to know me, or my motivations,' he said, prodding her in the back.

'No, no, I don't. But you always struck me as the sort of guy who loved art. If you could just let me—'

Before she could finish, his hand grabbed her shoulder, stopping her right outside the ArtScreen control centre.

He tapped a four-digit pin into the keypad and opened the door.

'After you,' he said, standing back.

She walked in and realised she'd never actually been in here before. The windowless room was small and claustrophobic, the only light coming from a row of LED panels, built into the ceiling. Against one wall was a large metal cabinet containing, what looked like, computer servers and other IT equipment. At the far end was a long, metallic desk seating three security guards – each watching a number of split-screen CCTV monitors showing live feeds from different parts of the museum.

'Emily, this is a surprise,' said one of the guards, standing up to greet her.

'Hello, Van Leer, I might have known you'd be behind this.'

'I must admit, I thought, we'd put you out of action for the evening.'

She ignored him, frantically scanning the TV screens to see if the paintings were still in situ. Spotting a TV feed labelled '55', she breathed a quiet sigh of relief – *The Lights of the World* were hanging exactly where she'd left them.

'I found her near the back door,' said Harry.

'Did you, indeed? Was she alone?'

'Yes, as far as I could tell.'

'Okay, thanks Harry. Now, get back downstairs and see that the rear entrance is clear, will you?'

'Right you are,' he said, closing the door behind him.

'Emily, come and have a seat. It's going to be quite a show, I promise you,' said Van Leer.

'No thanks, I'll stand.'

'Oh, but I insist.' Van Leer nodded to the two security guards, who stood up and grabbed her by the arms, shoving her into one of the chairs facing the control desk.

'We've got a superb view of proceedings from here, don't you think?'

'Wonderful,' she said, watching the guests enjoying their pre-exhibition champagne in the Randolph Gallery. The time on the display showed 7.35 pm. Julian would be starting his speech in a little under ten minutes. She didn't know when or how the gang were planning to remove the paintings, but it surely wouldn't be long before they showed themselves.

Being held captive for the second time in twenty-four hours wasn't exactly what she had in mind when she set out from Bristol, earlier; but at least she was in the thick of things. Whether that would turn out to be a blessing or a curse, only time would tell.

Chapter Sixty-Three

Oxford City Centre

3 April 2000

Hovering high above the rooftops of Oxford, DCI Cordell looked down at the endless trail of brake lights wending their way along the Woodstock Road. With even the lesser-known rat-runs jammed in every direction, it looked for all the world like a giant centipede had bored its way to the surface and was desperately trying to extricate itself from the streets of Jericho and Summertown. Occasionally, small gaps would appear in the blood clot blocking the city's main northbound artery, only to be filled, seconds later, by a pulse of hopeful drivers, edging forward a few precious yards – longing for the open road.

Shortly after taking off from Kidlington airfield, Cordell received an urgent call from CID, explaining the likely cause of the gridlock. Apparently, just before 6.30 pm, an anonymous female – thought by voice experts to be from London and in her mid-thirties – had called the offices of the *Oxford Mail*. The junior editor of the sports desk took the call and managed to scribble down the message, verbatim. When the young woman had finished describing the location of the three car bombs, each containing a deadly ricin canister, she asked him to read everything back to her, then said, 'You have precisely one hour until people begin to die,' and hung up.

Attempts to trace the call had proved fruitless, but the threat seemed chillingly real. The three cars containing the bombs were parked exactly where she'd said they'd be, and according to enquiries made with people living and working nearby, none of the vehicles had been there the previous evening. But what the police really wanted to know was, who was responsible and what were their motives? None of which had been volunteered by the caller.

The regional Anti-Terrorist Unit, aka bomb squad, had been immediately despatched to all three locations and, once 'uniform' had evacuated everyone in the vicinity, were then engaged in the delicate process of trying to defuse and remove the devices.

As the helicopter circled over St Thomas' Street, Cordell popped another couple of painkillers and glanced over at the dusky pink streaks forming along the western skyline. As he cradled his throbbing hand, he knew the next hour would be a defining one. The battles he'd had with his own conscience over the years, and there had been many, would all come down to this – a chance for justice and beauty to finally win out over darkness and abomination. And goodness knows, he'd given his blood for it.

He thought back to a comment DS Lloyd had made earlier, about it being a coincidence that the bomb threats had occurred on the same evening as the planned robbery. Cordell wasn't convinced. Given everything that had happened in the past twenty-four hours, he didn't believe in coincidences. This had something to do with Luke Waltham, he could feel it. And in a strange way, he kind of expected it of the man.

'Sir, I've got DS Lloyd for you, again,' said the pilot. 'I'll patch him through.'

'Lloyd here, sir, do you read me?'

'Yes, I read you, sergeant. Now where the hell are you?' said Cordell.

'I'm at the museum – just taking a quick break from serving canapés to the guests.'

'You took your time, what kept you?'

'We got snarled up in the traffic, but eventually managed to get through, using a combination of blues-and-twos, and the odd mounted pavement.'

'Well thanks for sparing the time to keep me updated.'

'Sorry, sir. I'm just having a quick wander around the first floor, to see if I can spot anything.'

'Okay, but for God's sake, stay out of sight, man. Now, what about Hyams and Nash, have they joined the rest of the guests yet?'

'Yes sir, they arrived a few minutes ago. Getting nicely stuck into the champagne, from what I could see.'

'Right, well tell them to knock it off. I need them razor sharp, once they land eyes on Waltham and his crew.'

'Will do, sir. What about you, any news on the car bombs?'

'We're flying over one of them, now – the bomb squad are trying to defuse all three, and according to my watch, or should I say, yours, sergeant, they've got about a minute until they're due to go off.'

'Rather you than me, up there, sir, I have to say.'

'Yes, thank you for those words of comfort,' said Cordell, peering down at the team in hazmat suits, below. 'My hunch is that our Mr Waltham is behind all this chaos.'

'Surely, total gridlock is the last thing he wants, when he's trying to make a quick getaway.'

'Well, maybe. But he's succeeded in diverting a lot of police resources away from the Ashmolean, that's for sure.'

Cordell spotted the large, padded figure of the bomb disposal officer giving the thumbs up to his colleagues.

'Looks like they've just given this one the all-clear.'

'Glad to hear it, sir.'

'Right, now get off the line. I need to check in with Sean Ellis-Smith and the SO-nineteen boys.'

'Okay, sir. Oh shit, hang on – are you still there?' said Lloyd, almost in a whisper.

'Yes, what is it? And speak up, I can barely hear you.'

'Someone's just walked out of the lift. A young lady, ... I think it's—'

'Spit it out, sergeant.'

'I think it's Emily Bradshaw, sir.'

'Is she slim, attractive, light brown hair tied back in a ponytail?' asked Cordell.

'Yes, sir.'

'You've got to be kidding me. Well, go and grab her, before she gets herself into trouble.'

'Err, I'm afraid I can't do that.'

'Why not?'

'One of the ArtScreen security guards is frog-marching her down the corridor. It looks like they're headed for the control room.'

Cordell put his head in his hand.

'Hang on, ...' whispered Lloyd, '... he's opening the door, and she's gone inside.'

'That's all we bloody need. I told her to stop off at Kidlington and ask to see you, before she came to the museum. Did she?'

'Afraid not, sir.'

'Fucking brilliant. Okay, get yourself back to the ground floor, before someone spots you.'

'Will do, sir. Over and out.'

Cordell looked out of the window and shook his head. Great, another kidnapping, he thought to himself, and ordered the pilot to head straight for the Ashmolean. It was 7.35 pm.

As sure as he was that he'd rumbled Luke Waltham's plans, there was just something about this man and his penchant for the unpredictable that worried him.

And, if he was being completely honest, even with an unparalleled birds-eye view of the city, and all the requisite Thames Valley Police resources at his beck and call, ... he still didn't have a bloody clue what was going on.

Chapter Sixty-Four

Ashmolean Museum, Oxford

3 April 2000

Detective Constable Hyams shook her head, disapprovingly, whilst secretly admiring the confidence with which her colleague could blag his way through virtually any given situation. Even when surrounded by high-brow people with whom he had absolutely nothing in common, he still came across as strangely erudite and attentive, and more than capable of bull-shitting his way through a conversation about Renaissance Italy or postmodernism. A rare talent indeed. And yet, for all DC Nash's natural charm and good looks, just how deep the seemingly bottomless well of composure went when the chips were down, she was none too sure. No doubt she would find out before the night was through; but at this precise moment, Hyams observed, he had his game face on.

On the far side of the Randolph Gallery, Nash spotted a woman standing alone. He straightened his tie, grabbed two glasses of bubbly from the waitress, and in true Bond-like fashion, sidled up to her and began castigating the abhorrent lack of cultural appreciation in today's young people, as if it were an affront to him personally. The woman nodded appreciatively and reciprocated with a flattered, yet knowing, smile.

Hyams looked the woman up and down. She was in her late forties (trying to look thirty-something), wearing a smart maroon jacket with a plain white blouse and black trousers (tight), vintage ruby-coloured earrings (cheap-looking), and had ash-blonde hair, cut to the neck (roots showing) and tanned skin (probably from a bottle). The woman laughed, casually playing with a strand of her hair. Nash responded, leaning in close enough to smell her perfume (Chanel No. 5, most likely). Hyams, meanwhile, sneered and turned away, pretending to admire one of the Roman statues, nearby.

'Tramp!' she said, quietly, and sipped her champagne.

'Are you a Friend?' came a voice from over her shoulder.

'Sorry?'

'I was wondering if you were a Friend of the Ashmolean.'

'Err, yes, ... I am.' said Hyams, taking a step back from the man, who was standing a little too close for comfort. 'Are you?'

'Oh yes, for the last twelve years, in fact. The Ashmolean is a fascinating institution. It started in sixteen seventy-seven when Elias Ashmole, a well-connected antiquary, government official, collector and student of alchemy, donated his unique collection of stuffed animals, birds, shells, fossils and even "a piece of wood from the cross of Christ" to the Oxford University. Of course, one mustn't forget John Tradescant the Elder and his son, who started the collection ...'

She nodded sagely and was about to ask something mildly intelligent when she felt a tap on her shoulder.

'Babe, you've got to come and see this Caravaggio,' said Nash, dragging her off in the direction of the unmanned reception desk.

With little or no resistance, she mouthed a quick, 'sorry', to the man, who smiled and wandered off to drain the energy of some other poor, unsuspecting guest.

'John, you're a lifesaver. That guy was literally about to bore me to death.'

'Ha. It did look like you were about to slip into a coma, there, for a second. And we can't have that, when you're meant to be on guard duty, can we.'

'Cheeky bugger. So, where's this Caravaggio, then?'

He laughed out loud. 'How the hell should I know? I made it up.'

Hyams rolled her eyes and tutted. 'We're not here to enjoy ourselves,' she said, giving him a friendly slap on the shoulder. 'We're supposed to be keeping an eye out for the robbers.'

'Now, I had an idea on that front,' said Nash, putting his champagne glass down next to the statue of a rather aristocratic looking Roman senator. 'While this lot are nibbling on their canapés, why don't I leg it upstairs and take a quick look round?'

'No, not a chance. McHardy gave us strict instructions to blend in, not go running off on our own little secret mission.'

'Oh, stop worrying. I'll be in and out before you can say Pre-Raphaelite Brotherhood.'

'They'll be watching you through the cameras, you idiot. Just stay put and—'

Ignoring her completely, Nash turned on his heels and went tearing up the main staircase.

'John – JOHN!' she called, but it was too late.

*

'Well, well, who do we have here?' said Van Leer, peering at the live CCTV feed. 'Looks like someone's decided to treat themselves to a private viewing.'

Emily watched as the young man ducked under the ceremonial ribbon tied across the doorway and began taking a leisurely stroll around Gallery 55. But there was something not quite right about him. For some reason, he seemed more interested in the doors and alarms than the multi-million-pound paintings hanging on the walls.

'What the hell's he doing?' said Van Leer, clocking his strange behaviour.

As the man moved towards the back of the room, not even bothering to glance up at *The Gates of Dawn* in front of him, Emily knew this was no ordinary guest – more likely, one of Cordell's men, working undercover.

Acting more duplicitous by the second, the young man walked over to the anteroom doors and tried the handle. Finding them locked, he gave it a firm rattle and looked up for signs of a bolt. Emily could barely watch, knowing full well who was lurking on the other side.

He then turned away and took out his mobile phone, waving it around and looking somewhat mystified.

'You won't get a signal in there, my friend,' said Van Leer.

Emily gave him a quizzical look. 'It was fine the other day.'

'We've put in a mobile phone blocker. So don't bother trying to call for help.'

'You've thought of everything, haven't you?'

'We like to think so. Hold it,' said Van Leer, sitting up in his chair. 'Did you see that?'

'See what, guv?' said one of the guards, next to him.

'I didn't see anything,' said Emily, quickly.

'Rewind,' said Van Leer. 'I want to see that again.'

The guard pressed a button on the control panel and replayed the last ten seconds of digital feed from the hard drive.

'Stop – there. He glanced up at the camera for a second, then looked away,' said Van Leer.

'So what?' said the guard.

'It was the way he looked at it, then realised he shouldn't have done it; as though, he knows who we are. I think our mystery guest might be a copper.'

He snatched the walkie-talkie in front of him.

'This is Van Leer. Looks like we might have an undercover copper right outside the door. Move in and take him. Over.'

*

Hearing the transmission, Tyburn grabbed the ArtScreen handset lying on top of his bag.

'Got it,' he said, motioning to Danny to cover him. 'Waltham, … just leave this to us, okay?'

He nodded and stood back against the wall.

Tyburn turned the key, flung open the anteroom door and rushed into the gallery. The young man spun round, and before he knew what was happening, felt the butt of Tyburn's AK47 strike him on the side of the head, sending him sprawling across the floor. Tyburn bent down and landed a succession of punches to his face; then grabbed him by the arms and dragged him inside.

'Who is he?' said Danny, locking the door.

Tyburn ignored him and knelt down to frisk the motionless body. He stopped and pulled up the young man's trouser leg to reveal a police-issue SIG Sauer pistol.

'He was right. The fuckin' cops are here.'

'What do we do, Marcus? Shall I waste him, while we've got the chance?' said Danny.

Tyburn fished inside his holdall and threw him one of Emily's garden ties.

'Tie his hands behind his back,' he replied, fuming as he walked over to the wall and punched it. 'FUCK!' he shouted, and spun round to face Luke. 'How does your grand plan cater for this, eh, Waltham?'

'It doesn't. That was always the risk we took, I'm afraid. We'll just have to hope he was working alone.'

'Yeah, some chance.' Tyburn picked up the ArtScreen walkie-talkie. 'Van Leer, any more police out there you haven't told us about?'

'Negative. Looks all clear from up here.'

Tyburn took his finger off the *Talk* button and threw the handset on top of his holdall. 'I haven't come this far to let a bunch of coppers get in my way.'

'Nor me,' said Danny. 'I say we go ahead as planned.'

They both looked at Luke Waltham. 'Fine. It's probably too late to back out, anyway.'

Tyburn walked back over to the door and, with both hands clamped firmly on the AK47, steeled himself for what was to come. He didn't know where the anger came from, nor did he care. It gave him the edge, the power – made people fear him. And oh, how he loved that feeling. He flicked the safety catch on his rifle and leaned against the wall.

These were the moments he lived for – stealing things and hurting people. It was time to have some fun.

*

On the dot of 7.45 pm, a phone rang at the sports desk of the *Oxford Mail*. The office was still buzzing from the bomb alert, an hour ago. The junior editor who'd taken the original call was sitting in the coffee lounge, having his statement taken by a member of CID.

All of a sudden, there was a shout from across the office.

'Oi! Pipe down, will ya?' barked one of the reporters, frantically waving at his colleagues. Everything went quiet. 'It's the ricin lady,' he said, his hand clamped over the mouthpiece.

He sat down at his desk and scribbled on the notepad in front of him. One of the detectives from Kidlington came over and sat down at the desk, opposite.

'Keep her talking,' he mouthed, making a circular motion with his finger, but the reporter was too busy taking down what the woman was saying.

He stopped and looked up at the detective. 'Where?' he said, and began scribbling again. 'Alright, can you just tell us—' but the "ricin lady" had already hung up.

He put the phone down and checked his pad.

'Not another one?' said the detective.

'Afraid so.'
'Where is it this time?'
'The Ashmolean Museum.'
'Oh, shit. That's not good.'
'No, it's not,' said the reporter, looking a little mystified.
'What is it?' said the detective.
'It's strange, but ... I could hardly hear a word she was saying.'

Chapter Sixty-Five

Ashmolean Museum, Oxford

3 April 2000

'On behalf of the city and the University of Oxford, I take great pleasure in declaring *The Lights of the World* exhibition ... open,' pronounced the mayor, and cut the ribbon leading to Gallery 55.

The sound of applause from the gathered patrons seemed to galvanise DC Hyams. She looked at her watch and tutted.

'Where the hell is he?' she said, realising it was ten minutes since DC Nash had decided to venture off on his own personal reconnaissance mission, despite her protestations.

Having joined the near one hundred guests in Gallery 54, she'd taken up position inside the doorway at the top of the stairs, just in case he did decide to make an appearance. And boy, was he in for a bollocking when he did. She kept checking her phone, but there were no messages; in fact, no signal at all, which was strange.

She watched as the mayor and his wife, accompanied by Julian Mountfield, made their way over to Hunt's *The Light of the World*, followed by a stream of excited guests, eager to see the much anticipated and venerated collection. Hyams was about to join them in the main picture gallery, when the doors leading out of the west wing slammed shut behind her.

'What the ...?' she said, pulling on the brass doorknob, just as a heavy bolt snapped shut on the other side.

'Hey, open this door!' she yelled.

People standing nearby came over, wondering what was going on.

'What's happening?' said a man next to her.

'I'm not sure. I think we've been locked in.'

'What? That's ridiculous,' he said, rattling the door knob.

It wasn't long before a murmur of disquiet spread through the two galleries.

Hyams checked her phone – still no signal. *Oh my God, this is it. And thanks to Nash doing a bloody moonlight flit, I'm going to have to deal with this, alone.*

All of a sudden, a volley of shots rang out from the next room, followed by a chorus of screams. She rushed over to the connecting doorway to Gallery 55. Two men wearing black balaclavas were standing at the far end, brandishing AK47s.

'Everyone stand in the middle of the room with their hands on their head – NOW!' shouted one of the armed men.

Hyams ducked out of sight in the first gallery and turned to the group of frightened guests standing close by.

'Listen everyone, I'm a police officer. I want you all to stay calm and do exactly what they say.'

Some nodded, their eyes wide with fear; others were too terrified to even respond. She put her left hand up to her face and whispered into the tiny high-gain microphone attached to her cuff.

'DC Hyams here, AURORA! ... it's started.'

There was a short delay.

'How many?' Cordell replied, into her discreet earpiece.

'Three – armed with assault rifles.'

'Alright. Where's DC Nash?'

'Err, not sure, sir.'

'What do you mean, you're not sure?'

'Sir, I have to go.' And she put her arm down by her side.

'Are you really the police?' said a young woman, looking petrified.

'Yes, yes. Now, remember what I said. Just do what they say.'

She walked over to the double doors and peered through the gap into the next room. *Keep calm, Hyams, remember your training.* She felt for her gun, then thought better of it. *Not yet. Pick your battles. Assess the situation, then react. You can't help these people if you're dead.*

She watched as one of the gang members in the next room fired another hail of bullets into the ceiling. Already terrified guests ran in all directions, ducking for cover or just freezing on the spot and waiting for death. One of the armed men looked over and ran towards the pair of interconnecting doors, knocking people out of the way as he went. DC Hyams was about to try and close them when she saw his AK47 pointing right at her head.

'Don't shoot, don't shoot,' she said, raising her hands in the air.

'You lot, ... get next door, NOW! I said move it!' shouted the gunman, and began shoving the last remaining stragglers into Gallery 55.

Everyone did as they were told – not even daring to look at the hooded man as they huddled together like sheep. Hyams immediately turned to her left and stood on the edge of the growing mass of people in the centre of the room. She placed her hands on her head and looked down at the floor, as instructed.

'Clear!' shouted the gunman, confirming the adjoining gallery was empty.

'Now we've got your attention, ...' said, what appeared to be, the leader, prowling round the edge of the room like a lion. '... I want you all on your knees, and if your head's not touchin' the floor in five seconds, I'm goin' to blow your fuckin' brains out! One, ... two, ...'

There was mass panic as everyone began to get down on their knees, some with more difficulty than others.

'... three, ...'

Those with physical ailments or bad joints took longer, grimacing with pain as they forced themselves to the floor, leaning forward as best they could.

'... four, ... I said, hands on your heads!'

Most complied, with their heads touching the floor. But a handful of, mostly elderly, patrons were left crouching and shaking with fear, desperate to do as they were told, but completely unable.

'... five.'

The ringleader let off another burst of gunfire into the ceiling, sending plaster and bits of roof timber cascading down onto the humbled guests.

That has to be Marcus Tyburn, thought Hyams, recalling the psychotic profile DCI Cordell had outlined at the briefing, earlier.

In three terrifying minutes, Gallery 55 had been transformed into something resembling a prayer hall. A corridor had formed round the edge of the room, as if to respect the sanctity of the eight paintings, while the penitent congregation – facing north, south, east and west – all prayed for mercy, and even the slightest chance of making it out alive.

'You, ... get away from the door,' shouted one of the gunmen.

Hyams slowly turned her head and watched as he walked over to the poor unfortunate woman, and kicked her in the ribs.

And you, you piece of shit, must be Danny Forgan, I'm guessing. Which, with Waltham, makes three scumbags in total.

Hyams kept a discreet watch as Tyburn scanned the room, then walked over to an elderly gentleman who was bent down on one knee and leaning on his walking stick.

'Didn't you hear me, old man?' shouted Tyburn.

The rather distinguished looking gentleman cowered as he felt the barrel of the AK47 dig into the back of his head. The young woman next to him whimpered quietly, waiting for the shot.

'I said get down on your knees.'

'I can't. It's my hip. I, I – just can't.'

Tyburn raised the butt of the assault rifle and slammed it into the man's shoulder, sending him crashing to the floor. The woman screamed and put her arm around him, sobbing loudly.

'Now, listen up everyone ... unless you want those fuckin' floorboards to be the last thing you ever see, I suggest you keep your heads down and your whiney mouths shut.'

A solemn hush descended over the room. Nobody moved. Some closed their eyes and tried to block out the reality. Others prayed to their god for divine intervention. But most just thought of loved ones and the hope of a life thereafter, when this whole damned nightmare would all be at an end.

*

From the relative calm of the ArtScreen control centre, Emily watched in horror as the drama unfolded before her eyes. Each time the men removed one of the iconic paintings from the wall and shoved it into the foam-lined compartment of the wooden crate, a little piece of her heart cried out. But what made her sick to her stomach was the utter brutality being meted out by Marcus Tyburn and his cronies on those poor defenceless people.

'Okay, young lady, it's time for us to part company,' said Van Leer.

A lump came to her throat.

'Oh, come now ... don't look like that. We're not going to hurt you. You can stay here and watch the show.'

'You won't be able to sell them – the paintings. They're too well known.'

'I think you underestimate the desires of the rich and powerful, Miss Bradshaw. There's always someone, somewhere who wants what they can't have. And it's down to the likes of us to give it to them, for the right price, of course.'

'Cordell knows who you are. He'll hunt you down. You think you can just—'

Van Leer quickly stuck a strip of gaffer tape over her mouth. 'Oh, you do like to have the last word, don't you?'

He nodded to one of the security guards who grabbed her by the wrists and held her down.

'Now, we're going to have to restrain you, I'm afraid,' said Van Leer, taping her wrists to the arms of the chair as she kicked and wriggled in protest.

'Please don't struggle. We don't want to bruise that lovely pale English skin of yours, do we?'

By the time they'd finished, both her ankles were tied together and her chest and shoulders bound so tightly to the chair's backrest, she could hardly breathe, let alone move.

Van Leer crouched down and put his hand on hers. 'It only remains for me to thank you, Miss Bradshaw. Without you, none of this would have been possible.'

She mouthed some unintelligible profanity and watched as the three men left the control room, locking the door behind them.

The painful memories of her captivity in the warehouse all came flooding back. She'd wanted to be so brave – to somehow save these great paintings. But in the end, she could do no more than sit there, helpless, as the conniving, malevolent forces went about their work.

She swivelled the office chair round on its base and watched the live feed from camera 55. The hostages were all crowded together in the centre of the gallery, heads bowed – obedient to the will of their captors. To a distant observer, it looked as though a sense of resigned calm had descended over the room.

How far-removed from her own feelings of outrage and frustration. Could nothing stop these marauders, these takers, from plundering her *pageant of light*?

Chapter Sixty-Six

Ashmolean Museum, Oxford

3 April 2000

The bespoke wooden crate containing *The Lights of the World* measured approximately ninety inches by sixty, with eight individual foam-lined compartments filling the space. Fitted with steel-reinforced edges, it was light, strong and built to precise specifications – an excellent piece of craftsmanship in itself. By the time the eight paintings were carefully located inside, it required two of the gang to manoeuvre the flatbed trolley on which it sat.

While Tyburn and Danny prowled around the perimeter of the gallery, ensuring none of the guests stepped out of line, Coos Van Leer, who'd joined them from the control centre, was busy screwing down the lid to secure the valuable contents.

'We're done here. Let's go,' he said, slapping the top of the crate.

There was no response.

'Come on, let's move it.'

But Tyburn and Danny's attention was drawn to a bright ray of light, shining down through one of the skylights, like a tractor-beam. Then came a strange vibration, penetrating the whole room as if a tube train was thundering overhead.

'Fuckin' flyin' pigs,' exclaimed Tyburn.

Then Danny spotted something out of the corner of his eye. A number of guests next to the radiators began to keel over. Then, more and more, until they all started falling in a great wave of comatose bodies.

'What the hell's going on?' he shouted, and turned towards Luke Waltham, who'd ditched his balaclava in favour of a full face gas mask, and was now clutching a little black box with a red button on the front – below which shone a bright green light.

'Oh fuck!' said Danny, assuming this meant that ricin was now being pumped into Gallery 55 – in which case, he and Tyburn were goners. 'You're killin' us with poison gas? Why the fuck would you do that?'

He laughed. 'No, we thought that was a bit callous, even for a pair of deceitful pricks like you two. It's actually a powerful anaesthetic – you'll be out like a light in a few seconds,' he said, and nodded towards Van Leer, who was also now wearing a gas mask.

Watching the exchange a few yards away, Tyburn raised his AK47 and fired a hail of shots into Waltham's chest. His eyes narrowed. Somehow, the bullets seemed to have passed straight through him. He fired again, but Waltham just stood there, smiling and shaking his head.

'You don't get it, do you ... you've been screwed over, gents.'

Faced with the sudden choice of fight-or-flight, Danny raised his Kalashnikov and fired at Waltham's head. 'Shit!' he said, realising it too was loaded with blanks.

He tossed the rifle on the floor and was just about to launch himself at Waltham when he saw one of the comatose bodies moving in the background. Miraculously, it stood up and began walking towards them, pointing a gun straight at Waltham's head. Danny tried to react, but found all he could do was stand there – his arms and legs refusing to function. He shook his head and waited for the confrontation, powerless, as the anaesthetic took control of his body.

*

DC Hyams' heart was pounding in her chest. She had no idea if she was doing the right thing, but having seen the two men discharge their weapons to no effect, the decision had been made for her.

When people started collapsing all around her, she'd had the presence of mind to hold a handkerchief over her nose and mouth to try and stem the effects of whatever substance it was. Not wanting to stand out like a sore thumb, she'd flopped over onto her side to obscure her makeshift mask. Then came the shots. Seeing all four gang members standing there, staring at each other, that was her chance. She'd grabbed the SIG Sauer from her ankle holster and, skirting the mass of bodies in front of her, made a beeline for the group of men.

And here she was, with her gun pointing at a man she assumed to be Luke Waltham. She pulled the trigger – the bullet striking him in the shoulder and spinning him backwards.

She quickly turned to Van Leer. 'Take off your mask and toss it over here. DO IT!' she shouted.

Begrudgingly, he did so, throwing it at her feet. As she bent down to pick it up, a wave of dizziness hit her. She put down her hand to steady herself, and saw one of the men lunge towards her. She fired again.

With a look of half-conceived shock, Danny Forgan clutched his chest and gazed down at the bullet hole streaming with blood. With his eyes barely open, he fell to his knees and hit the floor, face first.

Hyams stared at the body. She hadn't meant to kill him; it was instinct. Still contemplating what she'd done, she grabbed the gas mask and pulled it over her head.

In those few precious seconds, Tyburn ran over to where Waltham was lying and yanked the AK47 from his blood-soaked shoulder, making him howl in agony. Aiming the rifle at Hyams, he ripped off Waltham's gas mask and put it on, frowning at his mass of blonde hair.

With her pistol clutched tightly in both hands, Hyams aimed it straight between Tyburn's eyes. And there they stood, the DC and the psychopath – locked in a deadly embrace.

'Put it down, love, you're outta your depth,' said Tyburn.

'Ask those two if I'm out of my depth?' she said, nodding to her two gunshot victims. 'Looks like Waltham's double-crossed you, if you didn't get a gas mask.'

Tyburn's eyes narrowed. 'I don't know who that fucker is, but it ain't Luke Waltham,' he said.

Then came a thud as Coos Van Leer fell to the floor, quickly followed by the blonde-haired man – both drifting off into a deep fentanyl-filled sleep.

Hyams glanced at the AK47 Tyburn was holding. 'How do you know that thing's not loaded with blanks, too?'

Tyburn smirked. 'I guess there's only one way to find out.'

'Risky, ...' she said, steeling herself. '... if you want to walk out of here alive.'

For a second, he hesitated, no doubt mindful of the multi-million-pound cache of art sitting behind him.

'Unfortunately, you caught me on a bad day,' he said, and pulled the trigger three times, spewing a trio of cartridge cases onto the floor.

The short and relatively uneventful life of DC Hyams' flashed before her eyes. Why the hell had she been so reckless. Why couldn't she have just stayed where she was and succumbed to the anaesthetic, like everyone else. She waited for the unimaginable pain of the bullets piercing her body, but ... none came. Then she saw the look in Tyburn's eyes, bristling with anger.

She re-focused her aim and took a deep breath of clean filtered air. 'Hands against the wall, arsehole,' she yelled.

Now, she had control of Gallery 55. And apparently, much to her relief, this was not her day to die.

*

Emily glared at the split-screen monitor, not quite believing what she was seeing. Without the benefit of a rewind button, she tried to piece together what had just happened up on the second floor. The robbers had stormed in, forced the one hundred guests into the middle of the room and then proceeded to remove all eight paintings from the gallery walls. Then, just as they were about to make off with the spoils in a huge wooden crate, a bright beam of light appeared through the skylight. All the guests then started keeling over and, as if by magic, some random woman arose from her slumber and began randomly shooting members of the gang. She'd then donned a gas mask and, after a dramatic showdown with Tyburn, somehow managed to get him standing up against the wall with his hands in the air, like a captured fugitive. *They should pin a bloody medal on this woman.*

Emily span round in her chair in celebration. If she hadn't been gagged and bound, she'd have thumped her fist on the desk and run upstairs to help the brave soul. As it was, she was going nowhere.

Returning her attention to the TV monitor, she watched what appeared to be a helicopter searchlight light up the gallery floor and its eerie carpet of prostrate bodies.

The wonder woman with the gun suddenly looked up at the ceiling as a series of small explosions went off in the skylight, filling the roof space with smoke. Like the lid coming off a saucepan, the whole metal frame rose into the air, revealing the night sky and two men in gas masks peering down into the gallery. *Could this night get any more bizarre?*

One of the men fed down a steel hoist-cable with a large hook on the end, while the other calmly took aim with his Kalashnikov and fired a hail of bullets at the heroine's feet, sending her diving for cover behind the wooden crate.

'Oh my God,' mouthed Emily, behind her gag. She had to do something to help the poor woman, but what? She scanned the control desk. Then she saw it.

She wheeled the chair up to the edge of the desk and leaned forward as far as she could, wincing as the metal rim dug into her ribs. Nothing, but nothing was going to stop her reaching that little black button on the LIGHTS panel – the label for which said, #55.

*

Time to get the hell out of here, thought Hyams, cowering behind the packing crate – her gun no longer trained on Tyburn, who had turned away from the wall and was now watching the two masked men, standing where the skylight used to be.

Aiming blind, she held her pistol up in the air and let off a couple of rounds at the open roof space, behind her. Hoping she'd somehow managed to cover herself, she ran as fast she could towards the anteroom, twenty feet away. Then everything went black – someone had turned the gallery lights out. As she reached the doorway, shots rang out. With only the light from the anteroom to guide her, she burst through the open door and slammed it shut, locking it behind her.

Resting her forehead against the door, she felt a sudden sting in the side of her neck. Using her thumb and forefinger, she gripped the thin sliver of shattered architrave wedged in her skin and quickly yanked it out. After inspecting it and tossing it to the floor, she took out a handkerchief and held it against the wound.

She took a few deep breaths to try and calm herself, and turned around to check the rest of the room. She couldn't believe her eyes. Lying round the corner, almost out of sight, was DC Nash.

'Oh my God, what have they done to you?' she said, putting her pistol back in its holster.

She knelt down and felt for a pulse on his neck. He was alive. Having checked his airway, she took off her jacket, rolled it up and placed it beneath his head.

'Well thanks a bunch for leaving me to deal with everything,' she said, half-expecting a witty comeback as she sat down next to him.

Suddenly, in her ear came the familiar voice of DCI Cordell. Having ignored him for the last fifteen minutes, she knew he wasn't going to be happy, and braced herself.

'I'm here, sir,' she said, speaking into her sleeve mic.

'Hyams, what the hell's going on? I've been trying to reach you for God knows how long.'

'Sorry sir, I've been a bit busy down here.'

'I heard gunshots – is everything alright?'

She felt the wound on her neck, it was still bleeding. 'One of them had a pop at me, but I'm fine.'

'You sound a bit muffled, Hyams – can you check your mic?'

'It's not that, sir, I'm wearing a gas mask.'

'What? Why?'

'They've released some sort of anaesthetic gas into the gallery. I'm still feeling a bit light-headed.'

'Bloody hell. Is everyone okay down there?' he said.

'The guests are all spark out, sir. I think we'd better get the medical teams on stand-by – it's pretty potent stuff.'

'Okay, will do. Where are you, Hyams?'

'I've locked myself in a small annex next to the main gallery. Looks like this is where the gang were holed up before they burst in.'

'How many are there?'

'Four. One's unconscious, one's got a shoulder wound – also unconscious, and one ... is dead, sir.'

There was a brief silence. 'Okay, you said there were four?'

'Marcus Tyburn's still in there and he's wearing a gas mask, so who knows what he's up to. Actually, sir, I should have said six. Another two were about to enter through the skylight, by the look of things.'

'I can see a helicopter hovering over the museum, now. Just stay where you are, Hyams. I'll get some of the SO-nineteen guys up there to seal off the second floor. I don't suppose there's any sign of Nash, is there?'

'Yes sir, I'm sitting right next to him.'

'Well, tell him I'm gonna have his fucking guts for garters when I see him.'

'I would do, sir, but he's unconscious at the moment.'

But DCI Cordell had gone. She stood up and walked over to the door, pressing her ear up against it. It was difficult to hear anything over the sound of the helicopter, but there seemed to be an awful lot of shouting going on. Apparently, Marcus Tyburn wasn't about to give up the paintings without a fight.

Feeling utterly exhausted and very slightly anaesthetised, she sank to the floor and casually ripped off the gas mask, tossing it aside. Without any warning, she burst into tears as the emotion and stress of the last fifteen minutes came pouring out of her. She'd been gassed, shot at and damn near executed from point blank range. And if it hadn't been for that wonderful person switching off the lights at just the right moment, she'd probably be dead.

As she wiped the tears from her eyes, she gave a little laugh and made herself a promise – the next time she got a call to an armed robbery in progress, DC Nash would definitely be going in first.

Chapter Sixty-Seven

Ashmolean Museum, Oxford

3 April 2000

Wearing a black-patterned jumpsuit, balaclava and gas mask, Kate Waltham descended gracefully through the skylight of Gallery 55, the torch beam from her AK47 not leaving Tyburn's shadowy figure for a second. A few moments later, her father – the real Luke Waltham – followed her through the opening by climbing down a wire rope ladder into the darkened room, his own torch gripped between his teeth.

As Kate touched down, she unclipped herself from the winch cable and ran around the edge of the room towards Tyburn, her gun pointing straight at his head. Refusing to carry a gun himself, Luke followed close behind, confident his daughter would take great delight in discharging any "necessary force" to combat Tyburn, should the need arise.

'You're late, Waltham?' said Tyburn, shielding his eyes from the glare of the torch.

'Quite the contrary,' said Luke, walking over to the wooden crate. 'And I see you've packed up the paintings for us. How considerate.'

'Take off your mask, Tyburn, and lie face down on the floor,' said Kate.

'Go fuck yourself, bitch!'

Luke shook his head. 'I wouldn't speak to her like that if I were you, not when she's got that thing in her hand.'

Kate lowered the barrel of the rifle until it was pointing at Tyburn's crotch. 'Don't give me an excuse to emasculate you.'

Tyburn stood there, staring into her eyes, then yanked off the gas mask and tossed it aside.

'Enjoy the money while you can, cos I'm gonna hunt you down and rape you, while your daddy watches.'

Kate's trigger finger twitched, hovering next to the slice of curved black steel.

'We've got to get going,' said Luke, putting his hand on her shoulder.

'You know what's sad?' she said, tilting her head slightly as she gazed at Tyburn. 'That I won't be there to see the look on your face when they hand you a nice, long prison sentence. Now lie down, you piece of shit!'

Tyburn, begrudgingly, got down on the floor, staring at her shapely legs as he lay there with his hands behind his head.

With Kate standing guard over her captive, Luke wheeled the wooden crate round the edge of the room, and, having hauled a few unconscious guests out of the way, positioned the trolley directly beneath the open skylight. He then wrapped two nylon slings under the crate, gathered up the four metal rings of the basket hitch and looped them over the metal hook attached to the winch cable, checking everything was secure.

'Kate, come on!' he shouted.

For a few seconds she stood there, defiant, as Tyburn glared up at her. She calmly put her hand to her lips and blew him one last heart-felt 'fuck you' kiss, before running towards the crate.

Moments later, father and daughter clambered on top of the wooden box and began ushering *The Lights of the World* up into the swirling night air.

*

Since witnessing Emily's capture by the gang, earlier, DS Lloyd was intent on coming to her aid – only this time, he had backup. On DCI Cordell's orders, one of the Specialist Firearms teams had made their way upstairs, and were heading straight for the ArtScreen control centre – armed with, amongst other things, the four-digit security code.

'Police! Get down on the floor!' came the shouts, as they burst into the room, their assault-rifles raised in front of them.

Emily sat facing one of the armed officers as he approached – her eyes wide, hoping to God he wouldn't shoot.

'It's alright, Miss Bradshaw,' said DS Lloyd, walking over and removing the gaffer tape from her mouth. 'You're safe now.'

'Don't worry about me, you need to get upstairs. They're stealing the bloody paintings, for Christ's sake.'

'Okay, okay. We've got another team securing the second floor, right now.'

'It's too late for that. Look.'

Lloyd gazed at the TV monitor. 'I can't see anything, it's all black.'

'Hit button fifty-five on the control panel,' said Emily, pointing with her nose.

No sooner had Lloyd pressed the little black button, than the sheer carnage that was Gallery 55 appeared before their eyes.

'My God, what the hell happened?'

'I think they've been anaesthetised with something,' said Emily.

Lloyd spoke into his radio mic. 'DS Lloyd here. We need a team of medics up here, right away. I've got eyes on the second-floor gallery and there are, what looks like ... a hundred people lying unconscious and in need of urgent medical attention. Right; well, they need to get in there as soon as the SFOs have secured it.'

Even as Lloyd was cutting her loose from the chair, Emily could barely take her eyes off the CCTV screen.

'No, no, this can't be happening,' she said, watching in horror as the two robbers clambered on top of the wooden crate. Dressed in black and with their feet spread wide apart, they looked invincible, like the king of thieves, as they rose up through the skylight with the greatest collection of British paintings ever conceived.

*

The wooden crate began to rise slowly into the air. As they neared the rim of the skylight, the gallery lights came on. Luke Waltham winked at Kate and removed his gas mask. She smiled and did the same, before looking up and waving her torch at the winch operator to make it go faster.

Watching their every move, Marcus Tyburn quickly jumped to his feet and ran as fast as he could towards the rising crate.

'Kate, look out!' shouted Luke, but it was too late.

Tyburn leapt into the air and grabbed the edge of the box, tipping the whole thing sideways. Instinctively, Kate planted her feet against the cradle and leaned back as far as she could, to try to steady it.

'Shoot him!' cried Luke, grabbing the rigging as Tyburn hauled himself on top of the crate.

But before Kate could unhitch the AK47 from her shoulder, Tyburn grabbed her by the ankles and began hauling himself towards her, like a giant scorpion. She kicked and punched as hard as she could, but he was too strong. Getting to his knees, he grabbed hold of the rifle and yanked it from her shoulder. Desperate and fighting for her life, she sank her fingernails into his cheek, feeling the warm blood on her fingertips as she gouged out great chunks of skin. He roared with agony, then clenched his fist and punched her in the stomach, again and again. She bent forward – winded and defenceless, gasping for breath as the air left her lungs.

Seeing her in trouble, Luke launched himself at their attacker, but Tyburn saw him coming and swatted him off like a fly. Stumbling backwards with his arms flailing in all directions, Luke just managed to grab onto one of the sling straps to stop himself falling.

Turning his attention back to Kate, Tyburn punched her in the face, then began prizing her fingers from the nylon strapping, one-by-one. Dazed and gasping for breath, she stumbled sideways, desperately trying to grab onto something, anything, as she approached the edge of the crate.

'Daddy!' she gasped, and with one final empty grab at the strapping above her head, she toppled over the side.

'NOoo!!' screamed Luke, as he watched his little girl plummet through the glowing skylight. He scrambled to the other side of the crate, only to see her motionless body lying like a rag doll on the gallery floor, below.

'Go back, go back!' he shouted to the winch operator, but his words were lost in the maelstrom of swirling air, as they continued to climb. He let out a deep, heart-rending wail and glared at Tyburn, his eyes full of hatred. Then he saw Kate's AK47 – it was pointing right at his chest.

'Guess she didn't have angel wings, after all,' said Tyburn.

Luke was just about to hurl himself at his daughter's murderer, when something struck Tyburn's shoulder, spinning him round like a top, and sending the assault rifle tumbling into the street below.

Tyburn quickly wrapped his good arm round the nearest sling strap, trying not to pass out from the pain. As the helicopter began to bank away from the museum, he slowly reached up to the steel hook-clamp securing the four shackles above the crate.

'What are you doing?' shouted Luke.

'Givin' 'em back their paintin's.'

'Don't be ridiculous, you'll kill us both.'

'If I'm goin' down, you're comin' with me.'

Luke's head was a blur. He'd just lost his daughter and was about to see *The Blind Girl*, the painting he'd dreamed about since he was a young man, smashed into a thousand pieces on the streets of Oxford.

'No, please. I beg you.'

'You – beg me? The devil doesn't grant favours,' he said, and yanked out the safety pin.

Luke watched, helpless, as Tyburn's trembling, bloodied hand grabbed the release lever.

'Hang on tight, Waltham, you and me are goin' for a ride.'

*

Watching the drama unfold above the museum, Cordell heard a second crackle in his earpiece.

'Suspect is about to release the crate. I have a clear shot,' said the SO19 marksman – his cross hairs aimed squarely at Tyburn's chest.

'Take it,' said Cordell.

Tyburn never knew what caused him to let go of the lever, or tumble head first into one of the gardens behind St John Street, not a hundred yards from the museum.

'Target down, target down,' said the marksman.

Cordell's shoulders slumped. He rested the binoculars in his lap and looked down at his bandaged hand. The battle with Tyburn was over. It certainly wasn't how he wanted it to end – with one of them dead – but deep down, he knew, it was always going to be that way.

*

With tears running down his face, Luke glanced down at the glowing skylight of Gallery 55 as it disappeared beneath him – the agony of grief clawing in the pit of his stomach. He recalled the kiss on the cheek Kate had given him, before they'd set out that evening, and the promise she'd made – to only shoot Tyburn if he really caused trouble.

'If only you had, my love, ... if only you had,' he said, as they passed over the rooftops of St John's Street, where one of the ArtScreen security guards was now standing in the road, looking up at him. He watched as George Yates raised his arm into the air and fired six shots at the Bell's fuselage, hitting the aircraft in a series of rapid metallic clunks. Seconds later, a plume of black smoke began belching from the engine compartment, and Yates lay dead on the ground – a police sniper's bullet lodged in his skull.

Heading west over Worcester College, the stricken aircraft began to pitch and roll, tumbling earthwards like a sycamore seed. Perched on top of the crate, Luke clung to the nylon hitch-straps, a broken man.

With the wind rushing through his hair and the final flecks of daylight melting into the inky black horizon, the saddest of smiles appeared across his face. For now their race was run, and soon, very soon, he and his beloved daughter would be reunited, forever.

Chapter Sixty-Eight

Oxford City Centre

3 April 2000

As the bullet-ridden helicopter continued its *danse macabre* over the city's rooftops, Luke Waltham gripped onto the straps above the wooden crate, his knuckles raw as the cold air rushed past his face. All he could hear was the scream of the twin Rolls Royce engines, struggling to keep them airborne as the pilot wrestled for control of the cyclic stick. He peered over the edge of the box at the blur of street lights, spinning round and round like sparks from a Catherine wheel. Then something caught his eye – the lights of a train heading into Oxford Station. Beyond that, the glow of riverboats moored along the banks of the Isis. Could the pilot somehow manoeuvre them that way, perhaps even land the Bell in the soft river meadows, nearby? There seemed precious little chance of that – given the battle he was waging, just to keep them aloft.

Not usually one for spiritual sentiments, Luke found himself praying to an unfamiliar god; forsaking his earlier wish to meet up with Kate in the life hereafter. Perhaps, when all was said and done, he wasn't ready to depart this mortal coil, just yet.

*

In a lay-by on the north side of the station, next to the Oxford to Birmingham mainline, a group of railway workers were stood chatting when a strange noise came out of the sky. One of them looked up and pointed to some lights dancing above the short-stay car park. Transfixed by the balletic flying object, they stood watching as it approached them, howling like a banshee. Then, all went deathly quiet as the nose dipped, tipping the aircraft into an angled descent.

'It's gonna crash,' said one of the workers.

'It's coming this way,' said another.

Not fifty yards from where they were standing, the helicopter suddenly flared its nose into the air, transferring momentum into the rotor blades, then dived once more, scattering the railway workers in all directions. The wooden box and its curious passenger flew over their heads, just missing the rooftops on Abbey Road, and ploughed straight into a huge willow tree, showering leaves and branches onto the canal boats below. With nothing left to give, the helicopter followed suit, plummeting into the arms of an even bigger willow tree, nearby. The workmen rushed over and gazed at the scene of devastation as the pitch battle between nature and machine began to play out, right before their eyes.

*

Luke reached for the nearest thick branch and leapt from the top of the crate. After checking for cuts and bruises, he looked over at the neighbouring tree and watched as willow and steel fought for supremacy beside the dark waters of the Four Rivers confluence. The massive old tree put up a brave fight, cradling the Bell in a semi-vertical position – its nose pointing straight down on to a metal footbridge spanning the river. But branches and tree sap were no match for the scything blows of four rotor blades, and with the sound of splitting wood echoing round the river basin, the aircraft plunged nose-first through the canopy, hitting the water with a bone-juddering crunch. With its tail sticking in the air like a giant shark, and the landing gear jammed beneath the handrail of the footbridge, water gushed in through the open rear door, engulfing the cabin in seconds. From what Luke could see, the pilot and hoist operator didn't stand a chance.

The wooden crate, meanwhile, had also succumbed to the conflict, having been yanked from its original landing position, it was now wedged between two V-shaped boughs, some distance below where Luke was perched.

With the Bell's engines screaming their final death throes and a column of smoke, lit by the still pulsing anti-collision lights, spiralling into the night sky, it wasn't long before the curious residents from nearby Abbey Road were lining the towpath to gaze at the chaos playing out across the water.

Having waited for the aircraft and cargo to settle, Luke began making his way down through the darkened treetop, carefully testing each branch to make sure it would take his weight. He eventually reached the top of the crate, which had remained virtually upright in the second fall, albeit, with a gaping hole along one edge. Grabbing a nearby branch, he leaned over and carefully felt inside. One of the picture frames was missing a corner. Fortunately for *The Gates of Dawn*, the canvas appeared relatively unscathed – Aurora had had a lucky escape. But the weight of the stricken Bell pulling on the hitch-straps was exerting huge pressure on the crate. One more move and the wooden casing would be ripped to pieces, sending the eight canvases tumbling into the river.

As a cacophony of sirens came drifting up on the breeze, accompanied by the glow of flashing blue lights converging on the crash site, Luke sat pondering his next move. If he was going to make a run for it, it had better be now.

Fixing his sights on the grass bank at the base of the tree, he resumed his descent. Suddenly, up through the canopy came the sound of shearing metal. He looked over at the footbridge and watched as it relinquished its grip on the Bell's landing gear, sending the aircraft sliding into the murky depths of the Sheepwash Channel. As the nose hit the riverbed, it came to a standstill with just the rear boom and tail rotor sticking out of the water.

Luke glanced at the crate, still wedged between two branches. The winch cable looked tighter than a bow string, quivering as the nylon straps ate into the wood. As the box creaked and groaned under the strain, he thought about the eight paintings sitting inside – fragile and vulnerable. Among them, *The Blind Girl*, his inspiration, the picture his great-grandfather had given his life to possess. If the crate broke now, Matilda and Isabella would be lost forever, just like his beautiful Kate. Suddenly overcome with grief, and lamenting the loss of his daughter, the words of one of the Brother's sacred doctrines came into his head:

> Blessed are they that harbour the beacon of hope,
>   when all around them is desolation and despair.

His mind was made up; he would stay and save the paintings – to try at least – or his own blackened soul would never find peace. He clambered on top of the stricken crate and pulled on the wooden lid to try to loosen the remaining screws. There was a loud crack as one of the sides came away from the main carcass. He froze, ready to jump, in case the whole thing plummeted to the ground.

As the seconds ticked by, all remained static and silent, apart from the distant chatter of onlookers gathered on the far bank, and the haunting choir of police sirens echoing through the streets.

But Luke could detect an unmistakable tension in the air; a surreptitious fight for survival in the basin of the Four Rivers. And caught up in the middle of it – eight treasured ancestors of the romantic age: *The Lights of the World*, all delicately cradled in the arms of a giant willow.

Chapter Sixty-Nine

Four Rivers, Oxford

3 April 2000

No sooner had the police helicopter touched down next to the railway sidings than DCI Cordell jumped out and ran as fast as he could towards the distant plume of smoke. Reaching the iron bridge next to the mainline, he stopped and looked down onto the towpath running next to the Sheepwash Channel. There were no steps, not even a grass slope to scramble down, nothing.

'How the hell am I supposed to get down there?' he shouted, banging his good hand on the guard rail.

Spotting some lights further up the access road, he set off in the direction of a row of terraced houses. Picking the nearest one with a light in the kitchen window, he climbed over the small picket fence and went and knocked on the back door. An elderly gentleman clutching a brown china teapot, answered.

'May I help you?' he said, clocking the large bandage on Cordell's left hand.

'Good evening, sir. I need to gain access to the street at the front of your house. Do you mind if I—?' he said, flashing his ID card; and before the man could even reach out to inspect it, Cordell had barged his way into the hallway and was out the front door, running towards the alley at the end of Abbey Road.

A fire tender and police car had already arrived on scene; and, by the sound of it, more were on the way. Cordell turned the corner and was met by a large crowd lining the narrow cut next to the river. Some of the local residents had converged by the arched footbridge spanning the river, and were discussing whether it was safe to cross, to look for survivors.

'Stay away from that,' Cordell shouted, waving furiously.

'But the pilot's still in there,' said one man, pointing to the helicopter's submerged cabin.

'I don't care. These men are armed and dangerous. Now please, go back to your homes and let the emergency services do their job.'

Two Specialist Firearms Officers walked over to Cordell, followed by a station officer from the Oxfordshire Fire Service.

'Sorry sir, it's bloody chaos out here,' said one of the SFOs.

'Well, can I suggest you get a cordon set up and make sure this lot are pushed back out of harm's way.'

'Right you are, sir.'

Approaching the cycle barriers next to the footbridge, Cordell looked up into the trees on the opposite bank. Struggling to see into the canopy, he pulled a torch from his coat pocket and aimed the beam across the river. There, in the middle of an enormous willow, was Luke Waltham, perched next to the wooden crate with his head in his hands. Cordell panned the torch light down the taut metal cable, all the way from the basket hitch to the hoist on the side of the helicopter. The paintings' wild and crazy ride was over, but they were still just moments from disaster.

He turned to one of the firearms officers. 'I need to get over there.'

'Look, sir, why don't you leave this to us?'

'I haven't got time to argue, now give me your pistol, will you?' said Cordell, holding out his hand.

The SFO looked at his colleague, as if to say, *Is he allowed to do that?*

'Okay, cover me if you like, but I am going over there. And I would prefer not to be the only one without a gun.'

The SFO nodded and begrudgingly handed over his pistol. 'The safety's on, sir.'

'Thank you,' said Cordell, and stepped onto the footbridge – aiming the gun out in front of him with his right hand, whilst maintaining a somewhat less than secure grip on the torch with the other.

He stared at the gently arching boardwalk stretching out in front of him – it's ridged wooden planks flashing green and red from the Bell's anti-collision lights. Just as he was about to take a step forward, the bridge gave a loud creak.

'Shit,' he said, grabbing the handrail with his injured hand, then wishing he hadn't.

'I really wouldn't do that, Chief Inspector,' said the fire station officer. 'That thing could collapse at any second.'

Cordell waved him away and walked slowly towards the tailplane perched precariously against the side of the bridge, his eyes scanning it for any signs of movement. As he drew level with the cockpit, he reached over and peered down into the black waters of the Sheepwash Channel. The Bell's landing lights were still on, creating eerie reflections on the surface.

A voice called out from the willow tree, opposite. 'I need help up here, ... and we haven't much time.'

Cordell shone the torch up into the branches, the light beam picking out the lonely figure of Luke Waltham, shielding his eyes with his hand.

'Can you hear me, Chief Inspector?'

'Yes, ... I can hear you.'

'Well, if you don't want these paintings to end up in the river, might I suggest you get the fire brigade over here, sharpish. This thing isn't going to last much longer,' said Luke, pointing to the crate.

'Are you armed?' shouted Cordell.

Luke raised both hands in the air. 'Does it look like I'm armed?'

'What about the pilot and winch operator?'

'Dead, is my guess,' said Luke.

Cordell tucked the pistol into his coat pocket and walked briskly past the upturned fuselage, praying it stayed put.

Having reached the far bank, he made his way over to a narrow, railed section of the footpath and shone his torch up into the willow tree, picking out the pine-coloured crate about thirty feet up. The situation was worse than he thought – the box was lodged between two thick branches, with a huge hole in one side. More worryingly, the hoist-cable from the Bell was trying to pull the crate through the narrow gap, and judging by the creaking noises emanating from above, the whole thing could shatter into a thousand pieces at any moment.

'What do you suggest?' shouted Cordell.

'Can you unclip the cable from the helicopter?'

Cordell looked over at the Bell. 'Too risky – it's barely hanging on to the bridge as it is.'

'Okay, then you need to get a couple of fire brigade guys up here to help me break this thing open.'

'Do we have time?'

'Not if you keep asking me stupid questions, we don't!'

'Okay, okay,' said Cordell, hating the fact that he was having to co-operate with the perpetrator of this whole disaster, but what choice did he have? He walked back to the footbridge and shouted across to the team of firefighters watching from the other side.

'We need a ladder and some men over here, right away.'

'And a crowbar,' shouted Luke.

*

Fire Station Officer Andy Taylor stood in the cut at the end of Abbey Road, calmly surveying the scene on the other side of the river. The problem was a complex one. From what he could see, it was all a question of balance, with two competing forces – tension and compression – vying for control. What was needed was a way to maintain the equilibrium, buying his fire crew time to get in there and carry out the recovery, swiftly and safely. As with pretty much every situation they found themselves in, there were constraints under which to work. In this case, the darkness, the height of the tree, the water, the damaged footbridge and the fragile and precious nature of the helicopter's cargo. And, of course, time – that was always a factor. But he had an expert team and some of the best rescue equipment public money could buy. All he needed was a plan.

Obviously, there was no blazing fire or falling masonry to worry about. The crashed helicopter was their enemy, in this instance. With its nose resting on the riverbed and two thirds full of water, it was exerting massive tension on the hoist-cable, whilst leaning precariously against the side of the footbridge. From what DCI Cordell had reported, both of the aircraft's occupants were dead; which meant the stability of the bridge had become the priority – if that were to collapse, lives would be put at risk, and the chances of a satisfactory outcome would be next to zero. With the two thick branches acting like a vice on the box, the most important components were the nylon hitch-straps supporting the crate. He gathered his team of firefighters to explain what was going to happen, and soon they were running off to collect various pieces of equipment from the numerous fire appliances parked in Abbey Road.

'What's going on?' shouted Cordell.

'Don't worry, we'll be right with you, Chief Inspector. Could I ask you to move back from the riverbank? We'll need room to manoeuvre over there.'

Before long, the various members of the fire crew were back on site with ladders, extension cables, floodlights, cutting equipment, hoists, even an axe – which brought a frown of concern from Cordell. In a matter of minutes, and without a peep from the mostly submerged Bell, ladders had been erected, floodlights switched on, and a group of firefighters were positioned next to the crate, ready to get to work – much to the chagrin of Luke Waltham, who was duly escorted to the ground and into the arresting arms of Thames Valley Police.

'Ready, sir,' cried one of the firefighters, perched next to the crate.

'Okay,' said Taylor, giving them the thumbs up. 'Nice and easy, now.'

With the crown of the willow lit up like a Christmas tree, two of the firefighters brandishing rescue knives, began cutting through the nylon hitch-straps from opposite corners, while another three held the wooden crate steady from below. As the last two straps were severed, the winch cable took off like a bolt of lightning, sending the Bell's tail rotor toppling into the river. And, just like that, the aircraft and its crew were gone.

With three firefighters still supporting the crate, a fourth then proceeded to cut round the top section of the box with an angle-grinder, having been given strict instructions by Cordell not to pierce the foam-lined compartments.

The DCI stood anxiously twiddling his moustache as he watched the fire crew work their magic, overhead. The first painting to be safely transported back to terra firma was *The Blind Girl*. Cordell walked over and took it from the firefighter at the foot of the ladder.

'It's a remarkable picture, isn't it?' shouted Luke, watching from the far bank, his hands cuffed in front of him. 'I wonder, ... may I, Chief Inspector?'

Gripping the painting tightly in his good hand, Cordell crossed the footbridge and walked over to where Luke was standing.

'No, you may not,' he said sternly. 'You gave up that right when you and your gang violated the sanctity of the museum.' And he carefully handed Matilda and Isabella over to a uniformed officer for safekeeping.

Luke nodded. 'I understand. But remember, I stayed with them. I could have made a run for it, but I didn't. I had to protect them.'

'Don't give me that, Waltham. They're just artefacts to you, commodities to be sold on to the highest bidder.'

Luke shook his head. 'No, no, you're wrong. The Brothers had a gift, you see – an insight. These paintings are like windows into the very souls of men.'

Cordell laughed. 'And you'd know all about that, I suppose?'

'Does that surprise you, Chief Inspector? That I could be the kind of man who cares about such things? I wouldn't expect you to understand.'

'No, you're right, I don't.'

Luke bowed his head, looking almost tearful. 'I lost her, you know.'

'Who?'

'My Kate, she's gone.'

'Mmm, ... well I'm sorry about that,' replied Cordell, and nodded to the arresting officer to take him away.

They'd only gone a few paces when Luke stopped and turned back towards Cordell. 'Chief Inspector. May I share one last thing with you, before I go?'

Cordell ignored him, marching across the bridge to collect the next painting.

'You will thank me for it, I promise!' shouted Luke.

Cordell stopped and, with a shake of his head, turned around. 'Alright, Waltham, ... what is it?'

Luke beckoned him over with a mournful smile.

When the DCI was near enough, Luke leaned over and whispered in his ear. Cordell stood back and stared at him with restrained curiosity – it was a name he'd not heard in a very long time.

Chapter Seventy

Ashmolean Museum, Oxford

3 April 2000

Kate opened her eyes and looked up at the stars. For a moment, she thought she heard the sound of a distant helicopter, but she could have been wrong – her powers of deduction were being overwhelmed by the torrent of pain rampaging through her body. She thought about trying to sit up, but even the tiniest movement was met with agony. The whole left side of her body felt broken and her hip hurt so much, she was on the verge of passing out. Lying on her back and trembling with shock, she lifted her head and saw the mass of unconscious bodies stretching out in front of her – how ironic, if she were about to join them.

Crying with pain, she managed to drag herself next to a middle-aged couple, lying a few feet away. Just as she was about to try and roll over onto her stomach, the gallery doors flew open and in burst a team of firearms officers, screaming for the gang members to drop their weapons and put their hands on their heads. Obscured by one of the radiators, Kate thought about trying to pull off her balaclava, but the SFOs were approaching fast, so she put her arm over her head and waited. Any moment now, there would be an assault rifle pointing at her head, for sure.

*

On hearing her colleagues storm into Gallery 55, DC Hyams opened the door to the anteroom and put her hands in the air.

'I'm Thames Valley Police. We need a paramedic in here,' she said.

'You there, down on the floor. NOW!' shouted one of the SFOs, his rifle aimed squarely at her chest.

'It's alright, ... she's one of ours,' shouted DS Lloyd, rushing over to her.

'Thanks, skip' said Hyams, putting her arms down.

'What were you doing in there?' enquired Lloyd.

'Trying not to get shot, actually.'

'Right, fair enough. What about Nash, any sign of him?'

'He's in there, too – unconscious. And he doesn't look good.'

'Well, that's what happens when you disobey orders, constable.'

'I guess so,' said Hyams, looking sheepishly at the three gang members lying nearby.

Having confirmed the galleries were all-clear, the SFO team leader gave the nod for the team of paramedics and doctors to enter and begin treating the gassed and the wounded. Emily followed them, looking somewhat shocked at the stark reality confronting her – bodies everywhere and four empty walls.

'Constable, what happened to these three?' said Lloyd, pointing to the gang members, one of whom looked to have a fatal gunshot wound to the chest.

'It all happened so fast,' said Hyams. 'He came at me and, well, ... I thought he was going to shoot.'

'She's right. I saw it on the TV monitors,' said Emily, walking over to join them. She touched Hyams' arm. 'You were incredibly brave.'

Hyams smiled. 'Thanks. I had an idea some of their guns were loaded with blanks, but—'

'What makes you say that?' said Lloyd.

'Tyburn took a shot at this guy,' she said, pointing at the blonde-haired man. 'Then he picked up another gun and fired at me. Honestly, I thought I was a goner.'

She scanned the room, looking for Tyburn. 'That's weird, he's not here.'

'I saw him jump up onto the crate. He's long gone,' said Emily.

'Mmm ... not exactly,' said Lloyd. 'I heard on the radio, one of the SO-nineteen boys took him out. Apparently, he was about to detach the wooden crate from the helicopter.'

'Oh, my God!' said Emily. 'What about the paintings, are they alright?'

Lloyd shrugged. 'I'm not sure. We had reports that the helicopter went down by the river, a short time ago.'

Emily put her hand to her mouth, looking white as a sheet.

'As for Tyburn, he fell into one of the backstreets somewhere. Uniform will pick him up, or what's left of him.' Lloyd squatted down next to one of the other gang members. 'And remind me, who is this guy?'

'That's Coos Van Leer, head of security. He's the one who tied me up in the control room,' said Emily, rubbing her wrists.

Lloyd frowned. 'Strange – he's not wearing a gas mask?'

'No, I made him give it to me,' said Hyams.

'Do you remember the briefing, constable? Where we asked you to sit tight and observe?'

'Yes, skipper, I do. But when they started gassing everybody, I couldn't just sit there like a lemon, could I?'

*

Emily left them discussing the rights and wrongs of operational protocol and wandered over to one of the gallery walls, staring at the blank space where *The Gates of Dawn* should have been. The thought that the paintings had all been destroyed, never to be seen again, filled her with such agonising dread, she could hardly breathe. This was all her fault. She was the one who'd put the pieces of the puzzle together. She was the one who'd convinced the various trustees to loan out their paintings. And she was the one who'd organised the exhibition from which they'd been stolen. What a terrible price to pay for her naivety.

Feeling utterly distraught, she turned around and looked at the expanse of bodies lying at her feet; then noticed one of them was wearing a black jumpsuit and balaclava.

'There's another gang member over here!' she shouted.

One of the paramedics came over and knelt down next to what was obviously a woman's body.

'Can you hear me?' she said, giving her a gentle pat on the cheek.

The woman nodded.

'I'm going to remove your hood, okay?'

Her hand came up and grabbed the paramedic's arm. 'No, leave it ... please.'

Emily couldn't help but notice the desperate look in the woman's eyes. But there was something else.

'I need to take it off so we can give you some oxygen,' said the paramedic.

Lloyd and Hyams came over to join them.

'That's the one that shot at me from the skylight,' said Hyams.

Emily looked up at the gaping hole in the ceiling. 'She must have fallen from the crate as they were winching it up.'

Without compassion, DS Lloyd bent down and pulled off the balaclava. The woman looked away, then slowly turned her face towards her audience.

'Hello, Emily,' said Kate, quietly.

Emily stared at her, wide-eyed. Her brain desperately trying to process what she was seeing. For there, lying on the floor in front of her, was her best friend, Rosa Martell. Her hair was a rich golden blonde, compared to the dark brown that Emily was used to; but there was no mistaking that aquiline nose, those gently curving lips and flashing green eyes, now sullied with anguish and deceit.

'Please, ... say something,' said Kate, wincing with pain.

Emily sank to her knees, her lips quivering. 'I don't understand,' she said, with tears welling up in her eyes.

'You two know each other?' said Lloyd.

The paramedic tried to administer some oxygen, but Kate batted it away, then reached her hand out to Emily. 'I wanted to tell you, but—'

'Tell me, what? That you're a liar ... and a thief.'

'No, no, you don't understand—'

'No, Rosa, I don't.'

Kate closed her eyes and turned away.

'Ah, ... of course. Your name's not even Rosa, is it?'

She shook her head. 'It's Kate.'

The paramedic leaned in once more and applied the oxygen mask to Kate's face. After a few moments spent breathing in the precious gas, she pulled the mask away from her mouth.

'I never meant to hurt you,' she said, straining to be heard.

Emily glared at her. 'I don't believe you. All this time, I was just a part of your grand plan. You must have thought I was such a fool.'

'No, it wasn't like that ... your friendship meant the world to me.'

'Ha! What a joke. You betrayed me the minute you met me. Whose idea was it, that scheming father of yours?'

A look of concern fell across Kate's face. 'I heard you say the helicopter went down. Is he dead?'

'We don't know. But I wouldn't get your hopes up,' said Lloyd.

Kate closed her eyes as the tears rolled down her cheeks. Then, she turned to Emily and held out her hand. 'You have to know, ... I had no idea Tyburn was going to kidnap you and Tom. I'm truly sorry.'

Emily shook her head. 'You're unbelievable. Just look what you've done to all these people. Have you no shame?'

Kate glanced at the sea of bodies around her. 'It's only sleeping gas, ... they'll be fine,' she said, exhausted.

'That's assuming none of them were exposed to a huge dose, or have heart conditions,' said the paramedic.

'You'd better hope not,' said Lloyd.

Emily looked around the gallery. 'And what about the paintings? You always banged on about, what a crime it was that great artworks got secreted away by rich collectors. And then, you do this.'

'What do you want me to say?'

'Nothing. I don't want you to say another word.'

Another couple of paramedics appeared with a stretcher. 'Let's get you to hospital,' said the young woman holding the oxygen mask. Kate nodded and closed her eyes.

'Then, we need to have a little chat,' said DS Lloyd.

The paramedics dosed Kate up with morphine, and were about to wheel her out to one of the waiting ambulances, when Emily leaned over and gently placed her hand on her shoulder.

'I want you to know, I will never forgive you for this evil thing you've done,' and she walked away to help some of the guests beginning to wake up from their ordeal.

*

With only the night cleaners for company, Emily sat quietly in the Randolph Gallery, her hands folded in her lap, lost in thought. She watched as they cleared away the remnants of the champagne reception she, herself, had organised for those poor people upstairs. How ironic, she thought – the Ashmolean would like to welcome you to, ... the worst night of your life.

The lift doors opened and out walked DC Hyams with a rather groggy-looking Julian Mountfield, his hands cuffed in front of him, and looking every bit a broken man.

'Please, may I—?' he said, spotting Emily sitting alone.

Hyams nodded and escorted him over to her.

'I'm so glad you're okay,' he said, blinking slowly.

All out of hate, she simply shook her head and returned her gaze to the cleaners.

'I know you'll never forgive me, but I want you to know, you'll get the paintings back. I promise.'

'Was it you, who told the police we'd been kidnapped?'

He nodded. 'I couldn't bear the thought of you being hurt.'

She thought about saying thank you, but couldn't bring herself to speak the words.

Julian looked at his feet. 'Emily, would you grant a condemned man, one last request?'

'What?'

'Would you stay on and look after the department for me? I can rest easy then, knowing it'll be in good hands.'

'I can't,' she said, pursing her lips. 'I'm going back to the Academy in Bristol – if Richard will have me.'

'Of course. I understand. It's just that … well, I know how much Henry would appreciate it. He thinks a great deal of you, you know.'

'Don't bring that lovely man into all this; not after what you've done to him.'

'Emily, you have to believe me, I had nothing to do with any of that. Tyburn's an animal. Please, just say you'll think about it?'

With a look of pure contempt, she stared at him and nodded. Then watched as one of the uniformed officers led him away.

DC Hyams came and sat next to her. 'Are you staying in Oxford tonight, Emily?'

'No, I'm going home to see Tom.'

'Of course. But we could do with a statement from you, at some point.'

'I'll call you tomorrow, if that's alright. I've had just about all the culture I can take for one day.'

And without another word, she got to her feet, walked out into the cool evening air and headed back to the railway station to try and find her car.

Chapter Seventy-One

Lake Tahoe, California

6 April 2000

Spring had come early to the densely wooded shores of Lake Tahoe, as all manner of wildlife was waking up from the long, cold winter in the mountains and forests of northern California.

Watching through the Aspen trees was the owner of a large, stone-built mansion, just north of Rubicon Bay – his Swarovski binoculars trained on two red-necked grebes engaged in an elaborate courtship ritual. Having witnessed the male and female birds swim towards each other in a v-shaped trail, then raise their bodies out of the water, breast-to-breast, and shake their 'three-cornered-hats' in a display called the 'penguin dance', he put down the binoculars and took a sip of freshly made coffee, before returning to the business section of the *New York Times*.

All of a sudden, the opening bars of Holst's *Jupiter – the Bringer of Jollity* filled the air. The tycoon picked up his mobile phone from the patio table and looked at the display. With a resigned sigh, he pressed the answer-call button and looked out onto a view that only billionaires could afford.

'What is it, Gregg?'

Hearing the response, he glanced over at the driveway leading up to the house and saw a parade of red and blue flashing lights moving silently through the pine trees.

'It's alright, I've seen them.'

At that moment, his young Swedish wife came running out of the house. 'Darling, the police are here.'

'So I see,' he said, and calmly watched as a gleaming white patrol boat, belonging to the South Lake Tahoe Police Department, drew up to the jetty at the bottom of the garden. The tycoon put down the phone and told his wife to go inside.

Unfazed, he picked up his porcelain coffee cup and proceeded to finish his Americano.

*

DCI Cordell stepped onto the boardwalk, flanked by two local police officers. With his dark grey raincoat flapping in the wind, he fixed his steel-grey eyes on the vintage Riva Ariston motorboat moored on the other side of the jetty. This wasn't just a different country he'd come to, it was a different world – one of unbridled power and wealth. He stroked his moustache with anticipation and marched up through the Aspen trees, ignoring the path that gently wended its way to the Queen Anne-style mansion, beyond.

'You do realise this is private property?' said Willard Knox.

Cordell eyed him up and down – from the crocodile-skin loafers to the Gucci polo shirt and cashmere sweater draped casually over his shoulders – he was everything Cordell expected him to be.

'I'd advise you to co-operate, sir,' said Cordell. 'It would be in your best interests.'

'And why is that?'

'I have a warrant to search this property.'

Knox put down his coffee cup. 'And you are?'

'Detective Chief Inspector Francis Cordell from Scotland Yard,' he said, removing the printed warrant from his coat pocket and placing it on the table.

'Ah yes, I thought I detected an English accent, inspector.'

'It's Detective Chief Inspector.'

Knox picked up the warrant and looked at it. 'You'd better come inside.'

Cordell stood for a moment, admiring the lakeside vista. 'A privileged view, Mr Knox.'

'Yes, I suppose owning the world's fifth largest pharmaceutical company does afford one certain luxuries.'

Knox led the way into the house. 'Would you like some breakfast, Chief Inspector? I can have Marisa rustle up some English-style bacon and eggs, if you'd like.'

'No, thank you. We need to press on,' said Cordell, and entered the sumptuously decorated living room, complete with vaulted ceiling and double-height windows, to fully embrace the spectacular views.

Leaning against the huge stone fireplace at the far end of the room was Gregg Banks. 'Press on with what, exactly?' he said, with his usual business-like tenor.

'It's alright, Gregg, they have a search warrant,' said Knox, handing him the document, then flopping back into the large L-shaped settee, his arms outstretched, as if he had not a care in the world. 'Perhaps I could be of more help if I knew what it was you were looking for.'

'It appears the good detective is searching for some stolen property,' said Banks, holding the warrant in the air.

'Actually, I'm interested in your collection of paintings,' said Cordell, studying Knox for signs of a reaction – he got none.

'My paintings; well why didn't you say so? Come this way.'

At that moment, three California state policemen, having been previously briefed by Cordell, walked in and started going through every drawer, shelf and cabinet.

'Are you sure your men know what they're looking for?' said Banks.

Not dignifying the jibe with a response, Cordell followed Knox through an octagonal hallway and into a beautiful panelled library, decorated with paintings, bronzes and rare pieces of antique furniture. Along two walls were a set of fitted bookshelves containing what looked like some of the finest and rarest editions money could buy.

'Do you like old books?' Knox enquired.

'Of course, but it's more your predilection for stolen artworks that interests me.'

Knox's expression changed in an instant. 'I'm not sure I like your tone, Chief Inspector. Everything in my collection has impeccable provenance, obtained from the most trusted and reliable sources. In fact, I insist on it. You know the importance of that, as well as I do.'

Cordell walked over to the back wall of the library where a number of paintings were hanging, including well-known works by American artists Grant Wood, Frederic Remington and Edward Hopper. 'This is rather fine,' he said, bending down to inspect an original bronze casting of James Earle Fraser's *The End of the Trail*, taking pride of place on a side table.

'Thank you,' said Knox, gazing fondly at the iconic portrayal of a Native American warrior, slumped over on his horse. 'You have a good eye.'

'Although, I'd been given to understand your tastes were a little more, ... European,' said Cordell.

'Really? Well then, I'm afraid you've been misinformed. Anyone who knows me will tell you I'm a diehard patriot, and always will be.'

Cordell wasn't listening. His attention had been caught by a beautiful Navajo rug lying next to the row of bookshelves.

'This is most impressive,' he said, lifting up the edge with his shoe.

Knox shot him a fierce glare. 'Please, don't do that. The weave is quite delicate,' he said, showing the first real signs of anxiety since Cordell had arrived.

'Oh, not that delicate, surely; otherwise you'd have it hanging on the wall.' And he flipped the corner back on itself, revealing a long thin crack in the oak-panelled floor. Far from being a natural cleft in the wood, the aperture ran in a perfectly straight line – uniform, machined, covert. Cordell knelt down and pulled back the rug to reveal a perfect rectangle marked in the floor, approximately four feet wide by eight feet long.

'What do we have here?' he said, inspecting it more closely.

'Oh, that's just one of the entrances to the old cellar. I had it blocked up years ago.'

'A cellar entrance – here in the library? A little unusual, wouldn't you say?'

Having studied the search warrant and affidavit thoroughly, Banks entered the library. 'I wouldn't go stamping about on it, if I were you, Chief Inspector. We'd hate for you to fall through the floor and ruin your perfectly lovely suit.'

Cordell could smell blood. He walked back into the hall and called for two of the uniformed policemen to help him conduct a search of the library. Knox and Banks watched nervously as the three men proceeded to pull out drawers and delve into cabinets. Even the lampstands and ornaments were given a good going over.

Airing his frustration, Knox finally broke the silence. 'I thought you were interested in artworks, not sweeping the room for listening devices.'

'They obviously don't have a fucking clue what they're interested in,' replied Banks.

'Patience, gentlemen. There is method in my madness, I can assure you,' said Cordell.

He wandered over to the bookcase and scanned the shelves, all the time twirling the end of his moustache, until, finally, his eyes fell upon a beautiful cream-coloured volume from the Kelmscott Press. With a bemused frown, he reached up and removed what was quite a familiar work to him – William Morris's *News from Nowhere*. Based on a utopian vision for a Libertarian society, the narrator wakes up and finds himself in a post-revolutionary future with no private property, no industrialisation and no money; just a pastoral paradise where everyone works co-operatively and takes pleasure in their labour.

'A surprising choice for a power-hungry plutocrat like yourself, Mr Knox?'

'Don't presume to understand my politics, Chief Inspector. Now if you'd please get on with ... whatever it is you're doing. I'm expecting guests, presently, and I'd rather you and your colleagues were, somewhere else, quite frankly.'

Cordell laughed, enjoying the fact that the seemingly unflappable Willard Knox was losing his cool. Handling the book reverently, he ran his fingers across the woodcut illustration of Kelmscott Manor, Morris's Oxfordshire retreat – a rural English icon. But what was a rare copy of the English edition of Morris's work doing here, so many miles from home? It certainly didn't fit with Knox's apparent embodiment of the "all American collector".

Cordell had a hunch. He placed the volume on the table and reached up into the gap it had vacated, feeling inside the bookcase.

'I hope you've got some good lawyers back home, cos, by God, you're gonna need them,' said Banks, stepping forward.

Knox grabbed his arm. 'Leave it, Gregg. Let him do what he's got to do.'

'Ah, here we are,' said Cordell, locating a small brass button set into the rear panel. He pushed it with his forefinger and heard a noise behind him. The large rectangular section of flooring began to descend and then, as if by magic, slide silently to one side, disappearing into a narrow recess beneath his feet.

Cordell and the two police officers walked over to the opening and gazed down at the stone steps descending into, what appeared to be, a small underground room.

'It seems my secret is out,' said Knox.

'It looks that way. Please, after you,' said Cordell, standing to one side.

Walking round from behind his desk, Knox stepped down into the brightly lit stairwell of his inner sanctum, followed by Banks and Cordell, with the two policemen bringing up the rear.

The subterranean chamber was no less than Willard Knox's own private art gallery. The walls were smoothly plastered and painted in a pale duck egg blue, while the floor was covered in the finest American oak. Small, yet intimate, the windowless space was approximately the size of a single garage, with what appeared to be mirrored sun tunnels built into the ceiling, to feed natural daylight from somewhere outside. It contained just three items of furniture – a burr-walnut art nouveau drinks cabinet, a Charles Rennie Mackintosh card table, designed for the Argyle Street Tea Rooms in Glasgow, on which was placed a laptop computer. And, finally, a 1956 Eames Lounge Chair and ottoman by Herman Miller, finished in black leather. Beneath their feet lay an eighteenth-century Aubusson rug from one of the French royal palaces.

Cordell stood in the centre of the room, taking in the space where one of the richest and most powerful men in the world came to indulge his most secret obsession – the unattainable. In his considerable experience, few other private residential spaces anywhere on the planet would have cost so much to construct and decorate. For adorning these walls were half a dozen works of art, stolen to order from various art galleries and museums across Europe. And there, commanding pride of place at the far end, was the painting Francis Cordell had travelled more than five thousand miles to recover – Picasso's *Blue Roofs*.

Cordell walked over and gazed at it like a long-lost lover. 'How much did you pay for it? Four ... five million?'

'Something tells me you already know the answer to that question,' said Knox. 'Please, indulge me, Chief Inspector – who told you?'

Banks leaned over. 'Willard, I really don't think you should say any more.'

Knox held up his hand. 'Come on, now. You've come into my house, uncovered my private gallery, which, incidentally, very few people know about. Don't I at least deserve to know who betrayed me?'

'Oh, it's obvious, isn't it? It was that bastard, Waltham,' snapped Banks.

'I think it's time we wrapped things up here,' said Cordell, pointing the way back up to the library.

As the police officers were about to place the two Americans under arrest, Knox quickly spun round, pulled a letter knife from his pocket and ran towards the Picasso – his arm raised, like a wild-eyed assassin. Seeing the glint of steel, Cordell launched himself at the billionaire, in a defensive tackle any NFL linebacker would have been proud of, knocking him to the floor. Cordell raised his fist and was about to punch Knox in the face when one of the police officers grabbed his arm.

'Alright, alright,' said Cordell, getting to his feet. 'Get this piece of shit out of here.'

While Knox and Banks were being handcuffed and read their rights, Cordell gently removed the Picasso from its prison wall and brought it back up into the full daylight. He'd saved a great painting, and five others, from the clutches of the criminal caste – all thanks, ironically, to Luke Waltham's last-minute tip-off about Willard Knox and his secret underground gallery.

*

With enough evidence to bring a string of convictions against both men, DCI Cordell walked outside to one of the waiting police cars and opened the rear door. Knox was sitting there, smiling arrogantly, his cuffed hands resting in his lap.

'Just for my idle curiosity, why the business with the knife?' said Cordell. 'Why destroy something you prize, so highly?'

Knox laughed and shook his head. 'I wouldn't expect you to understand.'

'Try me.'

'You want to know the real travesty, Chief Inspector? Never in your wildest dreams could you hope to own a painting like that. People like you think it your moral duty to save great works for the nation. You're happy to see them locked away in some stuffy old museum, to be pored over, day after day, by thousands of little brats and uncultured philistines. Whereas, I believe they should be savoured by learned men, such as myself, who truly appreciate the genius it took to create them.'

'So, your philosophy is, if I can't have it, nobody else will, is that it?'

Knox smirked. 'Something like that.'

'You, so-called, elites make me laugh. You call yourselves men of culture and learning, but in truth, you're nothing but a bunch of ignorant savages.'

'Oh, come now, Chief Inspector, let's not sink to petty insults. And by the way, I do hope you're taking the Picasso back to Oxford with you – I need to know where to find it, the next time I come looking.'

Cordell reached in and grabbed him by the collar. 'Listen, mate, the only art you're going to enjoy for the next twenty years is the graffiti on your cell wall,' and he slammed the car door.

As the police cars drove off through the trees, he turned and gazed at Lake Tahoe's crystal-clear waters. For the first time in, he couldn't remember how long, he felt a deep sense of gratification. He strolled down through the Aspens to the waiting police boat, savouring the crisp mountain air. Who could believe the arrogance of men like Knox, thinking it their God-given right to possess all the earth's great treasures? He'd been there himself, in his younger days; he'd seen the dark side of men, casting their web of poison across the whole of humankind, and it repulsed him.

But, having experienced his own personal awakening – his own regenesis, so to speak, he would fight them with every breath in his body. For in his eyes, darkness would never conquer light.

Chapter Seventy-Two

Summertown, Oxford,
7 May 2000

The dawning of a new summer had restored a long overdue sense of well-being to the Faber residence, with the scent of lily of the valley, magnolia and elderflower filling the air and warming the heart, as the sun beat down on the gardens of north Oxford.

'Alice will be delighted to see you both,' said Henry, recently discharged from hospital and enjoying the company of Emily and DCI Cordell.

'I do hope she's been looking after you?' said Emily.

'Oh, she's in her element, don't you worry. She now has the perfect excuse to boss me about – as if she needed one.'

Henry stopped his wheelchair outside the old greenhouse which was full to the brim with bedding plants, tomato plants and numerous empty pots waiting to house a variety of seedlings and cuttings.

'Alice, we have some visitors,' shouted Henry, trying to make himself heard over the edition of *Woman's Hour* blaring out from the radio.

'What was that?' she said, fiddling with her hearing aid whilst clasping a handful of potting compost at the far end of the greenhouse.

Henry cupped his hand to his mouth. 'VISITORS!'

After removing her gardening gloves, Alice placed them on the potting bench and poked her head out of the door. 'Ah, the lovely Emily, and Chief Inspector Cordell – how nice to see you,' she said, and switched off the radio before joining them outside. 'He's doing rather well, don't you think?'

Emily looked at the old curator and smiled. 'He certainly is. And all thanks to you, Alice, from what he's been telling us.'

'Oh, no. I just make sure he's fed and watered, and throw a blanket over him when he falls asleep in front of the television.'

Alice led them to a table and chairs beneath an old sprawling magnolia tree, it's branches laden with fragrant pinky-white goblets.

'Why don't I bring us some tea and cake, while Henry tells you about the garden? May is such a lovely month, don't you think?' And she headed off towards the kitchen door at the back of the house.

'Millais would have loved it here,' said Emily, admiring the immaculately tended borders of azalea, weigela and viburnum.

Henry smiled. 'Hopefully, it won't be too long before I can give Alice a hand with some of it.'

'Absolutely,' she said, placing a reassuring hand on his arm.

'On a different matter, ...' said Henry. '... I would like to offer you both my heartfelt thanks for recovering the stolen paintings. Particularly you, Chief Inspector – that was a very noble thing you did, saving them from the dark clawing waters of the Thames.'

'Oh, I had very little to do with it,' said Cordell. 'It was those brave firefighters who deserve all the credit. And, much as it pains me to say it, we'd never have found the Picasso without Luke Waltham's information on Willard Knox and his secret bunker.'

'Perhaps the thought of losing a daughter awakened his conscience?' said Henry, leaning over to smell one of the fragrant hybrid tea roses, growing nearby.

Cordell twiddled his moustache. 'You say that, Henry, but the man had no hesitation in bringing the whole of Oxford to a standstill, with that fake car bomb stunt of his.'

'Not to mention, gassing a hundred innocent people at the exhibition,' said Emily, sternly.

'Quite,' Cordell replied. 'That said, I might be wrong here, but I really don't think Luke or Kate intended to harm anybody. It was as if everything was being played out as an illusion, to throw us off the scent.'

Emily looked at Cordell, unconvinced.

He continued. 'And I've always wondered why he chose to take the paintings in such a flamboyant fashion. I mean, it would have been far easier to break into the museum when it was closed, just like they did with the Picasso. Then it struck me; perhaps it wasn't the paintings that motivated him, after all. It was the thrill of the hunt that Waltham craved – the sheer audaciousness of the robbery – to prove to himself, and the art world, that it could be done. But then I remembered – on the night we arrested him, he kept waxing lyrical about *The Blind Girl* and the other paintings, being windows into the very souls of men. As though, he couldn't bear to let any of them go. Oh, I don't know, who can say for sure – the guy was a mass of contradictions.'

Emily shifted in her seat. 'At least *The Lights of the World* were all recovered, safely. And he and his daughter got their just deserts.

Cordell and Henry nodded in agreement.

Emily continued. 'Now, if there's one person who does deserve some praise, it's that brave policewoman, DC Hyams – standing up to an armed gang like that. I could barely believe what I was watching, up in that control room.'

'Well, you'll be glad to hear, she's being recommended for the Queen's Police Medal, for gallantry,' said Cordell. 'It'll be quite an honour if she gets it.'

Emily gently thumped the arm of her chair. 'Good for her.'

'Hear, hear,' said Henry.

'And turning from heroes to villains, how is that piece of shit?' scowled Emily.

'Marcus Tyburn? He's still in hospital; under police custody, of course. God knows how he managed to survive that fall from the crate,' said Cordell.

Emily shook her head. 'It's a shame he didn't break his bloody neck.'

Cordell and Henry looked at her.

'Sorry, but that's the way I feel ...'

'Don't worry, he'll be going down for a very long time, once he's well enough to attend court,' said Cordell. 'And come to think of it, Henry, I think we owe you a debt of gratitude. You were the one who figured out what was going on at the museum. What was it that put you on to them, exactly?'

'Well, as you ask. I'd been working with Julian Mountfield for a number of years and like to think I'd got to know him pretty well. Then, he started holding private meetings with some people I didn't know – people I didn't like the look of. When I asked him about it, he got all cagey and made up some story about the museum seeking new sponsorships. One evening, I walked into his office when he wasn't there and saw the Millais letter lying on his desk. I knew it was a little underhanded, but I couldn't resist taking a peek. I could hardly believe what I was reading – it was astounding. So, I photocopied it and took it home to study it in more detail. Of course, I didn't mention it to Julian, thinking he'd tell me about it when he was good and ready. Anyway, weeks went by and nothing was said. I thought about owning up and asking him about it, but something just wasn't right. That's when I decided to conduct some investigations of my own.'

'How did you find out about the auction?' said Cordell.

'It was a stroke of luck, really. Julian was off sick for a few days, so I got Barbara, his PA, to forward all his emails to me, just in case there was anything important. One of them happened to be from Kate Waltham.' Henry looked at Emily. 'Sorry to dredge up her name, again.'

'That's okay,' she said, gesturing for him to carry on.

'Well, it was all a bit cryptic, but in the email, she talked about how the target had been secured, and that Draper's sketchbook would be included in the sale at Barton & Cole on November 2nd. I thought to myself, *I have to go.*' Henry put his hand on Emily's arm. 'I would have warned you sooner, my dear, but having been told by Tyburn, in no uncertain terms, what would happen if I went to the police, I was afraid they would really hurt you, or worse. Do you see?'

Emily nodded and gave him a reassuring smile.

'So, how did Tyburn know that you'd be there at the auction?' said Cordell.

'Oh, he didn't. Not initially, anyway. Unbeknownst to either of us, he was there to keep tabs on Emily. He must have spotted me looking at the sketchbook, then bided his time and cornered me when I left the auction room. I couldn't believe it when he tried to run you over in the car park – I'm so sorry.'

'Henry, it's alright, I don't blame you. But there is one thing I'd like you to explain to me,' she said, in a serious tone.

He braced himself.

'Why did Millais, Hunt and Rossetti chose an artist like Draper to complete the final painting? I mean, he wasn't part of the Brotherhood, was he?'

Henry looked at her and laughed. 'Well, I think it was simply the wish of a dying man. Millais knew he would be unable to complete the eighth *Light of the World* before the cancer took its toll, so he chose a gifted young man whose work he'd seen in the Upper Life School at the Royal Academy. Draper was a huge admirer of Millais, and just the sort of progressive talent the Brothers needed to carry on their good work.'

'A new artist for a new millennium,' said Emily.

'Precisely.'

'Do you still have the sketchbook, Emily?' asked Cordell.

'No, I offered it to Henry, but he graciously declined,' she said, giving him a wry glance. 'So, I donated it to the Ashmolean. It seemed like the right thing to do, really.'

'What a lovely gesture. Now, while we're on the subject of the paintings, there's something I've been meaning to ask you both. What was it that inspired the Brothers to base *The Lights of the World* on those seven precepts? Where did they come from – do we know?'

'That is an interesting question,' said Henry. 'You may recall the first part of Holman Hunt's letter to Millais and Rossetti talked about "devout adherence to the sacred doctrines" to enable man to "discover the true nature of his humanity". Well, I did some research and came up with something rather interesting.'

Emily leaned forward in her chair, as Henry continued.

'It's my belief that the seven challenges of the soul came from none other than, Mary Magdalene.'

Apart from the distant chirping of sparrows, and the occasional bumblebee buzzing in the rose beds, a stoney silence fell over the garden.

'Mary Magdalene?' said Emily.

'Yes. Her own gospel, in fact. It was originally discovered in Cairo and brought to Berlin in eighteen ninety-six.'

'I didn't even know she'd written one,' admitted Cordell.

'Oh yes. You won't find any mention of it in the Bible, but there are three known papyrus extracts of the gospel of Mary Magdalene, some going back to the second century; and one – the *Papyrus Oxyrhynchus* – happens to be held in the Ashmolean.'

Emily sat back in her chair. 'You're kidding. I didn't know that.'

'It's true. However, there is one slight flaw in my hypothesis. The papyrus fragments were not translated and made public until well into the twentieth century. So, you may ask, how on earth could the Brothers have known the details of those seven challenges, a full one hundred years before they were first published?'

'And how did they?' said Cordell.

Henry laughed. 'I haven't the faintest idea. I'm afraid they've carried the answer to that particular enigma, with them to their graves.'

'How intriguing,' said Emily. 'But we'll need to update our displays at the exhibition.'

'Oh, I wouldn't worry about that, quite yet. The subject will need lots more research before we get to that stage.'

'You're right. I'll get someone started on it first thing tomorrow.'

'Ah, Emily, that reminds me,' said Cordell. 'I understand you've accepted the assistant curator job, while they find a replacement for Julian Mountfield, is that right?'

She looked at Henry and nodded. 'To be honest, I couldn't see myself coming back to Oxford, after everything that had happened. But our Mr Faber, here, can be quite persuasive when he wants to be. Anyway, it's only a temporary post, until he gets back on his feet. Isn't that right, Henry?'

He gave her a knowing smile. 'We'll see.'

'And what about you, Emily?' enquired Cordell.

'What about me?'

'I wondered how you were coping, ... you know?'

She threw him a puzzled look.

'I think what the good detective is trying to say is, how are you faring without your friend, Rosa?' said Henry.

Emily looked up into the magnolia tree and folded her arms across her chest.

Cordell put his hand on her shoulder. 'I'm sorry, Emily – that was insensitive of me.'

'Oh no, it's fine. I've been trying so hard not to think about her, these past few weeks. Then, it just hits you when you least expect it.'

'We're all different, Emily. Each of us has to deal with these things in our own special way,' said Henry, in his gentle, compassionate tone.

'Do you know, I've been grieving for her as if she'd died on the gallery floor, that day. And, when I think about it, I actually lost two people I thought were my friends.'

'You mean, Julian.'

She gave a resigned nod. 'Although, it was different with him. I blame myself for not seeing through that whole charade of his. I was just a patsie; there to protect Julian from any suspicion of being Waltham's inside man at the museum. But Rosa, or Kate, or whatever her name was, she was my best friend. I hadn't known her for all that long, but I trusted her. The talks we had, the laughs, all those times I confided in her after Tom and I had had a fight. Everything, ... everything was a lie. And, if that wasn't bad enough, she sent me all those stupid notes, pretending to be some kind of omniscient Shepherd; what a joke.'

She took out a handkerchief and wiped the tears from her eyes. 'I'm sorry Henry, we came here to see how you were doing, and here I am, rabbiting on.'

'Emily, we've all been affected by what happened. But we help each other through it, don't we.'

Cordell looked down at the three remaining fingers on his left hand. 'I suppose this whole sorry business has left its mark on all of us, in different ways.'

'It certainly has,' said Henry. 'But, at times like these, it's love and friendship that pulls us through; helps us to lick our wounds and heal our emotions.'

Emily and Cordell both nodded.

'I've been an academic nearly all my working life, and just when you find yourself wondering, what's left in it for me, the universe introduces you to some delightful human beings who take you to a different place, entirely – as if you're peeling back the layers of a new reality. They say, as we get older, certain things become clearer to us, almost as though our consciousness becomes more attuned to a state of awakening. We start to understand the boundaries of our physical selves, the limitations of our five senses and what lies beyond them. As I advance in years, I've come to realise that we can all learn how to awaken ourselves, if we have a mind to. We just need to try and shake off our fears and inhibitions – let them fall away like chains, so that we can draw on the power of our own experiences, and pull back this ... veil of illusion that has clouded us all our lives. How enriched we would be, if we could just open our eyes and see the world for the bizarre shadowplay that it really is.'

Emily's mind went back to the evening at the Randolph Hotel, and the lucid dream when she, herself, became Aurora – bringer of the dawn. An indelible vision, the memory of which had never left her, and never would.

She looked into the old curator's eyes. 'That's a beautiful thought, Henry.'

'You're quite the philosopher,' said Cordell.

'Oh no. Just the ramblings of an old man.'

'Not that old,' said Emily.

'There is one thing, about which I do often wonder, though,' said Henry.

Emily wiped the last of the tears from her eyes. 'And what's that?'

'What would the three Brothers, and Draper, have made of the thousands of visitors streaming through the doors of the Ashmolean, these past few weeks? All, to marvel at their *Lights of the World*.'

Cordell laughed. 'Well, I don't know about Draper, but if what we read about the other three is anything to go by, I'm sure they wouldn't be at all surprised.'

'If only we could go back and ask them – wouldn't that be something?' said Emily.

Alice appeared from the back of the house and placed a large chocolate cake in the centre of the table.

'Go back and ask who, dear?'

AUTHOR'S NOTE

Generally speaking, human beings need inspiration in order to create anything of merit. For thousands of years, this imaginative impulse was born from laying eyes on the gods and goddesses who, some say, first breathed life into our existence. It appears, in that respect at least, I am no different. That said, I have my parents and grandmother Gowers to thank for the artistic vein that runs through our family; and, although not personally blessed with any creative gifts for the visual arts, I like to think I know a good thing when I see it. In fact, it was one of those visual experiences that led me to start putting my first fictional story down on paper.

The creators of paintings and sculptures have a power to communicate their message to others throughout the ages, every bit as much as the spoken or written word; more so, perhaps. Herbert James Draper's portrayal of the goddess Aurora – in his painting *The Gates of Dawn* – certainly spoke to me, and provided me with the desire to set out on a new path, as a writer.

In their relatively short time together the Pre-Raphaelite Brotherhood (PRB) created some incredible and, in its way, pioneering art. They have my personal admiration because they chose to swim against the tide, to go against the flow of accepted opinion – which, in their case, took the form of the authoritarian and hugely dogmatic Royal Academy. Of course, they were also gifted artists, creating wonderfully detailed and lifelike images in paint and stone, the likes of which had never been seen before. If you want to see a prime example of what I'm talking about, search out the painting, *Ophelia* by John Everett Millais – a greater portrayal of nature in art I doubt you will ever see.

I chose to base this particular story around well-known works by William Holman Hunt, John Everett Millais and Dante Gabriel Rossetti, who I collectively refer to in the book as "the Brothers". Although they founded the PRB in 1848, it eventually came to comprise seven formal members, also including William Michael Rossetti (poet and critic), James Collinson and Frederick George Stephens (both painters) and Thomas Woolner (sculptor). Other accomplished young artists, with similar aesthetic values, became associated with the PRB around that time, including John Hancock, Charles Allston Collins, Alexander Munro, Arthur Hughes and Ford Maddox Brown.

Herbert James Draper – painter of the eighth picture in the book – was very much a later follower in the Pre-Raphaelite tradition, as were other well-known names such as Edward Burne-Jones, William Morris, John William Waterhouse and Frederick, Lord Leighton. Draper remains, in my opinion, a much underrated and neglected artist. One only has to look at the majesty of the Livery Hall ceiling at Drapers' Hall, depicting scenes from *The Tempest* and *A Midsummer Night's Dream*, to realise that. See *Herbert Draper – A Life Study* by Simon Toll.

The eight paintings at the centre of the story are full of symbolism and allegory, as are many of the works by the PRB, which often depict classical or Shakespearean themes. It is well documented that the Brothers put a great deal of thought into the messages they wished to communicate; particularly when we remember that the pictures themselves often went 'on tour' around the country, attracting many thousands of visitors from all classes of society, who would be able to gaze upon their artistry and their doctrine. To provide some additional context, I have interwoven the threads of modern-day storylines with a number of historical scenes about the Brothers and their artworks – all of which are based on actual events, but contain my own interpretation and dialogue, adapted from documented records.

On the subject of artistic licence, whilst I wish it were true, any formal connection between the eight paintings in terms of the "sun marks", the sacred doctrines and their collective label as *The Lights of the World*, are purely fictional. Similarly, any affiliation between the Brothers and Herbert James Draper, in terms of a commission to paint *The Gates of Dawn*, is again, my own invention.

Turning to the basis of the sacred doctrines, my inspiration for them came from the Gospel of Mary Magdalene, an extracanonical text that was never included in the New Testament, and which first emerged from the sands of Egypt over a century ago (1896) in a fifth-century papyrus codex (book) called *The Berlin Codex*. This has since been supplemented by other fragments of Mary's Gospel, including *Papyrus Rylands 463* and *Papyrus Oxyrhynchus L 3525*, both of which date from the early third century AD, and are respectively stored in the John Rylands Research Institute and Library – Manchester, and Bodleian Art, Archaeology and Ancient World Library (prev. in the Ashmolean Library) – Oxford.

The particular doctrines I have chosen to portray relate to where Mary recounts the Saviour's own revelations about the soul's journey of ascension, and its encounters with the four powers (challenges) that seek to keep it bound to the physical world, below. These include Darkness, Desire, Ignorance and finally, Wrath – which itself has seven powers. Only by facing up to and overcoming these challenges, and thereby distinguishing between the 'deceitful image, below' (mortality) and the 'true image, above' (immortality), can the soul progress to the timeless realm of silence and rest. For further reading, see *The Gospel of Mary of Magdala – Jesus and the first woman apostle* by Karen L. King, and *The Gospel of Mary – A Fresh Translation and Holistic Approach* by Mark M. Mattison.

Using my own interpretation of these revelations, I was able to 'assign' each one to a particular painting, and thereby highlight the symbolism by which it conveyed certain social issues, on behalf of those in Victorian society who had no voice.

Researching this book provided me with the opportunity to get out on the road and visit some fantastic locations, including four great cities and a number of historic institutions – most of which happen to be in the south of England. Perhaps I'll attempt to redress the imbalance and venture further north, next time! When describing the venues and scenes in this book, I have tried to be as authentic as I can to the little details – buildings, rural outlooks, room layouts, etc. But it has, on occasion, been necessary to include some minor cosmetic changes, for the sake of the story. I would definitely recommend that you visit some or all of these cultural havens for yourself; for you will be duly rewarded with a feast for the senses, the mind and the soul.

More importantly, please take the time to search out the various paintings featured, preferably at one of the five venues (Ashmolean Museum, Birmingham Museum and Art Gallery, Keble College Chapel, Drapers' Hall and Tate Britain), or in a good colour reference book – see Bibliography section. Alternatively, you can view colour images of the eight *'Lights of the World'* on my website www.michaeljgowers.com. Seeing these wonderful pictures and analysing their particular symbolism will, I'm sure, only enhance your experience of reading this book – my first venture into the world of the *art thriller*.

Finally, it is my belief that we are all on a journey of discovery. There are many hints from history, both spiritual and philosophical, that this life is not just a physical, one-off experience, and if we could only tap into the vast well of consciousness we have all been blessed with, but which appears to have been suppressed at some point in our past, we would then be able to transcend to a more enlightened, harmonious existence – wherever and whenever that may be. Of course, life is a gift, and not one to be squandered. But we owe it to ourselves to fight off those malicious powers of which Mary Magdalene speaks in her Gospel, whether they emanate from deep within our human history, or have surfaced in more contemporary, 'artificial' guises. And let me be clear, to *fight* means to arm oneself with wisdom and understanding – to listen, to learn, to love, to think, to question, to create; to tolerate and connect with each other; to cherish nature and ourselves; to embrace the positive whilst comprehending the negative. First and foremost along that road, we should learn to just *be* – in every sense of the word. To take control of and empower ourselves, by looking inside and remembering who we really are, and where we came from. The ability to 'see with our eyes closed' is a phenomenon with which we have all been gifted. But, as the ancients used to say, *for man to truly 'live', he must first die – only then can he be re-born and truly awaken*. In other words, the human spirit can only come alive once it has a mind to reject the cloak of darkness that seeks to oppress it. Turning our backs on the ego, selfishness and materialism that has blighted our existence, is never easy. But for those willing to ignore the side-shows of modern life and look to their own guiding light – they, alone, will be able to *peer behind the veil* and feast their eyes on the absolute truth of human existence. Then, and only then, can they truly awaken.

*

'The Dawn-bringer' (p104) by Michael J. Gowers, 2023.

Light my path – show me a way, where there's no way, love …

(MUTEMATH – Love light a way)

SELECT BIBLIOGRAPHY

In writing this book, my research into the Pre-Raphaelite Brotherhood, Herbert Draper and in particular, the eight paintings central to the plot, was quite extensive. I have listed below those books that I referred to, more often than not; and which I found most useful.

Ashmolean Museum, *The Ashmolean Museum – Crossing Cultures, Crossing Time*, Ashmolean Museum, University of Oxford, 2014, ISBN 978-1-85444-289-5

Birmingham Museum and Art Gallery, *The Pre-Raphaelites at BMAG [Guide Book]*, Birmingham City Council, 2003, ISBN 978-0-7093-0247-6

Bronkhurst, Judith, *William Holman Hunt – A Catalogue Raisonné [Vols 1&2]*, The Paul Mellon Centre for Studies in British Art, 2006, ISBN 978-0-3001-0235-2

Bullen, J.B., *Rossetti: Painter & Poet*, Frances Lincoln, 2011,
ISBN 978-0-7112-3225-9

Catling, Christopher, *Kelmscott Manor [Guide Book]*, Kelmscott Manor, c.2010,
ISBN 978-0-85431-296-2

Clark Amor, Anne, *William Holman Hunt – The True Pre-Raphaelite*, Constable, 1989, ISBN 978-0-0946-8770-7

Crossley, Alan & Hassall, Tom & Salway, Peter, *William Morris's Kelmscott – Landscape and History*, Windgather Press Ltd, 2007, ISBN 978-1-905119-13-4

Ehrman, Bart D., *Lost Scriptures – Books that Did Not Make It into the New Testament*, Oxford University Press, 2003, ISBN 978-0-1951-4182-5

Fredeman, William E., *The P.R.B. Journal: William Michael Rossetti's Diary of the Pre-Raphaelite Brotherhood (1849–1853)*, Oxford University Press, 1975,
ISBN 0-19-812505-4

Hawksley, Lucinda, *Lizzie Siddal – Face of the Pre-Raphaelites*, Walker & Company, 2004, ISBN 978-0-8027-1550-0

Hawksley, Lucinda, *Lizzie Siddal – The Tragedy of a Pre-Raphaelite Supermodel*, André Deutsch, 2008, ISBN 978-0-233-00258-3

Holman Hunt, William, *Pre-Raphaelitism and the Pre-Raphaelite Brotherhood – Second Edition (Vols 1&2)*, Chapman and Hall, 1913

King, Karen L., *The Gospel of Mary of Magdala: Jesus and the First Woman Apostle*, Polebridge Press, 2003, ISBN 978-0-944344-58-3

Lochan, Katharine and Jacobi, Carol, *Holman Hunt and the Pre-Raphaelite Vision*, Art Gallery of Ontario, 2008, ISBN 978-0-300-14832-9

Marsh, Jan, *Pre-Raphaelite Sisterhood*, Quartet Books, 1985, ISBN 0-7043-2462-8

Mattison, Mark M., *The Gospel of Mary – A Fresh Translation and Holistic Approach*, CreateSpace, 2013, ISBN 978-1-4912-5329-8

Millais, John Guille, *The Life and Letters of Sir John Everett Millais (Vols 1&2)]*, Methuen, 1899, (2012, Cambridge University Press, ISBN 978-1-1080-5172-9)

Moyle, Franny, *Desperate Romantics – The Private Lives of the Pre-Raphaelites*, John Murray, 2009, ISBN 978-0-7195-2190-4

Parris, Leslie, *The Pre-Raphaelites*, Tate Gallery Publications, 1994, ISBN 978-1-8543-7144-7

Prettejohn, Elizabeth, *The Art of the Pre-Raphaelites*, Tate Publishing, 2008, ISBN 978-1-8543-7726-5

Rossetti, Dante Gabriel, *The House of Life [Poems]*, Dodo Press, 2009, ISBN 978-1-4065-0026-47

Todd, Pamela, *The Pre-Raphaelites At Home*, Pavilion Books, 2001, ISBN 978-1-8620-5444-8

Toll, Simon, *Herbert Draper 1863–1920 – A Life Study*, Antique Collectors Club, 2003, ISBN 978-1-8514-9378-4

Whitely, Jon, *Oxford and the Pre-Raphaelites*, Ashmolean Museum, Oxford, 2004, ISBN 978-0-9078-4994-0

Wildman, Stephen, *Visions of Love and Life – Pre-Raphaelite Art from Birmingham Museums and Art Gallery*, Art Services International, 1995, ISBN 0-88397-113-5

Wood, Christopher, *The Pre-Raphaelites*, Weidenfeld and Nicolson, 1981

"*music enlightened*"

The amazing visual tool that enables
almost anyone to understand the
fundamentals of music and create their own songs
and compositions.

No traditional music knowledge
is required.

www.musicwheels.com

25% discount at checkout with code:
"LoW25"